a   y   J   a   y   b   e   e

SM erotica specialist Kay Jaybee can usually be found writing in
coffee shops on the South Coast of England. Making Him Wait is her
third novel.

D1589794

ALSO FROM SWEETMEATS PRESS

The Candy Box
Sun Strokes
Immoral Views
Named and Shamed
Naked Delirium

MAKING HIM WAIT

A Tale of Denial, Discipline & Reward

◆◆◆◆

KAY JAYBEE

Ⓢ

SWEETMEATS PRESS

A Sweetmeats Book

First published in Great Britain by
Sweetmeats Press 2012

Copyright © Kay Jaybee 2012

ISBN 978-1-909181-17-5

Sweetmeats Press
27 Old Gloucester Street
London
WC1N 3XX
England, U. K.

Dedicated to the cafe proprietors in my life.

prick (*noun, vulgar slang*) a man's penis (OED)

tease (*verb*) to make fun of, to be provocative or playful (OED)

prick-tease(r): (*noun*) a woman who leads a man to the mistaken belief that she is likely to have sexual intercourse with him (OED)

It is a widely held belief that being a prick-tease is a bad thing. But is it?

You could argue that it is fun. That it is a welcome form of flirtatious attention and that, for some, being a prick-tease is the very essence of power.

P r o l o g u e

◆◆◆◆

Ignoring the buzz of her mobile phone, Maddie placed the worn stub of charcoal to the side of her easel and took a step back from the girl before her.

Maddie nodded with approval as her newest model – a petite blonde – flexed the muscles she'd been keeping stock still for the previous half hour.

"Control, Freya – at least the appearance of control – is everything." The artist reached out an affectionate hand to her muse.

Freya rocked a little on her bare feet as Maddie touched her lightly freckled cheek. "No need to look so worried, honey. You are doing brilliantly. It's a difficult pose to hold for so long."

"Thank you." Blushing an endearing shade of pink, Freya lowered the hands she'd nervously clenched before her, giving her employer another chance to see the neat triangle of her semi-shaved pussy.

Maddie, her jeans and t-shirt smeared and spattered with all the mediums of her trade, did not feel the need to mention to Freya that her own knickers were sodden, nor that beneath her holster bra, her nipples were rock hard.

A further buzz from her mobile alerted Maddie to the arrival of another text message. In fact a steady string of muffled noises from her mobile, coming from the pit of her handbag, had been announcing the arrival of texts every ten minutes or so throughout the morning.

Smiling to herself, Maddie continued to disregard her phone and considered the exquisite outline of her companion's porcelain frame. Most people came to Maddie to be drawn or painted, sometimes as a commission for a lover, husband or wife. Some, however, like Freya, came to the studio as a way of improving their self-confidence. Despite her generally shy demeanour, Freya had proved to be very good at posing as Maddie required and the artist had offered her an occasional job as a life model.

Sometimes Maddie felt she was more therapist than artist – specifically a sex therapist – as men and women alike shared their most intimate secrets while standing on the other side of her easel. Maddie's studio certainly had the air of an erotic fantasy confessional about it. She wasn't complaining, however. No other life would do for her now. The job satisfaction Maddie achieved from listening to the dreams and fantasies of others while she recreated them onto canvas, went hand in glove with the personal physical gratification it gave her.

Money being either plentiful or non-existent, depending on the current success of her commissions and sales, Maddie had been forced to develop an alternative form of payment for her models – a reward system for good work. Maddie could tell from the rise and fall of Freya's chest and the glistening damp skin at the top of her thighs, that she was more than ready to be paid for today's session.

Closing in on her model, Maddie simultaneously cupped Freya's slick pussy and left breast with her charcoal-blackened hands, causing an involuntary shiver to ripple through the younger woman's body.

"Your progress really is outstanding, honey. Few of my models can stay as motionless as you can." Congratulating Freya on her skill, Maddie left two dark palm prints on the girl's tits and tapped at the inside of her legs. "Open up. I think you have deserved a treat after all your hard work."

Gliding her palm over Freya's mound, Maddie slipped a gentle finger into the slippery canal of the model's frantically clutching sex, enjoying the murmured mew of contentment that escaped from her lipstick-free mouth.

Pumping gently, the artist brought Freya close to orgasm with steady increases and decreases of pressure – her own mind straying to her mobile. Maddie wondered where Theo was and what he was doing. She knew what he was thinking about. She always knew that. Theo thought about her.

Pushing her happily sex-drugged model onto an armchair, Maddie's own arousal kicked up a notch as she bent to lick Freya's nub, swiftly bringing her to the dawn of a shuddering release.

While continuing to take pleasure in the sweet taste

of another woman on her lips, Maddie considered how she'd phrase her responses to all the messages Theo had sent and how she'd tell him precisely what and who had held up her replies.

Inhaling Freya's climactic scent, Maddie's hands roamed up and over the small, orgasm-jacked body, her thoughts still with Theo. His work-calloused right hand was probably on his dick at that very moment. A heady hit of power consumed Maddie – a power as intense as the climax of the woman panting hard in the chair before her.

Maddie loved making him wait.

Chapter One

> Theo: Tell me where u are
> Theo: Tell me what u are wearing
> Theo: I bet ur fucking someone
> Theo: Who is it? Who are u fucking?
> Theo: I can see u in my mind – ur hair
> is in a ponytail isn't it?

Maddie had deliberately turned her phone to silent as she'd pushed her overfull supermarket trolley around the packed store. Sitting in her car now, she couldn't help but smile as she read the five messages while running a hand along her ponytail. She knew Theo couldn't actually see her. He'd be fixing up new lighting in someone's house somewhere. But her favourite electrician didn't seem to have the ability to consider her other than in a sexual situation.

"I do have to eat like everyone else, Theo!" Maddie spoke to herself and the steering wheel before tucking the phone away without answering his list of texts and heading back to her home-based studio to get ready for work.

An hour later, dressed in the attire she'd been requested to wear by that day's model – a black pleated mini-skirt, a long baggy shirt and absolutely nothing else – Maddie sat at her cluttered desk to read the handwritten notes she'd made after Sara's last session.

1. *Issues involving going commando*
2. *Has a partner (Jake) who wishes her to live out erotic fantasy scenarios for him*
3. *She wants to oblige, but lacks the nerve*
4. *Sara's compromise is to have a picture of herself going commando – she hopes it will give her confidence*
5. *Almost there – just need her to be brave enough to uncover her pussy for me to draw*

Working with Sara had been slow progress at first. Now, three sessions in, at least she was happy to walk to the studio in trousers or leggings without wearing underwear. Maddie wondered if Sara would hold her nerve today and wear her partner's favourite skirt with nothing beneath, as they'd arranged during their last meeting.

Relaxing back in her chair while she waited for Sara's knock at the door, Maddie picked up her mobile and sent Theo the reply she had no doubt he would be waiting for.

> **Maddie: I'm waiting for a client. She is beautiful. U would love her.**

His response came almost instantly and Maddie grinned as she imagined his workman's hands diving towards his phone as her message reached him.

> Theo: What's her name?
> Maddie: Now now honey – client
> confidentiality...
> Theo: Spoil sport
> Maddie: Ur dick hard for me?
> Theo: Yes
> Maddie: Good boy. U out on the road?
> Theo: Yes

Maddie checked the time. Sara was never late. In fact it was rare for her not to be at least ten minutes early. That meant she had approximately five minutes before Sara's arrival in which to play with Theo.

> Maddie: I am going commando. I want
> u to do the same.
> Theo: Fuck woman, I'm on my way to a
> customer!
> Maddie: Park the van and take ur
> boxers off.

The pause before Theo's reply confirmed for Maddie that he was doing exactly what she told him to. When his text did come through, it seemed almost as breathless as she guessed he was.

> Theo: Done. Now what? Tell me!
> Maddie: Sorry honey – got to get to

work – think of me fingering my client's
pussy – then later u may masturbate.
Theo: What!? U can't say that and then
go!
Maddie: I can. No playing until I say
so.

The moment she'd pressed the send button on her last text, Maddie threw her mobile carelessly onto the desk. She knew Theo would reply, but he'd have to wait. For now she had work to do. The double ring of the doorbell told her Sara had arrived.

As arranged, Sara had dressed just as Maddie had, including the similarly styled short, pleated skirt that she had declared to be Jake's favourite. One glance at her backside however, told Maddie that her client's underwear was still firmly in place.

Careful not to make Sara feel ill at ease, Maddie said nothing about her model's overdressing and gestured towards the stairs. "Come through, we'll get you more comfortable."

The nervous yet happy energy that was radiating from every pore of Sara's skin was a familiar condition to Maddie. Nearly all her visitors had the same excited yet apprehensive aura about them. Only when that apprehension had been replaced entirely with excitement, did Maddie consider them ready to be properly painted. Otherwise there was no way she could capture the essence of their sexuality on canvas.

Sara risked an anxious smile as she walked up the narrow stairway that separated Maddie's living quarters from her office-cum-studio – a studio which held everything that might come in useful. There was a double bed, a battered yet comfortable sofa, and a multitude of different chairs, so her clients could choose where they wanted to be while they posed for a portrait. As well as the furniture, there were stacks of discarded empty frames and potential props, a battered metal trolley holding Maddie's artistic supplies, as well as a kettle, toaster and small sink where she cleaned her brushes.

Next to the bed stood an old-fashioned chest of drawers. Unbeknown to many of her customers, its three drawers contained every instrument of domination and submission imaginable – from tubes of lube, condoms, countless packs of batteries, dildos, whips, paddles, vibes, ropes, blindfolds and gags. Thus, Maddie was always prepared for any request from her clientele.

Ignoring the flashing light on her muted mobile, telling her she did indeed have more messages from Theo, Maddie addressed her companion. "So, Sara, how have things been for you this week?"

"Okay, thanks. Jake is really pleased I'm for doing this for him." The smile that wasn't quite as shy as it had been in previous weeks became wider as it spread over Sara's neat asiatic features.

"And so he should be. Hundreds of women say they'll carry out their partner's fantasies. Very few ever actually have the will or courage to go through with their promises. I have always thought that, if you make a promise, then you must do whatever it was you agreed to. Even if it takes some time to fulfil your oath."

Sara knew Maddie was probably right, but she refrained from comment as Maddie placed the large canvas that held her work-in-progress onto the easel.

The artist let Sara nervously pace the room while she selected the handful of chalk pastels she'd need to finish the basic design of her work. With the background and outline of the picture already complete, Maddie could go no further until Sara was comfortable enough to show the feminine folds hidden under the black knickers she wore.

While Sara fiddled with the high wooden bar stool she would be leaning over once the session began, Maddie ran a critical eye over the canvas. She'd chosen pastels instead of oils or charcoal to best capture the mocha lustre to Sara's skin. Some blocks of colour were already filled in – her subject's jet-black hair shone from the page and the crisp white of her long t-shirt, rucked up at the waist, contrasted perfectly with the beauty and lustre of her flesh. The artist reached out a finger and ran it over her representation of Sara's toned thighs and legs, and the varnished wood of the stool over which she was bent. All that remained was the gap in the middle of the canvas. A space that Maddie fully intended to sketch today.

It was a shame, Maddie thought as she nodded encouragingly to Sara, who was gesturing towards the CD player in the corner of the room, that she was drawing her client's back view. Consequently, the girl's exotically feline, emerald eyes, which suited her perfectly and yet somehow seemed startlingly at odds with her skin tone, would be missing from the finished scene.

Once Sara had chosen some light, almost ethereal, music to play softly in the background, Maddie took charge. "Would you like to remind yourself of what we've produced so far?"

Standing next to each other before the canvas, the blankness in the middle of the nearly-finished piece virtually screamed out loud. Tentatively, knowing the importance of keeping her model relaxed, Maddie reached out and took Sara's hand in her own. "If this is going to be completed in time for Jake's birthday, then I have to draw the rest of you today, honey."

Sara tightened her grip on Maddie's hand, the pulse in her wrist hammering against the artist's. "I know. I haven't stopped thinking about what I have to do since I was here last week."

Gently taking Sara's arm, Maddie manoeuvred her to stand directly in front of the stool. Taking a pace closer, so that her chest was pressed against Sara's back, Maddie wrapped her arms protectively around the younger woman's waist.

"It isn't that scary, honey All you have to do is take off those panties and lean over this stool just the same way you did during the last three sessions. In only half an hour, I will have all I require to complete the picture, which I can do once you've gone. I can make it even quicker for you if you allow me to take a couple of photos."

Sara said nothing for a moment, secretly relishing the heat of the curvaceous body behind her. "I know but, well… what if you don't like what you see? What if I'm ugly down there?"

This was a fear that Maddie had heard many times before. She neither laughed, nor scoffed, nor judged. As an erotic artist, this was something she came up against a lot. Everyone seemed to be afraid that they might be abnormal or insufficient in some way, be they male or female.

"Honey, I have seen all sorts in this studio. Trust me. I am sure you are exquisite. Jake loves you down there doesn't he?"

Sara blushed coyly as she remembered the countless times her man had worshipped her with his tongue from between her spread legs. "He certainly seems to."

"There you go then." Maddie took hold of Sara's shoulders and firmly but gently turned her so that they were face to face. "I am happy to do what I suggested last week, if you think it would help."

Sara dipped her eyes to Maddie's skirt. She knew without asking that there would be no knickers under its short pleats.

The air of eroticism that was a permanent feature of Maddie's studio took on a sharper tang, as if it was now something solid that could be grasped. Sara had been thinking about Maddie as much as she'd been thinking about the prospect of having to reveal her pussy, and she was afraid of giving herself away. She knew that if Maddie looked at her pussy, she would see how it glistened – wet with the hope that the artist's slender fingers would touch her.

Realising Sara was lost in her own thoughts, and fairly confident those thoughts concerned sex with her, Maddie adopted a firmer tone. "You do want to get this done for Jake, don't you? If you have changed your mind about going commando, then I have to know now so we can change things."

Visibly pulling herself together, Sara took a deep breath. "No, I haven't changed my mind. Jake will love it – I just have stage fright, that's all." She forced herself to raise her eyes to meet Maddie's and, with her chest tightening, said, "And yes, if you are still up for it, then the plan we agreed last week would be good."

"Excellent." Maddie stood up straight and dropped her hands from Sara's shoulders. "Well, as you can see, I am wearing similar clothes to your own, as discussed. I, however, have gone commando. You, I can see, have not. I understand that it isn't exactly nice weather out there today, which is presumably why you didn't walk here panty free?"

Both women knew that the fact it was unseasonably cold for a summer's day was not the reason that Sara had failed to leave off her undergarments. But Sara was grateful for being given the opportunity to blame the dull drizzle for her last minute failing of nerve before she'd left home.

"Exactly. I didn't want to catch a cold."

Keeping up the pretence, Maddie picked up the high, pine barstool Sara was to lean over and put it exactly where it had been positioned during the other three sittings. "Well then, if you take off those undies and stand by the stool we'll crack on?"

Sara's hands shook as she edged down her knickers, trying not to notice that the fabric was rather damper than it should have been as she slid them to the floor.

Once the small scrap of black material was placed gingerly on the end of the bed, Sara walked to the stool and hovered uncertainly, wondering if Maddie really was going to do as she'd promised last week or if, now she'd gotten her model this far, she wouldn't feel the need to keep her side of the bargain.

Maddie picked up her mobile. "Do excuse me for a second, Sara. I must answer these two messages before we start."

Theo had been getting impatient...

> Theo: What are u doing?
> Theo: I have work too woman – and I can't concentrate with this bloody hard on! For fucks sake Maddie – tell me what u are doing right now!

Maddie smiled as she typed.

> Maddie: I'm about to calm a nervous client by showing her my pussy.

Keeping the phone in her hand, she walked toward

Sara. With each stride Maddie lifted the hem of her skirt a fraction at a time, aware how much she was teasing Sara with every centimetre of flesh she revealed. As she reached the end of the bed, Maddie, keeping her bare feet inflexible on the floor, flipped the remainder of the skirt up to show her rounded peach of a backside. Then, spreading her legs, she leant over the end of the bed, her chest buried in the duvet, her back arched upwards so Sara could clearly see her pussy.

The sharp intake of breath the model gave echoed around the room, but Maddie pretended she hadn't heard it. "Do you want to look closer, honey? You could reassure yourself that we are all the same underneath. We are all vulnerable, all written to the same design code and yet somehow we are all unique." The artist spoke softly, but with a matter of fact nature that belied the provocativeness of what she was doing.

Her fingers parted her butt cheeks so that Sara could see her vulva in all its majesty. "If all our cunts were the same, then I would be able to draw in any old pussy. And where would the fun be in that? How fabulous that we are all different – all those new, stunning, unique and tasty treats to explore."

Maddie said nothing else. Every word she had uttered had turned her on and she hoped that she was having the same effect on Sara.

Taking a step towards the artist, her heart thudding, her head bursting with a curiosity that wanted to touch as well as see, Sara crouched behind Maddie. Allowing the haunting music emanating from the stereo to wrap around her, Sara's eyes took in every fold and shining wet line of the inviting flesh before her.

Twisting her neck round so she could watch Sara examining her with wide, emerald eyes, Maddie eventually broke the silence. "You can if you want to."

"I can what?" Sara's voice was husky as she asked, even though she knew the answer to the question.

"You can touch. See what it feels like. It seems only fair because I shall be examining you intimately as I prepare to capture your sexual essence on the canvas."

"Will you need to touch me, then?" Sara couldn't quite keep the edge of longing from her voice. Maddie was sure that the girl hoped and feared in equal measure that the answer would be yes.

Expertly keeping her own desire under control, Maddie's reply was uncaringly breezy. "I would never dream of touching anyone if they didn't wish me to, but I find I can get a better idea of the type of stroke to use with my pastel or paints if I can feel the texture for myself. It is always up to the individual model entirely."

"Oh." That was all Sara could say and Maddie privately speculated how much sweet honey was already flowing from her model's private parts.

Sara's fingers were only inches away from the artist. It wouldn't have taken much for her to lean forward, touch Maddie's flesh and discover what another woman felt like for the very first time.

Finally, breaking the silence, Sara whispered, "I'm pretty sure my boyfriend would be willing me on if he was here. Jake is pretty much into everything, women, men, straight, kinky; and he's always had serious fantasy issues about seeing me with another woman."

Maddie smiled kindly. "I honestly don't think I've met a bloke who doesn't hope to see his woman with another female, honey."

Dropping her eyes to the floor, not daring to look at the artist's succulent folds any longer, Sara spoke as if thinking out loud. "But would he be quite so pleased, if he wasn't able to witness it for himself? I don't think Jake would like me to have a woman without him watching."

"Then don't tell him." Letting her matter-of-fact answer sink in, Maddie let go of her rump cheeks and while she lay waiting for Sara's decision, she quietly tapped into her phone.

> Maddie: I am laid across my studio bed
> showing another woman my pussy. I
> am so wet.

Knowing that Sara was too wrapped up in her own battle between wishing to touch and being afraid to, Maddie read and responded to Theo's instant reply.

> Theo: If u fuck her will u tell me about
> it afterwards?
> Maddie: If ur good. But she has to

decide.

Maddie broke the silence. "You don't have to touch me, honey. But if it would relax you before we begin the session, then please do. Otherwise we'd better get on."

"Actually," Sara came to a decision. "I think Jake would quite like it – if I told him. Which I might…or might not." Reaching out a hand, not allowing herself time to change her mind, Sara placed a single finger directly onto the very centre of Maddie's labia.

The sigh of bliss that shot from the artist's lips at the tender nature of the furtive touch was all Sara needed to embolden her to explore further. Now the first move had been made, she was immediately more confident and soon her hands were exploring Maddie's vagina, smoothly luxuriating in and widening her creases.

As she let Sara explore and abandoned herself to the exquisite touch, Maddie tapped out another message, her fingers misspelling things as her concentration began to fracture.

> Maddie: There's a par of bashful figers
> playing with my slit.
> Theo: Fingers? – Tell me more
> Maddie: She is exploring me
> Theo: Feel good?
> Maddie: Amazing.

Despite the fact that the light on her mobile was

again flashing to tell her Theo had sent another instant reply, Maddie put down the phone. Sara had brought her face so close to Maddie's nub that the artist could feel the other woman's gulps of air on her slit. Without even slightly betraying how badly she wanted Sara to manipulate her clit, Maddie asked, "Have you ever touched a woman before?"

"Never." Sara inhaled, loving the sweet, almost fruity, aroma that she found between her companion's thighs.

"Well, what you are doing to me is probably what Jake does to you, so I don't have to tell you how good it feels. You are obviously a natural."

A flush of delight enflamed Sara's chest as Maddie's words extinguished her few remaining nerves. As she said, "Thank you Maddie," Sara leant forward and blew a sharp gust of breath onto Maddie's clit.

"Oh my God!" Maddie shuffled down the duvet, pushing her mound closer to Sara's face. "I should tell you, honey, that if you don't stop that right now, I am going to have to fuck you properly before the sitting."

A massive grin crossed Sara's face as she blew over the other woman's nub again. With every instinct in her body telling her exactly what to do, she gripped Maddie's bare buttocks. Pulling the lush oval cheeks apart, Sara took a long lick of Maddie's pussy from bottom to top.

The model's mumbled sigh of "Wow, you're delicious – sort of fruity and almondy at the same time," hadn't fully left her lips when, without warning, Maddie twisted around and grabbed Sara by the waist.

Hoisting the model onto her lap, so their black skirts bunched up against each other, Maddie pressed her mouth against Sara's, revelling in the taste of another new set of lips. As she worked, she pictured Theo. She knew how badly he wanted her lips, her body and her sex. But unlike Sara, he hadn't earned his reward yet.

Trailing fast moving fingers over her Malaysian companion, Maddie pushed her palms up under the baggy white t-shirt, popped down the bra Sara wore and freed the succulent breasts from confinement. Sara required no further encouragement and quickly reciprocated the move, gasping as Maddie's heavier bra-free tits sprang to attention under her touch. The older woman's nipples, large and pleasingly rough, pushed up at Sara's hands greedily, as if asking to be pinched and rubbed.

All cohesive thought gone, the women fell back on the bed, a tangled mass of arms and legs, hooking around each other, touching every inch of flesh they could reach. Once the initial wave of lust had passed, however, Maddie regained her habitual self-control, flipped Sara onto her front, sat astride her legs and pinned her to the bed.

Maddie, seeing her guest through artist's eyes, made her first proper hands-on inspection of the backside she was supposed to be drawing. It was rounded, without an ounce of extra fat – suggesting regular gym sessions. She ran her palms over the proffered smooth skin, taking pleasure in how Sara's breathing changed depending on how she was touched. The artist smiled as she spotted a telltale blotch of darker flesh, the signs of a bruise fading away. "Jake beats you sometimes? For fun, I mean."

"How do you know that?"

"That's a paddle bruise. I would know it anywhere." Maddie kissed the faint mark.

Sara asked, her voice breathless, "You like paddles, too?"

"I like everything, honey." Maddie licked the bruise, working her tongue over and around where her temporary lover's boyfriend had made his mark. "I think we should include this in your commission – prove to Jake I didn't draw any old ass."

Sara could feel the pulse in her chest pounding against the bedclothes. "But you can hardly see it. How can you add it in?"

"Easy, we'll just put it back."

Climbing off the model and giving her a stern look that told her in no uncertain terms she should not move, Maddie went to the chest of drawers by the bed and pulled out a palm shaped black paddle. "This should work well."

With no other warning and no gentle strikes of preparation, Maddie brought the leather down hard onto the exact spot of the first bruise.

Sara gulped, her hands grasping at the rich purple duvet beneath her, as Maddie expertly punished her, making her simultaneously beg for the pain to be kissed away and for her never to stop the strikes.

Only when Sara's right buttock glowed with the

indicators of a coming bruise did Maddie stop beating and Sara stop pleading. With contrasting tenderness, Maddie brought her mouth to the shining new mark, licking it better. She snaked her right hand up between Sara's legs.

Raising her bottom a fraction, Sara eased her legs open to grant Maddie better access. A gentle cry escaped from the model as her artistic partner kissed her buttocks while sending a finger to polish over and around her slippery clit. Almost as soon as her nub was touched Sara started to twitch – her breasts, ass, and pussy feeling drawn together as if an electric current had connected them and turned the spaces between into one almighty erogenous zone.

"I'm cumming – oh fuck, I..." Sara's words morphed into groans as Maddie slotted a finger inside her, caressing her thumb over the model's nub, her lips still nibbling and nipping at Sara's rump.

As her model shook and cried out her release, Maddie brushed herself down and prepared to start work. Manoeuvring a dazed Sara over to the barstool Maddie, forcing down her own craving to cum, positioned the girl over the seat as required.

Leaving Sara to gather her breath, the artist picked up her pastels, ready to capture the sex-swollen lips on the gap in the canvas – lips that she was determined to taste as a reward once her work was done.

C h a p t e r   T w o

◆ ◆ ◆ ◆

He knew it had to stop.

Everyday Theo told himself that it would be the last day Maddie played games with his head. Not to mention his groin.

Angrily he stuffed his mobile into his overall pocket and tried to give all his attention to the lighting circuit he was fixing within the walls of his latest customer's new conservatory. As he examined the spotlight-style fittings, Theo cursed again – they were almost identical to the ones he'd added to Maddie's studio six weeks ago. It suddenly felt as if the bundled collection of wires and switches he had installed that day were entirely responsible for the constant state of frustration he'd found himself in ever since.

How was he supposed to focus on cable runs and on not short-circuiting the whole property, or worse, electrocuting someone, when all he could think about was the last text message the artist had sent him?

Carefully letting go of the thin wires, Theo leant against the wall where he was working and squeezed his hazel eyes shut. The memory that flooded his mind was abrupt and vivid.

He was standing in the centre of the wooden floor that formed the right hand side of Maddie's studio, gawping at what he saw. Lined up around two sides of the room, propped against the corresponding stark white walls of the artist's creative space, were a dozen or so completed and semi-completed, paintings and drawings of men and women in situations that went way beyond compromising.

Theo recalled how his eyes had lingered over every brush stroke, every strike of charcoal, which had merged – not with vulgarity, but sensuality – to create illustrations of sexily twisted bodies. Sexy, but with more than a touch of erotic, perhaps even pornographic, kinkiness. Everything about the pictures had seemed to be alive to him. He'd felt as if the participants were about to move for real; as if the models involved really had been screwing whilst the artist captured their essence onto canvas or paper.

When he'd eventually managed to drag his eyes away from the artwork, Theo remembered how he'd surveyed the remainder of the room, in a vague attempt to appear as though he was assessing the best place to install the extra lights, rather than scanning for additional artwork. He'd been pretty sure that Maddie hadn't been fooled, however and knew very well that his mind had been on things a great deal more exciting than optimum bulb wattage.

In contrast to where Theo had worked, the other half of the Maddie's workspace had been thickly carpeted and painted in a restful cream. A plush double bed, covered in a maroon duvet, sat next to a low plum-coloured chaise longue. Normal furniture that should have been items of relaxation, seemed hungry somehow. As Theo had stared at them, recognising them from scenes in the works of art he'd just seen, his cock had begun to stir.

Theo snapped his eyes open and forced his mind back to the job in hand. *Damn that woman.*

Stripping back some wires, Theo felt his dick quiver against the inside of his underwear-free jeans. Thanks to her texts he knew that at that exact moment Maddie was lying on the studio bed with another woman.

His hands quivered a little. Theo took a protracted exhalation of air. This was ridiculous – he had to have her. He simply *had* to. Nothing else would stop these thoughts – thoughts that he now recognised had tipped from being merely keen to being frankly obsessive.

Another text came.

The electrician retrieved the phone from his pocket. "Shit!" Theo cursed as his commando state became harder to disguise. Thankful that his client had gone out to work, he read the latest text for a third time.

Maddie: I made her cum.

Knowing he would have to masturbate before he had any chance of doing anything remotely productive, Theo walked towards his customer's bathroom.

He had his hand on the bathroom doorknob when another text came.

Maddie: Don't u dare wank – I haven't
given u permission yet.

Fuck! How does she always know?

The very first time Theo had seen Maddie, standing
in bare feet, stained faded-blue jeans and an over-large long
purple t-shirt, he'd felt it – her blatant, self-assured sexuality.
It seemed to escape from every pore of her body. He'd no
doubt she knew of the effect she had on other people. And
the fact she dressed down and had a level of self control that
would make a saint jealous, made her an even more attractive
proposition. She was a woman that almost everyone would
want – at least once – just for the challenge of trying to make
her lose control for a millisecond, if nothing else.

It should have been so simple. Theo was a tall, well
built, confident guy, with the sort of rugged, ugly-handsome
appearance which, over the past twenty of his thirty-five
years, had never failed to attract a host of willing partners.
Maddie Templeton, however, was something new. Without
even realising what was happening, Theo had found himself
entwined in (and trapped under) her spell. A fact that was
reinforced as he found himself obeying her command and
going back to work, his unsatisfied erection chaffing the inside
of his denim trousers. He swore under his breath.

Screwing the first of three light fittings against the
conservatory walls with rather more force than was strictly
necessary, Theo considered for the hundredth time, exactly
how he'd become such a puppet to Maddie's whims, when he
hadn't so much as kissed her!

Six weeks earlier

He had been running late, but as it was only a quote she was after, it had seemed logical to slot his potential new client in before beginning the day's work in earnest. Parking his van in the one remaining space outside the row of Victorian terraces in the city suburbs, Theo had easily found the door to number thirty-eight, but was mildly confused. He'd been told by Miss Templeton that he was to provide her with a price for putting additional spotlighting in her artist's studio, and yet this was an ordinary town house, not a business premises.

Knocking on the door, wondering if perhaps he'd written the address incorrectly, Theo was soon confronted by a slim shapely woman in clothes that were too big for her, but whose appearance alone reassured him that he had got the location right. The tell-tale smudges of ink on her hand as she reached out to shake his, along with the mild aroma of paint that wafted through the door, gave it away. Theo had never before considered the smell of oil and turpentine to be an erotic scent. He did now.

The woman's slim yet strong hand felt both warm and cold at the same time as she greeted him. Grasping his palm for a fraction longer than most people would have done, she welcomed him inside, explaining as she did so that she lived downstairs and had converted the entire upstairs of the terrace into a studio where she worked.

Following her into the narrow hallway and up the stairs that divided her home from her working quarters, Theo had found himself faced with a space that only partly matched the assumptions he'd made in his own mind. He had expected a large airy space, with the work of the proprietor covering the walls. He had expected that work to be landscapes, perhaps the occasional portrait, commissions of much-loved pets or family homes. That was not what he saw.

It was a few minutes before Theo registered that he'd been gawping at the pictures on the walls and those lined up around the edges of the room. He'd missed absolutely everything his potential client had been saying to him about lighting, including her questions about what he would consider a safe maximum wattage for daylight bulbs.

"What do you think, Mr. Hunter? Can you fit extra lighting in here, or would it mean tackling the entire wiring system? I realise the house is quite old and I couldn't afford to pay for a total rewire just now."

"Theo, call me Theo." As he'd spoken, Theo knew he sounded a bit lame, a bit like he was giving his name as a limp handshake, but the artist responded gracefully.

"I'm Maddie. You like the art?" She spoke with a smile that seemed entirely genuine, but was somehow knowing. He felt as if she and she alone, were party to a private joke.

"Very much." Theo walked nearer to the pictures propped on the wooden-floored side of the room. "May I look closer?"

"Of course." Maddie, totally at ease with showing a male stranger around her blatantly erotic art, spoke casually as she gestured to those to their right. "These are commissions and those to the left are practice pieces."

"It doesn't look to me as if you need any practice."

Laughing, Maddie appraised the electrician more shrewdly. "You are very kind, but no one is ever so good at something that they can't get better and besides, when I practise my technique, I train up life models at the same time. It's a win-win situation."

His voice became huskier as Theo replied rather more wistfully than he intended, "You have life models in here?"

"Sometimes. How do you think I manage to draw people with no clothes on?"

"I..." Theo stammered, aware that his usually un-embarrasable face was colouring. "I guess I assumed you used photographs." He pointed to a large pin board on the furnished side of the room. "You seem to have a good many umm...action shots, over there."

"True." Again Maddie was unruffled by his observation. "I like to get a few stills taken in case the models have trouble holding the poses they wish me to recreate. As you can see, a few of the positions can be awkward to maintain for the periods of time necessary."

"I'm sure."

Feeling far more awkward than he had done in years, Theo tried not to look at the art again. He dared not let his brain consider what sort of activities had taken place in the room in which he was now standing, or he'd never have been able to address himself to the issue of improving the room's lighting.

The job should only have taken twenty minutes to assess. But it took almost twice as long, such was Theo's self-consciousness as the quiet Maddie Templeton watched his every move. He was surprised to find that his hands were clammy and his shaft was pulsing within his trousers as he hunted down the fuse box to a cupboard full of shoes and coats in the far corner of the studio.

At last Theo pronounced his conclusions to the waiting woman, who was still standing with infinite patience at the end of the double bed. "I could put in two extra fittings on the far side but, as you said, the circuits in here are old. To avoid rewiring, your best plan would be additional free-standing lamps." Theo gestured to the three tall, thin stainless steel lampstands stacked out of the way in the corner of the room. "Although I appreciate that they can throw shadows you may not want."

The whole time he spoke, all Theo could think about was how easy it would be to push the artist back against the bed and shove his hand between her legs.

"So how much would the two spotlights cost?"

Theo tried to blank out the vision of his companion's naked pussy. "It would depend on how long they took to fit, but approximately eighty pounds, including fixtures, fittings, my time and VAT."

"And if I said yes, how soon could you get the job done?"

"Tomorrow."

Maddie's eyebrows rose. "Really? So soon? You don't

have a job already lined up for tomorrow?"

Feeling his crotch stir again, as the artist's piercing chocolate eyes reached into his soul, Theo knew she saw exactly how badly he wanted an excuse to return to her studio as soon as possible. He felt caught out, like a teenager whose first unwise crush had been discovered.

In his efforts to seem sincere Theo's words came out far faster than they should have done. "I'll finish the job I'm currently on today and I have a gap tomorrow morning. If you'd like this doing soon I can slot you in, otherwise it would have to be next month I'm afraid. Should you be happy with my quote, that is."

Hoping Maddie wouldn't comment on his lie and also hoping the clients he was supposed to see the following day would forgive him for being 'unexpectedly delayed' the next morning, Theo kept his facial expression as neutral as possible as he waited for her decision.

"Can you be here early?"

"Anytime you like."

"How long should it take?"

"About an hour; assuming it goes to plan. If the existing wiring fights back, possibly two."

Maddie raised the corner of her mouth into an almost smile and clapped her hands as she came to a decision. "If you can be here by eight o'clock tomorrow morning, then maybe you'll be finished before I start work?"

Theo returned her businesslike smile and reached out to shake the hand he was being offered to seal the deal. "Eight o'clock tomorrow morning it is."

Dressing with her usual disinterest, Maddie had wondered if the electrician would be early, or if he would make sure the job took longer than necessary. She had no doubt that one or other situation would occur, if not both. The studio always seemed to have that effect on tradesmen. Or on most people that visited, come to that.

Tucking her hair up into a loose ponytail, Maddie took a quick look at the clock on her bedside table. It was a quarter to eight. "So, he'll be exactly on time, then." Grinning to herself, Maddie addressed her reflection in her bedroom mirror. "He's rather nice. Should I give him what he wants?" She stroked down her shirt as she considered how it might feel to take his cock between her teeth. It had been way too long since she'd tasted male flesh and it occurred to Maddie, that she had rather missed it. *Shall I go for a quick fuck, or should I play the long game?*

The doorbell rang at precisely eight o'clock and Maddie strolled sedately through her hallway, saying to herself, "Perhaps I'll just see how this goes? See if he acts as I expect him to act before I decide what to do with him."

The approach of Maddie Templeton's outline through the glass panel of her front door made Theo's pulse shoot up a notch. Immediately he felt cross with himself.

All the previous evening, he'd gone over and over how ridiculous he was being in rearranging his work schedule just because he fancied a customer. How stupid to act so unprofessionally over a fantasy featuring a woman he'd known for less than an hour and with whom he hadn't exchanged more than a handful of words.

Eventually, Theo had managed to convince himself that he didn't want anything to do with a woman who could evidently observe other people having sex and be completely unmoved by the event. Falling asleep on the sofa, his television left talking to itself, the electrician's dreams had immediately made a mockery of the hours he'd spent convincing himself to do the right thing and cancel his newest client's appointment.

In the safety of his sleeping state, Theo had held Miss Templeton against the double bed, her arms above her head, her wrists trapped beneath his hands as he pumped his solid dick between her thighs, his eyes locked into hers. He'd turned her over and serviced her doggy style while she cried out his name. He'd tied her up and licked her breasts until she squealed and begged for the dick he teased her with to be inserted down her hungry throat.

Now, the creature that'd haunted his waking and sleeping life for the past twenty-four hours, was ushering him up the stairs. Theo barely dared to look at her. He feared that if the artist's shrewd eyes saw his face, she would read his every thought.

Maddie was more amused than offended that the electrician was hardly acknowledging her existence. Years of painting people in the throes of sexual excitement had taught her a thing or two. He clearly desired her even more than she had thought. *Maybe the waiting game then...*

Observing Theo as he set up his equipment, Maddie took pity on him. She was sure his hands wouldn't have been so unsteady if she wasn't hovering nearby, so she left him to it. Moving to the opposite side of the large room, Maddie set up her easel and chalk pastels for the continuation of her latest commission – a woman's open legs and naked pussy.

Briefly studying what she'd already created, the artist began to add dabs of chalk here and there to enhance the depth of colour of her subject's curves, increasing the shadows that contrasted with the summer-tanned flesh.

Lovingly tracing a finger over and around the pinky-cream vulva she'd outlined, Maddie smudged it just enough to produce the correct texture and tone to the flesh that, after the particularly rewarding session the day before, she knew to taste delectable.

Theo's head was thudding from the effort involved in not glancing towards either Maddie at her easel, or at the erotic moments caught forever on the canvases stacked directly to his right.

Having quietly prepared both sets of lights, Theo was about to drill into the wall when he thought he ought to warn his silent companion that he was about to create a lot of noise. After all, he didn't want to take her by surprise, make her jump and cause her to ruin her work.

"Excuse me." He spoke clearly, but Maddie was so engrossed in what she was doing that she didn't hear him. Realising he would have to actually go over to her, Theo got up and crossed the room, very conscious of the noise his work shoes made on the wooden half of the studio floor – a noise that was suddenly stifled as he stepped onto the carpeted side of the room.

Still Maddie didn't seem to notice him. He had intended to politely cough, or say "Excuse me", keeping himself entirely professional. Instead, Theo expelled an involuntary gasp. The artist was running a chalk-dusted digit over the folds of another woman's pussy.

It didn't matter that what he was witnessing was simply an artist forming the picture she'd been paid to draw. The way his nether regions were responding made him feel as if he was standing before two women fondling each other. It took several gulps before his throat was sufficiently moistened for him to actually speak. "Miss Templeton? Maddie?"

A few more seconds passed before Maddie lowered her hand from the picture and refocused her attention on the man beside her. "Oh sorry." Suddenly attentive, Maddie wiped her hands over her thighs, carelessly dirtying her clothes. "I get a bit involved in what I'm doing sometimes."

"Well, yes. I can see why." Theo tried to keep the licking of his rapidly dehydrating lips a secret, looking away and gesturing across the room as he did so. "I'm about to use the drill. I didn't want to start it up without warning and give you a fright."

Maddie's smile hit her eyes and Theo's chest tightened at the effect it had on him. He couldn't help thinking that perhaps she didn't give out many genuine smiles.

"That's really thoughtful of you. Thank you."

Emboldened by her gratitude, Theo felt more like his usual confident self in the face of an attractive woman. "It would have been a shame to ruin your work. It's exquisite."

Maddie glimpsed up at the face of her electrician from under her eyelashes. It appeared he had given up on his determination not to acknowledge the presence of her art. "You are very kind, but this one is far from finished. My model will be here later for another sitting."

Mentally digesting the fact that the owner of the succulent thighs and pussy that covered the page before him was going to be in the room later, Theo said, "Can I ask you something?"

"You want to ask me why I paint people in sexual positions rather than respectable vases of daffodils or innocent seascapes."

This time it was Theo who smiled. "You get asked that a lot then? Although actually, I was going to say a vase of tulips, not daffodils."

"Have you ever looked at tulips properly?"

The question surprised Theo – as did the step Maddie took so that she was standing nearer to him. "No, I don't suppose I have. They're just flowers in other people's gardens – or vases."

"Next time you see some tulips, take a good look at them. See how the petals sit together." As she spoke, Maddie clasped Theo's right hand and held it by the wrist so his fingers pointed upwards. "Think of your fingers as the petals."

Theo's heartbeat increased as her strangely hot-cold touch held him with a firmness that belied her slim but appealingly curvy frame. Then, placing her free hand against his raised palm, Maddie pushed her fingers very slowly between his, so they overlapped by a fraction. "You see? Your skin is marginally darker than mine and some of your fingers are rougher than the others. Also, some of my fingers are not as smooth as others."

Theo didn't respond, all his being was now centred on the fake flower head they were creating as the artist went on. "It's the same with tulips. The different length petals make one whole flower, but each petal is marginally different to the next. Some are rougher, some smoother, some tatty, some perfect, even though they are all basically the same – like our fingers."

Letting go of his wrist, but keeping their palms entwined, Maddie pointed to her current project. "Do you see how her folds line up? How the different shades of skin lay adjacent to each other? The shape of each section of skin isn't that different from the next and yet they *are* all different, just like with tulip petals."

Theo looked. He was powerless to do anything else. Over the years he'd had direct physical contact with his fair share of women – more than his fair share. This was the first time he'd really looked at a cunt, though. Whenever he'd been faced with a real pussy he'd not wasted any time actually examining it aesthetically, always too caught up in passion to do anything more than stroke, lick, touch and ultimately fill the flesh on offer. Too keen to experience the rush of conquest as he made the woman he was with cum against him.

Temporarily speechless, Theo eventually said, "I'll never see tulips in quite the same way again."

His words broke the moment of connection and Maddie let go of his hand.

Privately cursing himself for such a flippant response, Theo murmured, "I'd better get back to work."

Nodding curtly, Maddie picked up her chalk and refocused her mind on the work of art before her.

Mindful of the hard-on that was barely concealed under his overalls, hoping like hell Maddie hadn't spotted it, yet sure that she had, the electrician picked up his drill.

As he made the first of a series of holes in the plaster work, Theo wished the action of the drill entering the wall didn't make him think of sex quite so much. *It's just drilling for heaven's sake.* In the years he'd been doing this job, he'd never made the connection, but now it seemed obvious. As if his drill was mocking him by getting the screwing he badly wanted for himself.

Theo turned the tool off. This was stupid. It was this place – it had to be. The atmosphere of background sex and sensuality was affecting him. As soon as he left he'd be okay again. Surely this was a perfectly natural reaction to such a place and the woman within it?

Taking a deep breath, Theo repositioned the drill bit and resolved to be as focused in his work as she was; and then to get out of there as quickly as humanly possible.

Theo was triple checking that the new spotlights worked, when the ring of the doorbell resounded through the room. The heart rate that he'd finally managed to calm shot back up. The bell had to be heralding the arrival of the owner of the vagina he felt he knew considerably better than any he had ever personally visited.

Maddie put aside her chalk and strode for the door, calling over her shoulder, "Are you done yet, Theo?"

"Yes, I'll put the bill on the desk." Theo sped up his tidying, producing a mini dustpan and brush from his holdall of tools to sweep up the plaster dust he'd sprayed across the shiny laminate flooring.

The sound of happily chatting female voices got nearer as Theo replaced his bits and pieces in the bag and, with a faint sheen of sweat on his forehead, he stood to leave.

He'd told himself he wouldn't even peek at the woman with Maddie. That it was none of his business what the rest of her was like. He did look though. He had no choice. The young woman with shoulder-length brown hair, a chest of ample proportions tucked under a tight t-shirt and a slim pair of hips, made sure she knocked into him as she passed.

Only risking a nod of recognition towards the newcomer, who headed confidently to the bed, Theo addressed Maddie in his best tradesman's manner. "All done then, Miss Templeton," he told her, before he carried on towards the staircase as fast as he could.

Theo heard the artist call to her companion, "I'll be

back in a tick, honey. I'll just see the electrician off." But he kept walking down the stairs, not stopping until his hand was on the front door.

"Thank you, Theo. I'll get your fee to you asap."

He inclined his head and opened the front door. As his feet crossed back into the fresh summer air, Theo turned and had a final look at Maddie. "You never did tell me why you paint erotica and not vases of flowers."

Staring unblinking into his eyes, Maddie was thoughtful before saying, "Is your phone number on the bill you've left me upstairs?"

Taken by surprise at her query Theo said, "Yes, it is."

"Then I'll text you the answer to your question later, when I have a minute,."

Theo didn't have the chance to respond, for Maddie had already shut the door.

Two hours later, Theo's mobile announced the arrival of a text.

>Maddie: I paint sex because I love to
>fuck.

Chapter Three

"You've had post." Sara's habitual grin was wider than usual, her stride noticeably more confident as she entered the studio waving three letters in Maddie's direction.

"Thanks, honey." A mixture of pride and desire filled Maddie as she looked at her model. Their last meeting had plainly had a very positive effect on her. "Just pop them on the desk. It's probably only bills."

Running her eyes up from Sara's feet to her face, Maddie nodded approvingly. "So, you finally did it then?"

A little shyly, Sara asked, "How can you tell?"

"You seem different. Freer." Maddie walked slow fingers down the back of Sara's shirt and over her flared mini-skirt as if to emphasise the lack of panty line or bra strap. "It suits you."

Soaking up the warmth of the other woman's touch through the thin cotton of her clothing, Sara couldn't keep her girlish surprise at her own brazen bravery out of her voice. "Jake is delighted. I called him as I came over, and told him I was strolling through town, commando-style just like he'd always dreamt of."

"And?" Maddie eased her palm up to the inviting flesh at the back of Sara's neck, soothing it with her fingers.

Sara's voice betrayed an evident surprise at the strength of her influence over her man's body. "Apparently, I gave him an instant hard-on!"

"I don't doubt it." Maddie drew her guest towards the easel to examine the chalked image in progress. Sara was bent, ready and moist, as if waiting for her unseen lover to simply step forward and impale her with a rigid cock. "You only have to glance at this to see that Jake is a very lucky boy indeed. You have a beautiful posterior. See."

Sara studied the picture in detail. The skirt she wore was rucked up above the rounded, coffee-coloured backside that perched high on the wooden stool. Her legs were stretched either side, her feet sloped in a pair of strappy silver high heels Maddie kept exclusively for the use of her clients. Sara shuffled an inch closer as she took in the details of her hands. They had been caught in the act of gripping the top of her thighs, pulling apart her own cheeks so that the damp folds of her vagina were tantalizingly on show to the companion you couldn't see – but you knew was there – just waiting.

Her voice was a whisper of amazement. "Is that really me?"

From the moment Sara had walked to the studio commando-style, Maddie had picked up on how happily sexy she evidently felt. *Perhaps even a little wanton...* Now, as she watched Sara observing her own kinky representation, Maddie could feel how anxious her model was to be taken by her – by anyone – and soon.

"You wanted me to capture the essence of your boyfriend's fantasy, so it really is you. If you don't feel it's you, then now is a good time to say."

Sara, her slightly awkward stance telling Maddie that she was attempting to hide a leak of sex syrup that was trickling down her leg, muttered in awe, "That's the odd thing. It feels exactly like me. I knew it would look like me, but – how do you get it to *feel* like me?"

Maddie merely smiled at the compliment, took her hands from her client, picked up her black pastel, gesturing to the stool as she did so. "Shall we make it even better?"

"Lets!"

Maddie deliberately pretended not to notice the efforts Sara made to disguise the tightness of her tits. Her body language made it transparent to the artist that Sara hoped there'd be a repeat of the fucking they'd shared the previous week.

As her model placed a cushion over the stool to protect her chest from the hardness of the wooden seat, Maddie reined in her own rising physical craving. As much as she desired Sara, Maddie also wanted her to remain erotically high and moist – her state of arousal being the very essence she wanted to capture within the work. With a few gentle adjustments to Sara's position, which sent shivers of lust through the model, Maddie set to work.

After fifteen silent minutes, Sara called a halt. "Getting dizzy here. Can we have a break?"

Helping Sara rise, so the blood that had rushed to her head returned to where it was supposed to be, Maddie agreed. "Take five."

Ignoring the way in which Sara perched hopefully on the foot of the bed, Maddie continued to stare at her work. "What were you thinking about when you were laying over the stool?"

Sara seated herself more comfortably and considered whether she should make something up, or if she should tell Maddie the truth. One glance at her surroundings reassured her. There couldn't have been much this woman hadn't heard before.

"The whole time I was bent over I could feel the air on my ass. I don't think I've ever been conscious of the air before."

Her shining eyes told Sara she understood, but Maddie made no verbal response as her model continued. "I guess I was mentally jumping between erotic musings of the sex we had last time and what Jake might be planning to do to me when I get home. From the tone of his voice when I told him I was going commando he is going to have to struggle not to fuck me against the nearest tree when we meet at the pub later."

Rinsing the chalk stains from her fingers, Maddie shot a smile in Sara's direction as if to confirm that she had been listening and headed to the pile of post on her desk. Opening the first envelope, Maddie threw it to one side. "As I thought – bills."

Restless, Sara got up and paced the room, stretching her neck and arms as she moved, flexing life back into them in preparation for the next session.

Picking up the third brown envelope from the pile, Maddie carelessly ripped at the opening. "Well, I've had the electricity and phone bill, I'm guessing this one will be for the gas."

Frowning as she was greeted with two sheets of high quality, folded cream paper. Maddie murmured, "Not the gas bill, then." Her companion was forgotten as her eyes widened in response to what she was holding. Reading faster and faster, flashing through the words in her excitement and yet unwilling to believe that she had understood the letter correctly for fear of being disappointed, Maddie finally looked up. "Sara, honey, can you read this for me. I'm not quite sure I believe this."

Somewhat disconcerted by the artist's expression, which could have been joy but could equally have been cynical disbelief, Sara took the thick watermarked sheets from her fingers. As Sara read, a beam lit up her face. "This is fantastic! Congratulations."

"It is real then. I'm not dreaming – wishful thinking and all that?"

Maddie's uncharacteristically uncertain expression told Sara just how important the letter she held was. "It is totally real. I've been to that place – it is incredible. Shows some really good stuff. You will do it, won't you?"

"But it's in only two months! That's no time at all.

It can take a year, if not longer, to produce the volume and quality of material they're asking for."

Seeing the ultra-confident Maddie unsure of her own ability endeared her to Sara even more. Putting an arm around the artist and sitting her down on the sofa, Sara pointed to the second paragraph of the letter and read out loud.

"Your work has come to our attention from a variety of sources, not least the feature spread in Art World Magazine from nine months ago. I regret the delay in approaching you with a view to proposing an exhibition of your work in our gallery, but we have been undergoing a major refurbishment and our schedule has not been as fluid as we'd like.

If you are agreeable and can produce twelve original pieces of art (any medium, including installations, as long as they are no larger than 3x3 metres) in the admittedly short time span of eight weeks (we would require all work available to hang/ place by 15 August), for a one month exhibition, ending on 15 September, at The Stripped Banana Gallery in Hoxton, London, then we would be delighted to accommodate you.

Please could you confirm the acceptance or refusal of this invitation as soon as possible?

Best regards,

Marco Philippe, Proprietor"

Excited on the artist's behalf, Sara gave Maddie a big hug. "This is incredible. You are going to do it, aren't you?"

"Twelve pieces of art in eight weeks! I'm not sure I can."

Sara edged closer, her bare legs nuzzling against Maddie's body-hugging leggings. "But you don't have to do twelve. Look over there." She pointed to the work dotted along the walls. "That's all original art and it's brilliant. It makes me wet every time I see it," she giggled.

"They're just practice pieces and a couple of unfinished commissions for customers who bailed on me."

"Practice pieces? Really? But they're really good. Surely, as long as the models don't mind, you could use them. I bet they'd agree. I mean, who wouldn't want to have a picture of themselves in an art gallery. If you use some of those, it means you have some of your work completed, or at least already started."

Laughing and buoyed up by Sara's enthusiasm, Maddie allowed herself the rare luxury of showing some of the excitement she felt inside. "I take it you'd let me use your picture when it is finished then?"

"Absolutely! Jake would love to think that hundreds of people would see me, without knowing it is me – if you see what I mean! Very much the sort of thing to appeal to his voyeuristic side."

"I think hundreds of people might be a bit of an exaggeration, but thanks, honey. Your pastel is so nearly finished, so that is one off the list. Although that would make it a rather delayed birthday gift for Jake."

"Trust me, he wouldn't care about that. The present part really is me being prepared to do this for him in the first place."

Maddie nodded in understanding, but remained more concerned with what Marco was asking of her. "But I still need eleven more pieces."

"Have you ever been to The Stripped Banana?"

"About two years ago, they had an amazing collection of eccentrically shaped pottery vessels, which would never have any practical use, but their very shine and lustre made you want to touch, want to stroke and even put your ear to their convoluted spouts and openings – just to see if you could hear voices from within."

"They sound lovely." Sara got up and, making the most of having the upper hand for a moment, dragged Maddie to the stacked-up art on the other side of the room. "Are you seriously telling me that you can't use some of these?" She picked up a large square canvas between outstretched arms, showing a striking blonde woman from the neck down to her neat oval navel. A pair of male hands were at her waist, the press of his fingertips on her flesh suggesting he was about to lift her up and twist her round. "This one I love. You can just imagine all the things they are about to do to each other."

"That's Freya. I've been teaching her life modelling. She's good."

"She's also gorgeous." A small stab of jealously needled at Sara as she guessed from the glimmer in Maddie's eyes that she had taught Freya a lot more than simply modelling.

"She is." Maddie said no more about the blonde model, but crouched level with the remaining illustrations and began looking through them more critically. "Do you really like some of these, or are you trying to stop me panicking?"

"I like them all. I think you should just use them and relax."

"Blinkered, but reassuring!"

Sara laughed. "It's really weird seeing you like this. You're usually so sure of everything."

Maddie immediately pulled herself together, cross with herself for fleetingly letting her insecurities show. "Sorry. I shouldn't be bothering you with all this. I am supposed to be painting you now."

Sensing the instant switch back to Maddie's normal mood, Sara dipped her head coquettishly. "So paint me, then. Make me part of your show."

There was no mistaking the "use me" expression on Sara's face and Maddie took the invitation for exactly what it was. Moving with determined speed and fishing a piece of worn white chalk pastel from her shirt pocket, Maddie pushed the crouched Sara back onto the hard shiny floor and ripped open the girl's white top. Then, without taking her eyes from Sara's, Maddie set the pastel to work on the underside of her right breast.

Sara's groan of gratification, as the hard dusty cylinder moved with heavy pressure over and around her chest was reflected in the rise of her hands, which longed to take hold of Maddie's body in return.

"No." Maddie's voice was unyielding and Sara immediately obeyed her temporary mistress when she added,

"Give your hands to me."

Tugging free the silk tie that she'd been using to keep her hair from her face, Maddie deftly fastened it around Sara's wrists, before placing them so they rested at the V of her pussy.

Sara's cat-like eyes shone with an intensity of sexual hunger that ricocheted through Maddie's own core and she let the artist in her completely take over. Her hand moved as if on autopilot, her own awareness of where the chalk stub was landing coming only from the expression on the model's face and the mewlings escaping from the corners of her mouth.

Only once did Sara lift her head, trying to examine the maze of criss-crossed white lines which were becoming more and more entwined around her tits. A glare from the artist however, sent her head instantly back to the floor and she didn't dare move again.

Maddie was in some sort of fierce trance. Yet somehow she was in full control, as she sat across Sara's legs, pinning her in place, her hand and chalk operating as one, hitting every available nerve, turning Sara's entire torso, neck and sides into one almighty erogenous zone that was every bit as sensitive as her chest.

Sara's naked pussy had changed from merely damp, to an oil slick of wistful desire between the crushed folds of her mini-skirt and the weight of Maddie's butt. As the chalk met her right nipple, Maddie had to press harder to prevent her subject from catapulting her off her over-sensitised body. The stimulating effect of Maddie's art was doubly confirmed by a thrilled cry of intense joy from Sara, which echoed around the open space of the studio.

Maddie's mind raced with the thrill of domination over her obliging companion, combined with the rush she was getting from creating living artwork directly onto Sara's silk-like skin. Maddie could suddenly see it all so clearly – the finished piece that she hadn't really been conscious of fashioning until that moment.

Breathless, but in complete control, Maddie commanded, "Stay still." Jumping to her feet, she grabbed her camera from the desk and started to snap away at the prone figure laying supine on the laminate surface.

Sara closed her eyes to shield them from the flash of the camera, as shot after shot was taken. Maddie danced around the body, digitally capturing every angle from the olive-brown waist to neck.

Maddie then retook the chalk and returned it to the girl's chest. Circling the white stub with a heavy increase in force, she pushed the girl's skin uncomfortably beneath its tip. Colouring in the nipples and the sensitive skin of the areoles, Maddie made Sara gasp and squirm with every deliberate stroke.

No longer moving her medium without thinking, Maddie treated Sara's torso as if it was a painting ready for the topcoat of perfection. Each carefully considered stroke after stroke of compacted white powder was added to the maze of lines that had gone before, stopping only when Maddie's unusual canvas began to whine rather than moan, as her climax approached.

Abandoning the pastel, Maddie took more photos with the use of the camera's high-speed shutter, immortalising the living art below her. Then, deeming it time to add the finishing touches to her impromptu masterpiece, Maddie commanded, "Don't move. Whatever happens, DO NOT MOVE!"

Gulping, Sara tried to steal herself. It was obvious that her orgasm was only seconds away. Her stomach had been fluttering and clenching with the growing desperation to explode for the past few minutes and her nipples had stiffened further.

Kneeling at Sara's side, Maddie's own nipples became more apparent through the thin material of her top. Her expression gave away a glimmer of acknowledgement at how hard her model was trying to please her. And when Maddie's finger arrived at the underside of Sara's breast, smearing and smudging the chalk so that it enhanced her body's natural shadows, it was like having someone hot wire her entire body.

As the chalk marks underneath her other breast were blurred to the artist's approval, Sara couldn't help the rise of her hips and the fidgets of her tethered wrists that accompanied the now steady mewling that gurgled up from her throat.

Totally possessed by the new work of art she was crafting, desperate for Sara not to move and destroy the effect of the light across the zigzags of white lines, Maddie threw her arm back and slapped Sara's left thigh hard. Gasping with the shock of the unexpected burn from Maddie's palm, Sara froze to the spot, startled to find that she was already anticipating another hit.

Making sure that the spotlights Theo had so recently fitted were precisely aligned for the best reflection against Sara's body, Maddie retook the camera, knelt back over Sara's twitching legs and took round after round of shots.

Switching the camera to auto-shot, Maddie held it with as steady a hand as she could. Licking the end of a finger, she slipped it between Sara's legs and tapped it against the slippery clit that had been mutely pleading for attention for the past twenty minutes.

Sara could hold back no longer and, as Maddie drummed a rhythmical beat against her nub, the model squealed an incoherent range of high pitched sounds, her eyes screwed up against the harsh light of the studio and constant flash and whirr of the camera.

Only when Sara lay still and a patina of sweat had turned the chalk pastel marks from solid lines to running blurs, did Maddie put down the camera, free Sara's wrists and pull her upright. Wrapping her arms around her shoulders, wiping stray hairs from the model's climax-clouded eyes, Maddie murmured into her ear, "You still sure you're happy to be featured in the gallery show?"

Sara, disorientated, her flesh buzzing with the high of what had just happened, peered down at her torso. "That was amazing. I mean…wow…"

Maddie gave her companion a perfunctory smile.

"I'm glad it was good. But I have to know, honey, can I use one of the photos I have just taken for the exhibition?"

Confused at Maddie's apparent lack of physical response to what had just happened, Sara asked, "Are you going to print out a photo and frame it then?"

"Maybe. I think one of those on canvas, blown up really big would look incredible. Although the gallery said "any medium", so, maybe I'll print them all out. As long as the photos are as good as I think they'll be, I could make them into a collage. I'd show you first of course. If you hated it, then it wouldn't happen and you would remain completely anonymous – your face wouldn't be shown. What do you say?"

Privately pleased that Maddie was so keen for her to feature quite so prominently in such an important exhibition, and knowing that Jake would get a big kick out of his girlfriend being secretly on show, Sara inclined her head. "If I like it when it's done, then yes."

"It's a deal!" Maddie let go of the rather stunned girl and, as if the past half an hour had never happened, said, "Right, that's a long enough break, don't you think. Let's crack on and finish the pastel you've asked me for! Another twenty minutes of posing should do the trick."

Maddie re-read the letter from The Stripped Banana over a steaming mug of black coffee. It had seemed too good to be true but a phone call to the gallery after Sara had gone confirmed that their offer was entirely genuine. Maddie immediately began to mull over who else she could get to model for her.

Freya would probably do it and she was sure Sara would be up for more.

She'd need a man as well. Theo was the obvious choice, but would he agree? Maddie knew full well that she wouldn't be able to keep him waiting for much longer before he totally gave up on her ever making good her innuendos. The flicker of a smile played at the corner of her lips. Perhaps the fact she wished to paint his body would act as a new carrot to dangle before him?

Maddie's grin disappeared as she mulled over her options for quick art creations. Another woman would also be helpful too. She knew the ideal candidate. Her colouring was sufficiently different to contrast nicely with that of Freya and Sara. She was also excellent at holding poses and had the confidence of movement that always transferred itself well to paper. But did Maddie really want anything to do with Tania ever again?

Good at life modelling she might be, but the woman had the capacity to be an absolute nightmare.

Chapter Four

◆ ◆ ◆ ◆

As a final year art student almost a decade before, Madeline Templeton's end-of-degree show had been extremely well received. The pundits had hailed her as "the one to watch" and "a new and exciting talent" who "had that rarest of ability: the ability to capture genuine sensuality on an emotionless backdrop".

Maddie had hoped for great things. She'd worked hard, designed her own website and had taken a myriad of commissions for both private and public buyers. Slowly, as her work had become more specialised towards the erotic and downright kinky, the promised and hoped-for shows never came. Now the art exhibition she'd long since given up on was actually going to happen. Maddie decided not to believe that it was real until she had actually gotten all her work together and seen it in place at The Stripped Banana. Only then would she celebrate enough to allow herself some sort of reward.

Kneeling on the floor, Maddie banished her past disappointments to the back of her mind and asked herself if Sara was right. Could she use some of these spare pieces? They weren't that old and none of them had been displayed anywhere before. She hadn't looked at them properly for a long time. Most were only canvases on which she had tried to hone her skills.

Carefully giving the neglected pieces their own space so she could examine them against the whitewashed wall, Maddie angled Theo's spotlights towards each one in turn.

At the thought of her electrician, the speed of Maddie's heartbeat stepped up a notch — a fact she would never admit to him or anybody else. She swallowed back the thought of eventually getting astride his body and extracted her mobile from her pocket where she had kept it, on silent mode, all morning.

Activating the screen, she saw precisely what she had expected to see: a pile of texts, most of which were from Theo. Each was asking her when they could meet and suggested interesting things they could do when they finally did get together. Ignoring them, Maddie sent a text of her own.

> Maddie: When u were here, did u
> look at the artwork around the studio
> properly?
> Theo: Yes

Theo's reply came as Maddie was examining the yellow and gold hues of Freya's nymph-like body as it reflected back at her from the bold canvas.

> Maddie: The yellow oil painting of a
> woman's body from neck to navel?

Theo: Oh yes. Made me nearly as hard
as thinking of u does.

Lowering her phone, Maddie moved her attention to the next picture, but dismissed it as impossible for inclusion in her show. The couple involved were a high profile pair and appeared in such detail on the page that they were far from anonymous.

Keeping a mental log in the back of her mind, Maddie started to plan more seriously, expressing her thoughts to the studio at large. "I could use the horny-waiting-Sara-over-the-stool, then maybe I could use the picture of Freya I finished on Monday and the yellow one as well. A fourth one could come from the photos that I took of Sara... Hmm..."

Knowing her slit was still wet from her role as photographer, and beginning to feel the need to do something about it, Maddie tapped again at her phone's touch screen.

Maddie: Would u like to come and
see a few more of my works of art
sometime?
Theo: In ur studio?
Maddie: Yes. In about 2 weeks time
perhaps?
Theo: 2 weeks? That's a lifetime away!

Maddie could almost smell the rise in Theo's testosterone from where she stood.

Maddie: I would like ur opinion. I also
have a proposition for u.
Theo: My dick just twitched
Maddie: Ur dick is always twitching
Theo: And whose fault is that?

The artist's mind seethed with possibilities as she dismissed all the other canvases propped along the wall. Time may have been against her, but if she had willing volunteers who were happy to be paid for their time in kind, rather than with money she didn't have, then Maddie was sure she could do it. Invigorated with fresh resolve and spurred on by the gallery's declaration that she could use "any medium", Maddie avoided answering Theo's direct question.

Maddie: Can I draw u? Can I turn u
into a work of art?

Theo almost choked on the china teacup his employers had provided for him as he took a break from trying to sort out the frighteningly worn wiring in their thatched cottage. *Draw him?* In all the fantasies he'd had about Maddie – and there had been literally hundreds of them – Theo had never considered that she might actually want to commit his likeness to paper.

Placing his teacup carefully on the saucer, Theo wondered how he could possibly stay still long enough in front of Maddie while (presumably) in a state of undress, without jumping on her and ruffling her annoying calm.

Theo re-read the texts he'd sent Maddie throughout the day. She hadn't responded to any of them. Feeling cross with himself for appearing needy, Theo knew he had no choice. His new resolve of the night before not to contact Maddie again had only lasted for a feebly brief two hours. He was now more convinced than ever that the only thing that would extinguish the lust-fuelled torch he had accidentally started carrying, would be to return to the scene of the crime and to let the artist do whatever she liked to him. Theo shivered at the thought. Even the limited knowledge he had of Maddie told him that could be literally anything.

> Theo: How will u draw me?
> Maddie: It's a surprise
> Theo: Will u want me naked?

Theo found his throat had clammed up. How was he supposed to wait another two weeks?! The woman was a torturer. Fancy putting the idea in his mind now, when she didn't plan to see him for another whole fortnight! Typical Maddie!

> Maddie: Maybe

Taking a gamble, Theo responded.

> Theo: I will only agree if ur naked while
> u draw me.

He almost dropped the phone when her reply flashed up on his phone.

Maddie: Ok.

Maddie grabbed a battered old notebook from her desk drawer and wrote down the list that had been formulating in her mind.

Keen to design a show that would take its observers by the scruff of the neck and not let them go until they were hankering for a fuck, Maddie planned a display which would be every voyeur's delight. To provide a keyhole view into a world that was normally private, even though many were secretly desperate to share it with others. Her mind strayed towards Sara's partner Jake. Although she'd never met him, Maddie was sure from what Sara had told her about him, that she'd like him.

The fantasies of Sara's boyfriend were pretty standard compared to some Maddie had heard confessed in her studio. Pausing in her plans to briefly consider how Jake might have rewarded Sara for having the guts to go commando for him, Maddie felt a flicker of pleasure at the fact that she'd helped them fulfil his erotic dream – well one of them anyway.

"Maybe Jake would pose for me?" Maddie mused to herself. She could see a few possible pictures in her head – arms, legs, breasts, mouths, cocks, all entwined in a variety of interesting and yet believable ways. A grin flashed across her face as she thought of a potential image for Jake to take part in, maybe with Theo. If she was going to ask either of them to help in the way she fancied, Maddie knew she was going to have to use an awful lot of her own special type of persuasion beforehand.

She decided to leave the idea that was firming up for the 'ideal' twelfth picture at the back of her mind, accepting it may well just be wishful thinking. She scribbled the numbers one to twelve in the notebook and jotted down her ideas so far:

1. *Sara over the stool – legs wide, pussy wet (Pastel)*
2. *Freya in yellow – male hands at waist (Oil)*
3. *Sara – chalked (Photos collage? One photo? – assuming pics ok???)*
4. *Freya flexing (maybe use this – not sure?? – Charcoal)*
5. *Tania – if she agrees (Dom pose?? – Felt tips – poster style – would be v quick to produce)*
6. *Tania – (Domme and victim – Charcoal)*
7. *Theo – (Wanking – Pencil drawing) ??*
8. *Sara and Freya together somehow??*
9. *Theo – not sure how???*
10. *Sara – with Theo or Jake (unsure of medium)*
11. *Threesome – Jake (??)/Freya/Sara (Pastel)*
12. *Idea – won't write down in case I jinx it!!!*

Maddie put down her pen. She was sure she wouldn't stick to the list as it stood, but was glad to have something solid to work with. *Too many flat images. I need something...a centre piece. Something tactile.*

She sighed as she considered what she was asking of herself. Tactile meant sculpture. There was so little time. She also had to name everything. She hoped her models might help her with that. Creating the pictures was no problem, but Maddie had never been comfortable with labelling them. Then there was framing them, pricing them, placing them, advertising the exhibition and so on.

Snapping the notebook shut, the artist walked back to the easel, grateful that there was no one around to see her being so emotionally off kilter. It was a feeling she hated. As she peered hard at her latest erotic creation, the texture of Sara's flesh against her own still fresh in her mind, Maddie stiffened her resolve, squared her shoulders and, cranking her radio into life, got on with the perfecting of Sara's thighs.

There were five texts waiting from Theo by the time Maddie was satisfied that the pastel was ready to rest before coating it in sealing spray to stop chalk-dust falling from the canvas.

> Theo: U mean it? U will let me see u naked?
> Theo: Don't tease me
> Theo: Maddie? Are u ever going to make good on ur promise?
> Theo: Have u any idea how hard the sound of my text alert makes my cock?
> Theo: I HAVE TO FUCK U

As she read, Maddie knew her instincts had been correct. She'd almost left Theo too long. Time to make him happy. She needed to get him fully on side. Then she could safely make him wait just a bit longer.

> Maddie: Sorry. I've been cruel. Forgive
> me and I will suck that patient cock
> soon – promise.

As she waited for Theo's reply Maddie flicked through the address book on her laptop and sighed. She didn't really want to call Tania but she couldn't think of anyone better for the job she had in mind.

> Theo: How will u do it?
> Maddie: Slowly – exploring with my
> fingers first
> Theo: And then?
> Maddie: I will flick my tongue over ur
> tip

Typing her text absentmindedly, Maddie continued considering how to approach her ex. If she emailed Tania she would be spared the sound of her sexily husky voice. A voice that had caused Maddie to fall for Tania three years ago and had led to her living a very submissive life. A life which had slowly stolen all her confidence, until it finally made Maddie so resentful that it was no longer worth the explosively amazing sex that had accompanied it.

Maddie knew she was putting off the inevitable. If Tania agreed, she and her seductive smoke ravaged tones would be here, in the studio which Maddie had kept a Tania-free zone for months. If it hadn't been for the exhibition Maddie wouldn't even have contemplated contacting her ex. But Tania was the best model she knew and Maddie began going through the reasons to call her once again – *she is supple, can hold seemingly impossible positions for long periods of time and, to top it all, she is gorgeous and therefore rewarding to paint.*

> Theo: What next?
> Maddie: My tongue would wrap itself
> around ur length, tasting u
> Theo: More

Maddie experienced a shimmer of fluttering in her diaphragm. She had no doubt that Theo had a dick like wood knocking at the inside of his boxers and that he was moving fast towards the nearest bathroom as she replied.

> Maddie: My fingers will play at ur balls
> while I suck u deeper – up and down –
> again and again...

Putting down the mobile for a moment, Maddie lifted up her landline phone and, telling herself she was doing this for the good of her exhibition and her professional future, tapped in Tania's number.

Her relief at hearing the recorded voice on the

answering machine was palpable. "Hi Tan, it's Maddie. Miracle has happened and I have a gallery gig. Have to do some super fast pics though as the schedule is very tight. As you're the best model there is, I wondered if you were free and could help. Can you call me asap? Need to crack on if you're willing. Thanks, Tan. Bye."

Maddie's pulse was positively drumming in her neck as she retook her mobile and added to Theo's list of messages.

> Maddie: And then I will squeeze ur balls while I scrape my teeth along ur cock.
> Theo: I'm pumping hard here
> Maddie: Good boy. My tongue is lapping at u as I pump u off
> Theo: So hot
> Maddie: My hands are slapping ur ass as I work u
> Theo: Harder. Hit me harder
> Maddie: Slapping u as ur cock hits back of my throat

Maddie could see the tableau their texts were weaving clearly in her mind's eye. A tableau which, for her, was mingling with memories of her S&M relationship with Tania. A relationship which had been emotionally hopeless, but physically unbeatable, as it had included a rather open element, with both women having additional men in their lives.

A quake of the desire she'd been suppressing since Sara had walked into the studio underwear-free, first thing that morning, prickled at Maddie's sex as Theo texted again, his urgency all too clear.

> Theo: I'm close
> Maddie: Not yet Theo. Not til I say so

Maddie rummaged in the second drawer of the cabinet next to the bed, pulling out a substantial vibrator. Crashing face down onto the bed, she wriggled out of her leggings and widened her thighs, pushing the latex toy inside herself effortlessly, the slick she'd been producing all day acting as a more-than-adequate lubricant.

> Theo: Maddie! I have to cum!
> Maddie: I said not yet

Clamping the vibrator between her now closed legs, its bunny attachment placed strategically over her clit, Maddie delighted in the impending tease of the currently inactive device. Her swollen chest rubbed tantalizingly against the bed as, resting on her elbows, her mobile in hand, Maddie continued to text Theo while pleasuring herself.

> Maddie: I have a big thick heavy dildo
> where ur cock should be
> Theo: Oh hell girl
> Maddie: Ur mouth should be on my clit

As Maddie pressed send, she slid her right hand down and activated the bunny vibe, gasping aloud as the instant hit of ecstasy filled her from the toes up.

> Theo: I would kiss and lick u til u
> screamed if I was there

Maddie knew, as the vibe sent rush after rush of pulsating bliss through her, that she wanted him to make her cum in exactly that way – but not until after the exhibition. He'd have to wait until then.

> Maddie: U will. Soon
> Theo: I AM CUMMING

Closing her eyes, Maddie visualised Tania's arm swinging back, a paddle in her hand, whipping her ass. She could almost feel the familiar heat as she recalled how her ex had punished her "for being perfect" as she had so often when they were together. At the same time, Maddie vividly imagined the taste of the salty cum Theo intended to shoot into her hungry throat, all because she had turned him on via a string of texts.

The knowledge of her influence over him acted as Maddie's trigger and her orgasm washed over her in a flashing sequence of increasingly kinky memories, ending with that of Sara, semi-bound, chalked and pleading to be fucked hard against the studio floor.

A minute later and Maddie, already back to her usual

composed self, informed Theo that she had climaxed as well.

Theo: U did?

Even though his question was only texted, Maddie was sure she could detect the element of scepticism in his words. It confirmed for her that if she didn't start to appear keen for some *actual* rather than *virtual* sex from him soon, she was never going to keep him waiting until after the exhibition, when she hoped to have his body as her reward for a job well done.

In truth, Maddie knew she would have been disappointed if she missed out on the chance to screw Theo. But she had always gained the majority of her erotic fulfilment from playing the long game. It was always a risk making a man wait, but a calculated risk that Maddie usually managed to gauge successfully. With women things were different. Playing games with women *always* led to trouble. Men, in Maddie's experience, simply rolled over if you said the right thing at the right time. Over the past ten years she had perfected the skill of seeming totally disinterested, but flirting like hell at the same time, until both she and the male in question got what they wanted. The artist sighed. As long as you kept the balance of attention and indifference level, it was depressingly easy. Until now she had a feeling that Theo might have been more of a challenge.

Maddie: Of course. I often think of u
when I cum.

Theo: U do?
Maddie: Yes.

Maddie knew that this was less of a lie than it had been when she'd played this game in the past. Theo had been creeping into her thoughts more and more lately. There was something about him that she couldn't quite define. He intrigued her.

Theo: I am in a thatched cottage,
standing next to a 4 poster bed.
Maddie: Nice
Theo: The bed is mocking me. U
should be on it.
Maddie: Would u let me tie u up on it?
Theo: Or I could tie u?

Maddie laughed into the echo of the studio as she typed.

Maddie: No hun. I do the tying. Ur face
down – I can see u
Theo: Tell me
Maddie: Ropes at wrists and ankles,
tied to the bedposts
Theo: And?
Maddie: I'm licking ur backside
Theo: And?
Maddie: My hands are parting ur butt
cheeks so I can get my tongue over ur

rim
Theo: Really?
Maddie: Oh yes.

There was a pause and Maddie wondered if she'd shocked him. Surely not? It was such a clichéd scenario so far. Perhaps she was the only woman who'd ever suggested licking his rim? She hoped so. As Maddie sat waiting for him to respond, the space where her vibrator had been suddenly seemed frustratingly empty again. Leaning back in her desk chair, Maddie slipped a hand back under the waistband of her leggings.

While her fingertips danced over the thin line of neat hair that ran with shaved precision around the edges of her pussy, Maddie's eyes fell on the rarely used Chinese Ink set which sat in an attractive walnut presentation box beneath a haphazard heap of papers on her desk.

She'd been awarded the handmade set twelve years ago as a prize for winning a painting competition. In all that time she had only used it once, saving it for a special project or a rainy day. Now, as her middle finger circled up inside her warmth, Maddie knew precisely what she wanted to use the ink set for. After all, what could be more special than her first solo gallery show?

The beep from her phone cut through her expanding exhibition plans, as the canal her finger was exploring became wider and slicker all the time.

Theo: Will u spank me?

Theo's question made the artist smile as she replied.

> Maddie: Of course
> Theo: Will u hurt me?
> Maddie: There will be pretty pink
> patterns on ur bum
> Theo: Bruises?
> Maddie: Naturally.

Maddie's finger was joined by another and she began to move them faster, tiny slurps escaping from her slippery cunt.

> Theo: And?
> Maddie: I will lube ur anus up with my
> spit.
> Theo: So u can do what...?

Despite only having met him on two brief occasions, Maddie could see Theo clearly in her mind. She was sure his cock was hard again already. But would it stay hard after what she was about to suggest? He'd never mentioned anal play to her and Maddie was fascinated to see how he'd react to her idea.

> Maddie: Slide in a finger. I want to fuck
> ur ass

When there was no express reply, Maddie, her breathing ragged with each shift of her pussy-slick hand, sent another message, changing tack slightly.

> Maddie: Where are u now – exactly?
> Theo: Still in the bedroom
> Maddie: Pull ur boxers back down and
> lay on bed
> Theo: They'll know!
> Maddie: Not if ur careful. Do it.
> Theo: OK
> Maddie: Good boy. I am there – I am
> lubing ur hole with my spit
> Theo: Ur so dirty
> Maddie: Oh yes. Where are ur hands?
> Theo: One on phone. One on dick.
> Maddie: U hard again?
> Theo: Yes

In the cottage's main bedroom, Theo cupped his cock with his right hand, wishing the artist would hurry up. His customers might well walk in at any moment.

> Maddie: Has anyone ever fucked ur
> butt?

The electrician paused, his dry throat grateful for a sip of the tea that was still to hand, before he typed with a combination of excitement and uncertainty.

> Theo: Only with a mini plug
> Maddie: Anyone ever asked to screw it

properly?
Theo: No

Theo's stomach flipped over, but his cock grew harder than ever, despite its recent release.

Maddie: I want to change that.
Theo: U don't have the equipment
baby
Maddie: Oh Theo! I most certainly do
have the equipment!

Feeling the bulk of his dick swell in his hand, Theo closed his eyes as he pictured Maddie standing behind him, her hand gliding over a fake shaft she wore on a harness around her slim waist. Her pussy would be visible and each time she caressed her toy cock, she would tease it back towards her clit, giving herself a spark of pleasure.

Opening his eyes again Theo typed: Will u use it on me when u draw me?

Maddie: All in good time Mr
Electrician. The wait for some things is
always worthwhile

Theo was about to text back when a call asking if he was alright came from the hallway outside the bedroom. He jerked his jeans and boxers up with lightening speed.

Opening the door, hoping he didn't appear too dishevelled, Theo apologised to his clients for how long he'd been, making up an excuse about not being able to track down a vital cable. But all Theo could think about was what Maddie had planned for him. *Did she really own a strap on, or was that idea just the product of his over active imagination? Maybe she had butt plugs...*

Five minutes later, having reassured the elderly couple that all was well, Theo texted Maddie back.

> Theo: I can't wait 2 weeks – I won't.
> Maddie: Next week then. Sunday.
> 11am

Infused with visions of fucking Theo's back passage, Maddie felt the wave of a second quietly bubbling orgasm ripple over her. Pulling her sopping fingers from her sex she licked them clean, savouring her own flavour. She was enjoying thinking up what possible excuses Theo might be giving to the owners of the cottage for spending so much time in their bedroom, when there was a loud double knock at her front door.

In the wake of her second satisfying climax, Maddie sauntered downstairs and insouciantly swung her front door open. Maddie's countenance froze as she took in the figure loitering on her step, a cigarette in one exquisitely manicured hand, a suitcase in the other.

"Hi Mads. Thought I'd come and help." The tall, perfectly proportioned, sun-tanned woman in impossibly high heels stubbed out her cigarette, pushed past the artist and climbed the stairs to the studio before Maddie had the chance to form a word of greeting or complaint. All she could do was stare in horror at the outsized suitcase and what it implied.

Marching up the stairs, Maddie's ex-girlfriend called over her shoulder, "I thought I would stay here for a bit. You know, board and lodgings in return for modelling. After all, you can't afford to pay me, can you?"

Chapter Five

◆ ◆ ◆ ◆

Maddie knew she couldn't stay in her bedroom much longer. There was too much to be getting on with to stay pointlessly skulking in her tiny sleeping quarters. Tania had only been there for a day, but Maddie felt as if her studio had been totally invaded and she hated not being able to work whenever she wanted to.

Kicking at the edge of her bed in a fit of peek, Maddie wished she hadn't been so rash in contacting Tania. If the schedule for her exhibition wasn't so tight, she could have had fun searching through the small ads for someone else. Yet, as she jumped restlessly around her bed, Maddie had to admit that, as overbearing and selfish as Tania might be, the preliminary sketch Maddie had started working on the night before had underlined for her that few others were as supple and controlled when modelling. Tania also wouldn't demand money for her time – although she might well demand something else beyond board and lodgings.

"I am not having this. I have waited too long for my big break to allow Tania to mess this up for me." Maddie spoke sternly to her reflection in the bedroom mirror. "I am in control here. *Not* her."

She was grateful that neither Theo, nor any of her clients or models could see her so unsettled for the second time that week. Maddie wrenched her shoulders back and, allowing no room in her head for anything other than the artwork she had to complete, she advanced to her artistic domain.

Always sluggish in the mornings, Tania was exactly where Maddie had known she would be. Curled up in the studio's double bed, covered in only a single thin cotton sheet, which suggestively highlighted every contour of her lithe body.

Tania's crystal-cut eyes might have been closed, but Maddie was convinced that she was awake. This was an old ploy. Her I'm-all-curled-up-and-am-adorably-ravishable-when-asleep look.

Maddie's vulva quivered without permission from her brain, forcing her to exhale slowly. Allowing her body to both register and accept its desire to let Tania make love to her in her own special way, but also to understand that was not going to happen, Maddie made herself focus entirely on her easel.

The previous evening, determined to get Tania out of her life again as soon as possible, Maddie had placed Tania in position: standing in her bright cerise silk underwear, her red hair piled high in a swishing horsetail on the very top of her head, her arm raised and a black riding whip held aloft.

While Tania waxed lyrical about how fantastic and

successful the past months had been, about how many "just fabulous darling" photographers she had posed for and then slept with and how her current tan had been "topped up on Mauritius, babe – you should try it", Maddie collected up some black and pink felt-tip pens of varying nib thicknesses and lined them up next to the easel.

Then, closing her ears to Tania's self-obsessed boasting (most of which Maddie suspected was exaggerated for effect) and denying her own body's treacherous insistence that it could benefit from being on the receiving end of Tania's expert whip action, Maddie phoned Freya. Having explained about the fast approaching art exhibition, she invited the blonde to pose for her the following afternoon alongside Sara. This meant that Maddie only had a short time in which to finish the 1920s style poster she was creating of Tania in mid-lash.

"For heaven's sake! It's ten o'clock in the morning. Get up will you! I'm on a deadline here."

"All right, all right!!" Tania affected her trademark pouty sulk that instantly managed to annoy the hell out of Maddie, even though she hadn't had to put up with it for months.

"Stop behaving like a spoiled brat. You're nearly forty, not ten!"

"Ouch!" Tania sat up in the bed, deliberately allowing the bed sheet to fall so that the artist was treated to a view of two ample tits pointing invitingly in her direction.

Maddie couldn't help but laugh. It was all so obvious.

"Still collecting all your seduction moves from bad porn films then."

"You used to like bad porn films."

"I still do, but I don't want to live in one!"

"Ouch times two!" Tania waggled a finger towards Maddie as if she was telling her off for being naughty. "Don't be nasty darling, it doesn't suit you. Why don't you pop over here and I'll give you a little spanking." Tania cocked her head to one side. "You know you want to. Your succulent bottom has been dying for the slap of my palm since I walked through your door. No point in denying it – I can tell these things."

Maddie had no intention of denying it. "Of course I bloody do! I want to do a whole lot of things. But what I want to do and what I allow myself to do are entirely different things. Right now I have to finish this poster. So will you haul yourself out of that bed, put some underwear on and get into position."

Groaning, Tania swept her long sleek hair into its usual high ponytail and padded naked, with deliberately tempting wiggles of her rear, across the carpet. "Alright if I use the bathroom first, is it?"

"Just don't be your usual two hours!"

Tania snorted derisively and, continuing to sway her hips provocatively, walked towards the stairs. As she reached the top rung she turned. "How come you've gone so cold? You were always in control of yourself, but not like this."

"I had a good teacher." Maddie's pulse thudded in her throat, annoyed at the effect her ex-lover's succulent flesh still had on her.

By the time Tania reappeared – stark naked, but now washed and made-up in such a fashion that would pass muster on any Hollywood film set – Maddie had prepared, undercoated and set aside two canvases to dry for later use.

Tania, who was taking her time putting on the bra and panties she'd been drawn in the day before, took a swig of her now cold coffee. Then, blatantly basking in the irritation of her companion, she picked up her whip and, as if she had never moved, adopted exactly the same posture as the day before, down to the last millimetre.

Maddie couldn't help but be impressed. This was why she had got Tania back here. She might be a self-serving pain in the backside, but she was bloody good at her job.

As the strokes of her pens squeaked satisfyingly over the board, fuchsia-pink lines overlaying and highlighting strokes of black with neat precision, Maddie found that her pen knew where to go from memory alone. She had drawn, painted and chalked Tania so often that her usual meditation-like state of concentration simply wasn't required.

The silence of the room, broken only by the swish of Maddie's pens against the board as they captured the muscles in the model's raised arm, was disturbed as Tania asked, "So, do you fuck all your clients and models these days or just some of them?"

Refusing to be stung by the sluttish implication of Tania's words, Maddie replied, "I have been known to use sex to help some of my clients and models relax."

"How convenient for you." Tania's voice was light –
too light – and Maddie could detect the old familiar, carefully
contained, brittle jealousy racing to the surface.

"It is, isn't it? Save's me the stress of having a paranoid
lover."

"I was not paranoid!" Tania snapped, without
moving. "I believe in monogamy, that's all."

"Of course you do, Tan." Maddie put down the thick
marker she'd been using to outline the curve of her ex's legs
and picked up a thinner one to accentuate her surgically
enhanced lips. "And your version of monogamy is so much
more interesting than everyone else's isn't it?"

"You can't still be sore about that, darling."

Maddie found she was pressing her pen too hard
and cursed as the black ink bled a fraction across the board.
"Shit!" Lowering her hands, Maddie squinted at the mark she
hadn't intended to make.

"You aren't still sore, are you, Mads?"

Seeing that Tania wasn't going to let it go, Maddie
gritted her teeth. "Of course I'm not. Why on earth would I
mind you sleeping with my boyfriend while I was out buying
you a birthday present? Now will you shut up. I need to sort
out this mess I've made."

"Consider yourself lucky to have had a girlfriend who
also let you have a boyfriend as well."

"You had one, too!"

Taking no notice of Maddie's interjection, Tania kept
talking. "I did say you could join in!"

"Only after I'd caught you tanning his ass! And, if you remember, we agreed *no* overlapping of partners – *no* boyfriends to be included in threesomes!"

"You like threesomes! And ass whippings!"

Maddie, having managed to disguise the pen blot she'd made between additional streaks of Tania's ponytail, noticed the tension in her shoulders suddenly dissolve. Their conversation was pointless. "Look, Tan, we had an agreement and you broke it. But you know as well as I do that we had other problems." The artist sighed, scrubbing pointlessly at some black ink that had marked her sleeve. "It doesn't matter anymore. You did me a favour in the end. I learnt a lot from you, my horizons have widened and my art has improved as a result. For that I owe you." She added a final stroke to the paper and, taking a step back from the easel, closed their discussion with a firm tone. "Rest your arm and come and see. I think I should leave this one before I over-work it."

Tania, always interested in seeing any image of herself, did what she was told for once. Winding an arm around Maddie's waist as if their recent conversation had never happened, she beamed: "Very 1920s – French Cabaret. I love it. You still have the gift, darling. It is wonderful."

◆ ◆ ◆ ◆

Freya and Sara arrived at the same time, chatting excitedly as they let themselves in, flushed and flattered at being asked to take part in Maddie's forthcoming show. Although they'd never met before, Maddie was relieved to see that they were getting on so well. She wasn't at all sure how they'd get on with Tania, though.

The would-be models had dressed exactly as Maddie had requested. In their black jeans and buttoned up white shirts, they smiled nervously at Tania, who was lounging full length on the sofa in ostentatiously expensive, bottle-green, designer trousers and a cream linen top that miraculously didn't seem to either crease or pick up dirty marks despite the dabs of charcoal which always seemed to get all over the room.

In an attempt to stop her relatively novice models being intimidated by Tania, Maddie called them to the other side of the studio, where she'd lined up the three pieces of art that were ready for the gallery.

Freya's eyes widened as she took in the oil painting of her body. "I don't remember it being like that. It's so vibrant!"

Maddie took Freya's hand as she saw the growing pink blush on the blonde's freckly face. "It is and, if you agree, it will feature in my exhibition."

Sara, whose eyes were on the pastel drawn representation of her most intimate area, spoke without looking at either of the other women. "It is an incredible piece. You are beautiful, Freya! The picture has to be included."

"And so does that one!" Freya pointed to where Sara was staring so intently. "Is that you?"

The artist's eyes strayed from one of her companions to the other. Temporarily forgetting that Tania was in the background, she reached out her free hand to Sara and felt the simultaneous increase in both the girls' pulses. Their arousal as they observed each other's nakedness, captured forever before them, was palpable. Maddie noticed how their pupils dilated as they continued to regard themselves and each other on paper. This boded well for the artwork she intended to create that afternoon.

Maddie was about to explain how she wished them to be placed, when a set of thin-fingered hands snaked around the threesome contemplating the art. "Seeing as Maddie doesn't seem inclined to introduce me, I'd better introduce myself. I'm Tania – her professional model."

"Hello." Freya smiled shyly while Sara simply inclined her head, uncertain of the over-confident woman who had wrapped an arm around her shoulder.

"I have a brilliant idea, Mads. You wouldn't mind if I positioned the girls for you, would you?" Tugging gently at the two models, Tania was leading them towards the sofa before anyone had the chance to protest. "Don't worry girls. Maddie will tell you – I am better at choreographing than she is. I have worked with some of the best in the business, after all."

Sara peeped nervously at the artist, whose face had taken on a furrow of annoyance. Freya, her intrinsic timidity still evident, also looked to Maddie for reassurance and was relieved when she broke the awkward silence.

"Tania, I have already decided how I would like the girls to pose – as long as they agree of course. *I* do not make my models do what they don't wish to do."

"Nonsense." Tania brushed away Maddie's words as if they were unimportant. "Taking people outside of their comfort zone makes for much better artwork."

Biting the inside of her cheeks, Maddie took a silent count of three before pointedly lifting Tania's arms away from Sara and Freya. "I appreciate your help, but I have this sorted, thank you."

"You have got to learn to trust me, darling. I have worked with professionals, you know." Tania manoeuvred an uncertain Freya nearer the sofa. "Now be a dear and sit on the edge for me."

"I *am* a professional," Maddie hissed at her ex. "If you can't stop interfering I am going to chuck you out, whether I need your modelling skills or not."

Tania laughed. "Don't be so ungracious, Mads. Honestly, I don't know what's happened to you since I left. Your manners seem to have deserted you."

Freya and Sara exchanged a startled glance. Tania was so *not* the type of person they'd expected to be one of Maddie's past partners.

Flashing her eyelashes as if she was a child after a lollipop, the redhead continued. "I think the least you could do, as I am granting you a favour here, is to see what my idea actually is. You might even love it."

Knowing that Tania wouldn't give up until everyone in the room was thoroughly embarrassed or exasperated, Maddie turned to her invited guests. "Would you mind sitting as Tania has asked for a minute. Then we can get on with what I've already planned."

Giving Tania a glare that would have sent a lesser mortal cowering, Maddie gestured towards the sofa. "Well, show us then if you're going to!"

Ignoring her ex's angry tone, Tania took hold of Freya and pushed her so that her bottom remained perched on the very front edge of the sofa with her neck and shoulders resting on the back of the sofa. Then, lifting the blonde's arms, one at a time, she placed them so they stretched out along the top of the seatback.

"You are a treat to position, Freya." As Tania let go of Freya and turned her attention to Sara, Maddie could already see where this was going. And, annoyingly, it was going to look incredible. *Damn Tania.* Maddie really didn't want her ex's set to be an improvement on hers.

Holding her tongue for the time being, Maddie nodded reassuringly to Sara as she was instructed to sit astride Freya's marginally parted legs. The artist wondered how the young women, unfamiliar to each other, felt as they were manoeuvred into a blatantly kinky position. How would they cope, sitting in close proximity for a prolonged period without being able to so much as kiss each other?

Despite the relative speed of creating a chalk drawing compared to an oil painting (which was out of the question due to the length of time it would take for the canvas to dry), chalk was not an ideal medium for too much detail – and suddenly this was looking like it was going to be a very intricate scene.

Uncaring that Sara was struggling to ignore the heat of Freya's denim clad legs as it radiated up from beneath her, Tania moulded her into the shape she required. One of Sara's hands was placed at Freya's neck, so it appeared as if she was pushing at her chin to hold her still. Sara's other hand was then semi-raised, her palm outstretched as if she was about to slap the pale woman's right breast.

Freya and Sara's bodies both gave involuntary shivers as they realised what their pose implied. Their eyes caught each other's for a split second. They looked away with a haste that told everyone in the studio precisely what they'd been thinking.

"So," Tania joined Maddie at the end of the purple seat. "If you drew them from here it would be brilliant, don't you think? Especially if they were naked."

Maddie rolled her eyes to the ceiling. "You're confident I'm going to go with this idea, then."

"Of course I am. It's brilliant."

Reserving her judgement, Maddie picked up her easel and moved it about until it was in the optimum place from which to begin work. Increasingly conscious of the tension between the two young women on the sofa and how tired Sara's raised hands probably were already, Maddie asked if she could take their photograph to speed up the decision making process.

Agreeing in harmony, neither model dared to so much as breathe in case they moved. The usual relaxed atmosphere that complemented the underlying sexuality of the studio was completely absent in the presence of Tania.

Four camera shots later, Maddie examined the camera's playback. "Why not grab yourselves some coffee, girls. I have to think. This is a rather different scene from the suggestive clench I had envisaged and would be complex to draw."

The moment the models had moved to the other part of the studio, Tania sidled up behind Maddie. "You hate that I'm right, don't you," Tania said softly as they stood regarding the now vacant sofa.

"Yes I do."

"We could call a truce. You did ask me here to help."

"As a model – not to launch a takeover bid."

Tania stroked her fingers over the waistband of Maddie's flowing floral skirt. "I just want this to work for you darling. You are too good an artist not to have the best gallery opening possible."

Suppressing her body's reaction to Tania's touch, Maddie continued to gaze at the empty sofa. "Thanks, Tan. Guess I'd better swallow my pride and do this piece then. It did look hot."

"Of course it did."

Maddie couldn't help but laugh. "Modest as ever."

"I'm honest, darling. Just honest." Tania inched her hands up into the space beneath Maddie's t-shirt. The covetousness of her ex's touch instantly inflamed Maddie's usually cool-blooded body. Quickly extracting herself from Tania's grasp, she called to Sara and Freya to join them.

"As much as I hate to admit it, the camera cannot lie and the set up that Tan has put together is a very clever one. Kinky, yet sensual. But I will only go with it if you guys are still happy to help."

Shyly avoiding mutual eye contact, Freya and Sara murmured their agreement. Freya then asked the question that was on both their minds. "How much will we be wearing?"

More than a little tempted to order the women to strip completely naked, the artist in Maddie curbed her libido. "I think it would be sexier if you kept your jeans on.

Freya, you would have a bare chest, so that it appears as if the slaps are going to land directly on your right breast. I think that would be more suggestive and therefore more exciting than if you had a bra on.

Sara, I think your chest should also be bra free, but your shirt should remain on. Open though, giving the viewer a glimpse of your nipples, but not the full story, if you get what I mean."

"You sure they shouldn't be naked, darling?" Tania interjected, her opinion confirming Maddie's suspicions on what her ex would like to do to the models once the session was over.

"I'm sure." With her back to Tania, Maddie focused all her attention on the models, her voice kinder and softer. "Are you okay with this?"

Again neither woman spoke. Even with their outer garments still in place, it was clear that they were extremely turned on. Four ripe nipples could clearly be seen poking at the inside of their tops. Maddie wondered how wet their crotches were. Quite, she would guess; and the artist was glad they were to be spared the indignity of revealing their pussy dampened knickers to each other, or worse, to Tania.

"If you will excuse me and Tania for a moment, ladies. Help yourselves to more coffee." Maddie took hold of her ex by the elbow and steered her down the stairs to the front door.

Speaking no louder than a whisper, Maddie, her hand still at Tania's elbow, said, "You're making the girls uncomfortable. It would help if you left us to it for a while."

"But I helped you! That's a hot scene I've designed! They obviously want to rip each other's clothes off. You know as well as I do that a healthy dose of sexual tension between models translates well to paper."

"I am grateful, Tan. Really I am. But they are novices at this. I need them to relax and you aren't helping with that. Please! Go out for coffee or something for an hour."

"And what will be my reward for doing as the artist in charge asks?" Tania leant back against the glass panel in the front door, crossing her arms to boost her surgically augmented cleavage.

Maddie rolled her eyes. "You are still the most impossible woman I have ever met."

"I'm very glad to hear it." Tania pulled Maddie closer and kissed her full on her lips.

Needing to keep her ex onside for a while longer at least, Maddie allowed her desire to override her reflex to step away. She reciprocated the kiss with more force than she'd ever shared with Tania in the past.

"Ummm...you really have learnt a few things since I last saw you."

"Let's just say I got tired of being the sub. As much as I loved it, I decided to revisit the other side of the whip for a while." Maddie swept a strand of hair from her eyes as she moved back towards the stairs. "After all, I was always in charge – until you came along."

"Do I really have to leave? I could join in – stand over the blonde girl and hold her tits still for you. Easier to paint if they're still..."

"Tania! Go for a bloody walk, will you? Just for an hour. That's all it will take to calm their nerves."

"Is it, indeed?" Tania shrugged, admitting defeat. "I will go, but only because you asked me nicely and *only* if you promise to give me a blow-by-blow account of what they get up to while I'm out!"

"Honestly Tan, they *aren't* having sex up there – you're as bad as Theo."

Tania turned back abruptly. "Who the hell is Theo?"

Having practically pushed Tania out of the door, telling her that Theo was just a tradesman who'd done some work for her and hadn't been able to keep his eyes off her artwork, Maddie exhaled a momentary sigh of relief.

Reassured that the models were okay by the sound of music from upstairs bursting abruptly into life, Maddie took the opportunity to send Theo some messages before getting on with her work. Texts that she hoped would ensure he was still baited firmly to her hook.

> Maddie: Would u like me to hold ur cock while u kiss me?
> Theo: Yes
> Maddie: Would u like me to play with ur cock with my fingers?
> Theo: Yes
> Maddie: Could I make u cum all over my chest?
> Theo: YES
> Maddie: Would u like it if I tied u up and used ur body?
> Theo: YES- u know I would!!!
> Maddie: If I stripped u naked in a wood and tied u to a tree would u like that?
> Theo: IF we were alone- yes
> Maddie: Do u think u could handle a 3-some?
> Theo: YES- Fuck yes!!!!!

C h a p t e r   S i x

◆ ◆ ◆ ◆

Although loud, Maddie was glad the girls had put the radio on rather than sitting in awkward silence until she returned. As she re-entered the studio however, she saw exactly why the music had been blaring so loudly. She was more annoyed that Tania had been right, than at seeing her models sat as she intended to draw them, but with their mouths fastened together.

The voyeur in Maddie was glued to the floor. Every part of her was instantly alight with the salacious pleasure of witnessing such an intimate moment. The muffled moans the girls were trying to hide with the radio's retro pop were as stimulating as the vision itself. Maddie revelled in the sight of Sara raking her nails through Freya's hair as, in turn, the blonde cupped Sara's face, pulling it to her own in a way that obliterated the very air space between them.

It was with a perverse sort of pride that the artist watched their desperately hungry grope. She knew that neither of them had explored being with a woman before they'd come to her studio. Now it seemed they couldn't get enough of the female touch. Unlike Tania however, Maddie didn't believe this addition to the girls' sexual tastes was due to her alone. It was the studio. Its atmosphere did things to people, including herself. A fact Maddie would never dispute.

An idea came to the artist. A thought that prickled at the tip of her clit and made her nipples harden. It would have to wait though. Art first. Fun later. Fun which should satisfy the girls and would hopefully keep Tania happy long enough to let Maddie get on with some work.

Watching until the girls paused for oxygen – their foreheads resting together, faces shy yet beaming – Maddie clapped her hands sharply. They jumped in surprise, guilty expressions replacing their excited ones. The models' hands fell to their sides and they automatically hopped off the sofa, their previously tidy hair now a tangle of knots.

Maddie made no comment about what she'd observed, knowing that leaving it unspoken would keep the atmosphere pleasingly heavy with halted sex. Instead, Maddie simply said, "Right, best crack on then. Time is short. If you could sort your hair out for me, please, we can get ready to start."

Knocking the volume of the stereo down a few notches, Maddie added in a less hectoring tone, "I'm sorry about Tania. She has a good eye, but she can be something of a handful. I swear she'd like to swipe the paintbrushes out of my hands and do the art herself. Just as well she can't draw."

With an encouraging incline of the head from a flushed Freya, Sara asked, "Who is Tania, then?"

"Now that is a very complicated question." Maddie threw a handful of chalks carelessly onto the easel. "Tan is best described as a thing of the past that happens to be a necessary evil if I am going to get all the exhibits created and ready on time for The Stripped Banana."

"We saw the poster you've done of her. It's amazing. Very '20s Art Nouveau. A bit Toulouse-Lautrec. A bit Beardsley. And yet still very Maddie Templeton."

"Thanks, Sara. That's the angle I was aiming for. I really want a variety of styles in my show, each reflecting the erotic theme."

Picking up a one-metre by two-metre prepared board, Maddie propped it in place. "Now, if you two are quite composed and ready," Maddie peered at them sternly, noticing how difficult they were finding it to stand so close to each other without moving. "Then we will begin."

"Sure we are." Sara relaxed her restless legs as best she could. Undoing her shirt buttons, she took off her bra and was unable to disguise her sigh of relief as her tight tits were given their coveted freedom. Her sigh was duly accompanied by a gasp of appreciation from Freya – a gasp that was prolonged when Sara shrugged her shirt back off her shoulders, leaving it to flutter enticingly over her chestnut nipples.

Maddie observed the widening of Freya pupils as Freya removed her own top, her cream bra falling to the floor with an abandon that would not have seemed possible only a few sessions ago. Sitting exactly where Tania had instructed, with arms outstretched, her fairy-cake breasts pert and inviting, Freya's parted, denim-clad legs revealed a darker apex that had grown damp with excitement. Maddie silently cursed that the angle of the drawing would not allow her to show where Freya's sex had lubricated itself in reaction to her truncated coupling with Sara.

Once they were in place, Freya's mouse-like voice asked, "Is this okay, Maddie?"

Combating the dryness of her own throat with a glass of water as she remembered how delicious those magnificent breasts tasted, Maddie found herself looking forward to experiencing again the differing textures of the women before her . In the meantime she calmly replied, "Spot on, Freya. Now, Sara, if you could climb on board?"

Eagerly sitting on top of her companion, Sara then hesitated. "How shall I hold Freya's chin? I don't want to hurt her."

Picking up Sara's hand, Maddie placed it on Freya's chin. "If you could tilt your neck back, Freya, it will look as if Sara is forcing you to stay still."

The blonde obliged, allowing Sara to grasp her. The contrast in their skin tones was as flattering and vivid as Maddie had hoped it would be. The atmosphere between the models was positively electric as Maddie readied herself to capture the pulse of their lust in her work – a pulse that energised her in every way and made her glad that she hadn't bothered wearing knickers under her skirt. Any form of undergarment would have been wet through by now.

After raising Sara's hand into the correct position so that it appeared the blonde was about to have her right breast slapped, Maddie selected a charcoal grey pastel and began to sweep the outline of the women onto the board before her.

Half an hour later, pleasing blocks of colour had taken shape and Maddie put down her chalk. "Stay still for another minute if you can. I'll just take some more photographs so I can work on the details at my leisure."

When she'd finished with the camera, Maddie allowed the girls a rest while she downloaded the photos to her laptop screen. Examining every shot, Maddie became lost in thought. Something was missing. Something about the images wasn't quite right.

"Girls," she beckoned to the models. "I have something else to ask of you, especially you Freya."

Still pretending that they didn't hope to do anything more than pose together, Freya and Sara joined Maddie at the computer screen, their eyes going to where the artist was pointing.

"You see, if I am to capture the idea that your breast is the subject of sexual chastisement, then it has to appear as if it has already been hit at least once."

The muses exchanged glances. They could see where this conversation was going as Maddie continued. "I suppose I could guess and simply shade your nipple and the surrounding skin a deep pink, Freya. That would work and it is certainly what I'll do if you don't fancy what I am about to suggest, but..."

Sara interrupted. "You want me to spank Freya's boob a few times so that you can draw in the resulting bruising accurately – just like you did to my backside the other day?"

"Yes." Maddie shrewdly examined one woman and then the other. "What do you think, Freya? Obviously I am aware that the thought of touching each other intimately is not unappealing."

The blonde, who'd struggled to keep her hands off Sara during the entirety of the last session, replied, "You'd be amazed what I'd do for art since I met you, Maddie."

"Sara?" The familiar rush of the blood surged through Maddie's veins as she deferred to the other model, already sure of her answer.

"Why would I reject the chance to have a proper touch of those tits?"

Maddie checked the time on her wristwatch. Tania had already been gone forty minutes and she knew the chances of her staying out for the full hour were slim, especially if Tania thought she might be missing out on something.

Adopting her headmistress pose, Maddie put her hands on her hips. "We must get on. Rewards for a job well done will follow *if* I deem them deserved."

The joint reply of "Yes, Maddie" sent fresh jolts of erotic frisson down Maddie's spine, and again she was glad that her flowing skirt hid the fact that her inner thighs were slick with her arousal.

Without further instruction, Sara and Freya returned to the sofa. This time, however, Freya's fingers were not gently placed against the back of the cushions. Instead, she gripped the material into creases as she braced herself for the smacks to come.

"The slaps don't have to be hard, Sara." Maddie stood behind the sofa, leaning over the seated blonde, so close to her that Freya could feel the artist's breath against her cheek.

Uncertainty crept through Sara. She had been on the receiving end of such treatment a number of times but she had never hit anybody herself and fear of causing actual harm to Freya engulfed her.

"We don't have all day, Sara," Maddie encouraged, trying not to appear too impatient. Although she was dying to see how Freya would cope with the coming smack.

In time, the desire to thrash Freya's flesh eclipsed the fear of hurting her. Sara swung her arm back and landed the tips of her fingers on the tiny pearl nipple.

Freya inhaled sharply, but Maddie shook her head. "No Sara, you need to hit out with the flat of your hand. Otherwise you will only succeed in continuing to excite Freya, while failing to make the required mark."

Determined to do better, Sara struck again, this time making Freya whimper through tight lips.

"Better." Maddie spoke as if she were merely commenting on the state of the weather. "But as we are in a hurry here, it might be a good idea if I showed you the best technique to achieve our goal."

Crossing to the opposite side of the sofa, Maddie crouched so she was level with Sara. Swiftly she brought her palm down onto the beautifully round breast, causing Freya to yelp and her whole body to shudder. A bloom of pink appeared on the afflicted flesh and tears dotted at the corners of Freya's eyes. Maddie, unsatisfied with the definition and depth of the freshly infused colour, struck again. Both her companions winced – one with a deliciously hot, pussy-clenching discomfort, the other in jealous sympathy.

Taking no notice of Freya's panting, nor of how hard Freya's nails were digging into the sofa, Maddie scrutinised the darker mark. "What do you think, Sara? You think you could strike her like that? One more hit should be enough."

Sara nodded. She'd been resisting the urge to knock the artist away and finish the job herself. As her Malaysian assistant raised her arm, Maddie took a firm hold of Freya's hands, pushing them against the top of the cushions to keep her stock-still.

The feeling of being trapped by two women sent additional shots of lust through Freya as she braced herself for the next blow. She hadn't been at all sure she'd be able to endure the strikes to her sensitive flesh. Now she found that the resulting fire that bubbled within her after each smack was a sensation she wanted to experience again – but harder.

Maddie was sure the slap from Sara had sent a new current of arousal coursing through Freya's abused bosom, into her neglected breast and down to her pussy. She had no doubt that the satin of Freya's knickers was stuck to her like glue, as Sara struck again and the gasps escaping from the blonde's throat grew in volume.

Returning her concentration to the shade of Freya's flesh, Maddie called out, "That's perfect. Stop now."

Sara however, either didn't hear her employer or

chose to ignore her. Getting into her stride, she spanked Freya again, loving the sensation of dominance that enflamed her own body as it coloured her companion's. As her arm rose again, Maddie leant forward and grabbed Sara's elbow in mid-air. "Enough now."

Freya gave a stifled sigh of confused loss as the blow she'd been anticipating failed to meet her burning flesh. Her body winced with the disappointment of not being struck; the white heat that was circulating through her torso and the throb of her right nipple, taking her close to the edge. "Please, Maddie, let her hit me again."

"How wet are you?" Maddie asked the blonde with a detached tone that belied her own lustful state, as she tried to gauge if there was time enough to let the girls have a quickie before she carried on with the artwork.

"Soaking." Freya spoke with quiet hunger, her blue gaze fixed on Sara's chest.

"Me too." Sara, her palm smarting, and surprised by how much she had enjoyed striking her colleague, shuffled forward, the aroma of sex and denim combining and wafting into the air as she moved.

Dusting her hands over her skirt, Maddie said, "Well then, we had better get this picture drafted as quickly as possible hadn't we."

Freya and Sara groaned in unison as they appreciated what Maddie was saying. They were going to have to sit in close proximity, their bodies frantic for the conclusion of what they'd started, without being allowed to move.

Returning to the other side of the easel, Maddie drew fast. The control she dictated over the other women had an even greater aphrodisiac effect on her than the touch of Freya's breast on her skin.

Tania was right, Maddie thought as she added colour to the bruise which was blooming on Freya's tender tit, *I have changed*. Maddie knew she'd always held the upper hand when it came to men. But since Tania had gone, she had kept things on a more equal footing with women, remaining in control of herself as much as possible, but allowing herself satisfaction when appropriate. The return of Tania seemed to have rekindled her dominant side, for there was no denying she was getting a definite kick out of making the women before her wait just for the sake of it – just because it turned her on. Maddie also knew what she wanted to happen next. Her pussy positively squelched at the thought, making her move her chalks even faster over the smooth board.

Only a few minutes into the sitting and Sara was struggling to keep her raised arm from shaking. The effort of keeping it still was bad enough, but the urge to bring it down onto Freya's other breast and even up the newly darkened skin was blanking out almost every other thought.

After a quarter of an hour, Maddie, pleased with the under-draft of her latest creation, put down her pastel chalks.

Listening for sounds of Tania's return, Maddie shared her satisfaction with her models. "I'm impressed. You have apparently both remembered what I told you about self–control. It is everything. It makes everything we do – once we eventually get to do it – even better. The wait, as I keep telling a certain gentleman I know, is as much part of the foreplay of sex, as is the first touch or the longed-for kiss."

Circling the motionless women, Maddie continued. "The sexual energy you two are giving off is intoxicating, to say the least. But I believe it could do with taming. Your skills need to be strengthened so you can learn to regulate your release, making it much better, much stronger."

Unable to stay silent, Freya cried out, "No, Maddie, please! Please don't make us wait any longer."

Tilting her head to one side, secretly impressed that Freya had the courage to speak out, Maddie spoke with deliberate precision. "You will do well to trust me. I can guarantee you won't regret it."

As much as they hated her insistence that they be made to hang on for the release they desperately craved, the models found being under the direction of the older woman more liberating than either would have cared to admit.

Trailing one pastel stained finger over the chin of each woman, Maddie went on. "Tania always makes such a drama out of being good at orchestrating the ideal sex scene for me to paint. And while I can't deny that she has a good eye for such things, she isn't always as skilled as she believes she is. I think we could create an even more interesting tableau that would make her flood her thong in seconds."

Sara, unsure if she was allowed to speak while Maddie was in mistress mode, put her hand up, as if she was a pupil wanting to answer a question in class.

"Yes, Sara?"

"You want to use us to taunt Tania?"

"That would be a perk. But I prefer to think of it as making an additional work of art." Maddie decided against elaborating further. It was time for direct action.

"Freya. Strip!"

Blinking just once, as if allowing a second to make sure Maddie was serious, Freya's fingers began to remove her clothing before her brain had fully engaged with what she was being asked to do. As the blonde pulled her jeans and panties down, Maddie could clearly hear the separation-suction noise they made as they peeled away from her sex.

"Now, return to the sofa'. After pointing Freya back to the seat, Maddie switched her attention to Sara, whose fingertips were already at the placket of her shirt. "Yes, remove that and your other clothes. I imagine that you are also uncomfortable between the legs…"

Sara was naked before Maddie had finished talking and, all reservations gone, she waited impatiently to be sent to join Freya.

"As I mentioned earlier, hard work deserves a reward." The artist weighed Sara's breasts in her palms as she spoke. "And although you were naughty and took advantage of my hospitality by indulging in some, shall we say, heavy petting when you thought my back turned, you have each shown an excellent level of self restraint since then, allowing me to produce the makings of another substantial piece of art for the gallery. A reward is certainly due.

"Freya, I would like you to stay here for a moment. Sara, follow me please." Walking to the chest beside the double bed, Maddie opened the middle drawer. "You may choose one."

The model gasped at what she saw, her fingers dancing over the contents of the drawer with all the delight of a child in a sweet shop. Lined with a roll of black silk, laid out with love and reverence, was a vast array of dildos, vibrators and clitoral stimulators.

"Or you may prefer to examine the drawer below..." Maddie half closed the first drawer and opened the next. On a similar bed of shiny jet material were three different styles of paddle, a short white cane and, running along the front of the space, a long slim red and black leather riding whip.

Curiosity getting the better of her, Freya rose from the sofa so she could also see what the other women were looking at – one with pride and the other with awe.

The blonde was still a step away from the others when Maddie rounded on her. "I don't recall giving you permission to move."

Freya froze as if she had suddenly found herself in the presence of a Gorgon that had every intention of casting her to stone.

Sara, her hands tracing the contours of the weapons before her, winced in sympathy with her new friend. Yet she could not avert her glowing eyes from the kinky possibilities presented to her. Her wish to administer some (if not all) of the toys on offer was far stronger than her dislike of the humiliating tone growing ever more apparent in the artist's voice.

Maddie pointed across the room, instructing the blonde as if she were a naughty puppy. "Sofa, Freya. Sit still. Cross your arms and legs and close your eyes."

Freya sat as instructed, trying to hide her nervous shaking at the prospect of what was to come. Her ears strained to hear her companions' words but they had stopped talking and Freya could only pick up the soft thump of their moving feet, the faint music from the stereo and the thunderous beating of her own heart.

With a finger to Sara's lips so as to keep her selection secret from Freya, Maddie hurried her decision with an urgent nod towards the drawers. Time was getting short if this was to be set up prior to her ex's return.

Knowing she could stare at the goodies before her all day and still not make a decision, Sara closed her eyes and plunged her hand into the second drawer, blindly selecting a red, leather-padded, wooden paddle. She surprised herself by wondering what colour it could turn Freya's backside, and whether the girl's bottom would bruise as quickly as her chest had done.

"Good choice."

Maddie's words sent further tremors of unease through Freya. *What has been chosen? What does Maddie keep in those drawers?*

Saying no more, Maddie grabbed Sara's hand and walked with her towards the sofa. Taking the paddle from the model, but keeping it hidden from view, Maddie gestured towards the waiting blonde. "I will look after this until we are ready. Now, I think you should sit next to your colleague."

Sara's forehead creased in confusion. "But I..."

With a sardonic smile, Maddie said, "You seem to have made an incorrect assumption. I did not say you would be the one to use the item you selected. I know I said a reward was due – and it is. But as I stated, you did seek amusement without my permission, and for that infraction there must be some penalty with the prize. Don't you agree?"

Sara sat as instructed, a lump forming in her throat as her caramel legs butted up against Freya's porcelain limbs. "Of course, Maddie."

"Good girl. I would like you to close your eyes as well please, Sara. Now, both place your hands on your knees."

The click of the front door closing was lost on the models as they waited side by side, feeling each other's pulse thud together in an anxious, horny race. Maddie, however, had not missed the sound. She knew, without even needing to turn around, that her ex was standing in the doorway.

"I hope you had a pleasant walk, Tan."

Freya and Sara's heads snapped up higher, though their eyes remained tightly closed. It was no longer just Maddie observing their naked vulnerable state.

"It was very nice, thank you." Tania understood the situation perfectly. This was her prize for giving Maddie some peace and she smiled at her ex as she crossed to her side. "I believe the agreement was that you would fill me in on what

I'd missed. I see I have missed plenty."

The artist handed the paddle over to Tania. "I thought about what you said earlier. You were quite right. You should be rewarded for helping me at such short notice. And, as I have no money to spare and the girls here are beyond desperate for a thorough seeing to, I thought I would let you have the pleasure while I get on with my work."

The way in which the models independently increased the hold on their own knees and tensed their legs, showed Maddie how apprehensive they were about this new development. Yet neither woman protested or moved.

"Why thank you, Mads. I would be delighted."

Leaving the three of them to it, Maddie sat at her desk and sent a text to Theo.

> Maddie: I am going to phone u now.
> Do not speak when u answer. Just
> listen. If u talk I will cut u off.

Without waiting for a reply, Maddie called his number. The instant Theo picked up she placed her mobile onto speakerphone, so that he would be able to hear everything that Tania and the girls were about to do.

Putting the phone down beside her computer, Maddie brought up the photographs she had taken of Sara the previous day. As each gorgeous shot appeared in thumbnail form on the screen, an idea blasted into her brain from nowhere for the next piece of art. She would have to work fast though. Sketch as if her life depended on it. Gathering four pieces of square white paper and a hard-tipped pencil, Maddie placed them at the ready. She then went back to choosing the best photographs of the chalked Sara, while enjoying the sound of Tania taking control.

"Freya." Tania pulled up a chair and sat so close to the girls that her linen covered knees met their bare ones. "You are to tell me *exactly* what happened while I was out."

The blonde's mind raced as she thought back over the last hour. "We posed for Maddie and then she showed Sara something in a drawer and then you came and..."

Tania cut through her answer. "I said tell me *exactly* what you and Sara did."

Starting again Freya gabbled, "Well, we stripped as much as Maddie wanted for the picture. My top came off and Sara took off her bra but kept her shirt on. Then Maddie began to draw but she wanted a more accurate scene so she and Sara spanked my breast until it was the right colour for the picture and Maddie drew it."

Licking her dry lips, Freya stopped talking. She half wished her eyes were open so she could gauge the expression on Tania's face, although she was equally glad that her eyes were closed so she didn't have to see it.

"That's a bit better." Tania's voice, however, told the other women in the studio that Freya's answer had been far from satisfactory. "Sara, perhaps you would like to tell me your version of events and bear in mind that I am holding the item you took from the drawer. When I say tell me *exactly* what happened, that is precisely what I mean."

Increasingly aware of Theo's breathing down the phone line as he listened to every word being uttered or moaned, Maddie, having narrowed down the chalked photos of Sara to three possibilities, contemplated how he was coping with what he was hearing just as Sara cleared her throat.

"When Maddie came back up the stairs from saying goodbye to you, Freya and I were kissing and..."

"That's better." Tania's tone mellowed from harsh to merely dominant. "Keep going – leave nothing out."

Speaking faster, Sara burbled out an account of every second that Tania had missed. As she concluded with her recount of being asked to choose a weapon from the chest of drawers, Freya's mouth dropped open. Maddie saw the lines of apprehension on the blonde's forehead double at the realisation that the paddle was now in Tania's control.

"...and then Maddie spoke to you and...well...you know the rest." Sara's chest was rising and falling with the effort of giving her accurate testimony.

"Very good." Tania leant forward and smoothed the leather of the paddle over the four adjacent legs before her, causing both women to exhale sharply at the same time.

This was Maddie's cue to act. Hanging up the call to Theo, she texted him

> Maddie: That's all u get for now, I have
> work to do

She picked up her collection of paper and pencils and an A4 clipboard to rest against. She'd always been the speediest sketcher at college. Maddie just hoped that the skill had not deserted her.

Ignoring Theo's text:

Bitch – u can't leave it like that

Maddie went to Freya's side. Her pencil poised in her hand, the artist decided to work on the blonde first.

"Unless I give you permission, you will not move." Tania lay down the paddle and reached forward with both hands, sharply pinching each woman's right nipple.

Freya's head instantly flew backwards and Maddie sketched the line of her slender neck, the slack of her jaw and the concentration she was employing not to open her eyes as Tania repeated the move, this time squeezing more of her tender, abused breast. The hiss Freya gave was still echoing through the room when Maddie dropped the first finished drawing and switched to Sara's side.

Tania stood, scraping back her chair a little so she could crouch before the women. Taking hold of each outside leg, she pushed them open, allowing herself some access to both bare pussies – pussies that were almost equally slippery. Understanding what Maddie was up to, Tania glanced at her, making sure she was ready; the redhead licked the ends of her index fingers and placed them directly onto the end of each clit.

The result was unswerving and electric as the frayed nerves of the models fire-worked through their bodies. Maddie stroked her pencil over her paper, capturing the illicitly opened eyes of Sara whose face spoke of nothing but the lust she felt at that precise moment.

Tania, her clothes still remarkably unruffled, swapped her index fingers for her thumbs and pushed a slim digit up inside each of the yielding channels.

Focusing on Freya's face as one finger slipped in and out of her cunt, Maddie again sketched fast, her style almost abstract, capturing the head-swimming detail of the moment as the models' fingernails dug into their own skin, their lips issuing a mingled mass of kink-driven grunts and sighs.

"Turn over!" Tania snapped. As she spoke, her hands fell from the women and, lifting the paddle, she ordered, "Kneel on the sofa. I wish to see those luscious backsides."

Clumsily, but with no hesitation, Freya and Sara clambered round onto the sofa's seat and rested their arms on its back, their chests knocking tantalizingly against the fabric. Sara linked one of her hands into Freya's as she waited for the strike to her backside she was sure would soon follow.

Maddie watched, unsure which angle to work from. Her mind was made up for her by Tania's expression. She clocked the stern dedication on her ex's face, wondering how Tania intended to work off her own thirst for sex once the girls had climaxed before her – a thought that brought a hungry clench to Maddie's own sex.

The paddle hummed as it was drawn through the air – a hum which ended in a hefty thwack as it landed squarely on Freya's bum. The paddle withdrew again, this time to land on Sara's ripe, upturned bottom.

The yelps of the models were laced with satisfied groans and, as the paddle found each of them for a third time. Freya began to murmur, "Oh yes…" as Sara stuck her butt out further, making herself an easier target.

Her sketches complete, Maddie put her work to one side and grabbed two dildos from the open drawer of toys. Throwing one to Tania, Maddie positioned hers at the aperture of Freya's pussy, while Tania abandoned the paddle and did the same to Sara. On a silent count of three, the older women drove their tools into place.

The effect of filling the girls was instantaneous. Keeping one hand on the inserted tools, the artist and her assistant eased their free hands between the trembling legs, pinching and kneading their fingers through the oozing honey that flowed from them both.

Freya howled and began to jack between Maddie, the dildo and the sofa, only a fraction of a second before Sara did. Their eyes now wide open and without bothering to wait for permission, they turned their faces to each other, entwining their tongues to suckle and kiss as their flesh was pushed into two body-ripping orgasms.

The intensity of their cumming forced the girls to pull apart so that they could catch their breath – green-eyed gaze locked into blue.

Easing away from the models, Tania and Maddie shared a knowing look as their victims slumped, spent but happy, across the back of the furniture.

Freya, her hair plastered across her sweat-sheened

face, smiled at Maddie through a drunken haze of post fuck dizziness and asked, "Will any men be posing for your pictures as well?"

"Oh yes, honey. I have one gentleman in mind. I'm sure you'll meet him very soon."

Chapter Seven

Having yet again rejected her ex's suggestion that they might as well share a bed seeing as Tania was there; and successfully stalling all Tania's attempted interrogation sessions about Theo, Maddie was finally alone.

Her evening of adding to and improving the pastel of Freya and Sara had been an irritating affair. Tania had stalked the studio bemoaning the lack of television and artificial entertainment in general, while Maddie worked, missing the peace of her usual out-of-hours solitude.

It was gone midnight and, although her right arm ached from a hard day's work, Maddie felt reassured that she had two projects rather than only one in production. If she could keep up this momentum then she might just make the gallery's requirements on time.

The following day she intended to work on both the new pieces and, as she got undressed in the privacy of her bedroom, Maddie prayed that Tania would be bored enough to go out and leave her to it.

Visualising all of the artwork she had created so far, Maddie's mind settled on the chalk swirl photographs of

Sara. At the time, she'd been convinced that a montage of all the shots she'd taken, built up into a huge square, would be perfect. Now she wasn't so sure. The pencil sketches of Sara, Tania and Freya in mid-ecstasy would look much better framed or maybe even arranged in a cube around a wooden block. A hint of satisfaction curled around the artist's eyes. "And if I take the best photograph of Sara all chalked up, I could then get it blown up onto a huge canvas...yes. That would work."

Relaxing against her pillow, Maddie savoured the quiet she normally took for granted. Idly, she wondered if perhaps she could persuade Tania to deliver the memory stick containing the photograph to the local printers, when she suddenly found her thoughts invaded by Theo. Rather than batting her uninvited musings away, Maddie began to smile into the semi-dark of her curtained room. *How had that fit body of his reacted to overhearing Sara and Freya talking to Tania about their preparation for sex?*

Having neglected her phone since she had given him an audial glimpse into her world, Maddie now fished it from a pile of clothes. She blinked at the screen. It must have held a nearly record-breaking amount of messages and missed calls. Every single one had come from Theo.

As he hadn't bothered leaving any recordings on voicemail, Maddie scrolled back to the first text he'd sent after she'd hung up on him early that afternoon. Reading each one, her self-satisfied smile died a little. But her body, which until that point had been content with the mild highs garnered from satisfying the sexual requirements of others, began to crave some personal attention.

It was with a sense of surprise that Maddie realised this was the second time in only a short while that Theo's messages had made her want to reach for her vibrator. With her brow furrowed and her flesh unexpectedly sensitive, she read through the accumulation of texts more carefully.

> 12pm – missed call
> 12.04pm – Will u answer the bloody phone
> 12.08pm – missed call
> 12.09pm – I am parked at side of road – too fucking hard to drive!
> 12.15pm – Have u any idea what u are doing to me?
> 12.17pm – U do don't u! U know exactly what ur doing to me.
> 12.19pm – missed call
> 1.00pm – I've had enough Maddie! U aren't going to play games with me anymore.
> 2.02pm – Unbelievable!! I am still horny. U are SO going to pay for this Miss Templeton when I finally get to fuck u – which I WILL.

Maddie drew in a low whistle as she read. Her clit spasming as she considered that perhaps she'd misguided Theo. Although he seemed to be made of sterner stuff than she'd imagined. *Either way,* she mused as she continued to read the catalogue of texts, *that doesn't mean I have to stop making him wait until I'm absolutely ready for him. As long as I'm careful how I handle things from now on.*

> 2.05pm – I am going to tie ur hands
> together and rip ur cloths off
> 2.09pm – I will spank ur bum with my
> palm until we are both bruised
> 2.30pm – For fuck's sake – respond
> woman!
> 3.07pm – I bet ur in bed with someone
> now aren't u – probably that tart with
> the posh voice I heard over the phone.

Tania hadn't ever struck Maddie as posh before. But she supposed her ex did sound that way if you ignored the smoke ravaged edge to her voice. There was no question that Tania thought herself a cut above the rest, and the flint-like self-loving conceit she always portrayed could be intimidating enough to make her appear upper class.

> 3.12pm – missed call
> 3.18pm – How would u like it if I
> was out screwing someone else –
> especially an ex!?
> 3.20pm – OK – so u prob wouldn't give
> a fuck. I won't hang on forever u know.

"And yet you have hung on, Theo. You have hung

on for six weeks." Maddie muttered to herself. But she was alerted by an unwelcome and growing frustration gathering in her chest, as the tone of Theo's texts abruptly changed.

> 3.37pm – I am good at licking pussy.
> 3.48pm – I can suck tits like u wouldn't believe
> 3.54pm – I bet u like having ur asshole tongued

Maddie's chest, pussy and backside all reacted together and the temptation to reply to each individual text in the positive grew stronger. Conscious that her palms were becoming sweaty, Maddie read on.

> 4.03pm – I wonder how long I could tease u with my dick before u beg to be full?
> 4.17pm – I bet u would take it up the rear

So, thought the artist to herself, her free hand unconsciously playing with the tip of her left breast, *you aren't averse to a bit of butt-play after all, Mr. Electrician. Interesting...I wonder if that goes for boys as well as girls.*

> 4.20pm – I want to spend an hour lubing up ur backside before I shaft it
> 4.30pm – I am so going to make u scream

> 4.37pm – Going to bury my cock in u
> so deep u have to bite the pillow
> 4.41pm – As I work ur butt I am gonna
> grab ur tits and...

Enough! Despite the lateness of the hour, Maddie began to type into her phone. She'd been so sure she had Theo back where she wanted him – waiting, perhaps not happily, but at least still prepared to wait. Now, with her own urgent hankering for a climax spurring her on, the pictures his texts were forming in her mind worked their own revenge. Maddie started a campaign to secure Theo's interest once and for all. If she *had* to come across as keen, then that was the price she was prepared to pay and, as Maddie unfurled her naked legs from the bed and stamped purposefully upstairs to the studio, mobile in hand, she knew exactly how to make this temporary deference work to her advantage.

Stepping quietly through the door, Maddie made sure that Tania was asleep before she pressed send on her next text to Theo.

> Maddie: I want u to fuck me over the
> bonnet of ur van.

It was a cliché – one of the oldest there was – but if she had learned anything from her discussions with clients over the years, it was that clichés were clichés for a reason: people like them.

Confident that Theo would still be awake despite the

lateness of the hour, Maddie scanned the room. It was time Tania saw how much she'd changed since Maddie had thrown her out. Walking with soft footfalls across the carpeted side of the room, Maddie quietly opened the top drawer of the chest she and Sara had explored earlier, took out four lengths of silk cord and laid them on her desk.

The artist glanced at the screen of her silent phone. She smiled. He was so predictable.

> Theo: I want u to bend over in front
> of me in a lane somewhere out in the
> open.

Maddie countered:

> I want that too.
> I don't care if it's raining either... I want
> to feel the rain trickling down the crack
> of my ass.

She then strode across the room and, with one sweep of her arm, yanked off the covers that had been keeping Tania warm. Without giving her ex time to come round, Maddie barked, "Get up!"

Blanking out the expletives that fell from Tania's lips after being woken from a mere hour's sleep, Maddie returned her attention to the phone.

> Theo: What time then?

Ignoring Theo's direct question, Maddie replied:

> I'm wet just thinking about it – and not
> just on the outside – juice is running
> down my legs

"Stand up. Come here. Say nothing," she said to Tania.

The erstwhile dominatrix stared quizzically at Maddie. No one had ordered her about like this before. Curiosity getting the better of her, Tania did as she was bidden but held a private resolve to play the submissive only for as long as she wanted to – *not* because Maddie said she had to.

Theo's reply was already flashing on the phone:

> Rain or dry, when ur bent over van
> bonnet, I will strip off ur jeans and
> knickers.

As soon as she'd finished reading, Maddie took hold of Tania's right wrist and marched her to the very middle of the studio's wooden floor. Standing beneath the spotlights Theo had fitted, Maddie ran the cool screen of her phone over the tip of Tania's right breast. Then, alternately agitating the mobile over one nipple and then the other, Maddie grasped Tania's face firmly, squeezing her cheeks and glaring straight into her eyes, before ordering, "Stay here."

Walking to the other side of the room, Maddie

returned her attention to Theo.

Maddie: What will u do to me next?

With a violent sweep of her arm, Maddie cleared the contents from the top of the battered metal trolley that held her spare brushes, paints and equipment. Then, kicking off the empty mixing tins from the trolley's bottom shelf, she wheeled it towards Tania. Despite the proud pitch of her chin and her resolutely squared shoulders, Tania was looking the most uncertain Maddie had seen her, and the defiant sense of disquiet from her ex lover's face sent a new blast of power through Maddie's system.

Leaving Tania to try and guess what the hell was going on, Maddie read the latest message from her electrician.

Theo: I will fuck u so hard the imprint
of the van's front grill will dig into ur
chest.

The artist smiled with a relief she would never have admitted to. For one unsettling moment this morning, Maddie had speculated that perhaps Theo was keeping her waiting and not the other way around. Now she had his interest again, it was time to rein him back in properly so she never felt like that again.

She abruptly changed the theme of the texts once again.

Maddie: U said my ex sounded posh.
She isn't. She's a pain in the butt,
hasn't an original thought in her head,
& could be mistaken for a leech. She's
standing in front of me – naked. Her
name is Tania. I'm going to show her
how I have changed since I threw her
out.

Laying the phone down, Maddie pointed from Tania to the trolley and back again, making her implication clear. "I advise you to continue to remain silent. I do not want to hear a single gripe from you. As you climb onto the trolley I do not wish to hear how other people fuck better than I do. I do not wish to hear what incredible sexual acrobatics you have been up to in my absence. Quite honestly, Tan, I don't care. It is high time you understood that the world is not at your beck and call and that you are not the Mistress while you are under my roof."

Tania's lips parted to give a biting response but a raised eyebrow from Maddie killed the words before they'd left her throat. The artist gestured towards the two-shelved trolley. "On you go."

"What?" Tania stared at the metal contraption. Each shelf was only one metre long by half a metre wide. "There's no way I can fit on there."

"Two things." Maddie's desire to dominate the woman in front of her interwove with thoughts of Theo. "One, I told you not to speak. Two, you claim you can get into any pose and hold any position for as long as the artist in question requires. Well this is what this artist requires. So get that perky backside on that top tray. Now."

She hadn't raised her voice, but Maddie's quiet command sent anxious (and decidedly erotic) shivers right down Tania's spine. This really was a new Maddie.

"You have until I have read and sent a text to get on. Ass down, face up."

> Theo: Sod how have u changed! Tell
> me what ur doing

Maddie imagined Theo's rugged face frowning, but also glowing with need.

> Maddie: U can receive photos on ur
> phone, right?
> Theo: Yes
> Maddie: Then be patient and u will see

Tania considered the trolley. Assuming that Maddie had an idea in mind for a gallery piece, the redhead's professional pride dictated that she should create it. The tremor at the top of her thighs also told her that she wanted to see how far Maddie was going to go with this, and Tania was interested to discover how good it might feel.

Taking a deep breath and with a bend of her knees, Tania jumped so that she was sitting on top of the trolley. Edging herself along in reverse, she positioned the small of her back in the very centre of cold metal tray. Slowly, so she didn't wedge her shoulders against the hand rails that ran along the long sides of the trolley, Tania lay so that her legs hung over one end and her head and neck hung over the other, her loose hair sweeping the floor. Forcing herself to relax as much as possible, Tania threaded her arms carefully through the side rails, letting them swing freely, trying not to think about how vulnerable she had allowed herself to become.

Secretly impressed at how easily Tania had gotten into position and resisting the temptation to take a photograph for Theo there and then, Maddie gathered up the silk cord she'd extracted earlier. Her face giving away nothing of her rising excitement, Maddie knelt by Tania's left side, picked up her wrist, bent her arm at the elbow and wrapped the cord in a figure of eight around her limb and around the nearest trolley leg.

Rather than get up and move, Maddie took hold of the trolley and wheeled it in a sharp circle, causing Tania to forget all about being quiet. She yelped in surprise, her stomach churning over and her hair dusting the floor like a brush.

Ignoring her ex's shocked protests, but noting mentally that she had now broken the no talking rule for a second time, Maddie tied Tania's right arm in place, before twisting the trolley twice more and securing her ankles to the remaining metal legs in a similar fashion.

The moment she was satisfied that Tania was unable to undo her fastenings simply by tugging at them, Maddie returned to her phone.

Theo had evidently become impatient again.

Theo: The wait better be worth it.

She didn't bother to reply. Instead, she simply lined up her phone's camera with the trolley, getting as much of Tania in the shot as possible, took the picture and sent the resulting image to Theo.

For once Maddie was not assailed by the urge to stop and paint the situation she'd orchestrated. This was not about obtaining a representation that would last forever. This was the creation of a personal antidote to all the times Tania had ordered her around – a way of working off the aggravation that had raced to the surface since her erstwhile girlfriend had re-crossed the threshold of her home.

At the back of her mind, Maddie's determination to rid herself of the feeling that she was losing her touch, spurred her on. If Theo wasn't happy to hang on his fish hook and wait like all the men that had gone before him, then she needed to toughen up and raise her game – and fast.

Theo: OMG!!! What u going to do to her?
Maddie: Wait and see

Tania tried to turn her neck to see what Maddie was doing. Never had she felt so exposed, yet the dull thud that was spreading through her trapped muscles wasn't preventing a giddy yearning for Maddie to make her next move.

Ever since she had received Maddie's answer phone message asking her to come and help with the exhibition, Tania had harboured faint hopes about resuming her life with the artist. Her body had wanted to take Maddie the instant she'd seen her open the front door. Yet this was a new Maddie, and the redhead had slowly come to the realisation that she was not the only one who wanted her. Whoever it was Maddie kept texting had to be a rival and if Tania had one rule, it was never to lose to a rival, even if it was one you didn't know and couldn't see.

With a purposeful resolve, Tania wove her fingers around the slim metal legs of the trolley, bit her lips together and decided to take whatever was thrown at her. She would prove to Maddie that she was the strongest woman she'd ever met and in the process, convince her ex that life would be much more interesting with her in it again, permanently.

Dismissing the temptation to use a selection of sex toys from her eclectic collection, Maddie grabbed a thin cushion from the sofa and, standing between Tania's widened legs, ordered, "Raise your hips."

After some awkward wriggling, Tania managed to push against her bindings enough to lift her backside an inch or two and successfully held the position long enough for Maddie to position the pillow beneath her bottom – effectively making her pussy an easier target for whatever the artist wished to do with it.

Switching the phone to its vibrate function, Maddie

placed it in the centre of Tania's flat stomach. Resting her bare legs against the insides of her prisoner's open thighs, Maddie reached forward, cupping and moulding the entirety of each breast in her palms. An illicit whistle of bliss issued from between Tania's clenched lips and Maddie added the extra noise to her mental score chart.

Absent mindedly rotating her left palm over the tip of Tania's left breast, Maddie began to text Theo, every press of the screen pushing against the gym-toned stomach.

Maddie: I am playing with her nipples.

Then, as if to prove her point, Maddie flashed off a quick photo and sent it hurrying after the text. Replacing the phone over Tania's neat oval naval, the artist turned her attention to the supine right breast, this time flicking at it with her tongue, feeling it grow within her mouth, savouring its rough texture compared to the perfect smoothness of the rest of Tania's chest. A whimper of satisfaction slipped from Tania's lips.

Maddie's eyes narrowed. "You keep making noises you have not asked permission to make." She slapped each of Tania's trussed thighs burningly hard in punishment, leaving a merging collection of hand sized blotches on the fake-tanned flesh. Tania howled with a pain that reflected gratification in her wide peppermint eyes.

The buzz of the phone as Theo replied sent shock waves through Tania's torso and thighs as the handset juddered, making her whine anew at the unexpected vibration.

Theo: Spank them. If it was u on that
trolley, I would spank ur tits

Mindful that she couldn't leave Tania with her head hanging down for too much longer, Maddie steered her tethered passenger towards the bed. Lining up the trolley against the foot of the bed, Maddie gently raised Tania's head and neck and rested them on the duvet, before checking that none of the bonds had loosened.

Satisfied that Tania was appropriately positioned, Maddie pressed her fingers against the touch screen and replied to Theo.

Maddie: What else would u do if it was
me on the trolley?

Knowing how much she used to love Tania smacking her own chest, Maddie relished the chance to turn the tables. Keeping the redhead's bright green eyes fixed on hers, Maddie swiped her fingernails sharply across the right and left nipples in quick succession.

Those green eyes began to water, but they didn't close as Maddie kept up the rhythmic pattern of strikes until the flesh beneath her palms felt singed to her touch. Maddie observed Tania's face as every expression, every truncated reaction sought to register. The artist changed tack, continuing to pinch each nipple between her fingertips until Tania's mouth fell open and she panted with the effort of maintaining her composure.

Again the vibration of the phone sent random pulses whizzing through every nerve of the bound woman, whose body was now rippling against the unyielding metal tray.

> Theo: I would sit astride u and make u
> suck my cock

"So obvious." Maddie spoke to herself as she took a photo of the now scarlet nipples before her. She knew they were hungry for a licking. She also knew that if she did feast on them, there was a high chance Tania would cum – and Maddie hadn't finished playing with her yet.

Pressing send on the latest photo, Maddie knelt at Tania's feet, snaking her fingers and palms over her ankles. Tania's toes were already cold from lack of circulation and Maddie rubbed them briefly before gliding her touch up the slender legs.

"I have to tell you, Tan, that you look rather appetizing. All available and ready for me to do just what the fuck I like."

Resisting the temptation to read Theo's response to the photo, Maddie continued her work. Reaching her hostage's knees, she scratched and danced her nails over them, making Tania jerk involuntarily as her kneecaps were transformed into two concentrated and unexpectedly sensual nerve centres.

As her hands progressed up towards her ex's thighs, Maddie examined the raised pussy that she hadn't visited for a very long time. She had no need to lean close to savour its aroma. The familiar sweet, yet somehow citrus, scent had been playing with her senses for the past ten minutes and now she could see why. Tania's poker face may have given little of her excitement away, but her sweet slit positively oozed with honey.

Maddie's face broke into a sarcastic smile. "My my, Tania, you've all but wet yourself. What happened to your famous self-control?"

Studying the green eyes before her, Maddie saw they'd begun to cloud and she knew that her ex couldn't take much more stimulation before climax. Tania was so used to dishing out the punishments and pleasures that her body had never been sufficiently trained in delaying its own responses when direct stimulation was applied.

Maddie wondered what Theo would do if he was there with her. *Would he want to impale Tania himself? Or let her suck him off while I played with Tan's clit until she bucked her way out of the bindings?*

Taking another photo, giving her electrician an intimate insight into the glistening folds of her ex, Maddie read his latest message.

> Theo: I think u should screw her with a
> strap on

Knowing she was going to need her hands free very soon, Maddie simply replied, In 2 mins phone me.

Locking the breaks on the wheels of the trolley and ensuring that it couldn't accidently move, Maddie lounged against the foot of the bed right next to Tania's face. "Tell me Tan, how badly do you want me to make you cum right now?" Even though she was physically fit, Tania's limbs were straining at every muscle. Although Maddie suspected that the discomfort of her muscles was nothing compared to the ache between her legs.

Pride, along with the private skirmish Tania was having with the unknown figure at the other end of the phone, dictated the need for denial. Even in the face of the physical evidence to the contrary, Tania replied, "Not as badly as you want to," her voice gruff, her throat dehydrated.

Again Maddie smiled. "I don't deny that I have every intention of availing myself of the orgasm I've delayed all day – and soon."

The phone rang and the artist laughed as Tania jumped at its prolonged buzzing against her flesh.

"If you'll excuse me, Tania." Maddie rescued her mobile before it jumped off its female table and pressed her mobile as close to her ear as possible to prevent Tania from hearing Theo's side of the conversation.

Too impatient for pleasantries, Theo dove straight in with what he had to know. "Has she cum yet?"

"No. She's close though."

"How about you?"

"Not yet, but I will soon. I am considering a few options as to how that may be attained." Maddie enjoyed watching Tania's eyes narrow as she spoke, all the while teasing her free hand over and around the proud breasts in an unending figure of eight.

"I assume you are not saying what those options are because you do not wish her to hear you?" Theo's voice was amazingly collected, but Maddie could detect the underlying hint of desperation.

"You understand correctly." Maddie continued her caress of the breasts as she spoke, making sure that her thumb caught the edge of a nipple every now and again, causing Tania to slowly lose the mask of control she'd been holding on to for the past twenty minutes. "Tell me, honey, how aroused are you? Fancy an orgasm duet?"

"Seriously?" Theo sounded more hopeful than Maddie suspected he intended to.

"Seriously. But you'll have to tell me how close you are to climax so we can cum together. Tell me everything." Her hand crept down to Tania's legs, which had begun to quiver with the effects of restraint and a clear wish to climax. Maddie circled a single digit around, but not over, Tania's clit as she listened to Theo.

"I'm like a fucking plank of wood – what the hell do you think woman!"

"Good." Maddie said no more as she made her move.

Climbing up onto the bed, Maddie knelt with her knees spread and her pussy directly over Tania's face. "I am going to put the mobile on speakerphone. My bitch is going to lick me out now, while you make her cum."

"Me? How?"

"I am going to bring her off with my phone. You are

not going to fuck her. You are going to 'phone' her, as it were. You will see what I mean. Are you ready?"

"Oh fuck yes. My hand is already on my cock."

"Good. Keep talking. Keep telling us what you are doing. I'd let Tania talk to you, but you're going to have your mouthful, aren't you Tan?"

The captured woman nodded as best she could, all pride evaporating in her determination to outperform whoever Maddie was talking to. All that mattered now was her climax and winning whatever competition she was in.

"The phone is going to her slit now – talk honey. Raise your voice so we can hear you. Shout even. Tell us what you are doing. Now."

Obediently, Theo's clear lust driven tones could be heard. She could hear him describing how stiff he was and how much he wished he was the one about to lick her out as Maddie lowered her pussy over Tania's head. Then, balancing her weight with a hand on either side of the trolley, Maddie shouted to Tania over Theo's wishes, "Lick me, bitch."

After a few false starts, Tania got her face to the gorgeous cunny that was presented to her.

As her ex's tongue swirled in and around her sex, Maddie's stomach knotted with the approach of her long delayed orgasm. She could hear Theo's ragged breathing as he listened to the noises coming from the studio, his voice husky as he described how his palm was wrapped around his dick, how he was pumping back and forth and how Maddie had been driving him mad all day with thoughts of what she'd been doing. Then suddenly he shouted, "What does Maddie taste like Tania? Tell me!"

Unsure if her ex had heard Theo's muffled question, Maddie moved the phone, turned it on its side and, using the end furthest from the battery, began to buff its edge over Tania's distended nub.

All the while the demanding voice of Theo could be heard yelling out, "I want to know what you taste like, Maddie! Tania, stop fucking her for a second and tell me! Is she juicy? Is she like fruit? Is she sweet? Salty? What the fuck does Maddie taste like?"

The result of the mobile touching Tania's pussy had been nigh on instant. Deaf to Theo and totally unaware of anything but the cool casing of the phone caressing her hot clit, Tania's hips rose as high as the silk cords would allow.

Grateful for the easier access allowed by the pillow beneath Tania's buttocks, Maddie massaged her ex's clit in time to the ever increasing licks and kisses to her own centre.

All the time, the faint words of Theo describing his path to release and his repeated demands to know what Maddie tasted like, came from the space between Tania's legs, until at last he was silent, and Maddie knew he had cum. Pressing the phone harder against the nub before her, Maddie forced Tania into a mutual orgasm, fast on the heels of Theo's climax.

Just as she howled out a grateful cry, the bound redhead rolled her tongue and forced it deep within Maddie's cunt, making the artist buck so hard that she almost dropped

the phone she'd been gripping so tightly.

Sliding slowly off Tania, Maddie could still hear Theo's breathing down the line as she knelt to free her ex's ankles. Relieved that the phone was still working despite being in contact with so much wetness, the artist called out to Theo as she worked, "Hope you liked that, honey."

"Hell yes! Although, I still want to know what your pussy tastes like."

"Well, be a good boy and I'll be in touch with you about coming over tomorrow. Maybe you'll find out for yourself."

Maddie then hung up her phone and continued to untie Tania, helping her to flex each limb and return the circulation to her extremities.

Putting a finger to Tania's lips to indicate the she didn't have any intention of discussing what had happened, Maddie left the studio without a backward gla Tania, speechless and massaging her wrists, was left s atop the metal tray as Maddie disappeared down the st

Chapter Eight

◆ ◆ ◆ ◆

Sitting at the patio table in the corner of the small flagstoned yard at the back of her terraced home, Maddie sipped at her first mug of coffee of the day. She closed her eyes and the bright oranges and yellows of the early morning lit up the inside of her eyelids.

Surprisingly refreshed, even though she'd only had three hours sleep, Maddie mentally lined up the works of art she had completed against those she had begun, and decided which pieces needed to be re-worked next. An image of Theo reclining against the studio bed, waiting with growing impatience for her to touch him, crept into her head and distracted her train of thought.

A strong frisson of erotic craving took her by surprise and Maddie knew it was imperative for her to finish the pictures she'd already started, before embarking on anything involving her electrician. His presence would be a distraction which would require all her powers of control to ignore. Furthermore, after the fun of the evening before, she felt she could now risk making Theo wait just a little longer.

Again she could see her artistic plans for Theo

evolving in the forefront of her mind – maybe with ink. *Ink and maybe paper moulding...* Maddie was convinced what she had in mind would make all the waiting worthwhile for both of them, not to mention the resulting exquisite works of art. He would just have to hang on a few more days – possibly a week. *At least*, she thought to herself, *despite my fears, last night has proved that Theo's very good at waiting.*

Deciding to work outside to make the most of the natural light, Maddie threw herself into action. Tip-toeing so as not to wake the sleeping Tania, Maddie fired off a text to Theo saying she was busy that day, explaining that her call to him would be delayed, but that she'd be in touch soon. Popping her phone onto the trolley she'd tied Tania to the night before, she plugged it in to charge up before filling her shirt pockets with pastels, tucking her easel under her arm and picking up the canvas board on which she had captured Sara and Freya giving and receiving tit slaps.

Setting herself up in the garden, the memory of the girls on the sofa so vivid that she didn't have to refer to the myriad of photographs she'd taken, Maddie launched a fresh ecru-coloured pastel against the curvature of Freya's right breast.

"You bruised me."

Maddie had been so absorbed in her work that Tania's arrival behind her took her by surprise. "Tan, you made me jump! For goodness sake, I could have ruined this!"

"I don't give a fuck about the bloody picture, look

at my ankle!" Closing a towel around her naked body, she banged her foot on top of the plastic table so that her ankle was visible for inspection. Tania pointed at a minuscule bruise, an expression of total fury on her face. "I was going to wear shorts today. How can I with that on show?"

Bringing her face nearer to the proffered foot so she could detect the minor abrasion to the otherwise flawless skin, Maddie peered up at Tania questioningly. "You interrupted me to show me an almost non-existent mark on your ankle. A blemish – if we can even call it that – that you enjoyed receiving – don't you dare say otherwise. You loved every bloody second of last night."

Tania was visibly taken aback. This was not how it was supposed to go. When she told Maddie off, Maddie was supposed to apologise and make amends. She wasn't supposed to dismiss her complaint as if it was of no consequence whatsoever. If her ex's behaviour the day before hadn't confirmed for Tania that Maddie had completely swapped sides from submissive to mistress, her attitude this morning did just that.

"So, if you don't mind I have to get on. Or the show you were so keen to help me with won't happen." Maddie picked up the ruby toe-nailed foot and relegated it to the floor. "If you want to be useful then you can take the memory stick that's on my desk to the printers. I've called them. They are expecting it and already know what I want them to do for me."

"So I'm a delivery girl now, am I?"

"Sulking like a spoilt brat isn't going to work on me anymore, Tan. So you can either help or piss off back to your own home. I never invited you to stay here. If you remember, I asked if you could help, that's all. You could have said no. You could have done one piece for me and buggered off. But you didn't."

The redhead jutted her chin forward as she said, "I was only trying to help."

"So help then! Get out of that towel, put on whatever clothes you like and get to the printers for me."

Stung, Tania turned on her heels and stalked out of the garden back up to the studio. Spotting the memory stick straight away, she placed it in her handbag before putting on some lightweight trousers and a pale, dusky green-coloured shirt that highlighted the shade of her eyes to perfection.

She was about to leave the house when Tania spotted Maddie's mobile charging on the corner of the trolley. With a cautious glance towards the stairway to make sure that Maddie wasn't on her way up, Tania picked up the phone and turned it on, whispering, "So, who are you then?"

Making herself comfortable on the sofa, Tania considered what Maddie's password might be. "I don't suppose you have been so considerate as to have kept the same password all this time, Miss Templeton?"

Tapping in the four digit number she'd used to hack into the same mobile six months ago, for the sole purpose of making sure Maddie's boyfriend learned to like her more than the artist, Tania smirked. "Honestly, Maddie, you really should change your password every now and then!"

Confident that she would remain undisturbed, as Maddie was sufficiently engrossed in what she was doing for the foreseeable future, Tania activated the call history of the phone. Determined to discover who she'd been providing so much entertainment for during her trolley experience, Tania scrolled to the top of the calls received list, tapping her sharp nails on the side of the phone as she read, "Theo." She nodded knowingly. "Theo."

The tradesman, Theo, who Maddie was so cagey about the other day. Of course.

Making a note of his number on her own mobile, Tania quickly scanned through all the text messages that Maddie and Theo had exchanged over the past few weeks. A resentful anger took hold of her as she read. In all the time she'd been with Maddie, they had never once flirted by text. Never had there been the tense sexual build up she could feel radiating from the messages exchanged between the artist and the electrician. *Well, it's time to put a stop to that.* Without a glimmer of conscience, Tania texted Theo.

> Tania: Hello Theo. My name is Tania.
> You 'phoned' me last night. Mads and
> I share everything – I am sure she has
> told you that – Want to meet for lunch?

Once her message had gone, Tania deleted it from the 'Sent' file and turned off Maddie's touch screen. She placed the phone precisely where she'd found it and left the studio, a resolute expression on her made-up face.

◆ ◆ ◆

Smarting from yet another of Maddie's texts delaying his quest to experience her body, Theo had no qualms about meeting Tania for lunch. His curiosity to see in the flesh the woman he'd viewed in such an acrobatic position the night before, overrode any loyalty to the artist. A loyalty he felt she didn't deserve anyway. Too many promises to meet up "soon" had been broken. Either that, or her definition of "soon," was completely different to his.

An hour later, sitting in the garden of a pub on the edge of town, Theo sipped thoughtfully at his pint of lager. His eyes searched out every female newcomer that entered the garden, wondering if he would actually recognise Tania when she was upright and fully clothed. But the second the slim redhead with the captivating hips sashayed through the gate, Theo knew it was the woman he'd been waiting for.

Straight away he saw why Maddie had found Tania attractive. But he could also see why she was an ex. This woman had *me, me, me* written all over her. She was, however, undeniably sexy. Faced with the creature he'd heard coaxed to orgasm by the rub of a phone and the stroke of his own pleasure, Theo's cock began to solidify within his boxers.

"You must be Theo." Tania extended a perfectly manicured hand.

"How did you know it was me?" Rising to return her greeting and feeling the silky smooth skin of her palm, Theo found himself grinning into her glowing face. He couldn't help comparing her to Maddie. He'd never seen the artist wear make-up, or anything but sloppy clothes that didn't matter if they got grubby, and her hair was generally shoved into an unruly ponytail. This woman was the polar opposite. He could imagine the scandalised expression that would cross Tania's face if anyone suggested that she went outside without at least two layers of foundation and a sweep of mascara.

"Maddie told me you were an electrician."

Theo regarded her sceptically. "Do I look like an electrician then?" Tania simply smiled, flirting unashamedly, and Theo knew he'd met women like this one before. The sort of woman who had to be with the 'in crowd,' and who couldn't function if the lion's share of attention wasn't on her. He would put money on her asking for Pimm's or champagne, with maybe Gin and Tonic as an outside bet. "What can I get you to drink?"

"Do you think they do Pimm's here?"

Although he'd summed up her self-centred character accurately, Theo proceeded toward the bar wondering why he hadn't texted Maddie to check she knew that Tania was with him. *Probably because I am sure Maddie doesn't know about this.* This meant that the woman he was buying a drink for had more than likely stolen his number from Maddie's phone. Theo found himself speculating as to how he could use this unexpected twist to his advantage.

"So why isn't Maddie here with you?" Theo placed the long tumbler of liquid, complete with ice cubes and bobbing cherries, in front of Tania, before sitting opposite his companion and sliding his legs between the wooden bench and the table.

"She's busy with the exhibition. She's always been very driven with her art. But honestly, I've never seen her like this. Maddie used to be so soft, so biddable."

Theo almost choked on his pint. "Biddable? You're kidding me!"

"Not at all. She was so kind. Now she uses people. Those girls that model for her. They idolise her, you know. But she does nothing but use them. Treats them like common whores, paying them with sex in exchange for their modelling." Tania shuddered as if to emphasise her distaste, privately exulting in the shocked look on Theo's face.

"I got the impression that the arrangement she has with her models was entirely mutual and that they were happy with the arrangement."

"Well, what would you expect Mads to say? That she fools them into thinking she cares for them and then has fun making them orgasm like they never have before. An act which, let's face it, she then uses to influence new pieces of art."

Theo took a drink from his pint. He hadn't thought of it like that. There was no denying that any act of sex Maddie was involved in could find its way into her artwork. *Surely that's not the only reason she has sex?*

Playing around with the cherries floating at the top of her glass, Tania continued. "I take it you realise that's all she'll want from you? Some art. Something to add to her precious exhibition."

What Tania was saying began to ring alarmingly true. *Is that really all Maddie wants from me?* All the sexual tension he was convinced he'd felt between them when he'd stood with Maddie in her studio, had that all been in his mind? Was it all wishful thinking on his part?

"You're wondering if Maddie really likes you, or if she's just using you too, aren't you?"

Theo said nothing, his eyes staring at the snake-like grin of the creature before him with renewed interest. Her face spoke of warmth and understanding and yet her smile failed to reach her eyes. Tania may well have been speaking the truth, but a voice at the back of his head was convinced that this was a woman who couldn't be trusted. *Why should that matter to me, though? What does matter is that she might be able to get me to Maddie quicker. Whatever the artist's motives are, I have been messed around and made to wait too long not to have her at least once.*

"It was the studio," Tania continued.

Pulled from his thoughts, Theo frowned. "I'm sorry, what was the studio?"

"The feeling you had when you were with Maddie. It was generated by the studio. It affects everyone like that. How can it fail to with all those erotic paintings and the pin board full of photos of sex in action? The place reeks of fornication – worse, it reeks of the *promise* of fornication. A promise which isn't always granted. And when it is, the artist remains aloof, rarely indulging, putting her own gratification on hold. I mean, what sort of woman can do that for hours and hours at a time? I tell you, Theo..." Tania reached out her hand and enveloped it around his as it cradled his glass. "...the woman is a robot."

Theo's eyes narrowed. It all sounded so plausible. It also sounded like sour grapes. He had increasingly felt like he'd been duped by one woman for days and he wasn't about to let this one do the same – although he had no problem with letting her think she'd pulled the wool over his eyes. He didn't care enough about Tania to mind that.

He wasn't exactly sure how Maddie had taken him in, though. She hadn't lied to him although she had certainly led him on. The woman was obviously a prick-tease, but did that actually mean she wasn't interested in him? Or was it just that his male ego didn't want to consider that he may have been played as a fool – that he might be, as far as Maddie was concerned, simply a more distracting sex toy than her vibrator? Something for her to play with for a while.

The shining eyes opposite him didn't seem to blink and he wondered if Tania could read his every thought. Gathering himself, Theo returned the silent, unashamedly lustful come-on his companion was giving him; his mind turning temporarily from Maddie's motives, to contemplating how long Tania's hair would be if it was let free from the high plait that swept up from the nape of her neck.

"When are you seeing Maddie next?" Increasing the pressure on his hand, Tania dipped two fingers of her other hand into her drink, before slowly and deliberately sucking off the sweet liquid. If the move hadn't had such a candid and profound effect on his groin, Theo would have laughed. It was positively textbook seduction. *Perhaps Maddie was right; maybe Tania doesn't have an imaginative bone in her body?* Did he care though? Maddie had been promising him sex for weeks and not delivered. This woman had been a feature of his life for less than twelve hours and, unless he was reading the situation very wrongly, she was up for it right now.

"I thought I was seeing Maddie today but she texted to say she was busy."

"Typical Maddie. Keep them waiting. Then keep them waiting a bit more. Especially men. It's a game she plays."

The heat from the midday sun, irritating Theo's neck, was made worse by a new sense of unease. He pulled at his white t-shirt to stop it sticking to his back. Extracting his pint and hand from Tania's soft grasp, Theo took a slow draft of the blissfully cool drink. "A game?"

"Yes. You know. Meet someone and then see how long you can keep them hanging on for sex before they get bored of waiting. Only then will she strike."

"Why?" Theo licked his lips which, despite the lager, were becoming dry in the face of the prominent nipples he could clearly see hardening through Tania's top. The knowledge that she wasn't wearing a bra was having an extraordinary effect on his already interested groin.

"She believes that the longer the wait, the better the eventual sex."

Theo remained silent. After giving him a moment to assimilate the thought she'd planted in his head, Tania lent further across the table and replaced her hand on his, noting with satisfaction the direction of his eyes. "Theo, you don't appear to be able to stop staring at my chest. Would you like to see it?"

Snapping his eyes back up to meet hers, Theo came to a decision. Maddie had delayed their meeting yet again and he was tired of his only physical pleasure being a solo affair. What did he owe Maddie anyway? She wasn't exactly denying herself while she waited for him! And if Tania was offering herself up on a plate, then why shouldn't he indulge? Anyway, he wanted to see if her chest really was as gravity defying as it appeared to be.

"I've already seen your breasts. Last night – via the phone."

"I like to think that perhaps they are better in real life." Tania somehow managed to look coy as her fingernails briefly slid teasingly along the back of his hand, before returning to her drink.

Theo drank the remnants of his pint and stood, holding out an arm to Tania. "May I escort you to somewhere more suitable, ma'am?"

Unable to prevent the brief flash of triumph from appearing on her face, Tania quickly composed herself. Hoping Theo hadn't spotted her lapse, she covered her delight with a small curtsy. "Why sir, you may."

Linking his arm with hers, Theo spoke in a taut

whisper. "I'm not going to be able to go far. My desire to see your tits without that flimsy shirt in the way has already had a...prominent effect."

Tania laughed, tugging him closer to her side. "Is that right?"

"I want to pinch the nipples I can see poking at your shirt and taste them on my tongue." Voicing his wishes somehow made them even more urgent and the twenty-minute walk to his flat suddenly seemed to Theo like a day's quest. He wanted her now. Right now.

Seeing the door to the Gents, Theo finally let go of the sexual hunger he'd be fighting for what seemed like forever. Pushing Tania through the rough wooden door of the single cubicle, he locked it securely behind them. "I can't wait any more. If you want out, go now."

Delighted by his impatience, Tania grabbed at Theo's t-shirt by way of a reply, raking her hands up his chest as he grabbed the back of her plait and used it to yank her closer. With no real interest in kissing her on the lips, Theo shoved her shirt up and feasted his eyes on Tania's naked breasts. His teeth fastened themselves around her left breast, while his palm squashed and kneaded its counterpart with rhythmical precision.

Tania groaned softly into the stale air of the grubby room. The salacious, sneaky happiness she felt from getting the better of Maddie combined with the blissful shocks Theo was sending through her body, made the less-than-romantic surroundings irrelevant.

More concerned with speed than finesse, Theo dashed his hands over Tania's hips and thighs as he kissed and licked her skin, moving his mouth steadily south. Only when he reached Tania's waistband did he pause to look up into the vivid glossy eyes that were fixed on him.

A silent nod of encouragement from Tania and Theo wrenched her trousers from her. His gaze delighted in the revelation of her tiny scarlet thong, which he tried not to snap in his haste to reach the pussy he'd seen only yesterday.

After fumbling in his wallet for one of the condoms he carried in the hope that Maddie would invite him to the studio, he had his jeans and boxers at his ankles and was rolling the rubber on before Tania had registered that, for the second day in a row, she was not directing the sex in which she was participating.

Even though she'd secretly liked being at Maddie's command, Tania needed to dominate for total fulfilment. For her, nothing was as good as gaining the upper hand over a horny male. *At least Maddie and I still have that in common*, Tania thought as she twisted her lithe body away from the unsanded wooden door, sidestepped Theo's exploring fingers and took his sheathed length firmly within her fist.

"Now then," Tania purred, her smoky voice low so they wouldn't be overheard. Tania used Theo's dick like a rudder – backing him onto the closed toilet seat. "You appear to be in a hurry, Theo." Moving her hand carefully up and down, letting Theo feel the strain build within his cock, Tania sat astride his legs, trapping his rigid shaft between their bare stomachs.

"Of course I'm in a hurry!" He slipped one hand over the globe of her right breast and worked the other to her mound, knocking her legs wider as he did so. His thumb immediately attached itself to Tania's clit and his middle finger buried up as far inside her as their cramped position would allow. "We are in a public lavatory, possibly with a queue of eavesdroppers building and I am with a virtually naked, very hot, woman."

Tania giggled and murmured with glee as Theo's digits circled her nub. Matching his movements with the speed of her pumps, she leant forward and spoke with ill-concealed smugness. "Now why would you want Maddie disappointing you every five minutes, when you could have me whenever you want?"

As if to emphasise her point, Tania rose up on her toes, thrust her hips forward and lowered herself in one deft movement so that she engulfed Theo's thickness in its entirety.

His voice was almost guttural as Tania's silky, muscular channel clenched at him with varying degrees of strength. "Why indeed?"

Theo said no more, requiring all his concentration to focus on the expert way the woman hammering against his legs was milking him. He equalled her urgency with alternate sharp tweaks of her darkening nipples and finger slaps to her clit.

As Theo's climax rose in a glorious crescendo of relief, the pictures that he'd seen on his mobile phone the night before of the woman now screwing him – her head thrown back, her breasts offered up like sacrificial cupcakes – merged with visions of Maddie and all the things she'd promised to do to him.

Vaguely conscious of the growing mew's coming from Tania as she nuzzled her face into the side of his neck, Theo let the imagery in his mind take over. Tugging at her plait, he levered Tania's face away from him so he could view her eyes as he came violently within her. Then, gripping her clit between his thumb and forefinger, Theo pinched her nub hard, sending Tania into a lip-biting orgasm of her own.

As the redhead convulsed against his taut thighs, a expression of victory consumed and annihilated the calculated sultry guise on her tanned, oval face. A victory that was abruptly wiped away when Theo asked through his panting lips, "So, what does Maddie's pussy taste like, then?"

C h a p t e r   N i n e

Maddie checked her phone for the fourth time.

There were no messages. There had been no messages from Theo for almost twenty-four hours. She had expected him to get in touch first thing yesterday morning to express his disappointment, or maybe even his fury, at having their meeting postponed yet again. She'd been looking forward to reading a few texts begging her to meet him, suggesting ever more outrageous things they could do to each other. But Maddie had heard nothing.

She was unprepared to accept that she had pushed him too far, and she was fed up of trying to justify Theo's silence with an imagined electrical emergency, a lost or broken phone, or a serious illness. Still, she couldn't deny an irritating and totally uncharacteristic whim to send him an "are you okay?" text. She distracted herself from such sentimental musings by opening up the battered notebook in which she was planning her exhibition.

After hours of shading and fine tuning, the impression of Sara and Freya on the sofa had been completed the previous evening, bringing Maddie's total of finished works to three –

four if she included the photograph of Sara covered in chalk swirls. Placing neat red ticks next to the finished works on her list and adding notes about framing, hanging methods and so on, Maddie turned to her laptop.

Opening up her most recent folder of photographs, Maddie's uncertainty at Theo's apparent disinterest faded in the face of the kinky photo thumbnails of Sara, Freya and Tania. Relieved to feel the familiar rush of erotic control return to her veins, Maddie immersed herself in her work, unconcerned for the moment that she hadn't asked her models' permission to use their images in the show.

The more she stared at the pictures before her – closed eyes, necks flung back, lips caught mouthing words of ecstasy, the clearer the need to use them in her exhibition became.

An hour later, Maddie was printing out fifty inch-square photographs on her thinnest and most flexible photo paper. She knew precisely what she would do with them. The image she had in her head was deliciously sexy, but it involved Theo.

Reining in her thoughts, Maddie checked the clock. There was only half an hour before Sara arrived to embark on the next project. Knocking her newly printed photographs into a neat pile and placing them to one side, she checked her phone again, just in case she had missed the buzz which indicated the arrival of a text. There was nothing.

"Damn!" She'd been so sure that Theo was dangling from her hook once more. Shaking her head, Maddie realised with a jolt of surprise that she wasn't simply missing the thrill of controlling the electrician via her phone, but also the flirting with him as well. There was something more intriguing about him than any of the other men she had played with over the years. Maddie halted her thoughts in their tracks. "No, he is nothing special to me." She spoke aloud as if addressing the studio itself. "I am merely concerned that he will disappear before I've had the chance to use his body for art. That's all. It's harder this time because of the exhibition. Because of the show, he is having to wait longer than most."

Slamming the mobile into the top drawer of her desk to stop herself from glancing at it every five minutes like some pathetic love struck teenager, Maddie resolved to stand firm. Surely Theo would be back in touch when his pride was feeling less bruised.

Laying a collection of dry paint encrusted sheets over the laminated part of the floor and pinning some old curtains up on the whitewashed wall, Maddie scrunched her hair into a ponytail, before propping a huge grey-undercoated sheet of plywood against the wall. She had just extracted four tins of coloured emulsion from under the studio's sink and lined them up next to the board with a vast assortment of differently sized brushes, when the doorbell indicated Sara's arrival.

Eager to see the pastel of Freya and her on the sofa, Sara bounced up the stairs, chattering ten to the dozen. "I have no idea how you captured just how fucking sexy it felt to spank Freya – but you did. It's amazing!"

"Thanks, honey. I'm glad you approve." Maddie

busied herself with moving her finished pieces safely to the other side of the studio. "You ready for today's work? It'll be messy."

"Can't wait."

"Today, I think we should have music." Turning the stereo up to a floor-board-shakingly high volume, Maddie gestured Sara towards the plywood, raising her voice above the heavy beat coming from the sound system. "Did you wear old underwear as I suggested?"

"Yeah, it's a bit faded and grotty. I have better stuff in my bag in case it is too awful for you."

"Trust me. Awful is ideal. After today, I don't think you'll want to wear it again."

Facing the wall-sized board and the tins of emulsion, Sara signalled her understanding of what lay in store for the session. "I see. When you said messy you weren't kidding!"

"I never joke about my art, honey." Maddie's tone was serious and hinted at pre-occupation as she levered off one paint tin lid at a time with a rusty old screwdriver.

Sara looked at her quizzically. "You okay, Maddie?"

Keeping the disquieting, unexpected direction of her thoughts concerning Theo to herself, the artist replied, "Bit caught up in arranging things for the gallery, that's all."

Placing the final tin lid to one side, Maddie stared down at the collection of scarlet, crimson, rose-madder red and egg-yolk yellow. "If you could strip off your clothes for me – apart from the grotty undies – put these on and then stand with your back flat against the board."

Retreating to the bed, only mildly self-conscious at the state of her greying bra and panties, Sara put on the pair of fake glasses and baseball cap Maddie had passed to her. Tucking as much of her shiny, jet black hair beneath the cap as possible, Sara stood before the plywood.

"Could you put your hands on your head, with your elbows making definite triangles? I would like some nice shapes to work around here."

Obeying, Sara laughed, "I haven't had anyone draw around my outline like this since I was a kid at primary school."

"If it was like this at primary school," Maddie said as she picked up the pot containing the darkest of the red paints and inserting a wide wallpaper brush into the dense fluid. "Then I think your art teacher would have been fired very, very quickly!"

Sara opened her mouth to reply but immediately wished she hadn't as Maddie launched her arm back and, in time with the music, sent an arc of paint flying through the air, spattering some of it across the model's face.

"Sorry, honey, I should have said that you might want to keep your mouth closed in case some emulsion goes astray."

Blinking in response, and disinclined to move her head or risk another audible reply, Sara tried to ignore the unpleasant taste of scarlet paint that had hit the inside of her mouth.

As the vibration of the music travelled up through

their feet, Maddie moved her whole body in time to its rhythm. As the tempo increased, her spatters of paint became heavier and more targeted around the edge of Sara's body, thudding and pattering against the grey board behind the model, and splashing repeatedly over her semi-naked body.

After about ten minutes, Maddie was beginning to regret wearing her jeans. They may have been old, but they were also very warm and the more she danced about in front of Sara, flinging two brushes worth of emulsion at a time now, the more uncomfortable she became. "Sara, if you think you can get your arms back in *exactly* the same place, you can rest for a minute. I have got to change out of these trousers – I'm roasting to death."

Sara gratefully lowered her arms, but didn't dare move the feet she'd planted firmly against the protective sheet. Her body quivered with hopeful lust as Maddie threw her jeans and shirt to one side. The vivid memory of her first sexual encounter with the older woman assailing her immobile body on the hard, laminate floor was a scene Sara had replayed in her mind so often that it had almost become her brain's default setting.

Standing only in a set of plain black underwear, allowing Sara a few more minutes rest, Maddie came closer to the board to critically assess the growing spots and splashes of scarlet that had already landed around the outline of her model's face and upper body.

Anyone coming into the studio unexpectedly would have been forgiven for thinking that Sara had been the victim of some frenzied attack. The blood-red splashes against her arms, face and torso, looked like a hundred different scars and scratches.

As Maddie examined her work, Sara found it difficult to keep her feet motionless when only one short step would take her straight into the artist's arms. The young model found it even harder to maintain her concentration as Maddie lifted her arms back into position, and trailed searching fingers along both sides of Sara's body to ensure it was in exactly the same place as before.

Determined to remain professional, even though she yearned for the artist to dominate her, Sara sought to take her mind off her physical longing. "No Tania today?"

"No, she's off sulking somewhere."

"Sulking?"

Maddie loaded two broad-bristled brushes with some crimson from the second pot. "She gets these toddler fits when she doesn't get the attention she thinks she deserves." As the contents of the brushes began to dribble down her own legs, Maddie prevented any further discussion. "I'd close your mouth again now if I were you, honey."

Putting all her strength behind the lunge, Maddie aimed the bristles to either side of Sara's left elbow, spotting the board and adjacent flesh with thick blotches of emulsion. Working with her usual economy of movement and keeping in time with the slightly slower track on the stereo, Maddie worked the new colour completely around Sara's head, arms, neck and stomach, before re-dipping her brushes and moving much nearer to the board.

With each fresh sweep and fling of the brush, the cold spatters that missed the plywood pitter-pattered against Sara's flesh. She hadn't expected it to feel so sensual. Sara found she had to bite her lip to prevent herself from sighing with desire each time some stray paint landed with a tantalisingly quiet thud against her bra – and then clamping down even harder with disappointment, when the stroke of emulsion missed her chest entirely.

So far, Maddie hadn't targeted the inside of her legs with any colour, and Sara found herself tensing expectantly at the thought of how it would feel when some of the viscous liquid eventually landed upon her cotton-covered pussy.

"Relax, Sara. You've gone all stiff."

"Sorry, Maddie," Sara mumbled, exhaling through her clenched teeth. Her eyes followed every movement of the artist's hands. Two much smaller brushes, their bristles doused in the lightest shade of red, rose towards Sara, leaving the model temporarily mesmerised.

Ignoring the rose-madder paint as it slithered from her hands, trickled along her arms and dripped onto her naked feet, Maddie stood so that she was almost touching Sara. Shaking out the brushes around either side of the model's body, the lighter shade of red speckled sporadically over the existing scarlet and crimson splashes, making a pleasingly striking pattern against the dove-grey background.

Sara exhaled again, her breath balmy against Maddie's shoulder as the artist repositioned herself to direct her rosy spritz around the left side of her subject's face and arms. Then, swapping to the right side, Maddie, whose focus had strayed to her companion's nipples, drew the red brush deliberately over Sara's cotton covered breasts in one swift swipe.

Sara gasped with surprise as the wet paint soaked into the thin fabric – highlighting the conical shape of her nipples – before quickly and tightly drying around them. In an effort not to ask Maddie to repeat the move, as well as avoiding another taste of emulsion, Sara kept her lips closed as the artist returned to her tins and coated two brushes in the scarlet paint. Then, kneeling about two metres from Sara's crotch, she layered the two shades of red up and around the outline of the lower half of the model's body in a series of bristle-flicked dots.

"If you keep your hands away from your lower half, you may relax your arms and shoulders again for a while." Sara gladly accepted the invitation and rested her palms on her waist, risking a bend of her neck, so that she could peer at the activity going on below her hips.

As Maddie worked, throwing brush load after brush load of varying shades of red around Sara's legs, she became intoxicated by the scent escaping from the flimsy cotton panties before her. Even though she had deliberately avoided all contact with Sara's most sensitive part, the model's knickers were already sodden – and not from any stray paint.

"How does your chest feel?" Maddie teased a brush over each of Sara's knees, tickling her flesh with the soft bristles, transferring some traces of vivid scarlet to her kneecaps.

"Tight. Swollen. I want you to touch them."

Pleased by the throaty yearning in Sara's voice, Maddie replied, "Is that so? And how about your pussy?"

"Wet."

"And yet I haven't touched you or the board down there."

"Will you?"

"When I'm ready."

Guessing how difficult Sara found it not to fidget, Maddie peered up at her from her position on the floor. "It is very important that you stay totally still now. One move and you could smudge the work we've already done."

Tensing into position, clasping her hands together so she didn't budge so much as one muscle, Sara closed her eyes. The temptation to reach out and steal one of the paintbrushes from Maddie's hands and wipe the residual paint across Maddie's body was beginning to hammer at her in time to the music. She had an overwhelming urge to see the shiny emulsion trickling into the tempting valley of the artist's cleavage.

"Not long now, I promise."

Sara wasn't sure if Maddie was saying it wasn't long until her part in the painting was finished, or it wasn't long until she would get the gratification she so badly craved. The artist was certainly moving faster and the spray of colour around her legs and feet landed thicker and faster, but with less care than before. Sara's skin had become almost as coated in paint as the board behind her.

Stopping short of the delicate V at the top of Sara's inside leg, Maddie retreated to the sink to scrub the excess splodges of scarlet, crimson and rose-madder from her fingertips.

From behind her closed eyes, Sara could hear the tap running and guessed that Maddie was at last about to start on the final colour. In her mind she could already feel the caress of the yolky-yellow paint as it adhered to her knickers and highlighted her sensitive labia. The model dug her fingernails into her palms. *Hurry up, hurry up!* If she bit into the side of her cheeks any harder Sara was sure that they'd start to bleed.

Searching through the debris that was still strewn on the floor, from where she'd hastily cleared the trolley the night before, Maddie picked up an old toothbrush and tested the flexibility of the short bristles through her fingers. The thought of what she was about to do sent a private flush of lust through her emulsion-streaked body and Maddie found herself going automatically to her phone to text Theo about it.

Opening her desk drawer, Maddie glimpsed the screen of her phone. There was one text. It was from Tania.

> Tania: Going to be back late darling.
> Unexpected photo shoot – for real
> money!!

"Bitch," Maddie whispered to herself. She slammed

the drawer closed again, annoyed at her own unwarranted weakness for getting her mobile at all.

Galvanised into action by a burst of inverted anger and frustration, Maddie snapped, "Right, Sara. Keep absolutely still – don't move!"

Hurt after her devoted efforts not to stir from her post, Sara swallowed quietly, unable to stop the small tears that unexpectedly leaked from the corner of her eyes, smearing and mingling with the paint that had clung and dried against her cheeks. Her tears stopped abruptly however, as Maddie growled, "Stop that crying. You'll ruin the picture if you get it wet!"

Shocked, and wondering what on earth she had done to make Maddie so cross, Sara hardly dared breathe, as the artist turned down the thud of the stereo's music, before kneeling before her model once more.

Abruptly, Sara shook. She felt as if a small rain cloud had burst directly over her pussy, as paint misted over her mound in a fine spray.

Partially re-applying paint to the toothbrush and wiping the excess against her own body in swipes of startling colour, Maddie held the brush as close to Sara as she could. The artist's face was so near to the girl's pussy that her nose nudged its cotton covering, setting every nerve in Sara on high alert.

Running a single digit over the bristles, Maddie sent another fine shower of yellow against the board and against Sara's panties. Repeating the action until she had a definite outline of red and yellow around Sara, Maddie merged the colours at the top of Sara's legs, until there was a pleasing orange overlap.

Feeding off the sexually charged aura emanating from her model, Maddie's resentment of her own weakness began to abate. The first part of the day's new project was complete – now she could expend some of the lust that had been building up in her since the morning.

Confident that Sara was too far down the road of arousal to object, Maddie took the paint covered toothbrush and rotated it over the delta of Sara's faded knickers.

As the brush made contact, Sara's eyes flung open and a long drawn out mewl of suppressed need shot from her throat. Accepting that there was no way she could possibly expect her model to remain motionless, Maddie took the girl's hands and carefully pulled her away from the board.

Still on her knees, grasping Sara's right hip, Maddie continued to press the yellowed brush over every inch of the once-white undergarment, fascinated as the liquid that had dampened the panties from the inside mingled with the yellow on the outside, making it blotch and swirl.

As Sara steadied herself by holding the top of the artist's head and curling her fingers into her paint-daubed hair, Maddie glanced up at her companion's chest, sure that it must be burning with a frantic craving to be free of the bra that had dried against her skin. Enjoying the twitch of the slender stomach, as each new touch excited her model, Maddie eased the top of the toothbrush inside the underwear, making Sara take a sharp inhalation of fresh oxygen.

A gush of pussy syrup made Maddie grin as she worked the flat side of the toothbrush's head over Sara's flesh. Then, lowering her tool at last and taking hold of either side of the ruined garment, the artist ripped it to the floor.

Sara screamed as some of the paint that had dried over the edges of her panties pulled out the fine hairs beneath. Her sharp yell changing abruptly to a ragged sigh as Maddie's mouth licked the wounds.

Pulling a swaying Sara towards her, Maddie sat her on the sheet covered floor, wrapped her arms around her and gripped the fastening of her bra. Sara braced herself for the sensation of a cast being removed, as once again the dried paint dragged tiny hairs from her flesh and pulled at her skin. The brief pain was worth it, however, and Sara's breasts seemed to sigh with a relief all their own. The almost solid bra hit the floor and her nipples reacted pointedly to their release from captivity.

Freedom was short lived, however as Maddie quickly retrieved the torturous toothbrush and, dunking it into the nearest tin, buffed Sara's right areola with thick red emulsion.

Sara gasped at the sensation, as the glutinous fluid tracked and trickled down every contour of her body, leaving crimson runways in its wake.

Maddie struck again, this time agitating the overloaded mini-brush across the left breast, watching with artistic appreciation as the paint coated the luminous flesh, following the sensuous line of Sara's hips and thighs, as it travelled south.

It was too much for Sara. This was what she had wanted and what her mind had been so full of as she'd stood to attention against the wall. Now that it was finally happening, she couldn't keep it a one-sided affair. Lunging forward, Sara grabbed the nearest brush, doused it into the yellow paint and swiped it across Maddie's belly, pushing the paint into her navel.

Maddie went to fight back, wanting to remain in charge of this situation. But Sara was too fast and hastily the artist's bra was yanked away and paint was lathered over her naked tits.

In retaliation, Maddie let go of the toothbrush and swapped it for a wallpaper brush. Coating the wider bristles in the now orange tinted scarlet paint, she dragged it over the wriggling Sara, who immediately pushed Maddie backwards.

Lying on top of the artist, Sara grinned at the sound of their paint spattered bodies suctioning against each other.

Allowing herself a moment to revel in the texture of Sara's thigh against her still-clothed cunt, Maddie used all her strength to roll, so that they moved together – a massive tangle of arms and legs. Brushes forgotten, their mouths attacked any section of one another that didn't taste of emulsion. Their fingertips and nails skipped over the rare areas of untainted flesh, hunting out the paint covered patches so that they could peel them away, sending sharp tugs of enticing, hair-pulling pain through one another.

Eventually their faces met and Sara didn't give

Maddie the chance to duck out of kissing her. Planting her full lips directly onto the artist's, Sara toppled them over again, so that they were lying together on their sides, on top of the sticky rucked up sheets.

Knocking off Sara's protective glasses and hat, Maddie surrendered herself to her model's ardent kissing until the urgency of the wet pussy against her leg could no longer be ignored.

Twisting away from Sara's embrace and ordering her to remain on her side, Maddie reached out to the only unused brush within grabbing range. Then, lifting up Sara's top leg and trapping the lower one where it was so her lower limbs formed a sort of 'v' shape, Maddie inserted the narrow brush handle into her sex, before clamping the raised leg shut, wedging the smooth wood in place.

"On your knees, girl!"

Scrabbling against the sheet to obey, Sara moaned through her panting breath as Maddie ordered her to move, the intrusion in her canal most welcome, but disappointingly narrow.

"Stick your bum high in the air. Part your legs."

The instructions were blunt and Sara's hips rose and parted without her brain engaging at all.

Maddie crouched behind her and, threading her left hand through the widened legs, she grasped the inserted brush's bristles and began to tease its handle around inside Sara's cunt, making it wider and more needy. With the other hand, Maddie plunged a different brush into the yellow paint and coated it over Sara's buttocks.

Ignoring the whimpering of her subject, Maddie told Sara to clench her pussy muscles so the brush didn't fall out. Then, grabbing a large sheet of paper from her desk, Maddie pressed it hard against Sara, making an imprint of her rump.

With extreme care, her desire for an orgasm put on hold in the face of her art, Maddie stood up, inverted the paper and rubbed it onto the space where Sara's backside had rested against the plywood.

Smiling with satisfaction at how good the print looked within the outline of Sara, Maddie let the paper glide unwanted to the floor. It was time to reward Sara for her patience.

Taking hold of the inserted brush again, Maddie heard Sara's utterance of relief as she moved it gently in and out of her. Then, with the flat of her hand, Maddie bounced her palm off the sticky backside, loving the smacking sucking noise it made, knowing full well that even light slaps against wet flesh would increase Sara's sensation ten-fold.

Stopping her spank session just long enough to dip her index finger into the nearest paint tin and scoop up a dollop of colour, Maddie swirled it directly over Sara's clit.

The sudden chill of the paint against her nerve centre sent Sara's beautifully abused body into a soul-wracking climax. As Sara shook, Maddie celebrated the orgasm by buffing and slapping her palms and fingers against the succulent rump.

Exhausted, Sara's muscles relaxed enough for the

brush to fall from its intimate cache, as she collapsed into a soggy paint-smeared heap.

"You were brilliant." Maddie soothed the black hair, heavy with paint, from the perspiring forehead. "Can you see the board?"

Sara eased herself up onto her knees. Her eyes shone as she saw the transformed grey board. A two-inch thick scattered and dotted outline of her body stood out in glorious tones of red. As Sara's gaze travelled down the plywood, the ruddy shades became paler. She was drawn to the smaller shockingly bright yellow in the space between her legs and the orangey imprint of her currently (and delightfully) sore butt cheeks.

"Later, I will have to add a few extra brush strokes in black around the curve of your ass. Then it will be a perfect back view."

Helping the model to her feet, Maddie cloaked her in a spare sheet. "Why don't you go downstairs and use my shower?"

Thankful for the chance to get clean, Sara asked hopefully, "Are you coming? You're messy as well."

Shaking her head, Maddie declined. "As much as I'd love to scrub your back, honey, I'm not done yet."

Sara had already been gone an hour when Maddie, finally satisfied with the last few thin strokes of black she'd added to the plywood, left her latest work to dry.

It wasn't until she'd fixed the last tin lid back in

place that she become conscious of how cold the studio had become. Grabbing her shirt, but ignoring her paint encrusted bra, Maddie threw it over her shoulders and cranked up the heating.

She was about to gather up the dustsheets, when she thought better of it. Still high from rewarding Sara and revelling in the quiet hum of unspent lust radiating through her own body, Maddie took her phone from the desk drawer.

"You may think this means you've won, Theo." Maddie looked up at her new spotlights as she spoke. "But this text simply means you're finally going to learn what you are up against."

With a well practised finger Maddie typed into her mobile.

Maddie: Hello Theo – I am covered in paint. Come and clean me up.

Chapter Ten

The text came through as Theo pulled his van into one of the few vacant parking spaces outside the block of flats where he lived. He was aware that he should have been grinning from ear to ear as the invitation he'd waited for so patiently had finally arrived. But, as he read Maddie's message, Tania's words of warning rebounded in his skull.

She only wants you while you're begging and while you are interesting enough for her to paint you. I mean it Theo. Maddie is a prick-tease. You will never get what you want from her.

Theo was certain that trusting Tania completely would be a mistake, but he also had no doubt that there was some truth to her warnings. As he got out of the van and headed towards his flat Theo decided that it was his turn to make Maddie wait. His dick however had no intention of letting this invitation pass him by and, as Theo climbed the stairs to the third floor of the building, his resolve slowly dissipated. *I wonder how much of her is covered in paint exactly?* Cursing his curiosity, Theo turned around just seconds from his front door and found himself walking back to his van, reversing it back out of the coveted parking space and driving far too fast in Maddie's direction.

Even though he'd only driven to the studio twice before, the route was burnt into his brain and, as he re-parked in the only free space on Maddie's street, Theo realised it was a miracle that he'd arrived without crashing. His concentration had been fully on what might happen once he reached his destination (and the woman who was there), rather than the traffic lights and the correct use of his indicators.

He kept his hands in place on the steering wheel for a moment, conscious of his heart hammering in his chest and the sheen of sweat on his palms. Despite his rush to arrive, Theo was now revisited by the urge to make Maddie hang on, even if it was only for a few extra minutes. Pride dictated he couldn't be seen to let her snap her fingers and he would appear – especially in the light of everything Tania had told him.

Allowing himself time to order his see-sawing thoughts into a more rational pattern, Theo began to wonder if Maddie had always planned to call him today as her last text had suggested or if, had he not gone quiet on her all day, she would have cancelled once again?

Theo banged his wrists hard against the steering wheel in frustration. What the hell was the matter with him? He never let women get to him like this. He took them out for meals, to the pub, the cinema; slept with them if they were up for it and then he ended it. It was a pattern Theo had fallen into as an apprentice at college ten years ago, and it was a pattern he had never had any inclination to break. In all that time, he hadn't been made to wait for anyone and he certainly hadn't had to second guess a potential lover's motives.

Staying in the van, he peered over to the opposite side of the terraced street towards Maddie's house and its part-wood, part-glass front door. Its ordinary looking blue paintwork seemed to loom out at him. But whether it loomed with promise, or with a fear of living up to the expectations of the woman within, he wasn't sure.

"Oh this is ridiculous." Theo took the key from the ignition and got out of his van, slamming the door behind him with far more force than was necessary.

He battled hard against the images of a naked Maddie smeared with droplets of paint – images that had been circling his consciousness since the text arrived. As his heavy safety boots thudded against the sundried pavement, Theo was struck with the thought that Tania might be inside the studio as well. He hadn't previously considered where Tania had gone once he'd finally extracted himself from her alluring embrace. *If she is in there, has she told Maddie that we've met – and what we got up to?* He suspected not.

As he approached Maddie's front door, Theo dragged a hand through his short, spiked hair and, determined not to let the artist get the upper hand, rang the doorbell.

If he hadn't felt horny before, the silhouette that approached him from the other side of the frosted glass panel hardened Theo's dick to instant wood and rocked his willpower as the door opened.

"Good evening, Mr. Electrician." Maddie stood to the side of her front door, shielding herself from all eyes but those of the man on the step, who seemed to be momentarily frozen to the spot. "Are you coming in or not? I'm getting cold here."

Theo wasn't surprised. She was naked but for her knickers and a shirt thrown over her shoulders and he suspected that she had dressed (or not) in that way just to taunt him.

He had expected, after reading her text, that Maddie's hands, and possibly her face, would be streaked with the occasional splodge of paint or charcoal. Theo hadn't been prepared for her to be positively covered in bright splashes of red and yellow emulsion. Coloured blotches clung to, and highlighted, every curve of the body he'd been fantasising about to the point of obsession.

Maddie shut the door behind Theo as he entered the small hallway. "I'm sorry I'm such a mess. It's been that sort of day."

Theo gestured to his work-dusted hands. "My days are always like that."

He followed her cotton-covered, paint-coated knickers up the stairs, already favourably comparing the feminine curves of the artist's backside to the gym tightened ass of Tania that had bounced against his thighs so recently. How he kept his hands from clasping the hips before him as he climbed the stairs behind her, Theo didn't know.

Maddie found herself struggling not to smile and give

herself away. She knew she'd wanted this man for some time, but the intensity of her joy now that he was finally back in the studio took her by surprise. Telling herself to stick to the plan she'd conceived, and reminding herself that the hiatus she'd enforced upon him would be worth it in the end, Maddie kept her expression neutral.

"I could do with cleaning up. I take it you could as well?"

Theo, who'd pushed his fists so far into his overall pockets that there was a risk of bursting through the seams, replied with an equal level of carefully cultivated care. "Seems sensible, considering the state of us after a day at work."

Maddie brought a hand up to her other arm, picking at the daubed paintwork. "Some of this is going to take some shifting."

"Is that the only reason you texted? So that I can help peel paint off you – presumably as a result of that?" Theo pointed towards the female outline that was still drying against the wall.

"That's Sara."

"Not Tania?"

Maddie's eyes narrowed at the way Theo said her ex's name. "I have a few models. Tania is merely a necessary evil. She is, as you saw via my phone, very good at staying still. It makes her an excellent muse."

"And the fact she's hot can't hurt either."

"True." Maddie followed Theo's gaze as it moved over the newest pictures in her studio. "All of those are for my exhibition."

"They're good. Have you got all your art sorted for the show?" Theo was impressed with how steady he was managing to keep his tone as he kept his eyes away from the artist and firmly on her created wares.

"No, but I am more or less halfway."

"Your pieces are certainly varied."

Maddie wasn't sure if this was a criticism or a compliment. "Is that a good thing?"

"Very. I visit galleries as often as I can. But some exhibitions are so samey, aren't they. Fifteen pictures of the same landscape all from marginally different viewpoints. Dull."

Taken aback that Theo was someone who visited galleries, Maddie told herself off for being such a snob. Tradesmen had every right to like galleries. She also knew she would be wise to stop underestimating this tradesman in particular. "I agree. That's why my theme remains the same, but the style of each piece is very different from the next."

"And the theme is? I mean, I assume the show will have a name?"

Conscious that this conversation was not the one she had expected to have with Theo – she'd assumed she would have him at her beck and call by now – Maddie knew it was time to grasp hold of the situation before he did. "You know very well what the theme is. As to a name, I haven't decided yet. Maybe you'd like to think of one while you lie down for me?"

Theo felt his shaft stir, but managed to keep his mask of disinterest in place as he enquired, "I thought you wanted a hand getting clean? Surely that would involve standing you under a shower, rather than me lying down."

"Ultimately that sounds like an excellent plan, but don't you think it would be more fun if you were as dirty as I am?"

Theo couldn't help but laugh. "No one could be as dirty as you are, Miss Templeton – in any sense of the word!"

"I wouldn't speak too soon if I were you, Mr. Hunter." Maddie picked up two dustsheets from the floor and, removing the duvet Tania had been using from the bed, threw the dustsheets over the revealed mattress. "Now if you'd like to see what I have in mind, then hop on the bed."

Theo took a pace towards the bed before he'd had time to think, but then he stopped himself. "And why should I?"

The artist laughed. "Your body obviously wants to do as I say, so why question it?"

"I'm not a toy, Maddie."

"Oh Theo," Maddie stood directly in front of him, forcing Theo to stare at the full firm breasts that he'd been trying so hard not to register. "You are *so* my toy. Now, take off all your clothes and lie on the bed. There's a good boy."

"Why?"

"Two reasons." Maddie placed her hands on the shoulder straps of his overalls and began to undo them. "First, I have been very naughty and kept you waiting for some attention for far too long – a fact that I intend to make up to you very soon. And second, you agreed to take part in my art show and what better time than now?"

"You want to paint me, lying naked on your spare bed?"

"Not exactly." Maddie lowered the bib half of his overalls and pulled the t-shirt she found beneath over his head.

Taking in the shape of his naked chest for the first time, Maddie saw that she had seriously underestimated this side of her electrician as well. His torso, which was decorated with a sprinkle of fair hairs just below the neckline, was trim, to say the least. No excess flab hung over his waistline and no muscle was undefined and yet, she was delighted to find, there was no false looking six-pack. This was just a very fit man, not an exercise freak or body-building slave, but a man who took care of himself.

"So what do you intend, exactly?"

Unsure how she was managing not to tug the remainder of his clothing off to see if his lower half was as hot as his top, Maddie simply repeated her earlier statement. "I think you should be as dirty as me, don't you?"

"You want to coat me in paint?

"Not paint and not all of you." Maddie trailed a finger around the top of the boxer shorts peeking out from the top of the jeans he wore beneath his overalls.

"And if I let you do what you want, do I get to do what I want afterwards?"

Maddie lowered herself to press her dry lips against the skin between Theo's belly button and the top of his trousers. "As long as it's what I want as well."

The electrician's body shivered, his response blatantly physical rather than verbal, as his dick strained toward Maddie's semi-crouched frame.

"So." Reverting to artist mode as she stood back up, Maddie gestured to the bed. "What do you think? Will you let me make you dirty in the interests of both my exhibition and for the guaranteed fun of cleaning each other up afterwards?"

Theo, his mind awash with Tania's warnings, could still feel the cool press of Maddie's lips against his flesh – even now that they'd been withdrawn. "And I will get to fuck the hell out of you?"

Maddie pressed the flat of her hand against the bulge that was now straining against three layers of clothing. "I promise you will get the reward you deserve."

Scraping off his shoes and removing his socks, Theo, his mind very much on what would happen after Maddie had drawn her picture of him, stepped out of the white, work-stained dungarees and stopped.

"Hot as you look Theo, for this to work I need you naked." Maddie almost regretted that she had to rush him – standing in his jeans, his chest and feet bare, he was far more of a mouth watering treat than she'd expected. She knew it would be a mistake to linger now, though. She wanted him stripped and she needed him stiff if the planned project was going to work.

With his dick beginning to cramp in its confinement, Theo didn't argue. Dumping his remaining clothes to the floor in one swift strip, Theo left the artist temporarily devoid of speech as his uncircumcised penis stuck out towards her as if it were a handsome finger of accusation.

Sensing that he'd impressed her, Theo turned his back, giving Maddie the chance to view his taut cheeks, before he did as bidden and lay down on the dust-sheeted bed, fixing his eyes on a point in the ceiling.

Without allowing herself time to think about how difficult it was going to be to resist sitting astride his cock immediately, Maddie fetched the bucket of paste and a soft-bristled brush she'd hidden beneath her desk. She then collected up the fifty square photographs she'd printed of Sara, Freya and Tania in the throes of ecstasy. "Are you ready to be moulded into a work of art?"

Theo rose onto his elbows as he saw what the artist was bringing towards him. "What the hell are you going to do, woman?"

"I am going to make you last forever." Maddie placed the flat of her right hand on his chest and pushed him gently so he returned to his supine position. "Unless of course..." She ran the brush over his balls, admiring how his dick quivered in reply. "You have changed your mind and no longer wish to be rewarded afterwards?"

Trying to appear as though he wasn't completely under her control, despite all evidence to the contrary, Theo spoke with far more calm than he felt inside. "I am only doing this because I can see how important your art is to you and I would like to help."

"Is that so?" Maddie grinned wryly at the man on her bed – his voice declared disinterest but his body looked like a coiled spring about to snap. "Well, that is very kind of you, Mr. Electrician."

"Keep your bloody gratitude! Whatever you are planning to do with the bucket and brush, could you just bloody well get on with it! You've been taunting me for weeks with promises you haven't delivered. Plus, in case you have forgotten, you are more or less naked and the fact I haven't taken hold of your tits and thrown you onto the floor shows just how bloody *kind* I am! But I am only human, for fuck's sake!"

"Your wish, Theo, is my command!"

Dumping the bucket of paste by her feet, Maddie deposited the pile of pictures unceremoniously into the mixture, pushing them down with the bristles of the brush so they disappeared just below the surface of the semen-like gloop.

Maddie pointed to his arms. "Put them behind your head. If they move, this ends and you leave my studio, erection or no erection."

His stomach churned slowly in uncertain anticipation – in perfect contrast to the pulse that was sprinting with lust-laden adrenalin through every part of his body. Theo obeyed.

"Good boy." Maddie leaned forward and, without giving Theo any warning, placed her dry parted lips around the tip of his manhood, relishing the taste of salty sweet flesh that met her tongue as she worked him gently, licking his head as if it was an ice lolly.

It was only the threat of Maddie stopping doing what she was doing that kept Theo's hands trapped beneath his short spiked hair. He closed his eyes to better experience every lick and touch, but quickly opened them again. The privacy of the dark behind his eyelids made the sensations even more intense than they already were and Theo knew he was in serious danger of cumming in the next ten seconds if she didn't stop soon.

Maddie had her eyes firmly shut, every one of her senses searching for the moment when she had taken him as far as he could go without setting off his release. She'd already privately admitted to herself that this was the most delicious cock she'd ever tasted, and only the pressing need to turn the muscle between her lips into a lasting sculpture gave her the strength to release him from her mouth.

Smiling at the cacophony of swearwords that escaped from Theo as the warmth of her lips abandoned him, Maddie took the condom secreted in her knickers and rolled it into place. "You see, doing what you are told brings benefits doesn't it."

Shrugging her shirt to the floor and enjoying the approving sigh from the man on the bed, Maddie carefully smoothed a layer of cling-film around her companion's testicles, before doing the same to his thighs and stomach, making sure it stuck to every curve and dip of his body.

Theo began to raise himself up onto his elbows again. "What the hell are you doing?"

"I told you, you'll find out. Now…" Maddie tucked the end of the film neatly under Theo's backside. "I have to concentrate, so I would appreciate it if you didn't make any noise until I'm done."

More concerned with the way he was being treated around his testicles than in heeding the warning rasp of Maddie's voice, Theo asked with an edge of concern, "Is that cling film supposed to warm my skin up like that?"

The artist's face plainly showed her disappointment in the man on the bed as she retrieved something from the chest of drawers next to her. The shiny metal tongue-depressing gag was wedged between his teeth before Theo could register what was happening.

Maddie stared at him, her expression shaded in regret. "I should remind you, Theo, that you only get rewarded if you do as you are told. Naturally, therefore, you get punished if you do not."

With a warning stare at the shocked Theo that told him exactly how unwise it would be to move in the foreseeable future, Maddie dipped the brush into the bucket.

Working fast, so as to prevent the papier-mâché solution from setting before she was ready, Maddie scrubbed a base coat of paste over his groin, covering every inch of the cling-filmed area. Then, fishing the first square photograph from the mixture, the artist lovingly flattened it over his lower belly.

Suddenly, even breathing seemed too risky a pursuit. Theo wasn't sure what he'd imagined Maddie was going to do to him, but this certainly wasn't it. He had absolutely no idea how he hadn't cum, or how he was keeping his hands beneath his head. The perspiration that had developed across his palms was already making his hair itchy and uncomfortable.

Rather than lessen the sensation of the paste and paper squares that Maddie was building up into a haphazard moulding against the contours of his lower body, the cling film accentuated it – heating him up so that the sweep of the cold brush and paper teased his flesh further. With each additional wafer thin layer of photographs, the film squeezed and cramped his groin. Theo felt as though he was being slowly trapped in an elaborate pulsating cock case.

He'd had to stop watching Maddie as she worked. With each move, her scarlet and yellow paint-streaked breasts hung more invitingly towards his immobile body, occasionally brushing his chest as she stretched across him to gently caress a square of paper into place.

A fine line of dribble had begun to gather at the edges of his permanently opened mouth and Theo felt more out of his depth than he'd ever done in his life. Time seemed to stretch on and yet the slim, fast-moving hands tweaked and ironed more papier-mâché into place. Theo felt the weight of Tania's words in the base of his skull. *She only cares about her art.*

It was finished. Maddie trailed a finger around the edge of the sculpture which was drying fast against the hostage beneath. Catching rogue drips of paste, she wiped them onto the edge of the bucket. Already the viscid substance was turning transparent and the expressions of her female models yelled out in kinky delirium from the groin of her electrician.

The artist allowed herself a quick peek at Theo's face. Never before had she needed to force herself into such a state of absorption with her art. The fact she'd shackled this man's mouth subsumed and excited her, and she fought to stay focused on her work. His vocal helplessness urged her to stare at him, to lick his face, to try and read from the expression in his eyes the words he wanted to say. She didn't look though. And she didn't lick. *Art first.* She had repeated the words over and over again in her mind like a mantra. If she'd looked at him, Maddie knew her detachment would have faltered and that the sculpture which was to be the perfect centrepiece for her exhibition would never be completed.

Now she had finished and she could safely examine him. Her hands free of paste, brush and paper, Maddie felt her chest swell and she let the urge to kiss away the salvia that had trickled from his lips prompt her into action.

Taking care not to knock her work, she stroked a sticky hand over his forehead. "You have been such a good boy." Maddie felt the tacky temperature of his skin. The struggle he'd had to stay motionless radiated from his eyes in a mixture of lust and hate. "If you promise me you will stay still for a few minutes longer, I will free your mouth. Do you promise?"

Theo's nod was barely perceptible, such was the

evident stiffness of his neck and shoulders. But Maddie understood and gently unlocked the silver-clasped spring that had secured the gag in place.

"Rest a second. Let your jaw adjust." Maddie wiped some more moisture away from Theo's chin, before planting a selection of butterfly kisses on his cheeks and neck. Her hands took hold of each of his arms and slowly pulled them out from beneath his head.

Theo's murmur of relief tickled her face as it wafted from his lips in a heavy rush of air. A murmur that intensified as Maddie placed each of his clammy hands over her chest. "I need you to keep your lower body still, but your arms are yours to do with what you like – for now."

He unclamped his fingers by flexing them back and forth against Maddie's tits – tits he could hardly believe he was finally touching – and he focussed on the woman whom he felt had become his adversary as much as his figure of obsession. She was staring directly at him. Her expression seemed to say that sex now would please her, but also that her world would not end if it didn't happen.

He, on the other hand, was in no mood for any more games. Pinching the ends of her nipples so hard that her mouth fell open, Theo hissed from between his dehydrated lips, "Get that off me now – dry or not – or I am going to sit up and break it. And I will *not* be back for a re-sit."

Chapter Eleven

◆ ◆ ◆ ◆

Despite making his intentions very clear, Theo hadn't raised his voice and Maddie could only marvel at his poise. Granted, she had never treated any of her previous male acquaintances in quite this way, so comparisons with her past male conquests were difficult to make. But she'd certainly made them wait. None of the men she'd played this game with before had managed to keep such a firm grip on themselves and by this stage they would have been pleading for her to put them out of their misery.

There had been a couple of moments as she'd worked, when Maddie thought he might have cum beneath her. But the hungry sheen in his eyes told her that somehow, miraculously, Theo would hold on.

Maddie edged her hands around the outline of the papier-mâché. "Okay, Mr. Electrician, I confess to being impressed. You have remained remarkably still for me . So, if you would like to be rewarded with your freedom, then I will grant your wish. But you have got to stay totally motionless while I do this. Deal?"

"Deal."

Theo breathed deeply as Maddie began to release the flaps of the cling film from where she'd tucked them beneath his body. Replacing his hands beneath his head to prevent himself from lunging at her body, Theo sighed as wafts of blessedly cool air gradually crept up between his skin and the plastic coating.

The touch of her fingertips against his newly released flesh sent Theo's nerves on a parallel circuit to his dick and his brain at the same time. Every inch of him yearned for her to lie on top of him. "For fuck's sake, woman, can't you go a bit faster!"

"No I bloody can't. Not unless you want this to crack, so that I have to start all over again."

Biting his lips, Theo tried to relax as the woman who had consumed his every waking thought and a fair amount of his sleeping thoughts as well, continued to coax and cajole the sculpture from his testicles, as if it was child she was trying to separate from a much loved cuddly toy.

When the edges of the piece were finally free from his legs and stomach, Maddie took a firm grip of each side of her creation. "Are you ready?"

Theo gave a tight, "Yes," as he lay like a fallen statue, holding his breath. Maddie gave a solid heave and the papier-mâché, cling film and condom came away in one intact piece.

Placing the cast on top of the art trolley to dry, Maddie swiftly returned to Theo. Grabbing the previously degraded duvet, Maddie threw it over him. He'd already started shaking with cold and, although she liked to punish, she didn't think of herself as cruel.

Watching as he cocooned himself into a sausage of bedding, Maddie then went to study her sculpture properly. Nearly transparent already, the glue had added an extra gloss to the photographs that were staring up at her from the perfect replica of Theo's penis, balls and abdomen. Resisting the temptation to run her fingers over the length of the fake phallus before it was fully set, Maddie decided it was time to turn her attention to the real thing.

Spinning around on her bare feet, Maddie jumped a mile, as she walked straight into the bulk of Theo. "Hell, you gave me a fright. I didn't hear you get up."

Completely wrapped in the dark crumpled duvet, Theo had padded over to stand just behind her. "I want to see what you've done with me." Opening the duvet, he enveloped Maddie in its warmth, so that his chest was buffered up against her back, his cock poking at her backside as he stared down over her shoulder. "Oh my god! Who are they?"

Maddie, luxuriating in the closeness of his body, freed one hand from the bedding so that she could point to the individual portraits. "That's Sara and that's Freya. They are both new to life modelling, but are already very skilled. They could earn an extra wage if they were brave enough to life model for colleges and art schools."

"And I assume they have skills in other areas which you have also exploited, or have at least helped them to improve in some way?"

"If you are asking me if they have been rewarded

for their hard work with the odd orgasm instead of financial remuneration, then yes. I have been lucky enough to teach them other skills alongside the ability to stay still in awkward positions. A skill which I suspect you now appreciate is not always so easy to develop."

"Which is why you asked Tania to help you? Because she is good at keeping still?"

Hearing Theo mention Tania again felt strange to Maddie, and now that she'd seen exactly how handsome this man was beneath his overalls, she knew she had to keep him as far away from Tania as possible. If her ex-girlfriend suspected that Maddie liked Theo, even if only for the pleasure of relishing his sexual denial, then she'd go all out to ruin it and very probably try to steal him for herself.

"Yes, I needed a good model in a hurry. The third face you can see there is indeed Tania. Anyway…" Maddie twisted around within the confines of the duvet so that her face was level with Theo's. "What do you think of the sculpture?"

"You have made a model of my dick and stuck the pictures of two strangers who appear to be in the middle of having an orgasm all over it. Frankly I have no idea what to think!"

"Three strangers."

Theo recovered his error. "Well, after the other night I don't think Tania can be counted as a total stranger can she." To prevent further questioning, Theo brought his lips to the artists and was surprised when she responded fiercely, even if only for a split second, rather than simply pulling away.

"I believe I invited you here to clean me up?" Maddie whispered into his ear, conscious that, although Tania said she'd be back late, she had no idea exactly how late that meant. The last thing she wanted was her ex walking in on them.

"So you did." Theo dropped the duvet and took a step back so that he could view the full extent of the mess Maddie was in. "I can see how your model could have gotten into such a state, but how did you get so painty at the other end of the brush?"

"Sara attacked me with a wave of paintbrush-related lust."

"Did she now?"

"Oh yes. And very pleasant it was, too."

"Did she make you cum?"

"No. I don't allow myself a climax while I'm at work. The reward for hard work was hers, not mine."

Theo shook his head in disbelief. "How can you do that? How can you be so detached?" He darted a hand down to his companion's cotton panties, daring to cradle her pussy in his palm. "You are so wet. Have you been like this since you serviced Sara?"

"Since before then, actually." Maddie pointedly removed Theo's hand from her body and walked towards the steps to her private rooms downstairs. It was time to give him something more, to encourage him to come back.

The water from the shower plunged down onto their

heads with a force that began to blast the paint from Maddie's shoulders even before Theo had attacked her colourful streaks with the sponge.

Steam filled the glass-panelled shower cubicle, which was barely big enough for Maddie, let alone Maddie and a guest, and the jet of hot spray thrummed against their skulls and cascaded over their shoulders and chests.

The last shred of self-restraint in Theo snapped. Gripping the artist by the back of the neck, he twisted her around and pushed her hard against the glass wall. All conversation rendered pointless by the pounding of the power shower, Theo pinned Maddie in place, by balancing his weight on one leg and pressing his right knee into the small of her back.

With the help of the water, Theo took hold of the fraying edges of the previously dried on emulsion and began to rip each strip from her back. Abandoning the soft sponge, Theo scratched at the more stubborn paint with his stubby fingernails, uncaring as to whether Maddie was moaning with pleasure or pain as each blotch was erased from her flesh.

When he'd finally finished her back and shoulders, Theo shouted above the din of the water, "You had better bloody well stay still," as he lowered his knee from her back and crouched to the floor to begin to purge her legs.

It was only when he'd cleared every spot of red, yellow and orange from her limbs that Theo allowed himself to turn his attention to the rounded rump before him. Maddie was still clad in her cotton panties which clung to every intimate fold, while the paint rinsed free from the fabric and ran down her legs in diluted streams. Slipping the garment to the floor, the electrician clasped his hands around each of Maddie's peachy buttocks. With a full but firm cheek filling each of his palms, Theo felt the return of the erection that had subsided a little with the force of the shower's hot blast. And it had returned with an intensity that the word 'urgent' didn't really describe. He had waited so long. Now, finally, he felt as if the wait had been worth it.

"Stay there!" He barked the order directly into Maddie's ear, half expecting her to disobey him, as he left the shower and dripped his way out of the glass box. "Oh fuck, woman."

Theo stared at her. The view of Maddie from the outside of the shower was even more luscious than from within. Her eyes were closed. Her chin was resting on the fold of her arms which in turn were resting at neck level against the glass. Her chest was squashed so tightly against the transparent wall that they resembled two beige plates with large nut brown circles drawn in the middle. Her fair hair was plastered against her face and neck while her legs, which tapered from the top to the bottom, quivered slightly, suggesting to Theo that the artist was finally nearing the end of her self-restraint.

His dick stuck out towards its goal and Theo could feel every rush of blood within its veins. Diving back inside the cubicle, he turned Maddie round, staring into her spaced-out, lust-filled eyes as he dropped to his knees. Frustrated by the lack of space, he kicked out at the door behind him, not caring that the showers flow now escaped onto the bathroom floor. Theo nuzzled her legs apart as wide as they would go and, at last, found himself nose to clit with the pussy he had fantasised about in every conceivable way.

Tania had refused to tell him how the artist tasted, but now he was going to find out for himself. Inhaling Maddie's scent, Theo felt a primeval rush of satisfaction as his nostrils were assailed with the scent of woman. No false perfumes, no scented soaps, just a clean turned-on female.

Rejecting his plan to clear the remaining paint from the front of her body, Theo slid a finger into the canal that was running with so much honey that it seemed to rival the flow of the shower above.

As Maddie sighed, her muscles immediately contracted around his thick digit, making Theo swear in wonder under his breath. If she could grip his finger that tightly, how on earth would she treat his penis? Bringing his other hand to her clit, he watched in fascination as the shower water trickled through every crease, reminding him of the first piece of erotic art he'd seen on his first visit to the studio. He stared hard, trailing a finger over the fold. She had been right, every pussy was different. Theo brushed his nose over the side of her clitoral cloche, making Maddie judder between him and the glass.

He nudged her with his nose for a second time, catching the very edge of her clit as he pulled out his finger. The moans from above him pulled Theo back to reality as

Maddie jacked harder, pushing herself firmly against him and then moving away just as quickly as she came in a wave of quivers and groans, her body sliding down the glass as if exhausted.

"Bloody hell, Maddie, I hardly touched you!"

Maddie, secretly shocked at how fast Theo had made her cum, used experience to hide just how amazing she felt. *If he can do that with just a few light touches, how could he make me feel if I let him take me?* "As I said earlier, I have been denying myself for some time. Thanks, I feel better for that."

Maddie made quick work of the remaining paint on her body before turning off the deluge of the shower and stepping out of the cubicle. She threw a towel to Theo who stood incredulous. "Don't you dare think you are getting out of this shower without the shag you promised me!"

"Of course I am. You chose to be freed from the papier-mâché early. That was your reward. You only get one."

"What!" Theo felt as if he was going to explode, his dick's eagerness for attention sending spiteful thoughts about the naked woman before him to his brain.

"I didn't say you couldn't cum, Theo. I said that you had sacrificed the right to fuck me." Maddie pointed to the shower. "You can spunk in there. I will watch."

"But I was about to make you cum again. Don't you want me to lick you out?"

"No need to shout, honey." Maddie felt the thrill of control simmer in the pit of her stomach as she looked at his bewildered face. "I have no doubt your tongue will feel extraordinary when it finally reaches my cunt." She stroked the small shock of fine hairs on his chest. "If the orgasm you've just given me is anything to go by, then I am in for one hell of a treat. But it's getting late and we both have to go to work tomorrow."

He floundered like a stranded fish as Maddie slid her hand around the base of his cock. Suddenly Theo felt utterly defeated. "But I...I wanted to taste you."

Tugging at his length in firm strokes, her right breast rubbing against his side, Maddie said, "Perhaps I've been too harsh? I'll stroke you off rather than make you do it yourself."

In spite of himself, he came – suddenly and fiercely. Angry that he hadn't been able to stop himself from creaming into the shower basin before Maddie had even finished her sentence, and that his self-control – which had been astronomical in the circumstances – still didn't rival hers, Theo spun on his heels. His face had formed a thunderous expression. A tirade of frustration was about to spill from his lips, but it died abruptly as his eyes fell on the doorway.

"I told you she would use you, Theo." Tania turned from one naked figure to the other. "Backing out on promises in the interests of art again, Maddie? And there I was thinking you'd stopped playing the waiting game."

Maddie peeled a bath towel from the rack and wrapped it around her soaked body. Disguising her disaffection, she spoke with a practised lack of care. "You two have met? An electrical problem at your place, Tania?"

"It's more a case of Theo having the problem,

wouldn't you say?"

Correctly assessing the atmosphere in the room as positively arctic, Theo interrupted. "I don't know what fucking game you're playing, Maddie, but Tania thought it wise to warn me about it. About you. About the games you play." He strode over the towel he'd dropped at his feet and rushed from the room.

Unconcerned about passers by catching a glimpse of his naked outline as he passed the glass of the front door, Theo dashed up to the studio and replaced his clothes with more haste than style. As he dressed Theo could hear the raised voices below growing in volume.

"You broke into my phone and read my messages. Again!"

"You should have changed your password."

"Tania! What the hell were you doing even picking up my phone in the first place?"

Unperturbed at being found out, Tania shrugged and turned away, her high heels tapping across the floor as she left the bathroom, a quickly-chilling Maddie in close pursuit. "I had a feeling you were up to your old tricks, Mads. He had to be warned."

"You mean, I have found a nice, handsome, kind man and you can't stand the fact that he is interested enough to hang around to see what happens. When the hell will you get it! You don't have the right to everything that everybody else has. You have to earn things for yourself!"

Theo felt his body bristle with confused desire as he

listened. Maddie had just told Tania that she liked him and thought him kind and handsome! *Bloody funny way of showing it!* On the other hand, Tania was showing that her true colours weren't exactly rosy either.

The electrician had just reached the door at the top of the stairs when both women appeared at the bottom. Pushing her ex out of her way, Maddie walked halfway up the staircase. "I would like you to tell me the truth, Theo. When did you meet Tania?"

"Why should I tell you anything? You haven't exactly been honest with me."

"Actually, I have. It isn't my fault if you don't listen to precisely what I say."

Theo's brow creased. "What!"

"I told you you'd get one reward and you did – you agreed to early freedom from the mould. I told you at the very start you would have to wait for me, that I had an exhibition coming up that it's important to me. I also told you my art always comes first."

"Bollocks." Theo – his anger bending in on itself as he realised Maddie was speaking the truth – still felt humiliated. Yet, despite everything, he was desperate to touch her again.

"Someone has certainly been talking crap, but I think you'll find it wasn't me." Maddie turned round, her hands on her hips as she glared at her ex, giving Theo a full rear view of her mouth watering figure, complete with the scratch marks he'd made on her flesh as he'd cleaned away the flashes of paint. He knew then. He knew he wanted to punish her.

But he wasn't exactly sure why, beyond the fact that he had an unwavering desire to see her covered in more marks inflicted upon her in moments of passion. Marks he himself had made.

Tania's voice dripped jealous venom. "That's so bloody typical of you Maddie – turning your crimes into someone else's."

Maddie closed her eyes, unable to believe she had let this poisonous woman back into her life. Taking a slow breath, she asked again, "When, Tania?"

"Yesterday. The Red Lion pub garden. Then the Red Lion Gents' toilet. You really should let him screw you, darling. He is very talented in that area – even in a confined space."

Theo felt as if his head was going to burst. *Has Maddie been playing a game with me or has it been Tania pulling my strings?* He'd been so convinced by Tania's claims that the artist was a prick-tease...*and Maddie did openly admit that she slept with her models if she couldn't afford to pay them.*

He had to get out of the hallway. The house suddenly felt unbearably claustrophobic. Without saying anything, Theo pushed past the naked Maddie and irate Tania and left without a backward glance, pulling his van keys from his overall pocket as he made a hasty get-away.

His libido told him if he turned around now he could probably have both the women in that house at the same time. But his pride told him they'd made enough of a fool of him thank you very much and he should get as far away from Maddie Templeton and all her associates as soon as possible.

So lost in his thoughts was he that he didn't hear the tap tap tap of a pair of high heeled shoes coming up behind him.

Unlocking the van doors with his remote key ring, it wasn't until the passenger door opened at the same time as he crashed down into the driver's seat, that Theo noticed Tania had followed him.

Pressing a long red fingernail to his lips before Theo could speak, Tania said, "I don't care if you like me or not, but I know you need to screw. I know you need to work off the tension my deviously tempting ex has built up inside you. And more important than all of that, I know exactly how to get Maddie precisely where you want her."

For a split second Theo contemplated throwing her physically out of the van onto the pavement. But Tania's words had struck a sympathetic chord, so he merely muttered, "Oh, what the hell!" before driving off with an annoyingly smug Tania sitting, virtually purring, in the passenger seat.

Chapter Twelve

Suddenly freezing cold, Maddie dragged herself into the clothes she'd abandoned to the floor of the studio when Sara had been there. It felt like days ago, not just hours. *Bloody Tania!* Maddie was sure that her ex had followed Theo as he'd stormed from the house. She could only hope that Theo would have the good sense to tell Tania to piss off and leave him alone.

The heavy humidity of the day had burst into a hard rain that threatened thunder. As she stood at the window, listening to the raindrops echo off the slabs of her patio, Maddie was reminded of the shower water hitting her scalp as Theo had pressed his face into her clit. A sudden cascade of temper washed over her. *Fuckin' Tania. Why did she always have to ruin things?*

◆ ◆ ◆ ◆

Common sense caught up with Theo when he was about five minutes drive from his flat. Swerving to an abrupt stop at the side of the road, he clicked open Tania's seatbelt, leant over her lap and pushed open the passenger door. "Get out."

"What?" Tania stared into his clouded brown eyes, flashing her peppermint gaze at him bewitchingly.

The redheads flirting fell flat. "Don't bother with the fluttering eyelashes thing. It won't work. I want to be on my own. I need to think."

"Don't be silly, darling, you need company. You need a damn good seeing-to." She crept a hand over his thigh.

Pointedly, Theo removed her palm. "No Tania. Those are the things *you* need. I need to be on my own."

Pushing her bodily out of the vehicle, Theo slammed the door behind Tania and accelerated his van out onto the wet street, leaving the model standing in the rain, her features frozen in a picture of total shock. Theo couldn't help but wonder if it was the first time a genuine expression had ever crossed her pretty face.

Shunning his policy of not drinking spirits during the working week, Theo poured himself a shot of whiskey. Crashing down into his living room armchair and dragging a hand through his still-wet hair, Theo took a mouthful of the sharp liquor.

Three gulps later and the electrician was ready to try and make sense of what had just happened. One minute his dick was being turned into a sculpture and covered with the orgasm-racked faces of beautiful women. The next his 'Maddie' fantasies were at last coming true, her luscious body squashed sensually between him and the glass of the shower cubicle. Then somehow it had ended. Maddie had, unbelievably, been about to make him settle for a hand job and miss out – yet again – on impaling her body when, without warning, they were no longer alone.

Closing his eyes and lounging further back in the leather chair, both palms clasping his glass, Theo tried to picture what had actually happened. To recall precisely the words Maddie had spoken before Tania had exploded onto the scene like a revenge-seeking missile.

◆ ◆ ◆ ◆

The short white cane landed against the duvet with a crack that, had there been anyone to witness it, would have made them quake with fearful anticipation.

Maddie threw her arm back a third time and then a fourth. In the artist's mind, the indents she was making in the duvet were forming on Tania's backside.

Panting, her rage partly vented, Maddie threw the crop to the floor and stared at the marks she'd made against the fabric while she struggled to control her breathing. Only when she felt sufficiently calm did she risk taking a look at the sculpture she'd made of Theo. Picking it up with great care, Maddie examined it from every angle.

She was glad it hadn't set yet – the urge to spear herself on the replica of his gorgeously thick shaft was immense. Trying hard not to think about the electrician, Maddie took a pair of extremely sharp scissors from her desk and began to trim away the ragged edges of the sculpture. She was in the middle of deciding if it was too soon to peel the cling film away from the base of the piece, when her phone announced the arrival of a text. Her hands froze in the act of placing the sculpture back on the trolley. It was bound to be Tania either bragging that she was with Theo, or brazenly announcing she'd be back at the studio shortly as if nothing had happened.

Dismissing the voice at the back of her head that told her the text might be from Theo and not Tania, Maddie busied herself by extracting the battered notebook from her drawer. It was time to update the list of artwork she'd planned for her exhibition. Firmly placing a satisfying tick next to the completed works, Maddie struck a line through those pieces that looked as if they would no longer happen.

1. *Sara over the stool - legs wide, pussy wet (Pastel)* ✓

2. *Freya in yellow - male hands at waist (Oil)* ✓

3. *Sara - chalked ~~(Photo collage- assuming pics ok???)~~ (One large close up on torso- photographed onto canvas)* ✓

4. *~~Freya flexing (maybe use this- not sure?? - Charcoal)~~ Would be another single female pic – too repetitive in small exhibition*

5. *Tania – if she agrees (Dom pose?? - Felt tips - poster style - would be v quick to produce)* ✓

6. *~~Tania – (Dom and victim – Charcoal)~~ Cube of pencil drawings of Sara and Freya's faces*

- *(need to make cube to place them around.) -
half complete*
7. *Theo - ~~(Wanking- Pencil drawing)??~~ Papier-
mâché sculpture of dick with photos of models
faces* ✓
8. *Sara and Freya ~~together somehow~~ - Over the
sofa- tit slapping* ✓
9. *~~Theo - not sure how???~~ Large paint splattered
outline of Sara* ✓
10. *Sara - possibly with Theo/Jake (unsure of
medium)*
11. *Threesome – Jake (??)/Freya/Sara (Pastel)*
12. *Idea - won't write down in case it doesn't
happen!!!*

Maddie counted up the number of completed and
half-completed pieces. "Shit. Only eight." She sighed as she
considered the four gaps in her list. Maddie still had a clear
picture of one additional work involving her Chinese Ink set
and Theo, but she wasn't sure if it was even worth adding it
to her speculative list. If she was going to get this exhibition
off the ground, Maddie knew it was time to stop hoping
Theo would agree to keep modelling and get Sara to ask her
boyfriend Jake if he would like to have a go.

Unable to avoid any longer the text that waited on
her phone, and mentally drafting the message she wanted to
send to Sara, Maddie picked up her mobile, bracing herself
for a catalogue of nastiness from the polished fingers of her

ex-lover.

It wasn't from Tania.

It was from Theo.

Theo: May I ask u some questions?

Maddie stared at the phone, wondering if she should reply. It would be easy to pretend that she'd had an early night and hadn't received his message. After all, it was already almost half past ten. *But what questions?*

Maddie: Okay.

Far too keyed-up to even attempt sleep, Maddie picked up the duvet she had so sorely abused. Snuggling herself into its bulky comfort, she curled up on the sofa and typed her text to Sara while waiting for Theo to reply. She didn't have to hang on for long.

Theo: Am I just someone u have kept waiting so u can use me for art?

Maddie stared at the screen on her mobile. She was sure that if Tania hadn't turned up when she had then she'd still have been firmly in control of the situation and, although Theo may not have appreciated being made to wait a little longer to seek the reward he really wanted, she would have been able to ensure he came back for it very soon. She also knew, however, that although it had all begun as a game, there was something new about this man. If their time in the shower was anything to go by, he would be able to give as good as he got – when she allowed him to. She didn't want him to bolt before she'd had the chance to feel his lips on her clit and his cock between her legs.

Inhaling the masculine aroma that still hung within the folds of the duvet cover, Maddie began to type.

> Maddie: I've told u before- I kept u waiting because I think waiting makes the end result even better. The fact I want to draw u is a bonus
> Theo: A bonus for whom?
> Maddie: For me – and I hoped for u too
> Theo: I enjoyed my reward – as far as it went

Maddie smiled. She could feel her electrician thawing out and she was reassured that Tania wouldn't be with him, adding to the doubts she'd already injected into his mind.

> Maddie: I enjoyed the shower.
> Theo: U have a hot body. I expected to experience more of it though
> Maddie: Tania interrupted us before we were done.
> Theo: U expect me to believe u were going to change ur mind and fuck me?
> Maddie: No. But u would have learned why it would have been worth the wait.

Theo: Really?

Maddie took a slow steady breath. She decided to take a gamble and tell him the truth.

> Maddie: Truly. I was going to ask u to
> come to the gallery with me, and for us
> to wait until after the visit to have more
> fun. I want to get a proper idea of the
> space. I would value ur opinion on how
> to show my art.
> Theo: I suppose that could be true.
> Maddie: It is - or would've been.
> Anyway, u have a v hot body and I still
> want to draw it- will u let me?

The phone went quiet and Maddie pulled the duvet tighter around her shoulders. If he responded with a yes, then she could relax – not only about her art, but about the fact that she would see him again. The reward she had in mind for Theo after he had posed for her a second time was one she was very much looking forward to. It was also a reward for herself. It didn't seem to have occurred to him that she was being made to wait as well.

Her phoned buzzed again.

> Theo: Are u cross that I had sex with
> Tania?

Trying not to worry that he hadn't actually answered

her text about drawing him, Maddie was relieved that at least she could answer this question easily.

Maddie: No. I sleep with my other models, why shouldn't u have some fun? It was Tania I was angry with - using u to get revenge on me.
Theo: Revenge for what?
Maddie: I dumped her after she stole my last boyfriend.
Theo: Did u dump the boyfriend as well?
Maddie: No. He was seduced by her. Tan can be v convincing and is v beautiful. Who wouldn't want to screw her?
Theo: Would u again?
Maddie: Only on my terms
Theo: And those terms are?
Maddie: I dominate her.
Theo: Like on the trolley.
Maddie: Yes. U liked that?
Theo: U know I did.
Maddie: We could do something like that again – if u wanted to?
Theo: As a reward that would stand in the way of me fucking u, or as an extra?

Maddie's abdomen contracted at the thought of what

she and Theo could do to Tania if they got at her together.

> Maddie: An extra.
> Theo: Why should I believe u?
> Maddie: I have always told u the truth.

Again the phone went quiet. Maddie could feel her pulse pumping against the rectangular handset. She could hear her own voice in the back of her head telling Freya and Sara how important it is to stay composed and to understand how power and control over your own body is everything. As she waited for Theo's response, Maddie started to consider how, since she'd been offered the exhibition, her iron-clad self-control had weakened. She wasn't sure if it was due to the desperate need to do well with this one-off opportunity, because of Theo, or because of Tania. It was probably a combination of everything. Either way, the submissive in her was trying hard to elbow its way back to the surface, and Maddie realised with a shock that if Theo was on the other end of the whip, she wouldn't mind one bit. Not that she was about to let him know that.

> Theo: As I said, why should I believe u?

Maddie sighed, how could she convince him?

> Maddie: I have kept u waiting. I have delayed u. But I have not lied to u. U

didn't listen to what I said carefully
enough
Theo: Prove it
Maddie: How?
Theo: Tell me where to meet u
tomorrow – not at the gallery. Not at
the studio either. That place is a bad
influence.

Not the studio? Maddie's mind raced. Where could they meet that was private enough to do what she badly wanted to do to him? She couldn't afford a hotel and anyway, she really didn't have the time to go far afield. A walk was too romantic and too public and so was a lunch date. Then she smiled, the memory of a previously shared exchange of texted sexual fantasies making the decision for her.

Maddie: Do u know Elf Woods – about
2 miles from my place?
Theo: Yes. What do u plan to do to me
when we get there?
Maddie: Take u to a remote area so we
can be alone without the distraction of
my art
Theo: And?
Maddie: I will reward ur patience
Theo: What time?
Maddie: When u finish work?
Theo: Only 1 small job booked for
tomo – 2.30pm?

Maddie almost requested a later time – the need to crack on with her exhibition pictures becoming more pressing by the day. But she didn't want to alienate Theo further by refusing. Not now that she could see her opportunity to get him back on board so clearly in her mind – not to mention the image of Theo naked, gagged and tied to a tree.

> Maddie: Fine. Meet u in the car park then?
> Theo: If u cancel on me, then that is it Maddie. Game over.
> Maddie: I WILL see you tomo

Maddie turned off her phone, her heart thudding. Her imagination was already leagues ahead as she decided what to put in her backpack to take with her. Elf Woods was a popular place but it was also huge and Maddie knew it well. There were many secluded places where they could happily be left to their own devices, with only a remote chance of being discovered by dog walkers straying far from the path. *And let's face it*, she thought with a grin, *the possibility of someone discovering Theo in that state is part of the fun!* Suddenly, tomorrow couldn't come quickly enough.

◆ ◆ ◆

Peeling off his overalls, Theo threw them into the mess that made up the back of his van and scanned the half-full car park in Elf Woods. He had no idea what sort of car Maddie drove, but he was sure that she was already there.

From the moment he'd gotten out of his van he'd had the feeling he was being watched, yet he couldn't spot the artist.

"Should I be offended that you looked straight through me?" Maddie didn't smile as she walked up to Theo, but her eyes shone with the suggestion of pleasure. The strength of the midday sun had forced the electrician to dress only in a loose, white t-shirt and raggedly cut denim shorts – it was a good look.

"Sorry, you look so different!" His eyes appraised her favourably in her short, flared skirt and bust-enhancing vest top. "I haven't seen you without paint or charcoal smeared all over you before."

As the memory of how she'd felt when Theo had peeled the paint from her skin flicked at her pussy, Maddie's smile hit her lips. "I even have shoes on! Well, trainers anyway."

"And you appear to have brushed your hair. You aren't all crumpled."

"Is that a compliment or a complaint?"

Theo eyes shone playfully. "Both?"

Maddie, temporarily forgetting she was planning to tie this man up and beat him until he begged to be allowed to cum, found herself blushing. "Thank you. I think."

"What's in the bag?"

Theo's enquiry brought Maddie back to the reality of her plans. She began to walk as they talked, leading Theo into the woods in the opposite direction to the public footpath. "A few essentials – picnic, rug and stuff. Just the basics."

"Sounds good." Theo began to follow, but suddenly he stopped dead.

Something about the way Theo was staring into the trees sent a quiver up Maddie's spine. "You okay?"

Theo shrugged. "I keep having this weird feeling I'm being watched. It's nothing. Probably a deer." He caught up with Maddie, gallantly taking the bag from her shoulder and slinging it over his own. "So where are you taking me?"

"You'll see." Striding ahead again, Maddie's trainers picked their way over the network of tree roots. "Come on, Mr. Electrician."

They walked on in silence, the trees becoming denser as Maddie followed the route her memory had sketched out the night before. Twenty minutes later she pointed to a fallen tree on the ground in front of them.

"Here we are." Maddie sat on a fallen tree trunk which hovered just above the mossy, twig-strewn ground.

Theo stood in front of her. "And 'here' would appear to be the middle of nowhere."

"Yes. Perfect for what I have in mind."

"And that would be?"

"I told you. You really must pay more attention to the texts I send you, Theo. I am going to tie you to a tree." Maddie gestured to the trunk on which she was sitting. "This tree, actually."

Only the faintest hint of surprise tinged Theo's voice as he said, "And what makes you think that I am simply going to let you fasten me to that?"

Maddie undid the clasps that secured her rucksack and produced two long leather straps, complete with buckle fasteners. She ran them lovingly through her fingers. "Because you want to know how it feels to be on the receiving end of my attention. Because the dick that is so obviously challenging your shorts right now wants to sink itself inside me, and because I promised that I would tie you to a tree – and I always keep my promises."

"Eventually."

"Eventually." Maddie laid the leather straps over the round curve of the trunk. The afternoon sun hadn't yet perforated the canopy of trees and as she stroked the space on the trunk next to where she sat, Maddie found that it was still damp from the rain of the previous evening. "Come here, Theo."

Theo sat as instructed, his legs stretched out in front of him, one hand resting on his knee, the other lightly on Maddie's bare leg. "I see the remaining paint has come away now," he remarked.

In no mood for small talk, Maddie lifted his palm from her leg and placed it on his other knee. Then, facing Theo, she smoothed her fingertips around his waistband. Pushing the flat of her palms up under his t-shirt, absorbing the heat of Theo's torso, edging his top higher, until he automatically raised his arms and she could take it off over his head. "Turn around."

"Yes Ma'am." Theo appeared sincere as he obeyed, and the stirrings of power that had gathered at the pit of

Maddie's gut began to swell.

"Stay still." Maddie knelt to her pack, producing a picnic rug, which she lay over the trunk of the tree. Then, satisfied that Theo was waiting as instructed, she returned to her bag and took out the short white cane she'd used to attack the duvet only the night before.

She hadn't heard him move. Maddie shrieked as two firm arms wrapped round her waist and lifted her bodily off the ground. Kicking against him, Maddie struggled to be free, but Theo's grip held fast.

Dropping her to the rough ground, Theo placed one foot on the middle of her belly, pressing just hard enough to pin her down. "Did you honestly believe I would forgive you that easily? That I would simply roll over because Maddie Templeton told me to? After being teased, being forced to wait and being made to feel foolish?"

Maddie's heart beat so fast it felt as if it was going to break out of her chest. She could have twisted away from him. It would only have taken one quick lurch to the side. But she didn't move. What was worse was that Maddie knew Theo was aware she could escape...and yet she didn't. Instead, her mind was frantically working out how to retrieve the upper hand with maximum dignity.

Theo crouched over her, placing his hand firmly over her mouth and spoke directly into Maddie's eyes. "I hear that domination is fairly new to you."

The artist didn't have to ask whom he'd heard this from. Tania would no doubt have delighted in telling Theo all about the things they used to get up to together.

"Thanks to the magic of the mobile phone, I have seen you in the role of dominatrix. And after all the waiting you have forced upon me, I think I am entitled to see how you perform as a submissive."

Maddie could feel her body wanting to give into this man, mutely willing him to turn the tables on her. But her mind still rebelled. This should have been her moment to show him exactly how good it could be to be under *her* command. *It isn't supposed to be like this.* And yet her pussy was already leaking its slick honey through her panties, glossing the rounded curve of her thighs.

Sitting across Maddie's legs, Theo was struggling not to rush. The temptation to fuck her hard against the woodland floor was almost overwhelming. Stealing himself against his own desires, he said, "If I move my hand, do you promise to be quiet?"

Nodding, Maddie licked her lips as Theo removed his dry hand. In one movement, that same hand had scrunched her vest up under her chin and popped her luscious breasts free.

Without taking his eyes from her large round globes, Theo reached down and picked up a handful of fallen twigs. Bunching them together in one fist, Theo grazed the knarled wood over her nipples, making Maddie squirm. Her hands clutched at his bent knees, her fingernails digging into his flesh as deeply as she could, fully intending to hurt him.

Theo kept up the sensual torture of her breasts

until he could no longer stand the press of her nails. Then, snatching Maddie's leather ties from the trunk, he grabbed both her wrists in one hand and secured them easily – one in each strap. "Let's keep those talons out of the way, shall we?"

Before Maddie had the chance to respond, Theo pulled on the ends of the straps, just as he would a dog on a lead, and she swayed unsteadily to her feet.

Twisted away from him, she was forced forward and bent over the trunk. With her bottom stuck up and out, her chest and stomach squashed, Maddie found herself exactly where she had intended Theo to be. He circled the long leather leads around the width of the trunk, before reattaching them to her wrists and buckling the tethers in place; effectively trapping her against the rough bark.

"I assume this is what you were going to do to me?"

"Sort of." Maddie muttered into the trunk. Her annoyance at how easily he'd been able to turn the tables on her merged with thoughts of what he was about to do, how quickly she would be allowed to climax and how soon she could make him pay for this unscheduled change to her neatly laid plans.

"Only sort of?" Theo flipped up the back of her skirt and ran a calloused palm over the silky fabric of her pansy-blue panties. "Tell me how things would be different so far."

Maddie hesitated. The breeze that had been rustling the leaves above them was tickling the top of her sticky legs.

"I think you should tell me Maddie. Otherwise I might take my hand off your ass, and I don't think you want me to do that, do you?"

Swallowing hard, Maddie said nothing, reluctant to admit how good his touch felt against her backside.

"Maddie. I said, I don't think you want me to do that, *do you?*"

"No Theo."

"That's better. You see, you can be a good little submissive, can't you. I didn't think Tania was lying about that."

Theo increased the force behind his hand, rubbing harder over the gauzy material, pushing Maddie's pussy and exposed nipples harder against the fallen tree, increasing her desire for the wood to be replaced by the body of the man standing behind her.

"So, last chance. What were you going to do to me once I was bent over?"

"I was going to spank you with my cane." Speaking through gritted teeth, Maddie wished she didn't know how good it would feel if he did the same to her. The cane, hidden in her bag, had met her backside many times in the past. And it appeared that her backside had missed its unique caress more than she'd appreciated.

"I assume your cane is in the bag of essentials?" Theo spoke practically, and if Maddie hadn't been able to feel the excited bulge of his cock as his shorts brushed against her leg, she would have thought him nearly as clinical as herself.

"Yes." Her voice felt small and every muscle in her body clenched as she waited for the inevitable.

Theo's hands however, stayed where they were. "And would you have struck me through my boxers, or hit me directly on my bare backside?"

"Both."

"A slow build up. Very sexy. I approve." With extra slow hands, Theo peeled her knickers over the globes of her ass. "But then you are very sexy, Miss Templeton – I wonder if you understand how sexy you are?"

The artist closed her eyes, all of her senses condensed within the patches of skin beneath the electrician's fingers.

"I wanted to see you away from your studio." His hands stayed still, but his little finger played tantalizingly over her anus, sending more nerve endings alight. "Tania, for all her bluster, said something about the studio that is true. It smells of sex. It is sex. You go into that place and sex is everywhere. I had to see if I was obsessed with the studio's atmosphere, or the artist who operated within it."

Theo seemed to contemplate this as he gently slid her panties down to the forest floor. The sigh Maddie had been withholding escaped as the flimsy material finally reached her ankles and Theo placed a soft kiss on each of her butt cheeks.

"It seems a shame to damage such pretty panties – best remove them completely."

Maddie knew better than to comment. She knew a pre-spank line when she heard one.

Theo rummaged in the backpack, retrieving her cane. "Nice weapon, Maddie." He weighed it in his hands. "But, seeing as we are in the bosom of Mother Nature, I think we should make use of her bounty, don't you?"

Maddie closed her eyes. The thought of supple sprigs, even heavier than the ones Theo had used to graze her tits, rebounding off her backside was almost enough to send her into a premature climax.

"If you continue not to answer my questions, Maddie, then I might get cross." Theo picked up a new stick, slightly longer than a ruler. It was smooth and nature had already stripped its bark. "I asked you a question."

"Yes Theo, we should use nature's bounty."

"That's better. Good girl."

Hearing him call her his "good girl" had an odd effect on Maddie's pulse rate. It was as though her heart skipped a beat. Theo flashed his improvised weapon before Maddie's eyes – just long enough for her to see how flexible it was and to calculate how much pain it could cause if wielded properly. Maddie began to wonder how many times Theo had played the Master before.

"In view of how long you have made me wait, after the many hours I have wasted dreaming about you lying on top of me, grinding your body against my dick, you have sacrificed the presence of the protective layer of your panties for the initial phase of your long-overdue spanking."

The first strike landed before Theo had finished speaking, sending a sharp exhalation of air flying from Maddie's throat as a burning pain stung her left side, matched almost instantly by another sting across the right.

As he continued to smack the fallen branch across her

bottom, Theo eased his left hand between her legs. "So wet, Miss Templeton! Why are you so wet?"

It took a moment before Maddie could speak, and when she did it was breathless. "Because I am tied up and being beaten by a hot man."

"Very good answer, but not the correct one." Theo aimed the stick at the cleft of her buttocks and struck again. This time Maddie screeched. A wonderful agony flashed through her, forcing her to jerk back onto her toes and press her naked breasts harder into the coarse surface beneath her – which in turn sent new sparks of lust throughout her body.

"You are so wet because you are a very, very dirty girl. What are you?"

This was new ground for Maddie. She'd been told she was dirty before, but no one had ever forced her to say so out loud.

"I'm…" She swallowed her shame. "I'm a dirty girl." Confessing to Theo that she was indeed a dirty girl was as intoxicating as the thought of what might happen next.

"And if I continued to thrash you with this stick while I patted your pussy, do you think you would cum?"

Her croak of "Yes" was barely audible as she struggled not to climax there and then.

"And if I plugged you with the butt plug I've found in your bag, would that feel good?"

"Oh god, I…" Maddie couldn't finish the sentence. Everything ached – every part of her needed to be touched, kissed, hit, or filled and fucked.

"I will take that as a yes." Theo trailed the plug over Maddie's clit, rolling it in her escaped syrup, rendering her delirious with delight as he moved the toy against her sensitive flesh.

Theo dropped the branch cane. "No need for lube, dirty girl." He parted her buttocks as widely as he could with one hand, before pressing the thin plug only a centimetre into her anus and then withdrawing it again.

Gasping as Theo held the plug at the very entrance of her darkest place, Maddie squeezed her eyes closed. Her hands dug into the brittle bark, breaking it off in sections as her tension grew, longing for him to push the plug in fully.

"Forgive me taking my time. I'm just admiring your ass. It's so pretty, covered in the lines I've just made. They are all red and pink. I am sure the artist in you would appreciate how good you look, especially with your asshole winking at me greedily." He teased the solid rubber in small circles, but still he didn't press it inside her. "You know, Maddie, if you want this inserted, you're going to have to ask nicely."

Perspiration had begun to gather on Maddie's forehead. Where her clothes were rucked up around her neck and waist, she felt hot and sticky with discomfort. Never had she felt so empty and, without even registering what she was doing, she began to jut her rear out as far as possible, trying to swallow the whole plug with her ass.

Theo laughed. "Come on, Maddie. All you have to do is ask nicely and I will pop it straight into that beautiful butt. I bet you'd like the discomfort of that, wouldn't you.

That odd pleasure that both aches and satisfies all at once?"

"Yes, Theo."

"So?"

"Please fill my ass, Theo."

Silently he worked the rubber plug down into her, marvelling as her muscles sucked it in – he barely had to push at all. "Well, that looks good. Does it feel nice?"

"Oh...yes." Her words were more like protracted breaths now. Her muscles spasmed against the awkward but welcome intrusion, her legs beginning to cramp from immobility and her arms dying to be free so she could turn and allow him to fill her other passage.

"I'm glad." Theo's hands deserted her. "I just need to tidy up a bit, if you'll excuse me."

Maddie could hear him moving behind her, and she already missed his hands on her body.

Suddenly he was standing before her, her backpack over his shoulder. "That's better," he said casually. "All tidy now. I do so hate to leave a mess."

She blinked, unable to see him properly from her tethered position, her neck bent, yellow hair hanging over her eyes.

"I'll see you some time, Maddie. Carry on being a good girl, won't you."

"What? I..."

Maddie's words disappeared into the breeze that circled her prone body and played over her impaled bottom. Theo's footsteps crackled as he retreated over the leaf-strewn floor. Before he disappeared entirely, he shouted, "Time *you* learned to wait for a change, Miss Templeton. Hope someone finds you before it gets dark."

Chapter Thirteen

"Theo?"

Maddie didn't dare raise her voice. They may have been in a remote spot, but now everything had become spookily quiet and she was conscious that any noise could carry for miles through the trees. She didn't want to be found by the wrong person.

Agitating her hands in an attempt to be free from the ties, Maddie soon admitted defeat. Theo had used her own straps against her and she knew precisely how strong they were. Her wrists could only be raised an inch from the trunk. Her stomach was squashed flat against the curve of the wood, and her breasts had gone from feeling nicely caressed to sandpaper-chaffed by the textured bark beneath them. Each time she so much as wriggled, shots of sore desire triggered in her chest and deluged her pussy. This, in turn, automatically made her clench her back passage, thus sending fresh waves of lust-fuelled need from that direction as well.

He'll be back. He's just trying to scare me. Maddie's heart drummed within her ribcage and rebounded off the wood. *What if someone else finds me? They could do anything...* The artist's thoughts became more irrational, the perspiration that had dotted her skin turning to full blown sweat. Maddie had no idea how long Theo had been away. It was probably only a minute or two, but it was enough to send her imagination into overdrive. All she could think about was how passers-by could use her. She was just a convenient female. A thing to play with – handily draped and already wet.

Theo watched. Positioned a hundred yards away, hidden behind a thicket of beech trees, he admired the rear of the artist who'd been tormenting his imagination for weeks. As he stood there, his erection urging him to hurry up and service his victim, Theo felt rather than heard the arrival of the figure behind him. He didn't bother to turn round. He knew who it would be.

Whispering so that his words didn't float across the wood to Maddie, Theo was terse. "You are rather predictable, Tania."

"Sorry to disappoint you." Tania failed to hide the brittle edge to her hushed voice.

"I don't care enough to feel disappointed by your lack of originality. Maddie told me you had no imagination. It seems she was right."

"You didn't spot me following you, though."

"You make it sound as if effective stalking skills are something to be proud of." Theo kept his eyes on Maddie. She was trying to shuffle her feet into a more comfortable position, but he could tell it wasn't really working by the stilted way in which she moved. He smiled to himself. The tension that rippled across her buttocks told him that she was afraid the butt plug would fall out. She probably wanted to make sure it stayed within her just as much as she wanted to be free of it – although probably not as much as she wanted him to come back and fuck the hell out of her.

Fed up with Theo not paying her any attention, Tania moved in front of him, obstructing his view of her ex-lover. "You *didn't* see me though, did you?"

"Oh for god's sake, woman. No I didn't see you. I knew you were there, though. I had a feeling I was being followed and who else would bother? And for that matter, why are you bothering? You're just one of Maddie's models now. If your boasting is to be believed, you don't need the work and you're only doing this for her as a favour."

Pouting, Tania put her hands on her hips as if she was poising for a fashion photographer. "Wasn't I a good enough ride for you?"

Theo dragged the redhead forward by her waist. "You were a very good ride, as you well know. But you offered yourself up just to spite Maddie – that is not an attractive trait."

Tania opened her mouth to protest his remarks, but Theo pressed his mouth over hers. His kiss was cold and brief, but frenzied. "However, I think Maddie has to be taught a lesson and if you behave yourself, then I think you could help."

Taking satisfying note of how the electrician's body

reacted against her own, and more than willing to be involved in any punishment of Maddie, Tania peered over her shoulder toward her ex. "Help? How?"

She could have sworn she'd heard Theo's voice. But the mutter had stopped as soon as it had started and Maddie was beginning to think it had been her imagination. At least ten minutes must have passed and if he really had abandoned her, then he would be back at the van soon. *He wouldn't really drive away and leave me though, would he?*

Every time she seriously considered the fact he'd really gone, Maddie dismissed the notion. If she'd ever had any doubts about her ability to manipulate the man she'd chosen to play games with, now they were crystal clear. This was someone just as devious and controlled as she was. *And he is giving me a taste of my own medicine.* Maddie winced – she hated that phrase, but even her thoughts seemed to be operating outside of her control. She didn't like the idea that she had read the all the signs so badly and now she was paying for it.

Forcing herself to remain rational, Maddie began to work out how she could manoeuvre this unexpected twist of events to her advantage.

Maddie tried to put herself in Theo's place. If she were him she wouldn't have gone far. She would have hidden nearby and relished his growing anxiety. Maddie only wished that her restricted position, combined with the sensation of the buried plug, wasn't turning her on quite so much. Now there was a real chance that when he finally did return, she would beg him to make her cum. Her body had never been so close to totally disengaging from her brain and taking total control of her every function

Alert to every sound, every change in the atmosphere around her, Maddie prayed that the faint barking of dogs and the shouts of owners, were further away than she imagined. As the slow minutes ticked by Maddie knew the chances of being discovered by a set of hands that didn't belong to Theo grew. Each crunch of leaves, each snapped twig sent new worry and anticipation through her, adding to the flesh-hugging sheen of sweat that coated Maddie like a second skin.

Closing her eyes so that her hearing was more acute, Maddie froze. Someone was getting closer. Her fingernails took thicker chunks out of the trunk and Maddie tried to tuck her backside in as much as possible – a pointless task as she was fixed fast, perfectly presented to any voyeur, with her skirt up over her back and her ass plugged.

The footfalls weren't heavy enough to be Theo.

"Open your eyes, Maddie."

Maddie groaned out loud. "You!"

"I knew you'd be pleased to see me, darling." Tania squatted in front of Maddie and lifted her chin slightly, giving the tethered woman no choice but to look her ex straight in the eyes. "By the looks of you, any passing stranger would put you out of your misery."

Maddie didn't reply, her respect for Theo's methods raising another notch. This guy was as good at playing the long game as she was. When she eventually got out of this,

Maddie vowed she would make sure she told him so – or at least gave him a proper demonstration of her own techniques as a respectful comparison.

Tania's fingers reached over Maddie and began to dawdle across her back. Speaking conversationally she said, "I don't think I have ever seen a woman so wet. I guess your cunt is feeling pretty empty? Although I see your backside couldn't be fuller."

Taking her hands away from the artist, Tania pulled the picnic rug from the tree trunk, laid the tartan square on the ground, and sat down in front of Maddie's head.

Desperate to know where Theo was, but not wanting to ask, Maddie bided her time, distracting herself by mentally arranging what she was going to do to the electrician the next time she got him inside her studio – and get him there she would. With each second Maddie became more resolute. Just because he'd outmanoeuvred her this time, didn't mean he would again!

Two minutes later, however, and Maddie had to force herself to stop making plans for his comeuppance. Visions of Theo trussed at her mercy – a living work of art, his hands so close to the pussies of Sara and Freya that were frustratingly out of reach – were not making her heart beat any slower and she knew she'd never live it down if she came there and then with Tania watching.

Another two minutes passed and Maddie had to bite her lips, fighting the urge to ask Tania what the hell she was waiting for – *why doesn't she free me…or screw me!?* *Where the hell is Theo? Can he see everything that is happening – or isn't bloody happening! Does he even know she is here?*

"I have to say, Maddie, that I'm impressed." Tania, always easily bored, had reached the end of her ability to entertain herself. "Your self-control, despite your current utter humiliation, is as excellent as ever. I fear I would have asked where Theo was before now."

Awarding herself a mental tick, Maddie replied, "Of course you would. You only have staying power if you have a whip in your hand."

"What makes you think I don't have a whip?"

Maddie's insides did a somersault, but her face remained set in concentration and her brain worked fast. "I don't doubt it. Hidden inside the length of those unseasonal boots I presume?"

Tania pulled out Maddie's own short white cane. "Theo gave it to me. Sweet isn't it."

Wishing once again that she didn't remember how good it felt to be on the receiving end of Tania and a well aimed crop, Maddie played for time by asking what she really wanted to know. "Had Theo planned for you to be here all along?"

"No. I found you both. Isn't that lucky?"

Maddie wasn't surprised. "You truly are a loss to the British spy network, Tan."

"Jokes at a time like this? You are truly made of iron, woman!" Tania stretched her legs out from under her. "And, in answer to the other question you badly want to ask me,

Theo will be back once he has found the others."

"Others?" The heat of the sun was suddenly blocked out by the comprehension that Theo may have invited an audience to watch her get her comeuppance. "What others?"

"Oh just Sara, Freya and maybe Sara's bloke, if he's free. Fun stuff, don't you think, darling?"

The remaining saliva in Maddie's mouth evaporated. "You're bluffing."

"Am I?" Tania pulled up her long flimsy skirt and widened her legs. Then, making sure that the captured woman could see exactly what she was doing, Tania revealed her naked mound and began to stroke a single finger over her pussy. "You really shouldn't leave your mobile lying around. I got their numbers so easily, and I had no qualms about passing them on to Theo."

Each fresh touch of Tania's fingertip on her own hairless pout made Maddie increasingly jealous of the touch that she was currently denied. All her efforts to hear what was going on around her and to listen out for Theo, were forgotten in her effort to keep her head at the uncomfortable angle which allowed her to stare fixedly at the moving finger before her, willing the sensations Tania was experiencing to somehow transfer to her desperately empty core.

Tania rocked back, widening her legs further, so Maddie could see how wet she was as her middle finger disappeared inside her little pink valley. To Maddie, in that moment, there was nothing else. The harmony of the birds singing and the leaves stirring in the breeze were forgotten.

Nothing else mattered but watching the narrow red tipped finger delving in and out of the woman before her.

It was an abrupt snap of a twig, halved beneath a booted foot, that brought Maddie out of her hypnotic state with a jump – a jump that sent the butt plug deeper inside her. *Damn!* Maddie couldn't believe she had made such a rookie mistake, letting herself get preoccupied with Tania while disregarding everything else.

Focusing hard now, feeling as if she had been doused back to reality with a bucket of ice water, Maddie detected at least four sets of feet coming towards her. Tania had not been bluffing.

If she thought she'd been tense before, that was nothing to how Maddie felt now as Theo addressed her. "I trust you are enjoying the wait, Maddie." His palm pinched her butt. "After all, you seem to have made a great virtue of telling everyone here how important it is to wait before you are rewarded with any sort of climax."

Her face coloured from pink to scarlet as more hands joined Theo's, all the time the voice at the back of her head repeating the same few words – *make this seem like your idea, make this seem like your idea.* The delicate palms of Freya and Sara's velvet smooth fingers were immediately obvious. But another unknown hand was playing across her back, undoing the strap of the bra that had earlier been unceremoniously exposed by Theo.

Maddie attempted to turn her head again, but her neck was stiff from its declivitous angle, and she was unable to see whom the new hands belonged to. Sara's boyfriend, Jake, presumably. Such was the relief at having hands on her body, that Maddie was unable to prevent the heavy moan of bliss as she relaxed a little, slumping more of her restrained body against the trunk.

"Well my friends, it seems that our combined attention is making Maddie happy." Theo's palms progressed up from Maddie's ankles to her slick thighs. "The question is, does she deserve to feel this good?"

Tania, who hadn't joined in the fondling of her ex, continued her casual masturbation as she said, "I think we should let her cum."

Maddie blinked in disbelief. That was not like Tania!

"But only when she asks nicely."

That was more like the Tania she knew and most certainly did not love.

The artist steeled herself. She'd been holding off a climax ever since Tania had sat down before her. She knew she only had a few more minutes in her before she orgasmed, whether she gave her body permission to or not. What was worse, she was sure all her companions knew it as well.

Theo felt a stab of pride for the artist. He hadn't thought she would hold out once the assembled hands had begun to explore her. "Okay then," he nodded in Tania's direction. "We will time Maddie. If she can hang on for another five minutes before either cumming, or begging to be allowed to cum, then we'll untie her. Then she can choose which one of us gives her the attention she's plainly desperate for."

"And if she doesn't?" Tania asked with unseemly enthusiasm.

"She will be left where she is until sundown."

Freya gasped in sympathy, as Maddie fought down unbidden tears of frustrated desperation which threatened to gather at the corner of her eyes. She couldn't possibly wait another five minutes.

"Are you agreeable to those terms, Maddie?" Theo traced the outline of her buttocks as he spoke. "I am assuming you are. I mean, I can't imagine you're the sort of person who would dish it out without being able to take it."

The smirk on Tania's face was enough to keep Maddie's lips sealed. She didn't really have time to speak anyway, for Theo was still addressing his assembly. "As I explained on the phone, Maddie originally brought me here to treat me in more or less the same way that I am treating her now. She was even organised enough to bring some supplies with her." Maddie heard him pick up her holdall. She could foresee the immediate future flash in tableaux of delicious overstimulation, with portions of carefully delivered pain. She had to make a decision about how she was going to cope – and fast.

"What did she bring?" The male voice that was still unidentified dripped with erotic anticipation, knotting Maddie's shoulders into tighter balls of tension.

"The strap I have tied her with is hers, as is the rug that Tania is sitting on. There was also a short cane tucked away which Tania has taken possession of."

Tania waved the weapon obligingly on cue and again Maddie swallowed, her throat arid.

There was a faint rummaging sound as Theo continued to examine her bag. "Obviously, she brought the butt plug you see so artistically displayed before you. I have to say, Maddie really does have the most luscious backside I have ever seen. Just the right amount of flesh, yet with no flab whatsoever. There is nothing worse than a bony ass…"

Even in her anxious state, Maddie didn't miss this dig at Tania, who suddenly appeared as if she had sucked on a lemon. Even so, Tania said nothing.

"Ah, how lovely, she has packed a vibrator for us. How was she going to use that on me, I wonder?" Maddie closed her eyes against the world, letting the words and sounds wash over her. If she kept listening, she was going to break long before the five minutes were up and she was fairly sure Theo wasn't including this preparation time in his countdown.

It was the slap of a hand across her rump that told the artist they had stopped taunting her and were ready to begin. A cry of shock flew from her lips as the pain from the spank blossomed through her ass. Her cry bounced from tree to tree and was quickly followed by another one.

"I think we'd better get her gagged before we have the entire woodland walking community over here. Jake, shut her up will you."

A large hand lifted Maddie's head by her hair and, before she had been formally introduced to Sara's boyfriend,

Maddie found his thick salty cock filling her throat, muffling any possible complaint she'd been about to make. At the same time two sets of female hands came to her legs, dancing over her thighs. Taking it in turns, the women's fingers tripped lightly over as much of her pussy as they could reach.

Rising from the rug, Tania elbowed the younger models off to either side of Maddie's legs and removed the cane from where she had sheathed it in her boot. Maddie heard the swish as the cane cut through the air before connecting with her skin, and she made the mistake of tensing her buttocks against the coming strike.

Even the wide presence of Jake's shaft wasn't enough to stop her yell of agony. Maddie tried to distract herself from the pain by gobbling at him all the harder. The continued blows from the cane were highlighted by the two sets of fingers caught up in the fervour of the moment, each fighting with the other to tug and poke at Maddie's clit. Someone, presumably Theo, was manoeuvring the butt plug in and out of her, widening her back passage.

Maddie was vaguely aware of Theo telling the others that she had survived two minutes. But her world had condensed to a microcosm of fingers, cock and the crop that had turned her ass from warm to burning. All she wanted now was for Theo to find a way to fill her with his cock.

Her wish, however, was partly granted when two sets of hands lifted her posterior up off the wood. Theo shoved her own vibrator deep inside her desperate flesh with a force that made her gasp. That gasp, in turn, made her suddenly and inadvertently deep throat Jake farther than she'd ever taken anyone before.

With a grunt that was almost animal, his fingers clawing at her knotted hair, Jake came hard into Maddie's mouth. As he pulled away, leaving her gulping for air, creamy semen fell from her lips, dribbled down her chin and puddled to the floor.

Jake was no sooner free from her sore lips, than his space was taken by Sara, whose face came to Maddie's. Holding the artist with more care than her partner had, she began to lick and kiss away his cum, pushing her tongue into the slippery mouth, lapping at the artist's cheeks and kissing her savagely.

Maddie's vision was merely a haze of flashing colours as new sensation topped new sensation. Theo was possibly telling the group that there was only a minute left. Maddie wasn't sure and didn't really care as the beating of her tender cheeks abruptly ceased and the vibrator was withdrawn.

Tears of loss cascaded down the artist's face, trickling onto Sara, who licked them up as well, savouring the salty liquid on her tongue. The loss didn't last for long. Two sets of hands had grabbed her at the knees again and Maddie yelled with surprise and terror as her legs were lifted clean off the floor, supported so that they were stretched out vertically.

Her mind racing and her head spinning – an ever expanding rainbow of exotic colours fire-cracking behind her closed eyelids – Maddie thought she was going to faint with lust-overload as Tania slid the frustratingly slim tip of the cane up inside her, while Tania's fingers massaged her clit.

The artist's screams were sucked from her face by Sara, and she didn't even register Freya's pliant chest as it trailed over her naked back. Theo's fingers plucked the butt plug free and, in doing so, his final act caused the body beneath them to wrack with such orgasmic violence that Tania had to withdraw and Jake had to lower her legs somewhat sooner than they'd expected to.

Maddie could feel the sound of her climax as much as she could hear it. She felt weak and was hardly able to listen, let alone respond to the words Theo was speaking.

"I am disappointed to report that Maddie failed with only thirty seconds to go. This of course means she will have to remain here for a while longer. I will look after her. Perhaps you would like to leave us to our vigil, ladies and gentleman."

Maddie thought that perhaps Tania had tried to protest, but she wasn't sure. She didn't even care that she had to stay where she was. All she needed now was rest.

Chapter Fourteen

"Why did you bring the box of ink?"

Theo was sitting on the rug Tania had placed on the ground in front of Maddie's hanging head. Her body felt pulled and stretched – as if she'd been pummelled on a medieval torture rack. Shaken by the strength of her climax and fatigued from being in such an uncomfortable position for so long, Maddie no longer had the energy to raise her head properly. But peripherally she could see that Theo was holding her prized Chinese Ink set in his hands.

Opening her mouth to speak, Maddie's throat felt gummed up and tacky and the words she tried to form simply didn't come out.

"Here." Theo put down the box and leant towards her, a bottle of water in his hands. "You need to drink. I got Sara to leave this behind for us."

Awkwardly, Maddie managed to twist her head enough for a few drops of blessedly cool liquid to cascade down her throat. She could have downed the whole bottle, but the ache in her neck and the very real possibility of wetting herself after so long made her stop drinking as soon as her lips were dampened, her thirst only partially quenched.

The electrician sat down and took up the box again. "So, why did you bring these inks?"

Licking the remnants of moisture from her lips, Maddie spoke huskily. "I was going to write on your back."

"Write on me?" Theo was openly surprised. "Write what?"

"All the things I want to do to you and with you. The stuff I'd *hoped* we could do, anyway."

Theo kept his voice level, although he was more than a little excited by the idea of Maddie running an ink brush across his back. "And then what?"

"I was going to ask if I could photograph the words on your back and use it in the show."

"And if I'd said no?"

The effect of the water had worn off and Maddie's throat felt coarser than ever. "I would have asked one of the girls or maybe Jake, instead."

"You wouldn't have put it in the show regardless?"

Maddie felt hurt. "No!" Her indignation came out as a shaky squeak. "It's a public show. Anyone can see the pictures. I have sought permission from every model I am using and that includes *you*."

"Every time I think I have you sussed, Miss Templeton, you say something that makes me realise that I don't really know you at all." He flicked her fringe back from her glazed eyes for a minute, before letting it flop back down again. Thoughtful, he added, "For your ability to constantly surprise me – which I can tell you is no easy feat – I will award you the privilege of getting into a far more comfortable position."

Maddie murmured to him as he began to loosen the straps around her wrists, "We don't know each other at all, yet."

Theo smiled as he gently eased the fastening away from her arms and began to untwist the tie from around the girth of the tree trunk. He didn't bother to tell her not to run away – even if she had the inclination to do so, he knew she didn't have the energy. Once the leather was completely removed, he stood in front of her, gently and slowly lifting her by the shoulders, letting her slump against him. "I am going to pull you right over the trunk. Your legs might scrape on the bark a bit, but I suspect that if I let go of you now you'll fall down. Okay?"

Bracing herself, Maddie allowed Theo to pull her by the shoulders. She gasped with relief as her chest was peeled away from the lichen that had soaked up some of the perspiration she'd been producing in unladylike quantities for the past half hour. Dizzy, she was only vaguely aware of the grazing to her skin as her bare legs were manhandled across the wide trunk.

Guiding Maddie onto her back, Theo placed his companion on the rug. Its tartan twill immediately acting as a pleasant balm to the abrasions Tania had inflicted on her backside, and the scratch marks that littered Maddie's back from a multitude of fingernails.

Closing her eyes against the fading sunshine twinkling

and blinking between the leaves of the tree canopy, Maddie allowed her lungs to inflate properly for the first time in ages. She let out a long slow exhalation of air as her breathing became more regular.

"You were very close to making the five minutes without cumming, you know. I was impressed." Theo sat next to her on the woodland floor, soothing the pad of one finger over her sore, blotched, lichen-stained chest. Maddie was only mildly surprised to discover that her rucked and crumpled vest had been removed at some point during the mayhem.

"May I have some more water?"

Theo brought the bottle to her lips and Maddie propped herself up on one elbow. She drank more deeply now that the angle was less awkward, and she was free to disappear behind a tree to relieve herself if necessary.

Wiping excess moisture from her lips, her throat lubricated, Maddie lay back down and spoke in her more customary matter-of-fact manner. "I let myself go for once. I knew I was going to have to lose this one, or you'd disappear before we've had the fun I think we're due. So decided to make the most of it."

Theo shook his head in disbelief and admiration. Here she was, shattered, bruised, grazed, tear stained, soaked in sweat and pussy juice and yet somehow, despite being at the centre of a gang-bang, Maddie really had kept some control. Maddie had simply accepted what was happening and used the situation to her advantage.

"You liked it, didn't you." It wasn't a question.

Now that Theo could see her expression properly again, he saw quite clearly that in granting herself acceptance of the situation, she had let all her physical guards down and savoured every touch.

"Yes. It has been a while since I was used so interestingly."

"Interestingly?" Theo laughed as his hands continued to soothe the swollen breasts, watching in fascination as her nipples swelled and grew beneath his fingers. "You make it sound like some sort of work-related project."

Maddie sighed as she considered how to explain. "For me, every act of sex is a work-related project. I can't help it. I see potential art in everything." Her arms still felt limp and her legs heavy. But each new touch Theo placed upon her tits re-inflamed her body and again Maddie allowed herself the luxury of floating on a sea of pleasure.

Serious, Theo said, "Does that mean you don't have proper relationships?"

Picking her words with care, Maddie said, "Not really – not so far. As Tania's sub I was constantly vulnerable and all my non-commissioned art came out as trapped images. Women at the mercy of others, male slaves in collars and leads, heavy bondage – you get the idea. All consensual, but someone was always under the dominance of someone else." A tighter sigh escaped Maddie's lips as Theo's finger clasped her right nipple and her breath snagged in her throat before she went on. "I got bored with doing only that style of picture. It was at pretty much the same time Tania finally pushed her luck too far."

With his free hand, Theo opened the lid of the wooden box and took out a thin brush. "That's when you decided to go the other way? To be Maddie the dominatrix?"

"Not so much becoming a domme, as letting out my inner control freak. I had learnt how to wait for fulfilment as a submissive. After all, that is sort of the point. I decided to develop the idea and make myself wait for pleasure. Not because I had to, but because I wanted to. Then I began to see the benefits in making others wait...for them and for me."

Theo picked up a leaf and laid it over Maddie's left nipple, while continuing to fiddle with the other one. "Tania said you were already playing the waiting game with men back when you were with her."

"I imagine she did." Maddie's chest was becoming more sensitive by the second, her exhaustion dissolving with every new stroke from the electrician. "We both did it. It was fun and the men in question always discovered it was worth it in the end. Tania was in charge back then. I just did what she said."

Theo carefully unscrewed the top from the black ink. "I can't imagine that. You doing what you're told without questioning it."

"I bet you can't. But that way of life suited me then."

He dipped the brush into the ink and wiped the excess very carefully over the edges of the small glass bottle. "Did you love her?"

"I am not sure I even liked her very much. Tania isn't

the sort of person you love. She is the sort of person that fascinates, and I was hooked on her aura."

Maddie was becoming more and more conscious of her twitching pussy. Keeping her eyes closed, she turned her head towards Theo, knowing she was going to have to concentrate hard to keep up any kind of conversation. She reached out a hand to feel the bulge in his trousers. "Did you cum?"

"No." Theo inched nearer, letting the artist cup more of his denim clad groin in her palm, his length fighting to burst free from its confinement. "It seems your levels of self-control are contagious. Anyway, I wanted to watch you. If I'd cum, I would have lost concentration and missed the show."

"Oh my god! That's it exactly!" Maddie half sat up, opening her eyes in surprise at finding someone who genuinely understood. "That's why I stay controlled. I don't want to miss anything. I have to give myself permission to..." She stopped talking as her eyes fell on the ink brush in Theo's hand. "You have my brush."

Theo clambered to his knees and placed the flat of his hand in the centre of her chest, pushing Maddie gently back on to the rug. "If you remember, you are still supposed to be tied up. I only released you due to good behaviour. I could easily change that."

"And you still intend to continue doing to me, what I was going to do to you?"

"Exactly."

Maddie bit her bottom lip. "And does that include

accompanying me to The Stripped Banana to view the space I have booked?"

Theo climbed astride the artist's legs, the brush poised. "You really were going to invite me along?"

"I said I was."

"You also implied that after we visited the gallery, I wouldn't have to wait any longer to fuck you."

"Yes I did." Maddie fixed her eyes on the end of the brush. A bobble of jet-black ink was gathering at the hovering tip. "I hadn't predicted that you would take matters into your own hands first, though. It rather changes things."

The ink landed against her left nipple. Maddie jumped, yelping as the ink mingled with a small scratch there. Her hands rose defensively at the sting, but she lowered them again as she saw the determined gleam in Theo's eyes.

He inclined his head in approval. "It changes nothing. Unlike you, I haven't climaxed. And what's more, I am still waiting to fuck you." Theo drew the brush in a swift zigzag across her torso. "So, what were you going to write on me?"

Maddie kept her gaze focused on the brush. Suddenly she appreciated how Sara must have felt when she had been waiting for the touch of the chalk or the spatter of paint against her flesh, not knowing for sure where and when the next touch would strike. "That doesn't matter now. Why not write what you want? You have turned the tables after all."

Theo lifted up the front of Maddie's skirt and stared at her pussy. "You are still very wet, Ms. Templeton."

"Tell me something I don't know!" Maddie's dirty,

bark encrusted fingernails dug into the rug beneath her, scrunching the fabric in her palms. "What are you going to write?"

Theo re-dipped the brush in the ink. "I think we should keep this simple." He leant forward. "Keep still, this may sting a bit."

The thick ink, more viscous than it should have been after years of storage, felt wonderfully cool as Theo placed short, letter-shaped strokes around the curve of her right breast. But as his words hit the raw patches of skin, braised by the chafe of the bark, Maddie cried out as if she'd had lemon juice squeezed over her wounds.

"Shhh! You'll have the world and his wife over here, woman. Honestly, I didn't think I'd have to gag you."

"Fuck off! It bloody stings."

"Told you it would. Now stop being a baby – I've almost finished."

Gritting her teeth, looking daggers at Theo, who was using his free hand to stretch the skin of her breast taut so he could write onto it with easy flowing movements, Maddie groaned. The firmness of his touch summoned extra helpings of ardour from between her legs and the stirrings in the pit of her stomach felt like there were strings inside her, pulling together toward yet another climax.

Wiping the brush's excess ink over her stomach, Theo carefully replaced the lid on the glass bottle.

Maddie, who'd been controlling her breathing in an attempt to keep her diaphragm from rising and falling too much and thus smudging Theo's work, relaxed a little against the rug.

"Where is the camera?"

"On my phone. Front pocket of my bag. But what have you written?"

In Theo's hands, the flash of the camera repeatedly lit up the globes of her breasts. Then, standing over the artist, the electrician put the phone safely in his back pocket, undid his zip fly and extracted his heavy cock. Sticky with pre-cum, his was a cock that had been too long deprived. It was with less than a dozen strokes of his workman's grip that Theo promptly released spurt after spurt of his sticky seed all over Maddie's breasts, making the ink run in all directions.

"Now that," he said as he retrieved the mobile and took more photos, "is a work of art."

Staring down at her chest, the cum soaked words he'd written were now completely unreadable. "But what did you write?"

Theo grinned his most devilish smile. "Make me beg ..."

Muddied and bruised, there had been no way that Maddie could have gone to view the gallery in her state of disarray. Common sense prevailed over her anxiety to see the exhibition space, and she retreated home to a hot bath. Agreeing a time with Theo when he could come to be painted, they had left the woods in their own separate vehicles. Tania had also spent her second night away from the studio, and

Maddie revelled in the solitude.

Maddie bathed quickly and grabbed a sandwich to fend off her hunger before going directly to bed, her dreams a complex mixture of humiliation and orgasmic delight.

Towelling her hair dry the following morning, Maddie stood in front of her bedroom mirror and examined the marks that covered her body. Physical proof that she had been the one out of control for once. She was fairly sure she had managed to convince Theo that it had been her choice to let go of her body and savour the moment, even though that was far from the truth. And any lack of face she had sacrificed in front of Jake, Maddie knew she could recover with just one visit to her studio. It was Tania's part in it all that irked most. Maddie had no doubt she would never hear the last of it. She recognised now, far too late, that she hadn't needed Tania's help at all. Sara and Freya were proving more than their worth.

Maddie wasn't sure how she felt about Freya and Sara having been part of Theo's adventure in the woods. It was embarrassing to know that they had seen her on the receiving end of her own techniques. But it wasn't the end of the world, and they had probably learned from what they'd seen.

She sped down the hall toward the stairs, eager to make further changes to her list of exhibits. Two steps up and Maddie froze. There was someone upstairs. A cold frisson of fear flooded her. No one had a key to the front door except her. But the front door hadn't been forced and she was sure the back door had been locked. Creeping back down the hallway as quietly as possible, Maddie, her heart in her throat, tiptoed to the kitchen. No. No one had broken in through the garden. The windows and door were all firmly in place.

That only left one option.

Maddie turned on her heels and darted up the stairs, anger bubbling at her throat. *How dare she!*

Maddie was shouting before she'd even reached the studio door. "Tania! How the fuck did you get in? I changed the locks months ago and I know you don't have a key because ..." Maddie stopped in her tracks and stared at the woman sitting crossed legged on the wooden section of the floor, the cast of Theo's cock in her hands.

"I think you should calm down, Maddie. Such outbursts are so not your style and it would be awful if you were to upset me and I accidently snapped this." Tania flexed the papier-mâché a fraction in her hands.

"What the hell do you want, Tania?" The fact that she didn't have time to remake the sculpture was the only thing that kept her from ripping the cast from Tania's hands. "I assume you made a copy of my keys the other day when I asked you to leave me alone with Sara and Freya."

"I thought it would save you running down the stairs to let me in each time I rang the bell. If I can let myself in and out, then you don't have to stop painting, do you. I was saving you time."

"Bollocks." Maddie crossed her arms. "So, what do you *really* want? And don't give me the "I only want to help" line again. It won't wash, Tania. You have never done anything for anyone else unless it was to your advantage and nothing you have done over the past week has proved me wrong."

Tania's feigned a hurt expression, but Maddie wasn't fooled.

"What...do...you...want?" Extracting the sculpture from between slim fingers, Maddie placed it on her desk, ready to brush a coat of glaze over its surface. "You've already had the fun of having me at your mercy as part of Theo's revenge, so that can't be it."

With a sulky edge to her voice, that she thought cute (but Maddie thought aggravating) Tania said, "If you don't start being nice to me, then I won't model for you anymore."

"No problem. I'll get Sara or Freya to do the threesome scene I'm planning." Maddie noted the jolt of jealousy that sparked in Tania's eyes, as she sat down opposite her ex on the wooden floor. "In fact, when it comes to modelling, it has become clear to me that they are far more skilled and obliging than you are. So if you would like to retrieve your things from where you have thrown them, you can give me the key you made and leave."

The women stared at each other poker-faced, both knowing that neither of them was bluffing. Tania fired her next shot. "I could withdraw my permission for you to use images of me in the exhibition."

"You could, but you won't. You are too vain to pass up the chance to feature in a gallery show."

"Don't be daft, darling. I've been in loads of gallery shows. Missing out on yours won't hurt me."

Unblinking, Maddie fixed on the peppermint stare that equalled her own in stamina. "When you arrived, you told me how much work you'd been getting, and that you'd been featured in countless wonderful shows. So I took the liberty of doing some research. To my surprise I couldn't find any mention of the photographers you've told me so much about, nor of the fashion shoots in which you have supposedly done so well."

"Then you must have been looking in the wrong places." Tania's eyes gave nothing away. But the appearance of a single wrinkle on her forehead told Maddie that her ex-girlfriend was beginning to feel caught out, and that her assumption about Tania's boasts being fake had been well founded. Maddie had no intention of telling Tania that she hadn't had time to keep her own website up to date, let alone take the trouble to hunt down Tania's bogus claims.

"Perhaps I was just unlucky in my search. I would have thought that a 'name'..." – Maddie used her hands to draw invisible speech marks in the air – "...like yours would be easy to find. No matter." She saw the green of her ex's irises darken as she added casually, "I imagine you must be keen to get back to your own home. No doubt the next wave of contracts awaits you there."

Maddie felt a small surge of success as the redhead turned away, the first to break eye contact. Tania spoke with a subtle drop in confidence, detectable only by someone who knew her exceptionally well. "You still need me to help finish the pictures."

"I told you, I have others good enough to help me now."

"I didn't have you down as ungrateful, Maddie."

"Don't bother trying to play the guilt card, Tania. I am very used to all your methods, remember? Including stalking. Something I thought you'd given up. But, as Theo has confirmed, it is a technique you are still gainfully employing."

Tania's face glowered. She had been so convinced she could get Maddie back. Now she was unsure she was even going to get to stay another night. "You have changed."

"You say that with a venom that suggests it is a bad thing. It isn't. I learned a lot from you, Tan. I love the art we made together and I am grateful for that." Maddie stood and made for her chest of drawers. "Perhaps if you'd changed as well things would be different. It seems however that you are just as devious and self-centred as ever."

Tania stayed where she was, as if she was somehow holding the studio hostage by sitting in the middle of the wooden floor. But she was shaken and began to bluster. "If you make me leave now, then I am taking the sculpture and the poster with me. You can't use an image of me without my permission and Theo's cock has my face on it."

Maddie laughed at the absurdity of Tania's last sentence. "No need to sound so pleased with yourself. I know that already."

"And you don't have time to do them again, even if you say you do."

"True again." Maddie took four sets of handcuffs

from the drawer. "Which is why we require a compromise."

Tania eyed the cuffs dangling provocatively from Maddie's fingers. "Compromise?"

Maddie pulled a heavy, unused metal easel from the collection of props in the corner of the studio. The image she had of Theo strapped to it had been so strong in her mind. But art was all about adaptation and suddenly this seemed a far more positive way to proceed.

Placing the heavy metal frame next to Tania, Maddie snapped at her, "Well don't just sit there. Undress, woman."

A multitude of emotions crossed Tania's face. Maddie had no doubt she was wary after her experience on the trolley. Nonetheless, Tania's fingers began to undo her shirt buttons. Peering down her nose at the other woman, Maddie added, "Come on, Tan. I'm on a deadline here."

"What are you planning?"

"You'll see." Maddie took a moment to admire the undeniably glorious naked form before her and then pointed towards the easel.

As Tania turned, Maddie tried to suppress a smile – her ex's rear was undeniably perfect, but Theo preferred her own more padded posterior. She knew it was immature to gloat about that, but she couldn't help it.

Tania moved with more speed than she'd intended, suggesting to Maddie that maybe she wanted to be at her mercy again.

"Perhaps I was mistaken," Maddie said as she positioned Tania with her back pressing against the front of the easel. "It seems that while I have discovered a liking for being in control, you have been similarly blessed with the discovery that you like being at my mercy. A happy co-incidence, wouldn't you say?"

"Rubbish, darling. I'm just helping you out."

Maddie shook her head. Tania had reverted to type already. In an hour this whole thing would be her idea. "Of course you are, Tan. What was I thinking!"

Taking Tania's left arm, Maddie fastened it to the frame of the easel with one of the silk lined, short-chained cuffs. She did the same to her right wrist, before kneeling and repeating the process at each ankle, securing them to the easel's heavy front legs.

Already envisaging the work that she was about to create, Maddie turned her back on Tania and picked up her phone.

"Who are you texting?" Tania's voice was wary.

"None of your business." Finishing her message, Maddie put down her mobile and sat at her desk. "Now, if you would just remain quiet for a while, I must update my exhibition list and make an appointment to visit the gallery."

Chapter Fifteen

The artist worked calmly at her desk, enduring Tania's whines for almost half an hour. Eventually, Maddie got up and placed a board of prepared stretched paper on another easel. "Are you going to shut up so I can start work now?"

"For goodness sake, darling. I've been standing here for ages. I don't get treated this badly by the boys in New York."

"I bet the quite-possibly-non-existent boys in New York have the common sense to gag you first." Maddie fetched a cloth to clean a smudged fingerprint from the corner of the paper. "And if you cannot be quiet, I am going to do just that."

Tania had misunderstood the intent behind the fetching of the cloth, and Maddie was relieved that Tania's suspicion had, for once, made the model heedful of the warning. Maddie eyed her tethered, temporarily silent model critically. Drawing her from the waist down, Maddie began to sketch the outline of Tania's sensuous hips in fast bold strokes against the paper.

As she worked, Maddie saw that Tania's ubiquitous tan was showing signs of needing a top up – its bronzed sheen more likely to have been applied by spray than by the sun-soaked tropical beach she'd claimed it hailed from.

Having stayed quiet for all of two minutes, Tania shrilled, "How can you stand this silence? Why don't you put some music on or something?"

Maddie glared at her model but kept drawing, the sweep of her ecru pastel constructing a pleasing growth of shape on the paper.

"Come on, Mads, I'm bored."

Slamming her pastel down on the easel shelf with a deliberate bang, Maddie hissed, "Tania, I am trying to work! I don't have much time left to get everything done. I still have to frame things, gloss things, package things, suss out the gallery space and work out who the hell to invite to the private viewing – something I should have done at least a week ago and, if you hadn't noticed, I am not interested in your belly-aching."

"If you hadn't tied me up for bloody ages, I could have helped with some of that. I could have sorted your viewing invites for you, I could have..."

In no mood to acknowledge the truth in what Tania said, Maddie ignored her ex's verbal impatience and stormed back to her chest of drawers. Extracting a fiercely large ball gag, she wrenched her ex-lover's jaw wide open, pressed down on her tongue with one finger and stuffed the ball into her mouth. Snapping the gag's elastic straps around the back of

Tania's head, Maddie pinned Tania's ponytail to the back of her neck. "Right. Now perhaps we can have some peace and quiet!"

Concentrating on Tania's arms and shackled wrists, Maddie made sure she left space on the paper for her delicate hands, as well as a couple of extra elements she was determined to add to the image once her helpers arrived.

Forty minutes later, Maddie had done as much of the figure work as she could without the other models. She began to fill in the background of her piece with swirls of cloth-blurred terracotta and cream chalk.

Blanking out the pleading hate in Tania's eyes and the muted whines of the last ten minutes, Maddie sat down at her laptop.

The weight of everything she had to do in preparation for the exhibition's launch in just over a week was beginning to worry her. Arranging the prices, naming her work and sorting out the private viewing invitations were jobs she'd been trying hard not to think about. And there were three emails in her inbox from Marco at The Stripped Banana which remained trepidatiously unanswered.

Making a few new alterations in her battered notebook, the comfort of knowing exactly what she was going to create for the final pieces made Maddie feel a touch calmer.

> *Replacement for <u>piece 4.</u> Tania at the easel (pastel for speed – in progress)*
> *10. Sara – possibly with Theo/Jake (unsure*

~~of medium}~~ Close-up of breast with words
'Make me beg' written on (photograph —
just needs setting in the centre of a circular
mirror)

11. Threesome – Jake(??)/Freya/Sara (Pastel)
– maybe Theo not Jake??

12. Idea – won't write down in case it doesn't
happen!!! – Will make it happen!!! – work
it in pencil and charcoal – close up...

The idea for piece number twelve turned her pussy,
which seemed to be caught in a permanent state of arousal
since her time in the woods, to molten liquid. Her sumptuous
revenge against Theo couldn't come soon enough. Adhering
to her own principals, however, Maddie consigned to wait
until her other work was finished before she savoured that
moment. It would be a fitting finale to the completion of her
gallery pieces.

Trying to pacify her growing arousal, she carefully
took the six pencil-sketched drawings of Tania, Sara and
Freya's faces – as they'd cum together under Tania's guidance
– from a folder on her desk. Wondering where she'd get a
wooden cube the right size, Maddie toyed with the idea of
asking Theo if he could make one for her, but she quickly
dismissed the notion. Just because he was an electrician who
was gifted with his hands (a thought that made her blood flow
faster), didn't mean he was any kind of carpenter.

Scraping back her chair, Maddie headed to her prop

pile. Moving the stacks of chairs and forgotten picture frames bought from various jumble sales, Maddie recovered the circular mirror she intended to use to mount the photograph of her own breast. Automatically her hand rose to her to that place – it was almost as if she could still feel the sweep of the brush and Theo's firm fingers stretching her skin. Her nipple leapt to attention and Maddie found herself having to regulate her rapid pulse with some deep breaths.

The faint tinkle of chains told Maddie that Tania was getting restless. Ignoring her immobile companion, Maddie searched further, discarding various candlesticks, broken lamps and heaps of unidentifiable bric-a-brac. A more determined rattle from Tania's direction sent another jolt of lust through Maddie. She was just about to round on her ex to warn her that she'd never get the seeing-to she craved if she didn't behave, when her eye fell on a dusty, giant dice. Brushing it free of cobwebs, she weighed it in her hands. It was a six-inch cube. She had a vague memory of it belonging to a long-forgotten game of outdoor snakes and ladders.

Taking the cube to her desk, she laid the first picture in place. It was Tania, her expression caught in the full throes of dominating two beautiful women. Maddie glanced over her shoulder. Her ex's current expression couldn't have been in greater contrast to that of the picture. Grinning to herself, Maddie checked the time. The others would be here soon.

Placing the outsized dice next to the folder of pictures, Maddie strode up to the redhead. Ensuring that she had Tania's complete attention, the artist began to strip.

She was only wearing four items of clothing: her jeans, a half open shirt, knickers and bra. Yet Maddie deliberately made their removal as slow as humanly possible, delighting in the knowledge that she was the sole cause of the conspicuously hard nipples and slick pussy on the captured woman before her.

"Do you know, Tania? I really *do* think you could take to this role reversal idea." Maddie stroked the firm chest before her, tickling the tips of the nipples with the ends of her varnish-free nails. "I think that the trolley experience has given you a taste for submission. And, as you won't tell me why you are really here, I must conclude that you simply want to be near me so I can treat you any way I want."

The defiant fire that had previously blazed in Tania's eyes had morphed into an expression of unmistakable pleading. Changing the pressure of her fingertips from teasing strokes to harder pinches, Maddie sent more blood coursing into the tips of her ex's breasts. "You don't seem to be denying this. And yes, I do know you can't speak – but that has never stopped you from making your feelings known before.

"I was trying to explain to Theo the reason for making him wait. I think he got it. In fact," Maddie moved one hand lower, playing it in and around Tania's circular naval. "I may have finally met someone who will give me a close run for my money in the self-control stakes."

A muted whimper came from Tania's direction.

"What's that, Tan? You think you're as good at self-control at he is?" Maddie pushed a single digit up inside the redhead, swiping a thumb over her clit at the same time. The result was instant. Tania bucked in a clatter of chains on metal, her abrupt orgasm almost tipping the easel over.

"I think perhaps that proves that you aren't quite as good at self regulation and control as you think you are."

Maddie helped herself to her favourite vibrator from her collection and, right in front Tania's wide, lust-clouded eyes, she swiftly treated herself to a body sighing, stoically contained climax. Then, as calmly as if she had just relieved an annoying itch, Maddie washed off the vibrator, put it away and replaced her clothes.

Just as Maddie was doing up the last button on her shirt there was a knock at the front door. With a disparaging look at Tania, Maddie told her, "Time to pull yourself together, Tania. We have guests."

Sara, Freya and Theo barely acknowledged the presence of Tania. Jake, however, was instantly mesmerised by the site of a naked, shackled woman in the middle of the room. He nudged Sara while pointing speechlessly to the easel-bound woman, not knowing whether to be surprised, comforted or disturbed by his girlfriend's response of, "Tania probably annoyed Maddie. Don't worry about it."

Jake struggled to avert his gaze from Tania – a figure in total contrast to the woman he'd seen wielding a cane against the artist's backside. Yet, when he did look away, he was assailed by the overload of erotic images that adorned every part of the studio. Sara had warned him what it was like in Maddie's studio, but until now Jake had assumed his partner was exaggerating. Now he saw that, if anything, she had understated the situation.

"Jake?" Maddie's voice cut through his transparent approval of his surroundings. "Are you with us? Sara said you would be okay with helping out as a model. Is that right?"

"Yes. Yes of course. Sorry – this place is amazing!"

"Thanks." Maddie smiled as she examined Jake's physique for the first time. Although he'd been present in the woods, and she'd thoroughly enjoyed the stout ram of his cock in her throat and the scrabble of his fingers through her hair, she hadn't actually seen him properly.

Short, cropped ginger hair topped a squarish face with the type of features that made the artist wander if he played rugby or maybe boxed. Broad shoulders tapered to a stocky chest and trim waist and, thanks to the shorts he wore, she could see muscular legs dotted with a collection of Japanese character tattoos.

Holding his hand tightly, Sara peered up at her lover through her black eyelashes. "You'll love being a model here."

Maddie smiled gratefully at Sara. "Would you like to show Jake the pictures of you and Freya? They're over there." She pointed to the other side of the studio beyond Tania. "Freya, could I trouble you to get the coffee pot brewing? I think we're all going to need all the caffeine we can get to see us through what has to be done. It's so kind of you all to agree to help!"

Surprised to see the redhead, but unsurprised to see

her chained up, Theo's eyes loitered over Tania as he lounged against the doorframe. "So, Miss Templeton, you have clapped your hands and your slaves have come. Where would you like us to start?"

Ignoring Theo's dig, Maddie picked up the selection of chalk pastels she'd been using to draw Tania and spoke to those who were already busy. "You are all wonderful! With your help, I might just get this exhibition in on time!"

"Do you still want me to visit the gallery with you?" Theo asked as he watched the artist begin to draw.

"Yes, but first I need you to help me finish Tania off." Maddie called over to Jake and the girls, "Can you help me a minute, guys?"

Gathering around Tania, Maddie began to issue her instructions. "Freya, could you take out Tania's gag. She's been well behaved, so I'll allow her to relax her jaw for a second. Although…" Maddie aimed her words directly at the tethered woman, "if she makes any more complaints, then it will go back in.

"Jake and Theo, if you could strip off your bottom halves only. Keep your shirts on."

Theo didn't hesitate. But Jake looked imploringly at Sara, who nodded encouragingly at her boyfriend. Bolstered by Sara's encouragement, Jake instantly removed his shorts and boxers, his penis as erect as it had been when Maddie had sucked him off the day before. He really was a big boy. Maddie grinned – he was going to be a pleasure to capture on paper.

A spluttering from behind them told the artist that Tania's mouth was free. "I think Tan might benefit from a sip of that coffee, honey, if you could help her take a drink." As Tania took an undignified slurp of coffee from the mug Freya proffered, Maddie issued further orders. "I would like you boys to stand at either side of the easel. Do stand close. Remember, Tania's reach is restricted."

Theo and Jake moved as one, both hoping they had correctly guessed what Maddie would tell Tania to do next.

They had. "Tania, take hold of their cocks please."

Despite her restraint, the redhead was able to obey without question. Even if her jaw hadn't been stiff from the effects of the gag, this was one order she wasn't going to protest.

As one slim fist wrapped around Jake's length, his sigh echoed around the studio, causing him to blanch with embarrassment. Theo, however, was determined to show Maddie that he had himself firmly under control. He stood silently, with no readable expression on his face.

"Excellent." Maddie stood at her easel and aimed a pastel at the paper. "I'll go as fast as I can boys." Tania increased her grip and the growth of their stiff shafts became more obvious. "Now, no one move."

Maddie worked with swift, bold strokes, loving how the men's cocks were half hidden beneath their shirts, making the view all the more tantalising – the suggestion of sex all the more urgent. Maddie turned to Sara and Freya. "Can you guys check through my emails from The Stripped Banana and make a list of everything that needs doing for the show?"

The chorus of "Yes, Maddie," hastened her hands. She began to darken the members of the two men, while listening to Jake's increasingly heavy breathing as he struggled with where to put his hands.

"Nothing above your groin is going to be in the picture. So if it will make you more comfortable, Jake, you can put your hands behind your back."

Tania cleared her throat. She'd managed to remain quiet for an almost record-breaking amount of time. Now that her jaw was more relaxed, she spoke. "Quite a workforce you have at your fingertips, Maddie."

"Jealous?"

"A little," Tania answered sarcastically.

Maddie's head snapped up in surprise. "I asked if they'd like to help and they all said yes. No one has to be here."

"Except me, because I am tied down."

"Do you want to leave? I am sure Freya or Sara would happily stand in for you."

The other models looked up expectantly from the list of tasks they were creating, each hoping that Tania was about to have one of her tantrums so they could take her place.

"No. I was just saying."

Maddie raised a sceptical eyebrow and went back to her work. The detail required to recreate the men's testicles caused her to slow her pace as she drew – both men fit and hot, but so different from each other. She licked her lips as she smudged in some shadow across Jake's balls, adding a sprinkling of freckles to his lower torso. As she worked, she considered whether she should ask Jake or Theo to form part of the group-sex picture she was determined to do next.

A sharp, unexpected groan from Theo lifted all eyes back to him. Unbidden, Tania was flexing and unflexing her grip on his dick, and specks of pre-cum were gathering at his tip.

Theo looked at Maddie, expecting her to tell Tania to stop. But the artist blithely carried on working, her arm moving faster as she swapped chalk colours yet again.

Tania began to flex both of her hands, and a low whistle of desire escaped Jake's lips.

Maddie shot a quick glance at the redhead, whose face was now full of the familiar challenge of old. The artist said nothing, her face a mask. Things couldn't be working out better.

It was Theo who first raised one hand to Tania's chest, squeezing her right nipple until she yelped with warm discomfort. "You did say we could move anything above our waists, right Maddie?"

"Certainly."

Quick to catch on, Jake grasped Tania's other breast, pinching and kneading it in a hurried rush of localised activity.

Continuing with the loose style of stroke necessitated by the time constraints now upon her, Maddie had soon reached a stage in which only the finer details remained. But she said nothing of her progress as she shadowed and shaded, letting the boys escalate their own desire alongside Tania's.

Maddie knew that Freya and Sara had stopped what they were doing to watch the three at the old metal easel. Still, she kept going, adding as much detail as possible.

Tania's moans had grown into growls. Working as one, the men's free hands snaked up to her face and, on an exchange of glances, they each pushed a single finger between her parted lips.

Sucking as though she was pleasing a duo of mini dicks, the slurp of Tania's pseudo blowjob became the only noise in the room apart from the rough scrape of Maddie's drawing.

Jake, his face turned towards Sara, began to sigh heavily with each manipulation of Tania's hand.

Theo took a step forwards so that his cock was encased more firmly, earning him a stern glare from Maddie. She'd finished sketching in his superb length and was adding just a few final touches to Jake's wood.

A few moments later and Maddie had completed all the work which required the models' presence. In normal circumstances she would have refined, polished and gone over every section of the piece until it was flawless. Today, she was simply going to have to make a positive feature out of her lack of perfection.

Laying down the cream and beige pastels, Maddie could feel the tension in the studio twanging from wall to wall. Her timing was spot on. Without a word of explanation to anyone, Maddie carried the picture and easel a safe distance from Tania, Jake and Theo. Although the men were free to move, neither of them did so as Tania increased the suction of her lips on their fingers, and her grip on their shafts.

From behind them, Maddie retrieved her video camera and affixed it to a tall tripod.

She manhandled a sturdy coffee table from the edge of her props pile and placed it about two metres from the end of the bed. Then, she carefully lifted the tripod onto the table, so that any shots the camera took would give an almost aerial perspective. Aware that all eyes were now on her, Maddie relished the tense silence that had descended on the studio, certain that each member of the assembled gathering wondered if they would be included in the next piece of artwork.

Once she was happy with the camera's position, Maddie jumped down from the coffee table and gestured for Freya and Sara to come forward.

The young models moved with lightening speed. Maddie had to hide her smile at their keenness as she told them to remove all their clothes and sit on either side of the bed. Then, like some sort of pornographic choreographer, Maddie turned her attention to the half-dressed men. "I would like you both to come away from Tania now.

Theo, I would like you to come stand beside me. And Jake, if you would be so kind as to slip off your top and sit down next to Freya. No touching."

Again the movement towards the bed was swift. Theo, his eyes shining, stood next to the artist. A note of reluctance crept into his voice as he asked, "Shall I get dressed?"

Maddie dragged the coffee table a bit further back so that all three bodies could be seen clearly through the lens of the camera. "If you would, then we can get to the gallery."

Theo, his cock rock hard, stared at the ménage Maddie was creating. "So, I'm still waiting then?"

"I promised you some fun *after* the viewing."

He struggled to calm his penis enough to tuck it back inside his trousers. "And you always do what you promise, right?"

"Always."

Tania, who was beginning to feel totally forgotten, coughed pointedly. "Am I a permanent fixture here now, darling? Or were you thinking of setting me free sometime this week!"

"Impatient again, Tania?" Maddie undid the handcuffs at her ex's ankles.

"Of course I'm bloody impatient! I've been shackled for fucking ages and it doesn't take an artist to know that the picture you're orchestrating on the bed is unbalanced. You need a fourth person."

Maddie made a few further adjustments to her video equipment before slipping into her shoes. Only then did she release Tania's chained wrists from the second set of cuffs. Maddie picked up her notebook and handbag before concurring with Tania. "We are in agreement for once." She pointed to the bed and the redhead quickly filled the vacant spot next to Sara.

Tossing a condom to Jake, Maddie addressed them all. "Theo and I are going to the gallery. While we are gone I had intended for Jake, Sara and Freya to have a threesome. However, as much as it pains me to say, I tend to agree with Tania: a fourth person will add an extra dimension. Threesomes are a bit predictable these days. I will record this foursome and then, with your permission, I'd like to paint a still frame from the resulting film. Do I have permission from all four of you to use this image?"

The chorus of agreement was instant.

Maddie turned her attention to Jake. His breath was shallow and his chest had become blotchy with excitement. It was quite clear he was very close to cumming. "Will you be able to handle all three of them?" Maddie asked him.

He shrugged, but the sheen in his eyes told her he was very much up for finding out.

"Excellent," Maddie switched the camera on. "If you could stop the recording once you're done, please. Enjoy."

She didn't look back as the bed exploded into an orgy of hands and mouths. Theo, however, his erection chaffing uncomfortably within his boxers said, "I thought I was going to be part of the threesome? You don't break your promises – remember?"

"Do you see three people on the bed?"

"Well, no."

"There you are then." Maddie fished the tube map from her pocket. "Which way is best to Hoxton from here?"

Theo shook his head in disbelief. "You're a bloody

robot, woman. Don't you want to watch what they're doing to each other? I know I do!"

Maddie linked her arm through his as she tugged Theo away from the house and down the street towards the nearest tube station. "Of course I do. And I have every intention of watching it with you."

Chapter Sixteen

Despite the photographs of the gallery she'd seen online, The Stripped Banana had been completely refurbished and it was nothing like Maddie had imagined. She was actually glad that she'd torn herself away from her role as orgy supervisor to come and see the gallery for herself.

Soothed by the subtle tones of a piano concerto emitting from discreet speakers, Maddie stood in the very centre of the square white-walled room. The space, currently empty after the recent redecoration, had been partitioned into a more interesting layout with the use of white, wooden dividers. While expertly positioned spotlights blazed against the bare walls and floor.

"I'm impressed, Marco." Maddie let the acclimatised air waft over her as she accepted a cool glass of lemonade from the proprietor. "It has changed so much since I visited two years ago.

"Two years! Did we not please you, Mademoiselle?" Marco feigned mock disappointment.

"Of course. I've just been very busy – somehow the days fly by."

The dapper Frenchman smiled mischievously, his expressive eyebrows wiggling suggestively. "I am sure, in your particular genre of art, there are more interesting diversions then we have in here!"

Theo had remained silent up until that point. But he couldn't help adding, "You can say that again," which caused Marco's eyebrows to rise even higher.

Maddie walked to the opposite wall and ran her palm over the fresh, crisp paint. "I can see my board of Sara standing here, can't you, Theo?"

"Yes, but the light will need adjusting." Theo diverted his attention to Marco. "Do you set the lights yourself, or do you pay someone to do them for you?"

"I tend to do it. Although sometimes my guests," he gestured towards Maddie as an example, "bring in their own experts."

Theo leaned against the wall and crossed his arms before saying to Maddie, "I suppose that's the real reason you wanted me along, Miss Templeton. A freebie from your tame electrician?"

Maddie crossed her arms in defiance. Theo's electrician status hadn't crossed her mind as being useful here. "Not at all, Theo. I just valued your opinion on where to place the work."

"Is that so?" Far from convinced, Theo began to pace the room, his eyes rising to the ceiling and then running over the floor and walls. As though he was projecting and predicting possible shadows.

Marco, detecting an undercurrent he wanted no part of, carried on with his tour and pointed to the wooden dividers. "We have other partitions available, should you wish to use something else. There is a selection of different coloured and patterned screens in the store cupboard at the back, along with various sculpture-tables, chairs, stools and so on. Would you like to see?"

Having already visualised where most of the work would hang on the walls, Maddie nodded. "That would be great. I have a couple of small sculptures to show."

Marco rubbed his hands with the glee of a man anticipating a treat. "Do you have a list of your work for me?"

Maddie frowned. "I'm sorry, Marco, I haven't yet. But all the work is in the finishing-off stage."

Theo bit back the temptation to reveal the precise truth of her progress.

"To be honest," the artist continued, "I find naming my art harder than producing it!" Noting the disappointment on Marco's face, Maddie kept talking. "I can, however, tell you exactly what I have and how big everything is."

Mollified, Marco went to the reception desk and tapped a few keys on the computer. "Excellent. Talk me through them."

Leaving Maddie to describe the ten complete pieces, and to exaggerate wildly about the work she hadn't even started, Theo went to investigate the storeroom. It wasn't the dark, overfilled cubbyhole he'd imagined. It was a light and airy room, almost as big as the gallery itself. When Marco said it contained most of the things they might need, he wasn't kidding. The difficulty would be in choosing the right props from the ample selection. Too few and the gallery could seem barren; while too many would distract the eye from Maddie's artwork.

Deciding that he might as well be helpful as long as he was there, Theo began searching through a load of Victorian-style screens at the back of cupboard. The white boards currently on the gallery floor were okay, and they'd be perfect for a display of landscapes or seascapes. But to Theo they just didn't feel right for Maddie's sensual work.

Immediately rejecting three partitions as too patterned and busy on the eye, Theo came to a dark bronze screen, featuring a series of semi-faded photographs. This piece appeared to be genuinely old rather than mock-antique. Pulling it into a better light, he smiled. It was perfect. At least, he thought it was. Maddie, of course, might disagree.

Leaving the screen where it was, Theo began to extract various different tables from a stash on the opposite side of the room. Some were white, some wooden, some painted bronze, gold or silver, – Maddie could choose a couple of them to display her wooden cube and sculpture. At the thought of the papier-mâché construction, Theo felt an insurgence of the erection that had been so cruelly stuffed into his trousers before he left the studio.

Distracting himself as best he could, he diverted his attention to a box containing picture fastenings of all shapes and sizes. He wondered how Maddie was getting on blagging her way through her project list. He would have gone to check, but there was no way he could re-join them in the gallery until his cock was under control.

Moments later, Theo could hear Marco's over-enthusiastic voice getting nearer. As the door to the prop room opened, Theo retreated to the back of the store, sliding himself out of sight between the divider he had selected and those he was sure were unsuitable.

"Voilà, Mademoiselle Templeton," Marco spoke proudly. "I see from your list that you'll need two tables or display stools, a mirror hook, a selection of hooks for framed pictures, hooks for unframed canvas, and possibly some sort of stand for your cube. Will the cube be something that our guests can pick up?"

"Yes. I am hoping that by the time its protective covering is dry, it will be strong enough to withstand being rolled like a dice."

Marco rubbed his hands in excitement. "What a wonderful idea. How would you feel about placing it on a gaming table?" He immediately headed for the collection of tables. "It seems as though your colleague has already sorted a few items out for you." Marco lifted a tall, thin, bronze table to one side so he could reach those still stacked against the wall. "I must say, he has good taste."

Maddie surveyed the room. She was sure Theo must be in here, but she could see no sign of him. *Surely he hasn't disappeared through the back door of the gallery and left me to it? Unless, of course, he is convinced I've asked him here under false pretences?*

"Success!" Marco dragged out a folded poker table. "What do you think? A throw of your erotic dice on the baize might whet the appetite for a purchase or two from your show?"

"That's brilliant, Marco. Thank you!"

"And that, of course, brings us to prices. Not only do I require a list of names for your work by this time tomorrow, I also require a list of prices, plus VAT, and my small commission, évidemment."

"No problem. I can certainly have all that emailed to you by lunchtime tomorrow." Maddie spoke with far more conviction than she felt, concealing her need to conclude her business here and get back to work on the foursome picture as soon as possible.

"Then we are not too far off schedule!" Marco spoke triumphantly. "If you would excuse me, I will go and check on the order of champagne and canapés for your opening night – oh, that's the other thing. If you have any guests to add to my list, can you email me their names as well?"

"That, I can do now." Relieved that she finally had some genuinely accurate information, Maddie extracted her notebook from her bag, found the page of names she'd written down, ripped it from the book and passed the list to Marco.

"Superb!" The little Frenchman paused just as he was about to leave. "Oh, did I say, I usually like the artists to do something extra for the opening night? An exclusive special. A spectacle that is only available on that one night. Sometimes it is for sale, sometimes it's not – I'll leave that to you, okay?. Surprise me!"

Marco strode spryly out of the storeroom and back into the gallery. Maddie watched the door shut behind him, her pulse hammering in her throat. *Another piece! Another one – and something extra special.* Her mind raced. The final piece she'd planned could be incredible if she did it properly. But at the end of the day it was simply another picture – however kinky it might be. And she had a feeling that wasn't the sort of spectacle Marco had in mind, judging by the playful twinkle in his eye.

Possibility after possibility passed through Maddie's fertile mind as she stood there, stock-still, her eyes focused on nothing in particular. Each idea that ran through her head was dismissed as swiftly as the one preceding it.

"Well, that's something I never thought I'd see. Madeline Templeton in a state of genuine panic." Theo spoke softly as he stepped out from behind the partition, aware that his sudden re-emergence might make her jump.

Without even trying to conceal her concern, Maddie shrugged as an unfamiliar sense of defeat crept along her spine. "What will I do? There is no time left to do anything else."

He cupped her face in his hands and Theo found himself forgiving her for bringing him here just to look at lights – if that had ever been her intention. With Maddie, Theo was beginning to understand, you only ever got half the story. "So," he stroked her blonde locks and kissed the tip of her nose tenderly. "You are a human being, after all."

Maddie allowed herself to be swaddled in Theo's arms. She inhaled the scent of his sun-heated shirt, finding it strangely comforting. *What the hell was happening to her, allowing someone else to see her weakness!* "I mean it Theo. I have bluffed my way through with Marco – but I still have two items to create. As we speak, Sara, Freya, Tanya and Jake are in the process of setting the scene for the eleventh piece. But it will still take ages to draw – even at my mega-quick pace. I have to think of names, prices, frame everything, finish it all off. In normal circumstances it would take weeks to do that. In the meantime, I'm still not earning any money and my unusual method of payment isn't going to work on the bank manager, is it!"

"Maddie," Theo took her hand and pulled her gently toward the screen he'd selected. "While we're here, let's concentrate on what we can sort out. Then, once we have done that, we can sort the rest. Okay?"

The artist looked up at him. "We?"

"Is that okay?" He held her closer, feeling the heat of her chest against his as he added, "You don't have to do *everything* alone you know."

A furrow appeared on the artist's brow. The controlled and sensible side of Maddie was having trouble fighting its way back to the surface. "You're right. I should sort out one thing at a time."

Disregarding the fact Maddie had said "I" instead of "we", Theo pointed to the Victorian screen. "This could work. You may disagree, of course. But I thought the

sculpture would look good in front of it on that bronze table."
He pointed to the high, narrow, square-topped table that
Marco had moved to the edge of the organised clutter. "It
could stand against the screen. What do you think?"

Examining the screen first, Maddie ran her hand
gently over it. "It's fabulous." The heavy, tarnished boards,
hinged into three flexible sides, had once depicted photographs
of Victorian erotica. But as she looked more closely, Maddie
saw that wasn't quite true. The women on the screen were
not just posed erotically – this was pure pornography. Peering
closer still, she saw that it was the same scene – showing a
woman's face between another female's open legs – repeated
over and over again. "This hasn't just faded over time. It has
actually been scratched out. This damage is deliberate."

Theo tilted the screen so that he could see the
provocative vision more clearly. "What do you think?" He
stood the divider up straight, bringing his arms around
Maddie's waist as they examined it. "A jealous wife broke
into her husband's study, found this and went at it with some
sandpaper, or maybe even a knife?"

Maddie laughed. "Could well be. I wonder if she
discovered anything else?"

"Like him and his secretary at it over a desk?"

"A *very* personal assistant!" Maddie felt the tension in
her unknot as she leant back against Theo's chest.

"Do you think they had such things as PAs back
then?" he pondered.

"The rich had whatever they wanted, just like they

do now."

"Don't knock the wealthy, Maddie. We need them to buy your art!"

Again, letting the word "we" pass unchallenged, Maddie couldn't help but agree. "That's true!" She turned to face him. "Do you think Marco would let us take this into the gallery and see it in place? If I used the bronze table and this bronze-ish screen, then I could use bronze-tinted frames ..." Her words faded into thought for a second before Maddie added, "And maybe I could add some bronze colour here and there to my work. Yes, I think..."

She disappeared into her own musings again, her keen eyes roaming the storeroom as if in search of something else.

The closeness of Maddie's body was testing the endurance of Theo's impatient cock to breaking point. He felt her relax into him as she surveyed the contents of the room.

"I think all that sounds excellent," he said softly.

Undoing the middle buttons of her shirt, Theo slipped a hand into the gap. "But before we fiddle with tables and picture hooks, I have a much better idea. Well, a more immediate plan, anyway."

Her hand rose to slap his away, but Maddie stopped herself. This felt good, why not go with it? After all, she'd promised him some erotic entertainment once they'd visited the gallery and it may well be the perfect sweetener for what she had planned for him later... *I don't have to give him everything he's been waiting for.*

The artist's mind gave a sigh of relief. As long as she was still thinking about how to give him only a fraction of what he wanted, perhaps she wasn't completely out of control when it came to this man, after all. Anyway, she was feeling particularly horny – the overtly sexual image on the partition had surprised and intrigued her. Now, erotic and artistic possibilities consumed Maddie's thoughts as she let the electrician caress her skin. *I could use Theo and this screen together*, she mused. *But should Theo be the one to use it, or should it be one of the others?*

Reaching behind him, Theo grabbed the back of a chair and dragged it closer. Then, making short work of Maddie's lower garments, he pushed her onto the seat, spreading her knees in the process. "I have been made to wait to receive many things from you, Maddie Templeton. And one of the things I need to know – *really* need to know – is what you taste like. It has even kept me awake at night."

Maddie was about to speak but Theo silenced her. "No. For once you are just going to sit back. Imagine how those lovely ladies felt as they posed for that screen. Think about how they tasted – I know you love the taste of pussy on your tongue. I wonder if Sara and Freya feel the same way when they part their legs for you."

Her eyes skittered from image to image. Studying each identical print, her senses were heightened by the touch of Theo's thick fingers caressing her inner thighs His breath tickled the strip of hair around her sex as his face drew steadily closer. Focusing on the screen, she saw that the destruction against it had certainly been intended. Now, at least a hundred-years later, that damage had become art in its own right, despite the frenzied and very specific nature of the original attack.

The touch of Theo's finger to the very tip of her clit sent a sudden exhalation of air shooting from Maddie's lips. Her gaze stayed fixed on the scarred photographs, and she found herself imagining the story behind the image. *Had the two women been in love, or where they just models enjoying their work?* Theo began to blow directly onto her slit and Maddie had to grip the sides of the chair to stop her hips from rising toward him to hurry the pace.

As his tongue arrived at the outer swell of her pout, Maddie sighed softly. Focusing on the fair-haired woman pictured all over the screen, Maddie saw that her bottom was placed on a similarly styled chair to the one Maddie was currently perched on. Her head was thrown back, her face an expression of ecstasy far too accurate to have been faked.

The artist wondered if the screen's progenitor had been the photographer himself. Or perhaps it was the master of the house, who'd ignored the camera operator and sat with his cock in his hand; bringing himself off as the women, probably prostitutes, performed for him. Maddie's eyes closed as her pondering mingled with the sensations rising in her body. Her stomach experienced the familiar internal tug which told her she was much closer to climax than she ought to have been in such a short time.

The dart of Theo's tongue continued to avoid the tip of her engorging clit, and Maddie couldn't prevent the moan of longing that escaped her as she unconsciously eased herself forward on the chair, making access easier for Theo's lips.

"I'm surprised at your impatience, Miss Templeton," Theo breathed the words against the sodden slick of her pussy. "Tell me what you see on the screen."

Gathering her concentration, Maddie began to speak as if in slow motion. She was vaguely aware that she had never had a tongue job like this – and he'd only just begun. Their time together in the shower had evidently been a mere warm-up session for Theo's agile mouth. Her voice was far more breathless than she would have liked. "A blonde woman with huge breasts is leaning back in a chair."

Theo swiped the tip of his tongue over her clit, nearly making Maddie bounce out of the chair. "And?"

Her throat was suddenly desperate for moisture as she went on. "I think her chest must have been on the receiving end of some attention before the picture was taken…it seems darker in places than it should be. I bet the marks were red in real life."

Theo licked her again. "Excellent. Tell me why you think they're red."

"I think she was whipped. There are stripes on her."

Again he licked her with one firm stroke. Every electron of her being travelled to her core, leaving Maddie light headed. She began to speak faster, her lust-addled brain learning that Theo didn't touch her while he was listening to her, but she'd always receive a lick after she'd described something.

"I don't think she cried out though, I think she liked it." Theo kissed her directly on her clit and Maddie's next words came out in strangled gasps. "Although...perhaps...she begged...maybe she begged her master...to cane her while the woman...you can't see her face from that angle..."

Somehow Maddie kept talking, not wanting the gaps between her sentences to be longer than they had to be. "I think the other woman had black hair...I bet her lips were painted rouge red. I think...that was...the favoured...colour of the...day..."

Maddie was punctuating each word with a gasp now as Theo pushed in closer, his fingers inside her, stretching her, so he could angle his tongue up and into her.

"She...was...covered...in cunt...honey...and..."

The artist cried out, getting no further with her imagined description as Theo thrust two heavy fingers up inside her while nibbling her clit with a riot of sharp kisses. Any previous attention to her nether regions had been a mere flirtation compared to this and Maddie shocked herself by calling out to him. "Please, Theo. Harder."

A rush of success hit Theo and he responded readily, moving his hand back and forth at a faster harder pace, tasting victory over the woman who'd prevaricated for so long. With a guttural yell, Maddie thrust her hips as far forward as they could go, feeling as if she had locked every muscle against him. She couldn't move as jolt after jolt of climax rioted through her, allowing nothing but the muscles of her cunt and the tender skin of her clit to react. No other part of her existed.

Then, as quickly as it had begun, the sensation of delicious immobility died away. Theo lowered her slackening body to the floor, his face shining with the juice of her pussy.

As he lay next to her, Maddie lapped his chin clean – tasting herself as she did so – while Theo's fingers extracted a squashed condom packet from his pocket.

"Oh no you don't, honey." Maddie glowered at him, grabbing his wrists and moving them away from his groin. As she prevented Theo from opening his flies, she found she was fighting herself even more strongly than she was struggling against him.

Not willing to give in, Theo took hold of Maddie's shoulders and rolled her onto her back so that he was lying directly above of her. His weight was crushing, but his hands were gentle as he smoothed her hair. "You promised, Maddie!"

Maddie's head swam as his physical heat suffused through her. Her body felt that it had earned every touch; and the feeling of being squashed beneath her handsome companion, whose hands now squeezed her breasts, was undeniably sensual. It was simple, rough and beautiful – and so far, still chaste – on his part, at least.

Theo raised himself up and again tried to free his cock from his denims, his face glowing with the taste of certain victory. A victory which Maddie again delayed. "No.

Not yet."

"And yet everything about you tells me you don't want to wait any longer, either." Theo remained sitting over her knees, determined to push her to the point where she would finally relent and let him do what he felt like he'd been waiting forever to do. "Play with your tits."

It was an order she was happy to follow, and she wrenched off her upper garments with one swift tug. Her fingertips tripped and tweaked over her nipples, doling out caresses of pleasure and pinches of pain in equal measure. Theo's fingers swirled over her indulgent clit, and the appreciation on his face as the two of them forced her pleasure hastened Maddie's second climax of the afternoon.

Abruptly, Theo dropped his body back down onto hers. With a muffled groan that was almost lost in her shoulder, he convulsed over her, releasing a long delayed orgasm of his own within the confines of his boxers. His physical relief was palpable. But embarrassment and annoyance rose within him as he realised that, once again, Maddie had managed to get her kicks while he had failed to get inside her.

He said nothing, though. Too humiliated at the mess he'd made of himself, he sat astride her, still and quiet, as she recovered from her own orgasms.

The only noise in the storeroom was the rise and fall of heavy breathing. At first Maddie thought it was Theo. But, as she floated back down to the reality of the situation, she realised that the sound wasn't coming from above her, but from beside her.

"Impressive." In appreciation of what he'd just witnessed, Marco's accent was lilting more towards his native French than it had earlier. "A little vanilla for my taste, but satisfying to watch."

Not entirely surprised to see their uninvited guest, Theo only hoped that Marco hadn't noticed his own lack of control. In an attempt to divert attention from himself, Theo gestured to Maddie's breasts. "Magnificent, isn't she?"

"She is indeed. You have a gorgeous mademoiselle." Marco bowed respectfully, his trousers revealing a bulge he was obviously keen to address before he suffered the same fate as Theo. "No doubt you were contemplating the extra special feature for your show, Miss Templeton, and got carried away, non?"

Maddie's shock at being watched subsided with his appreciation of her her naked form. "Indeed Marco. I have many ideas and I am convinced you will appreciate them. I suggest you state clearly on your preview invitations that the evening will be for over 18s only, and not for those easily offended. It is, after all, an exhibition of eroticism and sensuality."

♦ ♦ ♦ ♦

"Why won't you tell me?"

They'd helped a buoyant Marco set up the gallery with the few items of furniture that they'd chosen, but Theo was becoming increasingly aggravated with Maddie. It was bad enough that she'd got one over on him – again. But at least his underwear had managed to conceal most of his spontaneous ejaculation. He was sure Maddie knew he'd lost control, but she'd granted him at least some pride by saying nothing about it.

He'd resisted the temptation to quiz her about what she was planning for the exhibition's "special feature" whilst they'd been in the gallery. But the minute they'd left the blessedly cool air of The Stripped Banana and stepped out into the early evening sunshine, Theo hadn't been able to contain his curiosity. His enquiry, however, was met with a blank expression and the denial that she'd thought of anything at all.

Theo was sure Maddie was concealing the truth, and he wasn't sure he liked why that might be.

"I won't tell you," she repeated for the third time as they reached Maddie's street. "Because I haven't decided yet."

"But you *have* had an idea," Theo persisted. "I can tell by the look on your face."

Maddie was beginning to lose patience. She turned on him, snapping, "I have a couple of ideas, actually. But I don't know how practical they are and quite frankly I could do with sorting them out in my head before I discuss them with anyone else. In fact," Maddie fished her phone from her pocket and dialled a number, "I need to query something with Marco."

Theo was about to ask what it was she was querying, but Marco had already picked up Maddie's call.

"Hi Marco, Maddie here. I've been thinking about

the special feature you requested. Can I ask, exactly how big is the item we discussed earlier?"

Theo listened closely, trying hard to overhear Marco at the other end as Maddie responded to him. "And do you have anything similar in a larger size?"

There was a pause as Maddie listened, a smile taking over her serious expression. "Perfect. Is it available for the opening night? Yes? In that case, perhaps you could have it placed on the floor, in the middle of the far wall. I will fill you in with the details later this evening – if that's okay with you?"

Unable to catch the Frenchman's response, Theo assumed he must have agreed. Maddie finished her call, placed her phone back in her pocket and walked briskly towards home without any further reference to the conversation at all.

Chapter Seventeen

For three days Maddie hardly slept. The phone had remained unanswered, the doorbell ignored and her email inbox could have reached endemic proportions and she'd never have known.

Everything that could be ready was ready. She had named her work (even those pieces not yet started) and handed over a list of prices to Marco, whose commission had hiked those prices higher still. Maddie was sure no one would pay such vast sums for her work, but she didn't have any energy left to argue with the Frenchman.

The pictures that required frames were now nestled in bronzed, wooden box-frames; and the canvases that were to remain frameless were highly glossed. The sculpture of Theo's manhood was rock-solid and shone with countless layers of varnish. Its edges had been trimmed and smoothed and the faces of Maddie's models gleamed at her through its shiny coat. It was only the fear of breaking it that had stopped Maddie from trying it out as an impromptu sex toy.

All the completed pieces were lined up along the edge of the far wall and swathed in multiple layers of bubble wrap. Maddie couldn't help but feel proud of what she had achieved in such a short amount of time. Proud too of her models, who'd helped her get this far. She only hoped their nerve would hold for her remaining works.

Mild concern prickled at Maddie. She hadn't contacted her assistants for three days. Although she was confident that Freya, Sara and Jake would come back and help her finish off, Maddie hadn't a clue how Tania would react if asked to return, having been frog-marched out of the flat three days ago.

As for Theo...Maddie sighed. She should never have let him make her cum like that in the gallery. But she certainly couldn't deny how amazing he'd made her feel. She was also well aware that he'd cum in his trousers, a fact that gave her an extra kick of gratification whenever she thought of it. She just hoped she still had enough control over Theo. To help lure him back, she'd promised to allow him to choose which freeze-frame she should draw from the foursome film.

Staring hard at her notebook, Maddie concentrated on the three things that remained unfinished. The foursome had to be drawn and then piece twelve needed charcoaling. Then, finally, she would be able to have some real fun in sorting out her preview feature of "live art" – a feature which she hoped to make somewhat interactive. It only remained to be seen who would be its main focus. Maddie smiled to herself. As long as everyone came to help, she was fairly sure she could manipulate the day's outcome precisely to her specification.

The doorbell rang. The courier Marco had arranged to collect her finished work had arrived. Doing her best not to cluck around her pieces like a mother hen attending to her chicks, Maddie watched her art disappear into the van. Then, with only thirty hours until the preview show and a solemn promise to Marco that all the artwork, apart from the special feature, would be in place by six o'clock the following evening, Maddie joined the courier in his cab and headed towards The Stripped Banana to set up as much of her exhibition as she could.

◆ ◆ ◆ ◆

Maddie couldn't believe what she saw when she returned to the studio and peered inside. The day before, she'd finally admitted that she would need some help if this exhibition was actually going to happen. She'd texted her models to ask for some last minute assistance but, having received no response, she hadn't held out much hope. Even her most dedicated supporters had their own lives and responsibilities, so she hadn't been sure if anyone would turn up at all.

In fact, as Maddie pushed open her front door, she was hit with the hum of industry. Freya was cleaning paintbrushes. Sara was stacking up the detritus from the floor that Maddie had thrown off the trolley ages ago. And Jake was sorting through the chaos of props Maddie had thrown everywhere in her hunt for frames. But most surprising of all was Tania, who was sitting at the laptop, typing as if her life depended on it.

It was a few seconds before the busy workforce noticed they were being watched.

Freya blushed as though she'd been caught doing something she shouldn't. "Tan... Tania let us in, Maddie. Hope this is okay. We thought that, with time being tight, if we got here before you did, we could all help a little bit. We didn't want to take over or anything but..."

The gratitude evident on Maddie's face stopped Freya's words in mid flow. "Thank you guys! Really. This is wonderful."

As Maddie dumped her bag to the floor and wandered across to where Tania was sitting at her desk, Jake stopped what he was doing and poured her a mug of coffee. "How is the gallery looking so far?"

"It's great. I'm sorry I wasn't here when you arrived. It took much longer than I thought it would with Marco."

The absence of Theo felt like a void in the room but Maddie reminded herself she had been prepared for this eventuality. And she had a contingency plan. She just hoped she wouldn't have to use it. However good it would be, Maddie reluctantly had to admit to herself that, without Theo, it wouldn't quite be the same.

Maddie picked up the list of erotic words and phrases she'd left by her computer to format into poster size. Tania had taken over this job, and Maddie scanned her eyes down the bold italic font on the paper:

Lick me
Deep throat
Delicious
Sensuous
Whip me...

Maddie felt the first true moment of affection for her ex since she'd invited her back into her life. "This is great. I really appreciate this, Tan."

Tania positively preened at Maddie's praise. "Good job I had a two keys cut, isn't it? Since you so vigorously took the other one off me." Before giving a Maddie a chance to reply, Tania asked what no one else dared to. "So, no Theo, then?"

Before Maddie could give the response she'd rehearsed for just such a question, the echo of footsteps on the studio stairs came to her rescue.

He didn't look at her. He didn't say anything and the expression on his face quite clearly told everyone he thought himself mad to be there. Yet he was there, leaning against the doorframe with the air of someone who had no intention of moving for the foreseeable future.

"Theo, are you a coffee drinker too?" Jake broke the charged and expectant erotic tension by waving an empty mug in Theo's direction.

"Thanks." Theo wasn't sure if he was pleased for Maddie, or annoyed at her. She'd gotten him here on the promise of going through the orgy video together. But now the studio was full of other people. He knew he was being childish, but Theo began to wonder if there was any point in him turning up at all. *Is it time to accept I'm never going to screw her? Over the past few days I've seen her naked, given her indelible orgasms (if I do say so myself), tied her up, fucked her ex and seen more erotic images than I ever have before. Would it really matter if I left now? She probably wouldn't notice anyway.*

Drinking his scalding coffee, Theo watched the bustle of activity around him with a new level of confusion. All three of the women in the room had been made to wait for sex with Maddie at some point. On top of that, Tania had been belittled and humiliated – even if she had both deserved and enjoyed it. Theo couldn't see why she still hung around, unless she had her own private agenda. Women like her usually did.

Freya was there because it was sort of her job, and Sara stayed because Jake stayed. He didn't need to wonder why Jake was there: this place equalled sex. Jake liked sex. *QED.*

The electrician took a deep breath and shook his head, his eyes studying each person in the room in turn. *And it isn't just them is it? I am here because I thought I would see some porn and have more sex. Which is why they are here too. We are hooked. All of us.* It was a sobering thought.

Maddie had told him that she understood her clients' thought processes and what made their fantasies tick – it was why she was so good at her job, she'd said. Theo hadn't really believed her at the time. He did now. *Every time we think we have the upper hand, Maddie simply changes the way of looking at things, so we're left feeling as if she was in control of the final outcome all along. Even in the woods she somehow got me thinking she'd allowed it all to happen, yet she can't possibly have known what I'd planned. I wasn't even sure until Tania turned up.*

His eyes fell on Tania. *Perhaps she was only being helpful so that she could worm her way back into Maddie's affections.* If that was the case, he was sure that it wouldn't work.

The printer under the desk whirred into life. Tania bent down to pull out a neat stack of paper. Placing it in front of Maddie with a confident smile, she said, "The list you wanted. It'll be better on the parchment paper but how's this as a rough draft?"

"Thanks, Tan. It's perfect. I'm grateful."

"Bloody hell – are you?" Tania mocked sarcastic surprise as she swapped the printer paper for the higher quality stuff.

"Don't push your luck, Tania." Maddie was stern, but her eyes flashed with humour as she spoke.

Walking over to Jake, Maddie nodded thoughtfully. "I am going to need two more frames with a bronze tint to them. Once we have them, I can crack on with choosing the right size paper to draw on. I really must hurry now."

Jake began to rifle through the neatly stacked collection. "I saw a few, I think – just depends on sizes." Systematically he pulled out four frames of varying shapes that had a bit of bronze to them.

Maddie homed in on one straight away. "This would do for the final drawing." Dashing across the room, the air of urgent industry displayed by her unexpected helpers lent wings to her feet. The simple wooden frame had been sprayed a soft matte bronze, and she held it over the prepared, but still blank, paper.

"That's perfect. Right." She put the frame to one side, heading for her easel while Jake continued to hunt.

In the meantime Sara had begun to make the dishevelled bed and Freya was sweeping the studio floor, while Tania tapped away at the laptop. The camera that had been used to film the foursome was still in position at the end of the bed. Theo, still loitering in the doorway, continued to observe in silence, convinced that Maddie had forgotten he was even there. He'd been seconds away from walking back down the stairs and out of the door, but Theo now found his dick stirring at the thought of being the first person to watch the camera's playback. *It's a job that needs doing. So, as everyone else is busy, I'd better do it.*

Freeing the camera from the tripod, Theo sat on the end of the newly made bed and began to familiarise himself with the machine's functions, before locating the playback button. It was only a minute before he gasped louder than he'd intended and Maddie's head turned towards him with a frosty glint in her eyes. "I thought I was the impatient one?"

The ice in her tone was not lost on the others, who busied themselves further, trying to ignore the fact that the convivial atmosphere in the room had suddenly turned sub-zero.

"I am helping like the others, who it seems rather

relished the task you set them when we went to visit Marco. No wonder they are charring so hard for you right now. They probably want permission to do it again. There is no way they would do it without your approval, is there? Even though they could. Permission for them to have sex together is not yours to grant – and yet somehow it is, isn't it Maddie?"

Everyone had come to a stop.

Maddie's face revealed nothing as she looked at Theo. Only a few days ago he had given her the best orgasm she'd had in a very long time. She knew she'd been distant on their journey home from the gallery, but she'd had a hell of a lot to think about. If he couldn't cope with that, then he was no better than Tania. It was one thing to get one over on her in the woods, to belittle her, albeit in a sexually gratifying way, in front of her friends – and the gallery experience had been incredible without question. But in her studio, she ruled. It was time to get her plans back on track and show Theo exactly what she had been making him wait for.

Pushing her shoulders back, Maddie announced in a firm voice, "If there is anybody here who doesn't want to be here, then you are free to leave."

No one moved.

"That includes you, Theo." Her dark eyes issued a clear ultimatum: leave now and that's it, or stay and I promise you the next best thing to heaven – which might be hell – but it'll still be worth it.

Damn. She's done it again. Twisted control back to herself. Theo didn't move, but folded his arms defiantly. "And if I leave, will you get the last piece of artwork done in time?"

"I will have to change it a fraction but I am sure someone will stand in for you." Maddie folded her own arms, copying his body language almost exactly. "In fact, why don't we change things a little anyway?"

"Change things?" The now familiar spike of erotic uncertainty Maddie engendered in him began to play at Theo's groin.

"Yes, because these good people…" She gestured to the silent group behind her, "have worked so hard, I can now see the wood for the trees – if you will excuse the pertinent analogy."

Images of Maddie tied to the tree trunk flashed through Theo's mind, just as she had intended them to.

"And, as the expression on your face showed as you perused my film, there are some good stills to draw from the foursome. So why don't we sort them out as I promised and then I can crack on with the final piece – well, piece twelve, anyway?"

"You said you and I would be viewing the film together." Theo couldn't stop himself sounding like a petulant child.

"We will. Right now. I didn't say we would be alone in the room when we did so."

"I hate you."

Freya and Sara drew in a joint gasp at the force behind Theo's words, while Tania merely laughed and Jake looked perplexed.

"I know you do, Theo." Maddie sensed that at long last, after days of being overwhelmed by work and confused by the feelings she hadn't expected to have towards Theo, she was fully back in the saddle. Now she knew precisely what to do to get all the works for her exhibition completed in the coming hours – including the additional feature that Marco had sprung on her.

Tania broke the tension. "You know what? I think we all deserve a bit of a party."

Maddie and Theo stared at her as if she was mad.

"Come on, guys, we've all worked really hard. I know there is loads still to do, but if you two don't loosen up a bit, it isn't going to get done." Tania looked from Theo to Maddie. "You don't have to be so surprised. I'm not a selfish cow all the time, you know."

Maddie whistled slowly through her teeth. "Sorry, Tania, of course you're not. But I really don't have time for a party. It's half five already. In fact I can't even imagine that I'll be getting any sleep tonight. A takeaway and a bottle or two of wine might not be a bad idea, though."

Tania beamed. "Great, I'll sort it. Come on, Jake. You can help me carry it all. Chinese okay for everyone?"

As Tania and Jake disappeared into the cool evening air, Sara and Freya descended the stairs to the kitchen to find a few plates and glasses, leaving Maddie and Theo where they had been standing, staring at each other.

"Show me." Maddie gestured to the camera in the electrician's hands.

Angry at how much he wanted to do what Maddie asked and confused at how easily she had reduced him to the wrong-footed person he now was, Theo stalked to the end of the bed and sat down. Flicking the video onto rewind for a moment, he paused the footage and passed it to Maddie, who'd sat down next to him.

The two-inch square viewer had framed an intriguing image. Theo had chosen well. "How much of the film did you see before I interrupted you?"

"Only a few minutes worth. That screen shot sort of shouted out at me."

"You have a very artistic eye, Theo."

"So I'm told."

Maddie regarded Theo shrewdly. "Who told you that, then?"

"My art teacher in High School. I did quite well."

Keeping her eyes on the image, her brain working out how to reproduce something so complex in as short a time as possible, Maddie responded, "And yet you are an electrician not an artist?"

"I wanted to be able to pay the rent."

"Very wise." Maddie gestured around her: "I can only afford to live here through an extreme stroke of good luck."

"You sleep with your landlord?"

"Amazingly, no." Maddie didn't rise to his dig. "My landlord was a nice old man and I used to help with his shopping, clean his house, cook him the odd meal when his carer couldn't make it. He had no family and he left me all this in his will."

Theo wasn't sure whether to believe her or not. "You're kidding?"

"Is it so hard to accept that I am quite a nice person, really?"

He was quiet for a while, before saying, "Sometimes it is."

Maddie laughed. "Fair enough."

Standing up, she carried the camera over to the window and stared at the viewing screen. Theo really had picked well.

Pressing a few buttons on the camera, Maddie saved the chosen image to its own file. She then placed the camera back on the tripod, and Theo was surprised to see the film burst into life on the whitewashed wall as Maddie set the camera to projector mode.

"I promised you we would see the whole film, Theo. Would you still like to, or are you fed up with me now? You can leave if you wish?"

Maddie's softer tone was not lost on Theo. "You know that I want to see it. But what's in it for you?"

"Apart from the pleasure of watching your body react while you watch it, you mean?"

Theo couldn't prevent a smile. "You are such a voyeur, Miss Templeton."

"I have never denied that." She pulled the curtains to darken the room and then arranged a few chairs to form a makeshift cinema. Sitting down, Maddie said, "Join me?"

Hating himself for doing so, Theo got up and crossed to the chair beside her. The evidence of his arousal had been all too clear from the moment she'd spotted him watching the film without her. There was no point in being coy about it now.

"No Theo, you should have the best seat in the house. I think you should sit in that chair." Maddie pointed to the wooden seat directly in front of her.

Wondering what on earth she was up to now, when she really didn't have time to waste, Theo protested. "You won't be able to see as well if I sit there.

"I will see just fine. Don't you worry about me."

Theo felt on guard and yet curious as to what physical excesses she was going to put him through. Despite himself, he could hardly wait. Although he was certain he would have to do just that. "Aren't you going to make me wait for the others to get here before we start?"

"No. They were there. They know what happened. Anyway, if I am not mistaken, and I rarely am in these cases, Jake and Tania will be fucking in a secluded doorway on the way to the restaurant; and the distinct lack of clinking cutlery from downstairs makes me think that Sara and Freya are similarly preoccupied in my kitchen."

"These were all normal people before you got your hands on them." Theo had meant it as an accusation, but it came out as a statement of fact.

"They still are. They are now just sexually honest, normal people. As are you." Maddie took the camera's remote control from her pocket. Pressing play, she sat directly behind Theo. Moving her chair so that she could sit with both her arms folded around his waist, her hands settled themselves on his denim covered bulge as the film flashed silently into life.

It began just as Theo remembered. Jake, Tania, Freya and Sara had not spent long sitting on the sides of the bed. Before the second frame of the film, Jake had pinned Freya down on the middle of the duvet. Face up, her hands pulled over her head by Tania, the blonde was the joyous victim of a mouth at each breast and a tongue between her parted legs within the first minute of the show.

Maddie was very conscious of the wetness seeping into her knickers as she watched, reminding her of how sodden she'd been when Theo had pinned her down on the hard gallery floor. She wondered if Theo was thinking the same thing, as she felt his cock leap within his boxers beneath the presence of her hands.

Freya's onscreen body jacked against her assailants and Theo found his imagination more than adequately compensating for the lack of erotic murmurings. Freya was rolled to the side and Sara took her place. This time Jake's heavy penis took centre stage as he crouched over his girlfriend's face, teasing her open lips with his shaft as she frantically tried to lift her head up to engulf him. Her efforts were thwarted by Tania, who was holding Sara's neck while she tweaked her breasts. At the same time Freya played at dipping a finger or two into Sara's honey and licking the gleaming syrup from her fingertips, a vision of heavenly approval on her angelic face.

Maddie pressed pause. "That's the one, then." She crushed the flesh beneath her palms harder, causing Theo to bite back a groan. "The way Jake's cock is just hovering at the lips while Tania's hand forces Sara down, her hips rising as Freya teases her centre...it's the ultimate in foreplay. I don't know how Sara didn't go mad with it all. Every part of her is being stimulated at the same time, yet none of it is enough to tip her over. Clever. They are quite a team, don't you agree?"

Theo couldn't agree. He couldn't say anything for a moment. All his concentration was focused on not cumming in his clothes for a second time.

Maddie started the film again. "Don't you think that Jake is holding himself together well? I thought he'd have cum all over the girls by now."

More jealous of the other man than he could ever have previously comprehended, Theo said nothing.

The scene had changed. Tania had been placed on all fours in the middle of the bed. Freya was kissing her as if her life depended on it, while Sara had crawled beneath the redhead – sucking at her hanging breasts as if she were a starving lamb suckling from its mother. Maddie suspected Jake was fucking her anus with his finger, but she couldn't entirely see due to the angle of the camera.

Theo's breathing was becoming more laboured. His hands were still holding the sides of his chair and his bottom hadn't so much as wriggled. His dick, however, felt as if it might explode from the stress of its confinement at any moment.

Maddie's chest felt heavy and tight. To ease her discomfort, she undid the bra beneath her shirt with one hand, keeping her other hand firmly in place.

The scene on the wall changed yet again with the collapse of Tania into a squirming mass on the bed. Jake had flipped the redhead over and was sitting across her belly. Pulling Sara towards him, so that she was also using Tania as a seat, Jake kissed his girlfriend passionately. Freya, just visible behind them, lowered her pussy over Tania's head. Her pale face was a contorted image of ecstasy, as the older model licked her to heaven.

With the silent Freya's pretty face still contorted in evident bliss, the scrape of the front door opening and the thump of shoes heading up the stairs diverted Maddie's attention away from the film. But not Theo's. He couldn't have torn his eyes away if his life had depended on it.

"Woah!" Jake let out a whistle as his eyes met the wall on which his ass could now be seen moving up and down, his dick thrusting in and out of Tania, while Sara licked Tania's clit and Freya remained resolutely seated on her face.

Dumping the food, wine, plates and glasses on the table, the models sat wordlessly in the vacant chairs to see the remainder of the movie.

Giving the newcomers a few minutes to watch the film uninterrupted, Maddie then disturbed their concentration. "Jake, I hate to be a pain, but I wonder if you could do me a favour?"

Without adjusting the direction of his eyes, not quite able to believe that it was him being projected onto the wall, Jake said, "Sure."

"I have to get on with some work. Could you take over here a minute please?"

Theo's shoulders and back stiffened. "What do you mean let him take over? What do you mean you have to work?"

"Don't be such a prude, Theo! You know damn well I have to keep drawing, and the pressure from Jake's hands will feel wonderful. It's him or no one. And the film stops now."

Maddie's challenge in front of the others was a masterstroke and Theo knew it. No way could he refuse and the glazed look on Jake's face – mesmerised by the screen and probably still high from his illicit fuck with Tania – told Theo that he would do anything as long as he could keep watching.

"Place your hands here please, Jake. Press hard. You are not to move them. He is to get no relief until I say so."

Theo bit back the protest forming in his throat. It would have been a pointless waste of breath. Besides, he wanted to find out exactly how Maddie planned this to end.

Keeping her hands in place until Jake's palms were on top, Maddie stepped away, leaving the larger more calloused male hands where hers had been. She smiled at the unmistakable gulp that left Theo's throat as his cock spasmed without his permission beneath the masculine touch.

Leaving the others entranced, their appetites sharpening – although not necessarily for food – Maddie took the containers back downstairs and placed them in the oven to keep warm. Then, retrieving a flashlight from the cupboard under the sink and pocketing a box of matches, she went back upstairs.

Not one of her models had moved. Judging by the way Sara was fucking Jake on the screen, and the manner in which Tania and Freya were going at each other over the top of them, the pre-recorded ménage was almost at an end. It was time to act.

Maddie tiptoed to the sink unit and turned on her kettle and her ancient toaster at the same time. There was a pop and, as always happened when she used her toaster at the same time as another appliance, all the lights tripped out and the studio plunged into darkness. "Oh damn!" she feigned. "Oh god, Theo. It's the lights. Can you do something?"

Theo hadn't even noticed and it was only when Maddie used her remote to pause the film that he realised that everyone was staring at him expectantly. "What?"

"All the bloody lights have gone off. How am I supposed to paint with no light? Can you take a look, honey?"

Staring down at the hands in his lap, Theo felt dizzy and unsettled. He shouldn't be that hard just because Jake was touching him.

"Theo. Please?" Maddie was calling to him beseechingly and he stood up with a feeling of resignation.

"It's just your circuit breaker Maddie, honestly." Theo headed to the cupboard where he'd located the fuse box on his very first trip to the studio. "Can I borrow the flashlight?"

Maddie, who was already lighting candles and placing them on saucers, passed the flashlight to Theo. Opening the door for him, Maddie waited until the electrician had one foot inside the coat cupboard before asking him, "Did you like a man holding your cock through your trousers?"

The question took him by surprise. "I preferred you doing it."

"But you didn't mind Jake doing it?"

His face coloured. "It was okay."

"That's good, because I want to draw you and Jake together for picture number twelve."

"What? How do you mean?"

"I want to draw him teasing your ass."

Theo's throat had dried. He asked the next question carefully. "Teasing my ass with what?"

"His dick of course." Maddie smiled sweetly through the half-light. "You already know how good the heaviness of his hands feels. His dick feels even better, I promise. I should know – you got him to put it in my mouth. Now I thought it only fair that I return the favour. I don't see why I should be the only one who gets a reward, do you?

"I tell you what, Theo, why don't you think it over while you are sorting the fuses?" And with that, the artist pushed Theo inside the small space and shut the door. "Jake, honey, just stand with your back to the door will you." Maddie raised her voice so that Theo would be able to hear her. "Theo, the cupboard door opens from the outside. You can come out when you agree to let me draw you boys together.

You'd like that wouldn't you, Jake?"

The ginger-haired man smiled towards Sara, who signalled vehemently to her boyfriend that it was okay with her. "Oh yes," Jake answered forthrightly. "Theo has a nice bum – I'd be happy to fill it."

"I bet you'd like to suck his cock too, wouldn't you?"

"Oh yes, I certainly would."

Chapter Eighteen

◆ ◆ ◆ ◆

Theo banged hard on the inside of the cupboard door. He probably could have broken it down with enough attempts, but Jake was a big guy and the door didn't budge. Swearing as he shone the beam of light onto the fuse box and easily reconnected the circuit, Theo rested against the back of the door, bent his knees and slid to the floor.

This woman was the giddy limit. Theo had nothing against men having sex with men and the male form had never repulsed him. He'd positively delighted in seeing Jake in the film working his fit body over the three women. If he'd been given the chance, Theo would have had no problem striping off next to him and joining in the action. But he'd never been drawn to actually having sex with men himself. And being next to another male, butt naked and playing with a woman, was a world away from screwing one. Theo banged his fists against his knees. *How naive have I become!? How did I not see this coming? Maddie had included female-only pictures within the pieces for her exhibition. It's blindingly obvious that she'd want a picture of gay male sex as well.*

A crescendo of moans from outside indicated that at

least two of the remaining models were amusing themselves while they waited for Theo to make his mind up. *So, I'm waiting again, then*. A thud against the other side of door told him that Jake wasn't necessarily on guard alone now and Theo wondered which of the women was being rutted against that huge cock – a cock that Maddie fully intended to draw poking at the entrance to his anus. His stomach felt tight and his penis stirred, despite his misgivings.

He didn't need to close his eyes to be bombarded with imagery of what might be going on without him, not to mention what Maddie intended to happen later. She seemed more and more like some sort of grand puppeteer pulling all the strings while her puppets danced to her tune. A prick-teasing Pied Piper.

The memory of Jake's hands as they'd pressed against his cock grew stronger and Theo had to fight the temptation to slip a hand into his trousers to stroke himself off. He didn't want to give Maddie the satisfaction of making him clean up the sticky mess on the cupboard floor when she eventually gave in and opened the door.

But what if she doesn't give in? Theo had a feeling that Maddie was capable of leaving him where he was for an awful lot longer than he could face being in a dark confined space without food, water or, more urgently, sex.

Standing at her easel, drawing the foursome scene, Maddie's hand swept across the paper. She'd adopted an abstract, cubist style which was not only faster to do, but somehow extremely erotic as it lent more to the imagination. Maddie had already pencilled an outline by the time Sara and Jake had finished their abrupt coupling against the door. She could only guess how arousing it must have sounded to Theo, as Jake's backside rammed against the cupboard in time to the pumping of his girlfriends hips.

The aroma of the Chinese food wafting up the stairs was becoming more enticing by the minute. Her stomach rumbling, Maddie called to Tania and Freya, who had just finished coating two more frames with bronze spray paint. "Shall we grab dinner now?"

Downing tools straight away, Freya washed her sticky, paint-spattered hands and asked, "You want it all up here?"

"Please. And a glass of wine each. I'm gasping. I think we have all deserved a little something – just one though. We're all going to need our wits about us."

Asking more shyly, Freya added, "Do I bring anything for Theo?"

Speaking loudly to make sure that Theo could hear her, Maddie said, "Bring a plate and a drink for Theo. But he may not actually get any food or wine if he doesn't stop being childish and ask to be let out soon."

The banging against the door had stopped and all Theo could hear was the faint murmur of chatting and the occasional scrape of cutlery on plates. The scrumptious smell of the spicy food was torturing his stomach, just as much as the desperate need to have someone stroke him off was torturing his dick.

He'd had enough of this, but he'd be dammed if he would give Maddie the satisfaction of shouting for his freedom. So, pulling his mobile from his pocket, he began to text.

> Theo: Send the girls away and I will
> pose – only pose – with Jake for u.
> Deal?

Maddie's reply came remarkably fast and for a moment Theo wondered if she had already considered that he might want to negotiate by phone message.

> Maddie: Is ur dick still hard?

Theo sighed as his groin twitched in response. *Why can't she just answer a direct question!*

> Theo: U know it is. Do we have a deal?
> Maddie: U were going to fuck me over
> ur van in the rain, remember?

The electrician's mouth went from dry to desiccated as he recalled their past text conversations.

> Theo: YES. Deal?
> Maddie: Remember going commando
> for me?
> Theo: Do we have a DEAL?

His dick was seriously beginning to hurt within the confines of his clothes and Theo began to wish he was going commando right now. Yet he was certain that, if he so much as undid the zip of his fly, he was in danger of losing the final vestiges of control.

> Maddie: Do u remember I promised to tie u up and lick ur butt?

Theo froze. She'd used the word "promise" in her text. *Maddie claims she always keeps her promises – eventually. Did she always have tonight in mind? Did she trip the switch on purpose to get me in the cupboard and out of the way for a while?*

Suddenly Theo could see where this messaged conversation was going. He remembered very well indeed the text exchange she was referring to. The idea of Maddie tying him down and spanking him had been one of the hardest to shift over the past few weeks. Was that how she was proposing to stage the picture with Jake? Him tied up against her bed, Jake poking at his butt with his tool? Sweat broke out on Theo's forehead and palms. He gripped his mobile harder, his fingers almost digging through the screen. Not trusting himself to answer wisely, Theo refrained from replying, the ache in his body battling harder against his pride with every passing second.

He bent his head over his knees and found himself staring at a pair of trainers Maddie had haphazardly thrown onto the floor. They were tatty and covered in a light sheen of dust and mud. His increasingly lust-addled mind knew he'd seen them somewhere before. *Where?* If he could just concentrate on where he'd seen them before, then perhaps he could distract himself enough to forget that he wanted to feel Maddie's hands on his body – or somebody's hands. Anybody's hands.

The edge of the phone began to cut into Theo's palms. He could see Maddie's bare feet in the trainers, her slim ankles leading up to her shapely legs. Pressing his eyes shut, Theo found his thoughts making things worse rather than better, as he was subsumed by a vision of Maddie over the tree trunk, trainers scuffing into the woodland floor beneath her. *How could I have forgotten those trainers, even for a minute?*

Theo was consumed by his determination not to beg for freedom and it was a while before he registered the total lack of noise coming from beyond the cupboard. *Perhaps Maddie has done what I asked? Perhaps we do have a deal? Where is Jake? Has she ordered him to sit quietly somewhere? Is Jake even still there? Maybe she was just winding me up and has no intention of painting me with Jake at all?*

Pressing the side of his head to the door, his ears straining for any sound, Theo lifted the phone, unclenching it from his hot fist. No fresh message from Maddie awaited his attention. He contemplated sending one, but it all seemed so pointless. The chances of her replying to a direct question were slim.

Theo peered down at himself with a mild feeling of disgust. *How the hell has she done this to me?* A few short weeks ago he was happy go lucky Theo with a string of short, casual and mutually respectful flings behind him. If a girl had gotten too heavy, he'd simply let her down as gently as he could and walked away. Then he'd visited Maddie's studio and everything had changed. And now, for a reason Theo wasn't sure he properly comprehended, he was shut in a cupboard, like a naughty schoolboy, in the home of a Machiavellian woman, allowed out only if he played nicely with another boy!

The electrician felt his penis stir again within his clothes. In normal circumstances a wait this long for satisfaction would have killed off even the strongest erection. These, however, were not normal circumstances and Theo was as solid as ever. For what felt like the hundredth time since he'd met Maddie, Theo came to a decision. A final decision. A decision he was determined to stick to this time. It was time to stop hiding from whatever Maddie was promising him. After everything she had put him through, he was going to fuck her if it was the last thing he did. And to achieve that, he would just have to put up with whatever she had planned tonight.

Standing up in the confined space, holding onto the wall for support, Theo wasn't sure he could walk with any dignity on leaving the cupboard. Yet, there was still no noise from outside and he wondered how he would get out if there was no one to open the door for him. Extinguishing a trickle of panic that threatened to get the better of him, Theo exhaled slowly. He was sure he could cope with anything Maddie could throw at him. He would make the most of whatever sexual indulgence was offered and then, when it was done, he would leave. There was no reason their paths would cross again.

Theo reached for the handle on the cupboard door, certain it would be locked fast. But the handle turned easily and the door simply pushed open. And without Jake in the way, it was no contest. Trying to shake off this additional, if minor, humiliation and wondering how long he'd been able to simply walk out of the coat store, Theo looked around. He blinked as his eyes adjusted to the dim light of the room. Despite the fact he had reactivated the electricity some time ago, the room was still bathed in flickering candlelight. The daylight had faded, but the candles made enough light for him to see by. So he left the lights off as he went to look for the others.

The quiet was almost deafening as he searched for signs of life. The curtains in the open windows billowed inwards in the evening breeze. Leftovers from the takeaway were abandoned on the table and a solitary glass of wine stood in the very centre of the debris. He drank down the clear chilled liquid, the coolness and the alcohol bolstering his spirits.

Surveying the room, Theo pointlessly wandered around both halves of the studio. There was no one there. No one sat on the bed, or the sofa, or the floor. No one was propped at Maddie's desk and no one was standing at the sink or by the door.

Where the hell... Then Theo noticed that, not only was

no one there, but Maddie's easel wasn't there either.

Unease crept over him. Wherever the easel was, he was sure he'd find Maddie, but what about everyone else? *Has she sent everyone away and taken her work downstairs? Why leave the candles burning?* For the first time in what felt like hours, his erection subsided slightly. As anxiety took over, his cock went from painfully rock hard to merely solid.

They had to be downstairs. Theo considered heading for the front door and leaving. But then he'd never get what he'd spent all this time waiting for. *What if something bad has happened? What if all this isn't one of Maddie's games and they are all in trouble?*

Walking down the stairs one step at a time, his sweaty hand slipping on the banister, Theo listened hard.

By the time he'd reached the ground floor of the terrace, all he'd heard was the occasional car passing and the chatter of the odd pedestrian as they walked past Maddie's home. No voices could be heard anywhere in the house. In fact, the quiet had become positively spooky.

The short hall that led to the kitchen, the bathroom on the right and the lounge on the left, were also devoid of life. Speculation that Maddie might be in the shower edged his cock back towards rock status. It occurred to Theo as he skulked through the hallway that, before he'd met Maddie, he had loved his endless imagination. His ability to recall every detail of every sexual encounter had afforded him effortless fantasy fodder. But now it was like a constant torture, a continual rubbing of salt into the wounds of frustration and unfulfillment . Even when he thought he *had* got what he craved, Maddie moved the goalposts and he found he'd gotten only what she'd wanted him to get, and no more.

The bathroom was empty and so was the kitchen. The backdoor closed and the early evening was fading into night. The gloam of the summer sky cast the small yard into shadow. That left the living room.

With his fingers on the handle of the door, Theo paused. Was there a faint scratching coming from within, or was he imagining it? Breathing slowly through his nose, he turned the round handle and, as quietly as possible, so as not to either startle or annoy whoever was inside, Theo took one pace into the room.

"You took your time."

Maddie was standing in the centre of her lounge, drawing at her easel as if her career depended on it which, Theo thought, it probably did.

"Well come in then." She spoke as though she had been merely hanging around for him to get home from work. "What do you think? Does this do justice to the scene you chose?"

Peering around the room, hunting for other signs of life, Theo moved his attention to the pencil-drawing on the easel. The longer he looked, the more he could see the filmic foursome emerge from the square lines and shapes she'd etched onto the paper. It was exquisite, clever and very hot.

"Well?" Maddie appeared genuinely concerned. "If you don't think it works, you must say. I'd rather put forward fewer pictures than a dud one."

"It's amazing." Theo felt even more wrong-footed than ever. He'd been built up for something and once again he'd been left hanging. "Where are the others?"

"Waiting for you, of course."

That hadn't been the answer he'd expected and Theo's pulse began to race again as he searched her closed expression for any indication of what she meant.

"Where? I've been everywhere." Theo found he couldn't take his eyes from the picture as Maddie shaded in the suggestion of shape around Tania's breasts – not that you'd know it was Tania – but the form was most certainly female and she was most certainly enjoying everything that was happening to her.

Maddie's eyes remained on her picture, her face a vision of concentration. Theo wasn't sure what to do. Did he stay with her, or was he supposed to go and hunt down the others, wherever they were?

As the silence between them grew, punctuated only by Maddie's pencil against the board, Theo felt increasingly restless and unsure of himself.

At last, after an eternity of non-communication, Maddie said, "I think that will do for now. My arm needs a rest and," she looked down her nose at his dick, "it seems that you need some relief from your current condition."

Ashamed with himself for not even attempting to deny it and privately questioning why he hadn't simply grabbed Maddie from behind and thrown her onto the sofa,

Theo continued to stare at the artist like a rabbit trapped in headlights. He didn't want to admit that he wanted to see what she had planned. And he wasn't remotely ready to admit that he was prepared to go as far as she could take him – Jake or no Jake.

"Come here." Taking hold of Theo's top, Maddie yanked it off and proceeded to remove all his other garments, except for his dark grey boxer shorts.

The artist smiled as she regarded the tip of his cock sticking desperately out of the top of the elastic waistband. Its head shone with pre-cum. If she really had finally found a man who could hold himself in check as long as she could, now was when she'd find out.

Opening the canvas bag that sat on the end of the sofa, Maddie peered thoughtfully at the selection of restraints within. At this point in the game, she'd intended to have Theo securely shackled and restricted. But now, as she ran her eyes over his hard torso, firm butt, strong arms and legs and barely concealed shaft, Maddie wondered if she needed anything else at all to enhance his appearance. Would it perhaps be more of a challenge if he was able, but forbidden, to move during the next half hour?

With only a faint sense of regret that she wasn't about to see him in neon purple handcuffs, she closed the bag, and hoisted it over her shoulder – just in case she changed her mind later. "Follow me please, Theo."

Theo, who at the very least had been expecting to be attached to a collar and leash, like some sort of slave about to receive punishment, felt an element of relief. Yet, he was still almost naked, with an erection that no amount of clothing would hide, and he was probably about to be made a spectacle of. To his horror, he found he no longer cared, as long as he could cum – and soon.

As they walked back up the stairs, the sounds of life coming from above were unmistakeable. Theo, unsure if he would even receive an answer, couldn't help but ask, "Where did they come from? I looked everywhere?"

"Apparently you didn't."

"But I did! I…"

Taking pity on Theo, who'd begun to look genuinely panicked, Maddie relented. "I asked them to hide from you. Just a little experiment. I wanted to see how you'd react to being abandoned. And you've proved to be a most interesting test subject."

Without waiting for Theo's inevitable response of, "But why?" Maddie strode into the middle of her studio and loomed over the group of four sitting together on the wooden part of the floor. Before them sat a dice.

To Theo's relief, the models were all in their underwear as well. But the presence of the dice unnerved him.

Seeing Theo's gaze fix upon the wooden cube rather than on the semi-naked women, Maddie knew she would be foolish to waste time grandstanding. He had already gleaned the significance of the dice and she mentally thanked Marco for giving her the idea.

"Ladies and Gentlemen. As you all now know, not

only must I draw one final picture for the exhibition, but I must also display one additional 'special' feature. A work of art which is not necessarily for sale, but will encourage those visiting the private view to make a purchase – rather than just get their rocks off looking at the pictures."

Maddie picked up the nearest candle and let its light fall onto the dice as she crouched before it. "I confess I was at a loss as to what to do. But Marco and Theo here prompted an idea. After a hurried conversation with Marco, we agreed I would provide a living piece of art. My problem is, I can't decide which one of you will feature in this extra work."

The atmosphere in the room thickened with expectation as the weight of Maddie's words sank in. A living work of art. As one, the artist's five guests had a single thought: *that means one of us on show in public – probably naked.*

"I won't insult your intelligence by explaining what that might mean, as I can see from your faces that you've all worked it out. The question you have to ask yourselves is, are you prepared for that person to be you? If you don't want to feature as the final exhibit, then you can go now. No one will think any less of you. You can leave with my sincere thanks for helping me so much, and of course you will be invited to the gallery's private view as a special guest." The artist surveyed the wide-eyed faces, jutting nipples, and stiff cocks before her. "You have one minute to decide."

No one moved, each hoping that they could enjoy what was to come; but hoping too, not to be the chosen one. The sixty seconds ticked by at lightning speed, while at the same time seeming to take an eternity. Finally, Maddie nodded with satisfaction. "Thank you. I hoped you would all stay."

Pulling forward the stool which Sara had lent over on her very first visit to the studio, Maddie placed a candle on its small round seat. "So, let us begin the selection process."

As she spoke, she set up her metal easel – the same easel, in fact, that had provided the backdrop for a shackled Tania and two throbbing cocks. Maddie placed some paper and a selection of charcoals against the backboard.

"Should we turn some lights on?" Theo suggested tentatively. "I've fixed the short circuit."

"And I thank you. But how I light the room is up to me, Theo."

Theo tried to not to appear too hurt by the artist's clipped tone, as she dragged a few more seats forward and placed candles upon them, bathing her easel in enough light to work by.

"While we determine who gets to be the feature piece, I will crack on with picture number twelve. So, Jake, Theo, come here please."

Jake stood quickly but clumsily, his cock nearly as desperate and needy as Theo's. Theo however, moved slowly. He knew what Maddie wanted from him, but he still wasn't sure how he felt about it. *Of course you know how you feel*, he told himself as he looked at Jake's cock. *You just don't want to admit it. You are a fool Theo Hunter. A bloody fool – and she knows it. In fact she knows what you want better than you do – she told you she did – and you should have believed her.*

Moving the candle from the stool, Maddie patted its seat invitingly. "Over here please, Theo. Arms down the sides, with your butt over the seat and feet on the floor. Oh, and shorts off now, please."

With his pulse thudding up and down in his throat, and his stomach doing cartwheels, Theo did as he was told.

Determined to be as still as possible so as to get this over with quickly, Theo gripped the bottom of the stool's front legs and steeled himself as he awaited the touch of Jake's shaft against his butt.

Theo held his breath as he heard the scrape of a low wooden crate manoeuvred into position for Jake to stand on. Jake's boxer shorts whispered against his thighs as he slipped them off – though Theo was as unable to determine whether it was a whisper of seduction or malice. Only when Theo felt the tip of the meaty cock probing at the notch of his anus did he exhale. A noise which did nothing to justify the conflict of emotions within him. In that one breath, Theo had accepted that he wanted Jake to push harder against him. He was sure Maddie knew it as well and he cursed himself for being so damn predictable.

"Excellent, thank you boys." Maddie's charcoal was already travelling across the paper, and the sound of it filled the room. "Right girls, could you bring some of the candles closer? Set them on some chairs around the boys. I want this piece to look as if it's bathed in candle light."

Finally satisfied with the ambient light, Maddie announced it was time to discover which of her companions would feature in the gallery preview. "Stand up, please, girls and come to this side."

The groan that came from Jake was echoed by Theo. By moving the women to the other side of the easel, neither of the men could see what was about to happen. Their rampant imaginations had instantly sent extra shots of need directly to their shafts. Jake had begun to push his engorged member harder against Theo who, without even thinking about it, lifted his rear a fraction to meet it.

Maddie's reaction was immediate as she leapt out from behind her work and slapped Theo hard across his rump. The slap was not entirely unexpected, but Theo still yelped as Maddie hissed, "You do not move while you are modelling, Theo. I thought you had at least learned *that* from me!"

Managing to turn his groan of frustrated lust into a soft grunt of defiance, Theo bit his tongue as Maddie added in a silkier tone, "I know how badly you want Jake to screw you, honey. But I think I may have mentioned how important it is to be patient and wait until the moment is just right."

Chapter Nineteen

Her attention firmly focused on the easel, Maddie addressed the other women without so much as a glance in their direction.

"Freya, you are number one. Sara, you are number two. Which makes you number three, Tania." Firmly in artistic mode, Maddie swapped a thin charcoal for a thicker one and began to sketch in the sphere of Theo's tight butt. "You will be number four, Jake; and Theo, you are number five."

"And I suppose you are number six?" Tania added, as she slouched lazily against the wall.

"You suppose wrong, Tania. Please don't interrupt me again."

Tania's peppermint eyes flashed a darker green as she swallowed back the response on the tip of her tongue.

"Should you roll a six, then you can nominate a colleague to receive some attention from my collection of toys." Maddie could taste the expanding anticipation as it hung in the air between her comrades. "As I will choose only one of you to feature in the gallery, I thought we could at least make the process fun."

Theo, the blood beginning to run to his head, couldn't resist comment. "Bollocks, Maddie. You had something like this planned from the minute I freed you from the woods! The exhibition, and turning this into 'fun,' is just an excuse for you to get some sort of control-freak kick – not to mention your revenge."

Freya drew in an audible gasp in response to Theo's verbal attack, but the rest of the room took on a stony silence as Maddie put down her charcoal.

Rather than launching into a verbal retaliation against Theo however, Maddie continued to explain. "If your number is rolled, then you will not be the subject of the special feature. In order for us to remember who is exempted, I will ask you each to hold a candle once you are eliminated. Right, Freya, I would like you to roll first, please."

Theo's brain was racing. *Why didn't she snap back at me?* He hadn't realised until now how much he'd wanted her to. He'd been so sure that she was going to whip his backside as her earlier texts had implied. Even to receive some brutal attention, was better than being suspended in this agony of inaction.

He didn't understand how Maddie could be successfully drawing him and Jake at the same time as ordering the women about. Surely that was taking multi-tasking to another level. *Maybe she's just pretending to draw – making me bend over like this with another man's cock at my ass just for her own amusement.* Only the continued swipe of charcoal against paper and the memory of Maddie confessing that she could no longer separate her art from sex, alerted Theo to the fact that he was descending into a state paranoia.

The bang as Freya dropped the dice on the laminate floor resounded around the studio.

"What number has it landed on?" Maddie asked casually.

For heaven's sake! Theo moved his head a fraction to see the dice. But that only assisted the tip of Jake's cock to nuzzle further into his anus. A deeper sensation of lust and a fresh douse of perspiration broke out across Theo's body.

Without even bothering to turn round, Maddie barked, "Keep still, Theo." Then, delicately wiping the tip of a finger over the outline of the cock she'd just drawn, the artist repeated her question to Freya. "Which number, honey?"

"Two."

"Okay then, Sara, you are safe." Maddie added some further definition to the dick on the paper. "I would like you to take a candle from one of the chairs and sit down. But first, it is your turn to roll the dice."

Sara picked up the wooden cube, rolled a four and took up position on the chair nearest the men. Her candle's flame was highlighting how hard her boyfriend had become as he pretended to take another man. It occurred to Sara that a few months ago this might have made her jealous – now it just made her outrageously horny.

"Number four, that's you, Jake." Maddie's hand still didn't stop moving. "As Jake is unable to step away from the stool right now, perhaps you could pass him a candle, Freya. And remember, I'm working from that candle light – if you could all keep them as still as you can I would be very grateful."

The petite blonde did as she was told, lifting a cream beeswax candle up by its wooden holder and passing it to Jake.

Theo, his breaths shallow as he forced himself to blank out Jake's touch bobbing above him, could feel the heat of the flame in his pseudo-partner's hands. If it had been important not to move before, it was imperative now. The last thing he wanted was hot wax dribbling into the crevice of his ass.

Tania, bored with waiting for the order to roll the dice, picked it up from where it had landed and threw it across the floor. "It's number one."

"Thank you, Tania." Maddie made no direct comment about the redhead's impatience, but her voice conveyed to everyone all the annoyance that she felt. "Freya, you are number one. If you could collect a candle and sit next to Sara."

Although Theo could only see bare feet and legs, he could feel the erotic expectation escalate in the studio as everyone closed in on the space around Maddie, the easel and the stool over which he was bent.

That just leaves Tania's number or mine to come up.

"And?" Tania's question filled the room. It may have come from her lips, but everyone was thinking the same thing.

What is going to happen next?

"And now I would like Jake to roll the dice. Pass it to him please Tania – he'll just have to drop it to the floor from where he is."

Obliging, Jake chucked the cube across the floor. "Tania, can you tell us which number it landed on, please?"

"One again."

"Roll again please, Jake. Freya is already out of the running."

Awkwardly, Jake dropped the dice again. "Six."

Maddie paused before she spoke, so she could concentrate on adding texture to the dip of Theo's newly drawn anus. "So, Jake, who do you nominate to play with a toy from my chest of drawers?"

"Do I get to choose the toy?"

"No. That is up to me."

If he was disappointed by this, Jake didn't show it He immediately responded, "I think it should go to Tania."

Maddie picked up a stub of a buttery-yellow chalk and began to recreate on the paper the candlelit glow that surrounded her subjects. "Sara, if you wouldn't mind going over to the chest of drawers for me. Open the third drawer and take out what you find."

Tania, unsure if she was pleased to have been chosen or if she should be wary, especially as her number hadn't come up on the dice yet, looked on with open curiosity as Sara pulled open the only drawer she'd never opened before.

"Bring the contents over and place it on the sofa

please."

Satisfied that Sara had done what she was told and that Tania had enough self-discipline not to run over to the sofa and inspect the bundle of knotted ropes, Maddie took a step back from her easel and scrutinised what she had created so far.

This project had gone just as well as she had hoped – both on and off the paper. She'd previously briefed Freya, Sara and Jake as to how she wished this project to conclude, and they were all performing their roles dutifully. Theo and Tania, on the other hand, would simply have to wait and see what was in store for them as the night drew on.

She was pleased with how she had captured the taut curve of Theo's butt flesh and the tip of Jake's shaft as it almost, but not quite, entered him. Maddie was confident that if she kept going at this rate, the charcoal would be ready in no time, and she could focus all her attention on the special feature.

Theo's head was beginning to thud from being upside down for so long and his hands were slippery against the legs of the stool. He flexed his neck, turning it slightly towards Maddie. "How much longer?"

"It is almost done." The artist picked up a cloth and began to run it over the drawn muscles of Jakes thighs, a little regretful that his tattoos were too low on his legs for inclusion. "How much longer you stay over the stool, however, is another matter."

Theo shut his eyes and tried to regulate his breathing,

reminding himself he was going to leave the studio the instant this was over and never come back. *She promised this would all be worth it and she always keeps her promises.*

Cleaning loose charcoal dust from her work, Maddie spoke to Tania. "Perhaps you would roll the dice for Theo. I suspect he's getting dizzy. I don't think he should let go of the stool just now."

Confused as to why she hadn't been asked to do anything with the equipment Sara had extracted from the drawer, Tania rolled the dice beneath Theo's face so that he could see how it landed. It was another six.

Annoyed that Theo had rolled a six, but relieved he hadn't rolled a five, Maddie kept her disappointment to herself. "Theo, I believe that gives you the right to decide who is treated to a toy from my supply."

Theo licked his lips. In his state of heightened arousal all he wanted was for some stimulation of his own. The application of pleasure to others was currently very low on his list of priorities.

"Come on, Theo, it isn't hard. Just chose someone."

"Jake."

Maddie was surprised. She had been sure he would pick one of the girls, or perhaps even her. "If I may call on your services again, Tania, seeing as you are the only one without their hands full, I would like you to go to the second drawer and bring out the black butt plug."

Theo felt the expectant judder from Jake ricochet through his body, as his cock quivered and poked harder at the yielding butt-hole. Colours began to flash behind Theo's eyelids as he lay as still as he could, not daring to move so much as a muscle in case it produced further friction between himself and Jake. He knew his imagination could set off the orgasm which was edging ever closer to eruption. Wishing he could stop wondering what it would be like for Jake to ease his length into him just an inch or so, Theo realised he should have asked for the toy to be applied to himself – right now a butt plug would be more than welcome.

"Right!" Maddie clapped her hands decisively. "I am pleased to announce that this sketch is complete. I will seal it and frame it later."

Maddie wiped the excess charcoal from her fingers onto Theo's backside, making pleasing black and grey smears across his firm cheeks. She lifted the easel out of the way and then strode into the space where it had been. Her hands were on her hips, her bare-footed legs spread wide as if she were some sort of obscure Ringmaster in the weirdest show in town. "You have all taken a turn at rolling the dice. Freya, Sara and Jake's numbers all came up and they are therefore out of the running for being the living feature on opening night – tomorrow!"

Three independent sighs of either relief or disappointment came from the candle bearers. Although no one, not even they, could be sure which it was. Theo groaned and Tania smirked, the faint flicker of almost-lost hope rekindling a little in the back of her mind. If the dice put her in a position of submission, then she could be the centre of the artist's attention, doing whatever Maddie said, without having to admit that she was rather enjoying being at her beck and call.

"Jake, lower your candle over Theo's butt a fraction." Maddie watched as the flame flickered just above the surface of her latest lover's skin. "Don't burn him, though."

The instant Maddie put the possibility of being burnt into words, Theo's muscles stiffened further.

"Theo, I am going to insert the butt plug into Jake now. Am I correct in thinking that you would much rather I pushed it between *your* cheeks? I imagine you're feeling... unfulfilled in that area right now."

"Not at all." Theo tried to appear nonchalant, but the husky edge to his voice gave him away as a liar.

"Is that so?" Maddie tilted the candle Jake was holding so that a growing reservoir of wax formed around its wick. "And yet your asshole is winking at me. Puckering like a hungry mouth. And I clearly remember you telling me in a text conversation we once had, that I could plug your ass sometime."

Theo did his best to blank out the memory of their text sex and said, "I think Jake would like the plug."

Maddie tilted the candle a little more and Jake sucked in his breath as the long drip of wax fell directly past the tip of his cock, missing him by a fraction of a millimetre, and pooled precisely into Theo's anus.

The electrician howled with shock, his hands letting go of the stool and his body rearing as if to stand. "What the fuck!?"

"Hold him, Jake," Maddie had anticipated the move and Jake's large palms pushed the other man back into place. "Did that hurt, Theo?"

"Of course it fucken hurt."

"It doesn't hurt any more though does it?" Maddie smoothed her fingertips over the fast hardening wax. "Now it feels rather nice, doesn't it? Like a mini butt-cap."

Unable to deny that it had only smarted briefly, Theo merely grunted. The sensation of the solidifying wax was bizarre, enflaming and frustrating, as it effectively sealed his rear entrance.

"I wonder, Mr. Electrician, how badly would you like Jake to peel that plug away and fill the hole with something more substantial?"

Theo clamped his lips together more tightly. This was no longer about his reluctance or desire to have sex with Jake. He knew now that it never had been. It was about his pride and about Maddie taking it from him.

Tania, her eyes occasionally straying to the item on the sofa, came closer to Theo, longing to touch the wax cap for herself. "May I stroke it, Maddie?"

"I don't see why not." Maddie opened the offer to the others. "In fact, why don't you all come and have a feel. The difference in texture between Theo's flesh and the candle wax is very satisfying beneath the fingers."

Theo mentally applauded Maddie. It was a clever move, making the gangbang he'd put her through in the woods appear psychologically basic by comparison. He didn't think about it for long, though – he couldn't. Four sets of fingers were playing around his anus, which paradoxically felt full and empty at the same time.

Conscious of the pressure of time, Maddie regretfully began to hurry things on, even though she could have enjoyed Theo's squirming for considerably longer. Taking the candle from Jake's hands she called to Sara, "Do me a favour and wedge the plug Tania's holding between Jake's butt cheeks."

Tania almost complained about having the impetus taken away from her yet again, but the fact that she was still in the running to be involved in the special feature made her hold her tongue.

"Now that Theo's rear has a shiny wax guardian, Jake, you are free to come over here and bend over this chair." Maddie picked up the seat that Sara had vacated and placed it in front of Theo. "Knees and hands on the floor please, Jake."

Jake moved away from his modelling partner as, despite the presence of the wax, Theo moaned at the departure of the cock that had teased and hovered above him for so long.

"You are to stay precisely where you are, Theo." Maddie addressed her electrician sternly, but her tone instantly softened as she moved her attention to Sara. "I think Jake may need lubing up a bit, honey. I am quite sure Freya has an ample supply of lube you could use."

Yanking down her own skimpy thong, Freya thrust

her vulva towards Sara, an inviting expression on her face. Sara's caramel hand dove between alabaster legs to the centre of the proffered mound, squeezing out a handful of pussy syrup and playing the sweet liquid around her fingers. Under Maddie's watchful gaze, Sara thoroughly coated the plug in Freya's liquid, before driving her fingers back inside the willing Freya, using the extra sap to oil inside Jake's tight rim.

Jake's hands remained pressed obediently flat to the floor as Sara positioned the plug next to his anus. She pushed gently, probing his secretive entrance with the tip of the toy, before applying just the right amount of pressure to make him take the probe's widest diameter. Jake groaned as his rectum finally closed over the whole piece, and Sara was privately amazed at how eagerly he'd sucked up the thick black rubber.

Satisfied that Jake was both enjoying himself and adding to Theo's visual torture, Maddie felt the erotic influence of the studio envelop her in its familiar embrace. It seemed to seep out of the very walls and surround her. Even with the unpredictability of the dice, this was going even better than she'd dared to hope.

Each person was hanging on her every command. She knew she could do anything she wanted to them at this point – that she could get every single toy she owned out of the chest of drawers and put them to use and no one would complain. It was *so* tempting...

Visions of them all gagged, bound at the wrists and ankles, lying before her with dildos, nipple clamps and butt plugs firmly wedged in place, filled Maddie's head. She smiled wickedly, but reluctantly accepted she had to stick to her plan or the exhibition would never happen. *Maybe another day.*

"Now that the last official picture has been completed, we don't need these candles. Sara, could you collect them up and turn the lights back on. I have no doubt that Theo has everything working properly again."

Theo sucked in a small sigh of relief. Unwelcome scenarios of Maddie waxing his chest or balls had been sprinting through his mind. At least that was one horror he could cross off the ever-expanding list of sexual nightmares Maddie might have in store for him. However, as the lights came back on and Maddie resumed her speech, Theo found his moment of relief was short lived.

"Theo, although he may not be ready to admit it yet, really wants the cock that has been teasing his ass for the last forty minutes to fuck him. Be in no doubt, ladies and gentleman, he *will* admit to that before the evening is out."

With her audience's undivided attention, Maddie proceeded with her monologue. "In the mean time, Jake is being rewarded for posing with Theo by having a plug pushed into his back channel. And Freya and Sara, helpful and patient as ever, are shortly to receive their rewards. This just leaves Tania. I can assure you, Tania, that your pleasure will come – but it is not going to come quite as quickly as you'd like it to."

"But that's not fair!" Tania actually stamped her foot.

"Life has a habit of not being fair!" Maddie pointed to the sofa. "Go and put it on. Freya will help you."

"Put it on? It's just a pile of bondage ropes." Tania

poked at the incongruous twisted strips of hemp on the sofa.

"That, Tania, is where you are completely wrong."

"It isn't just a few ropes?" Unease tiptoed into Tania's voice.

"No, Tania. As a special present for all the help you have given me, despite our personal ups and downs, I got you what you always wanted. It's a dress – well, sort of."

"But…" for the briefest of moments, as realisation dawned, Tania appeared almost afraid. Maddie had indeed come a long way since their relationship ended. But, more than that, Tania realised that her ex was nowhere near the end of this voyage of discovery. Everyone else in the room was simply along for the ride, and Tania realised that this terrified and excited her in equal measure.

"Take her into the bedroom, Freya." Maddie continued. "It goes on as we discussed." She gave the blonde a hard stare. "Freya, I am trusting you to come straight back here once everything is in place. The additional equipment is beneath the pillow."

Freya bobbed a sort of curtsy to the artist and, taking Tania by the hand, steered the taller woman towards the stairs.

"But I wanted to be here when Theo caves in!" Tania was torn between wanting to see what was to happen to her downstairs and not wanting to miss out on any of the action in the studio.

"Don't worry, Tan." Maddie dismissed her with a wave of her hand toward the doorway. "I'll fill you in later."

As Freya towed Maddie's ex downstairs, the artist faced the only other remaining female in the room. "Sara, I would like you to sit on the floor next to Jake and give his cock a gentle massage. I want him nice and solid for when Theo finally decides he wants to be filled."

Sitting cross-legged, Sara reached out her hand to play happily with the shaft she knew so well as it jutted between Jake's bent legs and the wooden seat.

Immediately Jake cried out, "Oh...yes..." The ecstasy on his face making it clear he thought all his dreams had come true at once.

"Just you left then, Theo." Maddie fingered the nape of his neck. "Jake's a lucky boy, wouldn't you agree?"

"I would." The angle of his neck meant he couldn't see the couple. But their sighs and mewls made him all too aware of exactly what they were doing.

"Why is he lucky, Theo?"

"Because he has a woman, who is both beautiful and kind, caressing his dick."

"And?" Maddie began massaging Theo's scalp through his short spiked hair, as she treated him to an inquisition similar to the one he'd enacted upon her in the woods.

"He has a girlfriend who loves him."

"And?" Maddie edged forward, her body pressed flat against the curve of his buttocks. "Why else is he lucky, Theo?"

Well aware of the response he was supposed to make,

Theo simply muttered, "Because Sara is prepared to live out *his* fantasies for *him* – that's why she came to you in the first place."

Ignoring the deliberate emphasis Theo had put on the word *'his'*, Maddie squatted on her haunches. "That is correct." She ran her nails down the backs of his legs. "And why else?"

Soft finger pads caressed his stretched tendons. Theo closed his eyes, wishing he could also close his ears to the increasing volume of noise coming from Jake as he was manipulated by his lover.

Maddie checked her watch. It had gone midnight. They would all need to get some rest – even if they didn't actually get any sleep – before the show tomorrow. "Sara, I think you've earned the right to select your own reward. Would you like to fuck Jake, or would you like to fuck Freya when she returns?"

Jake answered for her, his eagerness unmistakable. "Freya. Say Freya, baby. Do it in front of me."

Bending down, Sara tenderly kissed her boyfriend's lips. "Thank you, sweetheart. You're the best."

Theo also felt relieved. *If Jake is just watching, there's more chance of him remaining stiff enough to fuck me.* Theo's head shot up as far as it could go with the shock of his thought. He couldn't take much more of this. But how could he admit to what he now knew he had to have, without making it sound like failure?

He needn't have worried. Maddie had already seen

the flash of regret when Theo realised that Jake's cock might be otherwise engaged. She whispered into his ear, "Do you remember that I promised you a threesome?"

Theo's reply was strained but the tinge of hope in his tone betrayed him. "Yes."

"And I always keep my promises."

"So you keep saying."

"Well, if you admit that you want Jake to fuck your ass, I will make sure it happens right now."

The press of his stomach against the stool had morphed from uncomfortable to painful and Theo shuffled his feet in a vain attempt to decrease the pressure. "That's blackmail."

"No, it's helping you to understand what that handsome body of yours really wants. After all, that's what this is all about, isn't it, Theo?"

"And how the hell do you know what my body wants?"

"I just do." Maddie stood as Freya reappeared at the top of the stairs. "Is Tania tucked up in bed?"

"Just as you requested." Freya's porcelain skin was flushed and pink. "She didn't like it, though. She thought she was coming back up here once she was dressed."

"I bet she did!" Maddie put her arm around Freya's shoulders, admiring how the mini nipples pushed outward in her cotton bra. "You've done well and I am sure you'll be delighted to know that it is now time for you to be rewarded as well."

Freya blushed crimson. "Thank you, Maddie."

"Away you go then." Maddie patted her neat, round ass, luxuriating in the voyeuristic view as Freya wriggled out of her sodden knickers and walked purposely to Sara.

Her dark haired partner immediately took off her own tight bra and panties and pulled Freya onto the floor directly in front of Jake, their flesh contrasting exquisitely as they lay together.

"You may ease back onto your knees so you can get a better view, Jake. But keep that plug in place."

Jake's flash of gratitude to Maddie was short. He didn't want to miss a second of the action as the girls' lips joined together, their nipples chaffing, causing them to mewl into each other's mouths.

Taking Theo by the scruff of the neck, Maddie craned his face upward. "You know what you have to say if you want to join them."

The crick in his neck was forgotten as he saw the breasts of the young women squeezing and jousting together. "I thought that was Jake's threesome?"

"I suspect he does too. But it depends on you, doesn't it. It could be his or it could be yours."

Theo's head swam, having been facing the wrong way for so long. The circulation in his arms and legs felt strange – his fingers and toes numb. "Does this mean that I am to be the feature for the show tomorrow? I mean, it was inevitable, wasn't it?"

"Of course it was. Although it was fun playing with the dice and keeping you guessing, wasn't it?"

"But you stopped rolling the dice before we'd all been eliminated." Theo felt a begrudging respect for the woman beside him.

"Of course. I'd already got what I wanted."

Of course she had. The image of Jake's pre-violation of his ass was testament to that. There was no point in arguing. Anyway, Theo's attention had drifted to Sara and Freya.

The girls were lying directly on top of each other, their hands everywhere at once. Jake was as vocal as ever in his appreciation. Theo knew he could be there with them, if only he'd say the words Maddie wanted to hear.

Instead he said, "What have you done with Tania?"

"Oh she's fine, just a bit tied up at the moment."

"Literally, I assume."

"Indeed." Maddie dismissed talk of her ex. There was a private matter to sort out with Tania, but for now she wanted to see if Theo would give in. "The girls could be sitting on you right now. One on your cock and one on your face."

It was too much. An idea too far. Theo yelled the words he'd been trying to deny for the past half an hour, his libido taking full control of every sense within him. "Okay! Sod it! I want Jake to fuck me. Okay! Happy now? I want him up my ass!"

Maddie immediately helped Theo up. "So you want to have Jake inside you then?"

"Yes!"

She stroked the sweat from his forehead. "Well I'm

afraid that's not going to happen, honey."

"What? I..." Theo was stunned.

"I said you'd have to admit you wanted Jake's cock Theo – I did *not* promise that you would get it. When will you learn to listen to *every* word I say?"

Jake grinned at Theo, his cheeky wink telling Theo he had known how this would end all along.

The electrician was about to explode with exasperated indignation when Maddie pulled the small wax cap from his anus, making him howl with pain and shock.

Completely oblivious to Theo's vocal protest, the artist continued. "I did promise you a threesome, though."

Argument would have been pointless, and he dared not dawdle in case Maddie changed her mind. Theo didn't wait for her to speak again and he crawled on tired limbs towards the girls.

Recognising his exhausted state, Sara took over, rocking Theo onto his back, while Freya unfurled a condom onto his straining dick. Thirty seconds later he was climaxing deep inside the blonde, while Sara sat on his face and Jake, on the outside of the threesome looking in, shot his load all over them, a massive beaming grin across his rugged freckled face, the heavy plug still nestled tightly in his bottom.

Chapter Twenty

Maddie glanced at her watch. It was eleven o'clock in the morning. She flexed her arms and legs and took another slug from her extra-strong espresso.

Freya, Sara and Jake had left in the early hours of the morning. Maddie hadn't asked if they were going home separately or all together. Once they were outside the studio, it was not her concern. She was confident they would all be at the gallery by six forty-five that evening – in time for the preview to begin at seven o'clock sharp.

She had been less sure about letting Theo leave. Especially now that he knew she intended for him to be the spectacle of the living work of art. But Maddie wanted to see if he'd come back of his own free will, without being coerced. It *would* be worth all his waiting – their waiting. Of that, Maddie had no doubt. As long as Theo turned up at the gallery before seven o'clock that evening, all would be well.

Washing her hands, Maddie let the tension of her night's work ebb from her shoulders. At long last everything was ready. The final two works of art needed to be delivered to The Stripped Banana and then Marco would sort the rest.

All Maddie had to do was put on her best dress, cripple her feet in some impossible heels, plaster on some of her rarely worn makeup and chat up potential buyers.

Blowing the last of the fallen charcoal dust from the frame she'd clipped around the picture of Jake and Theo, Maddie went to check on her consolation prize. If Theo didn't show up, someone else would have to act as her special feature – and that meant Tania.

"I assume you've given Theo his freedom...for now." Tania lay face up on the bed, her head resting on the soft pillow beneath her loose hair. She didn't turn her head towards Maddie – but only because she couldn't, not because she didn't want to.

"I have."

Despite the submissive nature of her position and the lack of shine in her eyes, Tania's manner was as blatantly forthright as ever. "I guess you pushed him to the limit and he admitted he wanted Jake."

"Again you are correct." The artist began to examine the harness Tania wore, admiring how the thinly twisted hemp circled her breasts, highlighting and enhancing them, pushing her tits up so that the nipples looked like red berries ready to be plucked.

"And did he have Jake?"

"Of course not."

Maddie composed herself so she didn't weaken in front of her captive, before leaning forward to casually flick her fingertips over Tania's outthrust globes.

Giving every impression that she was perfectly calm and in control, the redhead mused, "Do you think he's got the message by now?"

Maddie had expected Tania to be either asleep or incandescent with rage. But finding her sanguine made Maddie wary. "Which message?"

"The message that it is very important to listen carefully to what Madeline Templeton says, or you might not get what you bargained for."

"Oh, that message. We'll find out later, won't we. When he does or does not turn up."

This got a more immediate reaction from the almost naked woman on the bed. Tania's neck jerked against the circle of leather that surrounded it. "You let him leave?"

"I let everyone leave. They needed their sleep'. Maddie walked to the end of the bed so she could admire her prisoner properly. "I want Theo to come to the exhibition tonight because he wants to, not because I have forced him to. I don't like making people do what they don't want to do." The unspoken, "unlike you" was left hanging in the air.

Patches of pink spotted Tania's foundation-enhanced complexion as her suppressed rage leaked out. "You're no better than me! You trick people!"

"No, they trick themselves by hearing what they want to hear rather than what is actually said."

"I can't believe you let them all leave – all of them! And I'm lying here, shackled like a dog!"

Maddies insides were heaving, partly with nerves about tonight, and partly because she had denied herself a climax for so long that her brain fizzed as though she were on a sugar high. Still, despite Tania's outburst, Maddie's face remained passive. "I would say, you're more like a bitch on heat."

Maddie stared harder, admiring what a good job Freya had done of capturing her ex-partner. "A tempting bitch, though. No question of that." Maddie's eyes traced the ropes that ran from the entwined breasts down to her nub. "How did Freya manage to get you like this? Not easily I imagine."

Tania refused to rise to the implication that the petite blonde had physically gotten the better of her. "She has obviously learnt a lot from you. Freya has picked up your way with words."

"Really?" Maddie felt a wave of pride towards the young woman. It hadn't been long ago that Freya had been so lacking in confidence that she'd taken the post as Maddie's model just to improve her own feeling of self-worth. Now it seemed that the once mousy Freya had been able to weave words of persuasion that tricked the infinitely more experienced Tania into being tied to Maddie's bed. "I guess Freya told you that once you were tied up, I would come to you."

"And you have."

"True." Maddie smiled. "Eventually." Before Tania had the chance to interject, Maddie went on. "I have to say,

Tan, that outfit really suits you."

Tania's green eyes lost some of the dullness that her long wait and hours of uncomfortable, fitful sleep had produced. Following the course of the ropes from Tania's neck down, Maddie took in every knotted section. The rope outfit was attached to the leather collar at Tania's neck. Two separate strands led to each breast. The lengths were twisted around Tania's back in both directions and then circled around each breast in a body-hugging figure of eight.

Knotted to the underside of the elegantly lewd brassiere, another pair of ropes travelled to either side of Tania's navel, continuing down to the left or right of her mound. These lengths went on to form two leg loops, which Tania would have had to climb into, like an insubstantial pair of shorts, when Freya coaxed her into the outfit.

Above the perfectly shaved pussy, affixed between the parallel strands, an additional short length of hemp extended from side to side. From its very centre, a small rope circle hung uselessly, as though waiting for something to be fixed into its circumference.

Tania's lower limbs were completely unfettered. But her arms had been stretched out to either side and her wrists tethered to the legs of the bed with long leads. Tania had been given enough slack to move her arms slightly, but not enough for her to be able to bring her hands to her body.

The leather collar around her slender neck was tight but not immobilising. It fastened with two short ties to the metal bedhead, making it possible for Tania to manoeuvre her head a fraction, but not to move much beyond that.

Dancing a finger over Tania's stomach in the spaces between the ropes, Maddie sighed ruefully, more or less talking to herself. "Maybe I should have used this as one of my main pictures? It would have made an exquisite oil painting. But then I didn't really have the time to do you justice."

Indifferent to Maddie's missed opportunity, Tania's skin rippled as the artist's hand continued to do a fingertip waltz over her exposed flesh. "I have to confess Tania, that the temptation to fuck you is immense."

"You aren't going to, though. Are you?" Unable to keep all of the hope from her voice, Tania did at least manage to keep her expression neutral, disguising a good deal of her desire for Maddie to give in to temptation.

"How well you know me." Maddie shook her head with feigned sadness. "I am going to have to stick to my principles, here. It hardly seems fair to have fun myself if I'm making everyone else wait."

"Don't be foolish, darling. You don't honestly think Theo hasn't had at least three wanks since he escaped from here? And I'm damn sure that Jake, Freya and Sara have been at it all night."

Maddie had no doubt that Tania was correct. "What Jake and crew do is up to them. Their work for me is complete and they are at liberty to do as they wish. As for Theo, he can wank himself into oblivion for all I care. We both know that isn't what he actually wants. And what he wants, he will get only if he comes to the preview this evening."

"You never used to be so sure of your charms, Madeline!"

The artist took hold of the ropes around Tania's chest and pulled them roughly, causing her ex to gasp. Tania's backside rose off the duvet and her chest swelled with the pressure. Maddie stared pointedly into the minty pupils of her prisoner. "Again, that is true. But I had a good teacher."

Abruptly, Maddie moved away. A memory was stirring at the back of her mind. A section from an erotic story she'd read years ago and had always fancied trying for herself. The more she thought about it, the more she was convinced it would form the perfect addition to Tania's outfit.

Leaving a confused Tania behind her, Maddie ran to her kitchen and dug out the sewing kit she kept for emergencies. Selecting a reel of white cotton and picking up one of the many paintbrushes she'd left lying around, she returned to the bedroom.

"What are you going to do with those?" Tania was both wary and hopeful as Maddie perched on the side of the bed.

As the intensely soft sable bristles made contact with Tania's right nipple, the redhead couldn't hold in her whimpers, her brown tips darkening as they became quickly engorged.

Unable to resist, the artist in Maddie pulled out her phone and took a photograph of the breast, fully intending to use the glorious image in a future painting. After a few more strokes of the brush had coaxed Tania tips to urgent peaks,

Maddie broke off a length of cotton and tied it securely around one protuberant nipple.

Tania gulped loudly, her breast swelling as the joint sensations of pain and pleasure sent gushes of liquid from her already wet pussy.

Happily observing the effect of her handiwork on her captive, Maddie copied the move on the left side, knotting the other end of the cotton twine to the nipple, effectively forming a trip wire between Tania's tits.

Tania's rib cage rose and fell with increasing speed as Maddie returned the paintbrush to the swollen tips. She was enjoying herself as much as she was enjoying the reactions on her ex's face – not to mention the radiant glow of perspiration glistening over Tania's whole body. A glisten most noticeable in the slick of pussy juice that had begun to anoint to the ropes around her sex. Maddie reached for her mobile. It was time to reel Theo in for the final time.

> Maddie: I trust u got some sleep
> Theo: Very little. U?
> Maddie: None.

Maddie felt encouraged, both by the fact he had replied and by the speed of his response. She could picture the electrician sitting with his phone on his lap, hoping that she would contact him.

> Theo: And Tania?

Rather than send a text by way of reply, Maddie dropped the brush with which she'd been teasing Tania's trapped chest and took another photograph so he could see for himself.

> Theo: OMG!!!!
> Maddie: Do u think she looks good?
> Theo: U do ask some stupid questions sometimes!

Taking up the paintbrush again, Maddie stroked Tania's mound between her open legs, making the bound woman groan from between clenched teeth.

> Maddie: If u want to see her like this in person, u will have to come to the gallery
> Theo: And if I don't?
> Maddie: Then u will never get what u have been waiting for.
> Theo: U are so sure it will be worth it. Worth my humiliation! How arrogant u are.
> Maddie: There will be no humiliation - it is art.
> Theo: U didn't answer my question - again.

Maddie abandoned the brush and Tania whined at the loss of stimulation. Ignoring her pleas, Maddie looked her in the eye. "It is time for me to get ready. You should rest. It is going to be a busy evening."

Confused bluster shot from Tania's artificially enhanced lips. "You can't leave me like this! I'm so close to cumming! And anyway, I have to change into my preview outfit!"

"Actually Tania, that won't be necessary. You are already wearing your preview outfit."

Maddie shut the bedroom door behind her, drowning out Tania's cries of protest, then replied to Theo.

> Maddie: It will be worth it. Not
> arrogance. A fact. U have been waiting
> long enough. So have I.

Nerves had begun to play at the pit of Maddie's stomach as she waved off Marco's courier with the last two pieces of her collection. Now, tweaking a stray hair into place and welding it down with an obscene amount of hairspray, Maddie took a final glimpse in the bathroom mirror, hoping she'd managed to get the balance right between sexy and serious artist.

The satin dress she wore was a plain, dusky bronze, cut long in an oriental style, hinting at the delights beneath without actually revealing any of them. Marco had decided to call the exhibition *Expectation: Shades of Erotic Fantasy*. And Maddie had chosen her dress to compliment her work, both in colour and theme.

She checked her watch. It was five o'clock. In order

to arrive first, she had to be at the gallery in less than an hour. Reminding herself that her nerves were due to anxiety about the exhibition, rather than a possible no-show from Theo, Maddie slipped into her hated high heels.

Maddie pulled her shoulders back and put on another thin layer of lipstick. It was time to fetch Tania and to let her know that the special feature would involve an unexpected participant.

◆ ◆ ◆ ◆

The Stripped Banana was fully lit and everything was in place. Having been enthusiastically greeted by an overexcited Marco, who passed Maddie a glass of champagne the moment her foot crossed the threshold, she allowed herself a solo walk around her exhibition, not quite able to believe she'd got there at last.

In situ, her collection looked even better than Maddie could have wished. The only things she didn't dare look at were the price cards neatly placed beneath each exhibit. The prices had been steep to start with, but Marco had told her he hadn't thought them steep enough and hiked them up considerably more. One sale would keep her solvent for the next three months, if not longer.

The Victorian screen Theo had picked out for her was positioned in the centre of the room. On one side of the screen, the poker table had been erected, the face-covered dice ready to be rolled across its surface if the visitors so wished. On the opposite side of the divider was the tall bronze table holding the sculpture of Theo's penis and testicles.

She couldn't help but run her fingers over it, wondering if she would get the opportunity to touch the real thing later on.

Here and there Marco had placed tall stools, each holding packets of condoms, leaflets about the gallery and Maddie's business cards. She smiled. It was a nice touch and confirmed to Maddie that Marco knew exactly what he was doing.

One wall of the gallery, however, was almost bare. All that hung there was the framed list that Tania had created for Maddie. The huge bronze letters sprawled across thick, cream parchment. Beneath the list was a table similar to the one on which her sculpture rested. On it sat an oval wicker basket containing four brushes and a pot of black ink from her precious Chinese Ink set.

It was the item lying on the floor next to it, however, that Maddie examined carefully: a transparent, heavy duty plastic case, just as she'd ordered.

Marco came up behind her, rubbing his hands with gleeful anticipation. "You will be pleased to know, Mademoiselle, that we have sold twenty five of the thirty tickets for your viewing."

"You're kidding." Maddie hadn't expected to sell half that many. Even with the word 'erotic' in the title, she hadn't considered herself to be sufficiently well known to pull such a crowd. With the guests she'd invited as well, The Stripped Banana would be at full capacity.

"I'm sure the fact that this is the gallery's re-launch has something to do with it."

"You are most kind and, may I say, you look dazzling." Marco bowed. "Now, all we need for this extra exhibit," he tapped the large perspex box at his feet with extreme reverence, "is your model."

Surrounded by her work, Maddie felt emboldened and her eyes flashed with provocative promise. "I hope you don't mind the liberty," she explained to Marco. "But I arranged for two models to take part in the extra show. It is, as I'm sure you'll appreciate, daunting to bare all in front of strangers. If one chickened out, I wanted to make sure that another remained."

Marco beamed. "A true professional!"

Maddie placed her empty champagne glass down on a tray. "I will go and collect my first assistant. I left her freshening up in your bathroom."

"All this time?" Marco was shocked that Maddie's companion had been left to fend for herself for so long.

"Oh don't worry. She had a long night, and an extended freshen-up is just what she needs."

"Ready?" Maddie found Tania sitting on a chair next to the sink. She was still draped in the full-length trench coat that had allowed her to travel to the gallery without raising too many eyebrows.

Even with her hands shackled behind her back in loose handcuffs so that she couldn't fiddle with the harness,

Tania still managed to sound defiant and haughty. Although Tania's slightly increased rate of breathing told Maddie that the model was nervous. "Why am I here like this? Theo is the special feature, not me."

Reluctant to reveal her concerns that Theo might not make it, Maddie held out her hand to help Tania to her feet and unfastened her cuffs. "You were the only one who actually wanted to be the centre of attention. It seemed churlish not to grant your wish."

"I couldn't care either way." Tania shook out her hair so it shielded her shoulders. The rope outfit – slinking with every move of her body – looked beyond sexy now that Tania was moving around.

"Bollocks! You love it."

Tania smirked. "Okay, I do love it. But I'm only doing this because it's you asking. No way would I ever do this for anyone else."

"Unless they were paying you."

"Ouch!"

Maddie checked the position of all the ropes, tugging them so the ellipses of Tania's tits were even more pronounced. The red marks where the ropes had dug into her skin for so long looked like shadows beneath the cords. "You will do exactly as I tell you. If you let me down now, Tania, then I will never forgive you."

Tania had her hands on her hips, and the collar at her throat now looked like an exotic choker as she tilted her head to one side. "And what's in it for me?"

"I will make sure you get the sex you crave."

"Big deal. I can get that whenever I want!"

"Come off it, Tania. The time for exaggerating about your life is over. You live in a grotty flat, you have no regular income and you survive by sponging off others – like me."

Tania's face blanched, but she held her tongue.

"You behave out there and I will keep to myself the fact that your age has halted your progress through the fashion world." Maddie inspected her watch. "We have no time for this now. Come on. I want you in place before Marco's guests arrive. Think of it as extreme modelling!"

Taking her ex-girlfriend by the hand, Maddie led her into the gallery, where Marco let out a low whistle of approval. "Wow!" His eyes fell upon the cotton tightrope that ran between Tania's breasts. Maddie watched as his pupils dilated nearly to the size of Tania's nipples – nipples now so flushed and hard that they were a rich burgundy.

Tania saw the box and her eyes widened with alarm. "Please tell me that I've guessed wrong."

"If you've guessed that you are about to take up residence in that box so that our visitors can appreciate your beauty without getting their fingerprints all over you, then you have not guessed wrong."

Tania stared at the six-foot by three-foot by one-foot clear plastic box, which had regular air holes drilled around the long sides. Her heart hammered so hard she could feel its aftershocks bounce through her cunt as she imagined being thrown into the see-through coffin trussed in her harness.

"Madame will be like Snow White in her glass coffin. Will I perhaps have the pleasure of a kiss to bring you back to life later?" Marco, at least five inches shorter than Tania, was already having trouble controlling his erection. Maddie wondered how he was going to get through the rest of the evening without having to disappear for some light relief.

Tania, basking under the gallery owner's attention, opened the lid of the box. Maddie smirked at her ex's predictability. "Hang on, Tan. Your outfit is not quite complete."

In full professional showing-off mode, now that a wealthy man's eye was on her, Tania gave Maddie her best smile. "Certainly."

Collecting her handbag from under the reception desk, Maddie approached Tania with a brand new vibrator cradled in her hands. "Guess where this goes?"

Disguising her anxious swallow so that Marco didn't notice it, Tania stood perfectly still as Maddie slipped the vibrator into the special loop that hung from the rope dress at the apex of Tania's thighs. The fit was perfect, its weight both pleasing and distracting. It seemed natural, from its angle in the harness, that the toy should slip easily inside her. Tania's hands immediately went to hold it, only for them to be smacked away by Maddie. "Not yet, Tan. Patience!"

A heavy knock at the gallery's main door took a reluctant Marco away from the vision of a harnessed Tania.

Jake, Freya and Sara, came in with a flurry of smiles, engulfing Maddie in hugs of congratulations. Bedecked in their finery, each of her models looked as striking as the works of art they had helped Maddie to create. They were about to view themselves in their various guises on the walls, when Jake's complexion flushed from his usual freckled beige to ruddy. "Oh my God. Tania!"

Maddie beamed. "Immaculate isn't she. Your timing is perfect as ever, guys. Could you all help me, perhaps? Tania will be trapped for the entirety of the viewing. I don't want her to be more uncomfortable than is artistically necessary."

Producing two short-chained sets of handcuffs from her bag, Maddie attached one to each of the captive's wrists. Freya held open the clear lid of the box, as Jake assisted Tania to lift her legs and step carefully inside.

On a nod from Maddie, Sara collected a square, bronze-coloured cushion from one of the many chairs dotted around the gallery and placed it so that Tania had something to rest her head on.

Looking at Tania with more affection than she'd had for a very long time, Maddie smiled as she issued her instructions. "I want you to lie down, Tan. There is plenty of room. Your head can go on the cushion; your legs will be bent at the knee and placed slightly apart so that your gorgeous pussy can be viewed to perfection."

Tania, feeling incredibly exposed, did as she was bid. The thought of being a Snow White figure for Marco kept her smiling enigmatically, a voracious desire radiating from her body.

Fixing Tania's wrists to the sides of the box by

securing the open cuffs to the conveniently placed air holes, Maddie looked down, satisfied with her first special feature. Only the vibrator remained free, lying provocatively over Tania's slick mound.

"We will leave the lid open until the last second." Maddie hoped her increasingly frequent glances towards the front door weren't too transparent. It was ten to seven and there was still no sign of Theo.

"Maddie?" Tania looked up at her ex, her eyes already silently begging for more attention. "You are going to put that vibrator where it belongs, aren't you?"

"If you behave." Maddie walked briskly away, leaving the others to sip at the champagne Marco was thrusting into their hands as he asked them questions about posing for such sensual pictures.

Suddenly Maddie had a feeling she knew where Theo would be.

"How long have you been in here?

"About an hour." Unlike the others, Theo hadn't dressed for the occasion. But then, if he went through with what Maddie had planned, he didn't require smart clothes anyway. "You look incredible, Miss Templeton."

"Thank you." She'd thought that her pulse would slow down with the relief of seeing Theo. But she was aware her heart rate had only increased in pace as his intense, hazel eyes devoured every inch of her, from the open toe of her heeled shoes, to her carefully brushed hair.

"I'll be honest, Maddie. I am not sure why I came."

"That isn't being honest." The artist made herself comfortable on a chair opposite Theo. She'd found him in the storeroom behind the gallery. The storeroom where he'd helped her find the various props and furniture. The storeroom in which he'd made her cum – twice. The storeroom in which he came in his pants.

He was sitting on one of the many seats the room had to offer, one leg folded over the other, his white t-shirt showing all the signs of having been worn all day, his denim shorts speckled with charcoal from where they'd been so recently thrown onto Maddie's studio floor.

"If you were telling the truth," she continued, "you'd have said, "I am here because I want to fuck you, Maddie. I want what I've been waiting for. I want to feel my cock between your legs.""

Theo pulled his mobile phone from his pocket. "According to this text, that is what you want as well."

Maddie read the last text she had sent him from his screen.

> Maddie: It will be worth it. Not arrogance. A fact. U have been waiting long enough. So have I.

She nodded solemnly. "All the time you have been waiting, I have been waiting as well. I've been working very hard. You are my reward."

"And what makes you so sure that I want to be

your reward for finally getting the gallery show you say you deserve?"

"You are here."

Theo was silent for a moment, then added, "And if I go into the gallery, what will happen to me?"

"You will assist me in selling some artwork. After which, I promise I will allow you to do anything you like to me."

The word "anything" echoed through the back of Theo's mind, bouncing around the sides of his brain as he considered what that might imply. "And if I get up and leave."

"Then I will not get to feel how wonderful your dick fits between my legs and Tania will become the main feature of the preview rather than just a sideshow."

"Tania? You do know that she is only hanging around because she wants you back."

"I did. Although thankfully, I think she has targeted her greedy ambitions elsewhere now. He is very well off and money, not to mention the power it brings, will always mean more to Tania than anything else."

"Not…Marco?" Theo couldn't help but grin. "Do you think we should warn the poor little sod?"

"Too late. I fear he is already smitten." Maddie flicked her fringe from her forehead. "Although I must say, Tania is looking particularly appealing tonight. So it's not that surprising."

Theo slowly uncrossed his legs and stood up. "Can I ask you a question, Miss Templeton?"

"Only if you're quick. The doors open in two minutes."

"Why me? Why have I been the one you made to wait? Why not one of the women?"

"They, unlike you, Mr. Electrician, are no challenge — where would be the fun in that?"

Chapter Twenty-One

◆ ◆ ◆ ◆

The reception area of the gallery was packed with people. The previously light, airy space was no longer airy as Marco, beaming broadly, and a diminutive waitress whom Maddie presumed had turned up while she was with Theo, handed out drinks and canapés.

Having deliberately kept the guests gathered in the reception area, away from Tania, Marco launched into his welcome speech. "Mesdames and Messieurs, I am delighted to welcome you to this, the official prelaunch of my gallery, The Stripped Banana and to its inaugural exhibition – *Expectation: Shades of Erotic Fantasy*. Art by the incredibly talented and I'm sure you'll agree magnificent, Miss Madeleine Templeton."

A round of polite applause echoed through the gallery and Maddie smiled on-cue as Marco continued. "Not only has she provided some pulse throbbing exhibits for us, but she has, for one night only, given us two very special additional features – some living art. When you witness these pieces for yourself my friends, I am sure you'll see why I felt it necessary to put an over-18 warning on your invitations. I will now hand over to Miss Templeton, who will explain all."

Maddie, gathering strength from the fact that Theo was finally in place next to Tania, took up the introduction. "I would also like to thank you all for coming. I hope you enjoy what you are about to see this evening. As Marco said, alongside my paintings, drawings and sculptures, I have some living art for you to enjoy this evening.

The first of these, *My Lady in Waiting*, speaks for itself, or should I say, herself. However, the second piece, *'By thy words we shall know him...'* is an interactive work and if I can call on your services, ladies and gentleman, we will create a work of art together.

When you enter the show, you will see a very fit young man with his back to you. He is not permitted to turn around – and I would ask you not too force him to move. Next to where he stands is a basket containing brushes and a jar of Chinese Ink. You may use these to write on his flesh, whatever you might like to do to him. Should you be stuck for ideas, I have provided some suggestions. You will see a list of helpfully provocative words and phrases framed on parchment next to where my model is waiting."

Maddie rose a glass to the assembled crowd. "Thank you and, once again, enjoy!"

The crowd immediately divided itself into those who headed straight for the living art and those who, for reasons of shyness or personal taste, turned to the inanimate art first.

To Maddie, the preview both sped and dragged. She talked nonstop about her art, her inspiration and why she chose to work with erotic images and not landscapes. She introduced her models and graciously accepted praise.

It was almost an hour before she managed to make her way over to Theo and Tania. Maddie couldn't prevent the smile on her lips turning from one of genuine happiness at hearing so many favourable comments, to a wide beam of pride when she saw how well Theo was coping.

He was exactly where she had left him, standing butt naked, facing the wall. A black, silk, cowl hood was draped over his head and shoulders so that he wasn't recognisable. His hands were clasped together over his cock, which was stiff but mostly hidden. And his back, arms, legs and sides were covered in words. Far from being reticent, the select crowd had gone to town. As she approached, Maddie heard a dauntingly elegant woman, who simply dripped money, giggling as she wrote on Theo's bare foot. Ink was running over her manicured nails, and she happily bemoaned the lack of space she needed to inscribe her desires on his buttocks.

Tania, on the other hand, was hot and desperate. Even though the gallery's air conditioning was at full blast, Maddie doubted it held much benefit for Tania in her plastic prison. Calling over to the waitress for some water, Maddie opened up the lid and dribbled some liquid between Tania's dry lips.

"Please, Maddie," she croaked.

Instantly, the artist knew what she was asking for.

"If I could have your attention once more, ladies and gentleman." Every eye turned to Maddie as she called across the room. No one wanted to miss what might be happening to

My Lady in Waiting. "I think you will agree that my marvellous model here has performed well and deserves a reward after such a long period of confinement."

There was a general chorus of agreement and for the first time Maddie noticed that many of the invited guests were not as physically in control of themselves as would befit a visit to a posh London gallery. Nipples were obviously tight, cocks were certainly stiff.

"*My Lady* here has endured her rope harness for many hours prior to our arrival this evening. If you look closely, you can't fail to see how the chaffing of the harness has highlighted her exquisitely tanned skin with a reddish bloom that matches her hair almost exactly. She truly is a work of art. However, the art I have provided for Marco, with the exception of this other handsome specimen," Maddie patted Theo's backside, "and the dice which I have seen many of you roll, is all rather stationary. I think some movement might be rather fun."

Tania, restrained, her oversexed flesh caressed by the rope harness for so long, and gawped at for the last hour, was a mass of coursing adrenaline and endorphins. She was too drugged up on her body's own chemicals to do anymore than whimper as Maddie lifted the vibrator that had been laying at the entrance of her sex-starved body. With no lubrication required, the artist eased the toy through the loop of the harness dress and into her model.

Fresh perspiration broke out on Tania's forehead and her arms rattled at her cuffs in frustration as Maddie reclosed the box's lid. She felt blissfully full at last, but it wasn't enough.

Producing a slender black remote-control from her bag, Maddie held it aloft as she spoke in a loud clear voice. "Marco, can you tell me please, have any of these good folks purchased any of my work?"

There was a sudden hush as the Frenchman replied, "Not as yet, Mademoiselle. But I have been in discussions with two gentlemen about possible sales."

"That's a shame, for I am going to let the first person to purchase a piece of my work from the newly styled Stripped Banana take control of this. This is a remote-control for the vibrator now buried within the core of *My Lady*. Whoever holds this has power over exactly when and for how long, the breathtaking redhead in the box will orgasm."

Jake, standing between Sara and Freya, a proprietary hand on each of their backsides (they were now not so much a twosome, but a threesome), broke the silence. "I don't suppose your models get a discount!"

Maddie laughed. "You guys get a free commission whenever you like – isn't that good enough for you?"

The ginger-haired man grinned down at his women. "Oh yes, that is very much good enough!"

A tall, grey-haired, black-suited man at the back of the group came forward. "May I ask a question?"

"Of course." Maddie treated him to her best flirty smile.

"My wife," he indicated the stunning platinum blonde Maddie had seen writing on Theo's ankle, "has taken a fancy to your sculpture. However, she won't buy it until she knows who the dick belongs to."

Maddie tapped Theo's backside for a second time, feeling his cheeks tense under her touch. "The member in question belongs to my helper, here. The faces which adorn it are those of my other models." Maddie waved an arm in the direction of Freya, Sara and Tania.

"So, my dear," The enquiring man turned to his wife. "Do you want it?"

"I'd love it. Thank you, darling!" She gave her husband a protracted kiss and then turned to Maddie, her face a picture of eager anticipation. "Does that mean I get custody of the remote control?"

"It most certainly does – and thank you!" Maddie was smiling so hard her jaw was beginning to ache. She has just sold her first ever exhibition piece for at least £1500, probably more, seeing as Marco had upped all the prices.

The woman strode towards the perspex box. She loomed over Tania, sapphire eyes narrowing – Maddie knew a dominatrix when she saw one and wondered how many whip marks her husband's back bore beneath his immaculately laundered shirt.

Holding the remote so that the captured *Lady in Waiting* could see it clearly, the platinum blonde paused to allow the other guests to gather around and get a good view. Only then did she begin. Maddie mentally applauded her – this woman had style.

Slipping the vibrator onto the mild setting, the blonde smiled as Tania's bent knees shook, the pulse of the longed-for movement taking effect. Her concentration focussed on nothing but her new toy, Maddie's buyer cranked the vibe through the next four settings with measured precision. Carefully observing the resulting tremors, the woman took obvious delight in making Tania whine, making her hips rise and her hands tug uselessly at her cuffs as the rhythm inside her vagina nearly reached breaking point, before cruelly and suddenly stopping the vibrations altogether.

The cotton line between Tania nipples visibly twanged as she wriggled within her prison, her nipples a blazing cerise, her clit engorged and pebble hard.

Maddie, who could see it wasn't going to take much now to trip Tania either into madness or ecstasy, opened the box lid and uncuffed her wrists, but left the vibe in place. Maddie turned to the blonde's husband. "If your wife is in agreement, I think *My Lady* has had enough of waiting – perhaps a kiss to her chest would be a kindness?"

The blonde didn't wait for him to ask her permission and snapped, "Do it. Tongue those tits." The crude words sounded gloriously erotic somehow, coming from a figure of such poise. As her husband got to his knees, fiddling his fingers over one nipple and his mouth over the other, his wife shot the vibrator up to full pelt.

Tania howled and bucked, her deprived, encased body climaxing to the cheers of the overheated crowd, the discomfort of the restricting rope harness as it bit into her flesh forgotten in the wake of the coveted orgasm.

Maddie took one step closer to Theo and, taking

advantage of all the guests' attention on Tania, pulled the cowl from Theo's head before leading him quietly into the storeroom.

"I take it from the noise that Tania is having a good time." His voice was quiet from so long without speaking, and Theo flexed his legs and arched the balls of his feet. "I was so sure you were going to make me vulnerable, like she was."

"You were intrinsic to making that happen, but I wouldn't have treated you like that. I keep telling you. I don't make people do what they don't want to do. Tania may protest and moan, but she loves it. She has always been a whore to the limelight and I have merely made one of her dreams come true."

Maddie ran her hand over Theo's solid shaft. "You look incredible. I don't think there is a millimetre of your back that isn't covered with an interesting sexual suggestion."

"Are you going to tell me what they've written?" Theo stepped closer, welcoming the touch of the artist's fingers as she played them sensuously over his balls.

"Let's just say that the gallery's guests aren't lacking in imagination." Maddie's face was so close to Theo's that the gap between them barely allowed enough room for air. "There is everything there from wanting to suck you off, to a desire to paint your toenails with turquoise nail varnish, to wanting to eat treacle off your chest."

"I'm amazed you let other people use your prized inks."

"I told you I wanted them to be used to write on you.

And now they have been. I never said I had to be the one doing the writing."

"I really should listen more carefully to what you say, shouldn't I?" Lifting his hands to the front of the satin dress, the electrician teased his fingers over Maddie's silken breasts, pressing just hard enough to make her nipples leap back at him. "So, you sold the sculpture of my dick then?"

"I would bet good money on that woman using it as a dildo. She is so going to fuck you until the whole thing disintegrates."

Maddie's words brought Theo back to the matter at hand with an urgency that felt painful. He had waited for her body for so long. But, with a massive strength of will, he pulled back.

Taking pleasure in the surprise on Maddie's face as he walked away, and knowing she'd assumed he would have ripped her clothes from her body as soon as they were alone, Theo drew a piece of crumpled paper from the shorts he'd left on the floor. "According to this list, which I complied this morning from the records of our texted conversations, you owe me:

A fuck over the bonnet of my van in the rain
Suck my cock
Sex bent over in a country lane
I am going to tie your hands together and rip your clothes off
Spank your bum until it's bruised

Fuck your ass while I hold your tits
A beating whilst tied up on a four-poster bed
Receive anal sex with a strap on..."

As he reached the end of his list, Theo stared hard at his companion. "So, that's what I've been waiting for. Or, should I say, what *you* have *made* me wait for. Tell me, Madeline, what exactly is it *you* have been waiting for?"

Returning Theo's determined gaze, Maddie took hold of the bottom of her dress. Tugging it off, so that she was standing only in her bronze, strapped high heels, she walked purposely towards him, never letting her eyes unlock from his. Resting her forehead on Theo's, her bra-free breasts buffing against his chest, Maddie replied, "I have been waiting for my very first art exhibition."

Theo's lips curled up at one side into a lopsided smile. "And what else have you been waiting for, Miss Templeton?"

She took the list from his fingers. "I have been waiting to be fucked over the bonnet of your van in the rain, to suck your cock, to have sex bent over in a country lane, to have you tie my hands together and rip my clothes off, to have my bum spanked until it's bruised, to have my ass fucked while you hold my tits, to receive a beating whilst tied up on a four poster bed and to give you anal sex with a strap-on. Do I need to go on?"

"And where on that list do you think we should start?" Theo bent his face to her chest and licked the very top of each nipple. Maddie's pussy convulsed as she revelled in the freedom of not having to control her body's desire and not having to stop herself before she reached the point of no return.

Her hands ran down his arms, smudging the inky messages of pornographic intent. "How about we..." They both froze as a massive crash came from the gallery. "What the hell was that?" The colour drained from her face. "A picture falling?"

Theo grabbed her hand, and they both ran naked to the gallery door. Flinging it open, they looked at each other, as if to check that they weren't seeing things. "Bloody hell." They breathed the words in unison as they viewed the bacchanalian scene before them.

Relief swept through Maddie as she stood, her hand clenching Theo's hard as they watched the orgy that had exploded amongst her exhibits. All her work was still safe. A fallen chair and table, which had failed to support two guests who were now sprawled on top of each other on the floor, explained the bang.

Maddie glimpsed up at Theo, her eyes shining with devilment. "On the other hand, we could save that list of things for later and just join in here?"

Theo's hazel eyes twinkled back at the artist shrewdly. "Is that a promise?"

"Oh yes."

"And you always keep your promises." Theo pulled Maddie after him into the middle of the gallery. Freya was there already, licking at Sara's breasts, while Jake had his arms around the waist of the woman who'd bought the sculpture. A quick scan of the rest of gallery showed that Tania had cornered her new quarry: a naked Marco was now in the box, with the much taller redhead lying neatly on top of him.

Maddie nodded. "Oh yes, I always keep my promises, Theo…eventually." She pushed the electrician onto the nearest seat, unfurled a condom from the selection Marco had laid out around the gallery and climbed astride him. Her long drawn out sigh of ecstasy as she finally felt his length move inside her was lost in the noise of the room. Then, Maddie called to the platinum blonde who was now free from Jake. "Do you want to see why I decided to capture this man in sculpture?"

The woman was at their side in seconds, watching as Theo and Maddie rutted, their desperation to enjoy each other lending more urgency than finesse to their coupling. As they moved, Theo whispered into the artist's ear, "Are you going to watch me screw her in a minute? Shall we both suck the juice from her body? Can I see you lick her tits?"

"I think we should do all those things. But first, I think we should have some fun making her wait."

Lightning Source UK Ltd.
Milton Keynes UK
UKOW030630211012

200892UK00005BA/6/P